The Cold War was over . .

wasn't it?

They promised peace . . .

prosperity . . .

and an end to fear.

They lied.

They tore down the Berlin Wall and carried away the pieces for souvenirs. The Russians and the Americans said there was a new world order — a new peace — that would last forever.

For awhile it seemed like it might even happen that way. But then mad priests and mullahs rose up from the hells to preach hatred and spread terror. Their followers attacked with weapons that maimed and killed thousands. They unleashed dread diseases everyone thought had been eliminated from the face of the Earth.

And always they pointed the finger of blame elsewhere. The Americans caused it, they said. Or the Russians. Slowly the hard won peace between those two great nations was stretched to the breaking point.

A few wise ones in Moscow and Washington, became suspicious. They wondered if there was something else behind the madness. Something unimaginably evil.

But time ran out and in one single, bloody day the Russian president and the American president were assassinated.

The Cold War returned.

And it lasted for a thousand years.

Until one day . . .

. . . In uttermost space . . .

THE HATE PARALLAX

ALLAN COLE

AND NICK PERUMOV

WILDSIDE PRESS

DEDICATION

*For my sweetie, Kathryn, who makes
everything possible.* —Allan

*To my wife, Olga, bravely bearing a crazy
writer for all these years.* —Nick

THE HATE PARALLAX

Published by Wildside Press LLC.
www.wildsidebooks.com

CHAPTER ONE

'Oh, East is East and West is West, and never the twain shall meet,
Till Earth and Sky stand presently by at God's great Judgment Seat;
But there is neither East nor West, Border, nor Breed, nor Birth,
When two strong men stand face to face, though they come from the
ends of the earth!'

"The Ballad of East and West"
by Rudyard Kipling

He was an old devil, a tired devil and as he pushed the starship through Uttermost Space his thoughts were on his long-overdue vacation.

This voyage would end soon — a few EarthDays at most. Even as he went through the first phases of SpellDown his mind was on the bonus he'd receive for a good docking. Surely more than enough for a DirectSpell return. Enough so he could engage the very best of port wizards, close his eyes and …

… Lo! he'd be on Avalon.

His name was Scratch and as Old Scratch he was known to more than a thousand Navigation Spirits, Control Brownies and Supply Goblins.

Scratch was an Engine Devil and with tremendous overlight speed he was pushing the starliner deeper into the Void. His power cut the very flesh of The Continuum and made hundreds of thousands of lesser spirits in huge armored tubes throw back thick spurs of overheated plasma.

But it was an Engine Devil's curse that whatever he received was less than he needed. He spent every second of every voyage swearing and sweating over each dram of power so he could hurl the ship to its distant goal.

However, on this particular EarthDay Old Scratch's thoughts were not on his common duties. His ship was the *HolidayOne*. His employers: StarFunInc, who ran a fleet of six bargain-fare vacation liners throughout the galaxy. The *HolidayOne* was the least luxurious and oldest of the six.

Still, it was a stout ship, a reliable ship and in good repair. Just now it was being used for the company's annual Honeymoon Special. There were more than a thousand couples aboard, nearly all young, lusty and merry.

Several times Old Scratch found himself turning an even deeper shade of his normal red when he accidentally eavesdropped on the private chatter and thoughts of the young people.

He could see nothing — strong spells barred his sight. But those good-for-nothing Brownies darting about the ship were eager to spy on the honeymooners and never missed an opportunity to tell the dull and credulous Goblins the hottest of the hot stories.

Supporting his authority, Old Scratch growled several times at the rowdies, but, but …

But … it only made him dream more of Avalon.

Avalon … Fire, hot enough to whip away this damned chill of Uttermost Space. First he'd enter the House of Flame, where he'd lie absolutely still for FiendDays on end, making his old bones glad with the delicious heat of it.

As Scratch dreamed of Avalon every weary joint and muscle twitched in blissful anticipation. Even for an engine devil three hundred years in space (never mind Uttermost or Innermost or Nearest) don't pass easily. Plus he could never be certain if the bonus would be enough to match his dreams.

The Company's chief bookkeeper was a many-degreed blackmaster of financial lies. At StarShift's end a hard working devil never knew how many LT's would be credited — or deducted — from his account.

Scratch dismissed this depressing thought, replacing it with a vision of the fattest possible bonus and what those great stacks of Legal Tender notes would bring.

Which was … Avalon!

His best fiendish friend, Ashgaroth, would return to Avalon in a wheel or two. Old Scratch smiled to himself imagining the good uproar they'd have at the "Three Hanged Monks" — the favorite tavern of Engine Devils Local 666.

There was a sign on the door that was the delight of every fiend who saw it: "Softskins Beware! Enter At Your Own Risk!"

Not that softskins — or humans — would be comfortable for a second in the "Three Hanged Monks." There were no tables, chairs, or even a bar — none of the ridiculous paraphernalia the Unfiendish require to live their clumsy lives in comfort.

A place where human time, EarthTime, CessiumTime, had no meaning. A place where a mentos shout brought a drink quicker than a decaying atom could parse time.

And the treasured silence that followed could last a hundred EarthYears.

Engine Devils were a proud race and disliked all things connected with their soft-skinned masters. Yet they served their masters well. Devils must obey. That was the rule. The Great Spell cast a thousand years before had decreed it.

Damned Spell! And nothing to do about it. Freights and charter runs, consignors and insurers, bonuses and salaries, cargo terminals and repair docks, and ...

" ... Spells-spells-spells-spells-movin' up an' down again!"

A damnably good poet, that Rudyard Kipling. Although he'd been a soft-skinned human — and therefore a natural disgrace for an Engine Devil to enjoy — Kipling brought much comfort to poor Old Scratch's life. Even his best friend, Ashgaroth, knew nothing of this secret vice.

Yes, "spells-spells-spells-spells" ... Spells to cut the way through. Spells to control that rowdy crowd of hotjet-fiends. Spells to protect the sophisticated and cursedly expensive machinery from the ruining breath of Uttermost Space. Spells of many kinds.

And each one sucked at Old Scratch's strength.

Frequently he hated his work, which Scratch disliked to admit even to himself. Frequently he dreamed about The Inner Hell — his home. Yes, Inner Hell, the Fiendish Worlds, whose might and pride had been cast down by soft-skinned Mages a millennium ago.

The Great Flame had perished and now a common Engine Devil (or SuperProcessor Devil, or PowerGenerator one) had to work hard to earn enough to buy a small bit of local Flame for himself.

Old Scratch was a great swearer. He would always grumble and growl, grudge and grunt. His curses were his shield against the incompetence of captains and navigators, port wizards and fiendish innkeepers everywhere. His complaints were about the common thorns in all Engine Devils' hides.

But Old Scratch was the past, present and future master of swearing — of putting tormentors in their place. Some of his curses became legend — as legend as the bureaucratic foulups causing them.

He was so surly, so full of lava-hot deprecations everyone cringed when they saw his name on the ship's MasterList.

What no one knew was that Old Scratch had one other secret vice besides his fondness for Kipling. Which was this: he hated his work, but loved it too.

He loved the shimmering of the uncounted stars with their fiercely burning crowns when his ship passed by. He loved the storms of hard x-rays near the Black Holes; the many-colored planets, blue, purple, yellow, red or green; the voices of his remote friends coming upon wings of FastSpells from afar.

And many other wondrous things, the very sense of an Engine Devil's life.

As for Avalon ... Old Scratch returned to his most gratifying thoughts. Yeah, "Three Hanged Monks." Pure bliss. Deep curtains of smoke and black stones floating in the air — air pierced by countless thunderbolts and filled with the most welcome warmth of True Flame.

Surely no human weaklings could stand this. Spells running to and fro, burning Fiendish punch, fire sparks dancing and flashing above Engine Devils Local 666.

Scratch sighed in anticipation. He'd be in Avalon soon enough.

But first he had to work.

*   *   *

Billy Ivanov was in love.

He was ten years old, a round-eyed innocent, and the object of his youthful desires danced before him in all her splendor. She was slim, she was curvaceous, she was torrid.

Her name was Lupe Morris — half Spanish, half Amer — and she had night-dark eyes and a smile that lit up every corner of his small world.

At the moment she was dancing with her new husband, who Billy thought looked like an ape. Joe Morris was his name and he was Amer through and through.

Thick of mind and body, with a voice that rattled the ship's hull when he called sweet Lupe's name.

The music was hot, hot, hot. And Lupe jounced in her form-fitting toreador outfit, rousing feelings in Billy wholly unfamiliar but quite pleasurable.

The scene on his cabin wall shifted as his eyes followed her across the dance floor, which was several decks below his lonely berth.

He whispered a command and the Vidsprite said, "Yessir," and scrambled back to give Billy a wider view.

The ship's main salon was crowded with honeymoon couples decked out in makeshift exotica for the traditional Costume Ball that was the finale of every StarFun cruise.

Some of the costumes were daring — nubile young wives jouncing in see-throughs, muscular husbands strutting in less than what a classical statue wears. A few costumes were modest, but these were worn by middle-aged or even quite ancient couples on their second honeymoons.

The passengers aboard *HolidayOne* were exceptionally middle-class. Some had saved for years for an economy berth. Others were making the trip thanks to the generosity of their relatives.

To everyone it was a once-in-a-lifetime experience. A trip to the sinful lights and uninhibited fun at a Frontier Zone resort.

Although if truth be known the resorts were mild-mannered and far from wicked. They catered to conservative tourists on limited budgets interested in mild titilation rather than in-your-face sin.

StarFunInc knew its market well. The company offered good food and plenty of it, constant but cheap entertainment and watchful employees to ensure no one got into difficulty once they reached the resorts.

To maximize its profits — and fill all its berths — the company booked passengers from both New America and New Russia. Crowded as it was, the dance floor was divided in half by beefy security men strolling the middle zone to make sure the two traditional enemies didn't mix and spoil the fun.

Billy whispered orders and the Vidsprite zoomed in on Lupe again, coming in so tight her pearly teeth glittered in the revolving ballroom lights.

"Hey, hey, heyhey!" the vidsprite said. "Look at that, master. Va-va-voom!"

Billy was embarrassed, but he didn't call for a wider angle. Then the tempo changed to something romantic and to Billy's immense disgust Joe the Amer Ape clutched Lupe close, rubbing his body against her.

"Off!" Billy commanded and the vidsprite scowled, then switched off, dissolving the scene of the ship's main salon. It was replaced by a canned shot of the swirling colors of Uttermost Space.

Billy was an educated child who knew there was nothing to be seen at Spellspeed and the images on the vidwall were a simulation, a Fantas, of what space would look like at postlight speed. If mortal eyes could have viewed it, that is.

Billy watched the ever-changing colors and shapes for a moment, then turned away, bored.

At first the voyage had been a marvelous first-time experience. He was a half-breed child; part Russian, part American and never mind how it had happened. To Billy his half-breed status was a subject of intense shame. He was traveling to the Frontier Zone with his grandparents, who were on their second honeymoon.

Billy was an orphan and his grandparents had no friends in New Russia close enough or understanding enough to see to a half-breed child's care. During the voyage he'd kept to himself as much as possible, instinctively allowing them privacy to enjoy this long-dreamed of adventure.

He was the only child on the ship, making him a bit of a curiosity, so he'd *Eloised* at will, exploring the crew quarters, officers' mess, and all the mysterious corridors permeated with the buzz and stink of spell machinery.

Billy had even been allowed on the bridge — a really *skushne* tour as it turned out, since as everyone knew humans did little to run a starship's machinery and were stuck with boring jobs.

He sneered at the memory — the silver-haired captain and handsome first mate strutting about as if they were really in charge, instead of merely being the glamorous and bemedaled servants of the paying passengers.

Billy wished he were an Engine Devil. Now that was *real* power! Thinking about it, he made engine noises and pushed at the air with his hands as if guiding the ship.

Except if this really *were* his ship, it wouldn't be a stupid old passenger liner. It'd be something huge and military like … like … a space fortress!

The boy instantly took command of the imaginary gun turret. He pointed a finger at the vidwall, imagining Joe Morris in an American military uniform.

"Take that, you dirty old Amer dog!" he falsetto-growled and he sprayed the vidwall with imaginary projectiles.

CHAPTER TWO

At that moment Old Scratch was busy sending out powerdown spells.

The *HolidayOne* was entering The Frontier Zone, formed of hundreds of newly developed and terraformed planets — cast across the fabric of space like the Pacific Isles on Old Earth.

The Zone was inhabited by all the sentient species of the Galaxy — both human and alien. Some worlds were warm, some hot, some green and some desolate. What all had in common was that jobs were scarce but living was cheap — if a being didn't miss luxuries from home too much.

In recent years Zone administrators had pushed tourism to help fill the gap, playing up the Zone's wild and woolly history to attract visitors. The advertisements, playing on vidscreens all over the galaxy, were aimed at the working class.

The resorts offered low cost entertainment — safaris into the safest areas of the wilderness, casinos where the odds for the house were low and as little as a single LT could be wagered, re-enactments of famous Old Frontier fights, and shows featuring aging entertainers.

All the ads were clever and the program was a big success, drawing tourists from the Old Colonies, New Russia, New America and even Mother Earth. And over and over again the advertisements stressed that the days of violence and danger in the Frontier Zone were long past.

Old Scratch entered the Zone with supreme confidence, guiding the *HolidayOne* to port.

The only reason to keep a watchful eye on his surroundings were the military bases, equally divided by treaty between the United Galactic States and the Russian Galactic Federation.

The UGS and RGF bases were huge armored spheres, floating in space and armed to the teeth — grim tokens of past bloodshed.

Old Scratch had reason to be confident for all captains considered the Zone as "Danger Declined One."

* * *

Something was wrong!

Billy shot up in bed.

He was sweating heavily, heart fluttering, stomach churning. He looked about the darkened cabin. His grandparents were still absent. The curtain closing off their alcove was open, the bed empty.

Billy couldn't figure out what was bothering him. No nightmare had troubled his sleep. Still, he was drenched with a feeling of tremendous dread.

Except for the distant throb of the spellengines the ship was silent. This was normal during the false night when all humans slept.

Billy turned his head toward the ship's bulkhead. He knew that just beyond the cantilevered layers of alloy and plas forming the honeycombed skin was nothing but empty space.

There could be no danger there, no monster, no hulking brute bent on tormenting little boys. Nevertheless he had a feeling someone was watching him. No … Not him … .

… It was watching the ship!

An evil thing. A thing of malice and dark intent.

Billy swung his legs over the side of his bunk. He started to rise and then … suddenly the feeling of dread was gone!

He giggled in relief. "You're stupid, Billy," he said aloud, unconsciously using his voice to push away the last webs of fear. "There's no one there."

Instantly he felt better. He got up, went to the bathroom, then crept back into his bunk. A moment later he was asleep.

This time he dreamed. He dreamed of Lupe and their first meeting …

…She was alone at the game table, eyes cast down, peering into the black mirrored surface. She motioned with a slender finger tipped with scarlet and the viddeck of cards spread out. She motioned again and the cards rose up, shuffling as if worked by invisible hands.

A few feet away, Billy watched, fascinated by his first close view of an Amer woman. There was no one else in the room to see him staring and so he felt quite safe. Not that anybody — even an Amer — would have been disturbed.

A ten-year-old child would be a threat to no one.

Despite the bitter hatred all Americans and Russians had for one another, children were exempt — both by policy and natural human inclination.

"Play," the Amer woman commanded and the cards spread out before her, making up a complex solitaire game.

Billy thought he'd never heard such a beautiful voice. It was soft and musical and edged with humor. He moved closer and he could smell her perfume — warm and tinged with lemon flowers. It drew him closer still.

He watched her play, delicate hands fluttering in the air as she commanded card to column. After a time he saw her frown, shake her head and let out a long sigh of defeat.

"You can present the seven of spades," Billy blurted in Russian.

The woman turned, frown deepening into one of confusion. She hadn't understood. Billy was dumbfounded by her beauty. She was in her early twenties and had a small, heart-shaped face with immense eyes — dark and mysterious as the deepest space. Her lips were full, naturally red, and her smooth skin was the color of a rare tropical wood.

At her look of confusion, Billy realized what he'd done and switched to English. As a half-breed child he'd spent many secret hours studying all things American. Especially the language, which he was much better at than his teachers realized.

"I'm sorry," he said. "I didn't mean to bother you." He pointed at the spread out cards. "The seven of spades can go on the eight of hearts."

The woman looked down. "So it can," she said, surprised.

She played it and the numerical barrier fell away. A moment later she'd won and she looked up with a smile so bright Billy lost his heart.

"Thank you very much, my young friend," she said. Although Billy didn't know it, she had a slight Spanish accent. "You are very observant, yes?"

Billy shrugged. "I like to play cards," he mumbled.

The woman laughed, thrilling him. "We must not warn the casinos," she said, "that a gambling man approaches and they are in much danger."

The boy blushed. "I'm too young to gamble," he protested. And then he hated himself for making such an admission.

The woman put out her hand. "My name is Lupe," she said. "Lupe Morales." Then she laughed, blushing. "I mean, Lupe Morris. Forgive me, I haven't been married long enough to become accustomed to my husband's name."

Billy felt an odd pang at the announcement that she was married. Then he felt stupid. What could it matter? He was only a boy. For the first time he truly hated his age.

But he bravely took the woman's hand, saying, "I'm Billy Ivanov."

Lupe's dark brows rose, but the smile remained. "Russian?" she said. She squeezed his hand, sending an electric thrill through his body. "I've never met a Russian before. And your English is so good!"

Billy despaired as she let his hand go.

"I'm only part Russian," he said. "The other part's American. Just like you." In the past this had been his greatest shame — now he was immensely proud.

"I'm pleased to meet you, Billy Part American Ivanov," Lupe said, shaking his hand again. Then she gestured at the game table. "Would you like to play?"

Would he! Billy instantly took up a seat on the other side. In a moment they were both engrossed in a game of hearts. Hours passed. Lupe proved to be an excellent player and Billy had to be careful she didn't catch on when he politely let her win.

For reasons he didn't fully understand, Billy always knew what cards his opponent held. He had other small talents, like sensing when someone was near and being able to find lost objects with ease. Although he didn't know it, Billy was a budding mage.

It hadn't been noticed yet, thanks to his status as a half-breed. Both of the two super power federations — America *and* Russia — had intensive programs and tests to discover mages and wizards at an early age.

Mages were rare. Wizards, who were much more powerful, were rarer still. And it was wizards and mages who made the Galaxy livable for mortals — commanding the demons and their minions to do their bidding. Combining magic with human ingenuity and technology to make starships for space, weapons for war, computers for science and business and even quick cookers for household kitchens.

But for Billy, all that was in the future — if he was to have a future, that is.

He stirred in his sleep, dreaming of Lupe. They played cards like they had that first time. He let her win and she rewarded him with a kiss, soft and sweet. Billy sighed, pulling the blankets tighter.

In his dream Joe Morris didn't rudely interrupt his wife and insist it was late and he wanted to go to bed. He didn't leer at Lupe, or put a possessive hand on her round haunch when she left with him.

And he didn't turn and fix Billy with those flat Amer eyes and say, "Night kid."

No, none of those things happened in Billy's dream. Instead Billy was tall and muscular and by God, significant!

And Lupe kissed him and purred his name in that funny way she had, making it two names instead of one: "Bil-ly. Bil-ly."

Just like that.

*   *   *

Old Scratch was satisfied. All was well.

His latest spell whirled in the very depths of the Continuum and the plasma spurs rushed from the ship's jet spiracles as if from the nostrils of Leviathan himself.

He allowed himself a little break.

And then …

What?

Had something passed by … just at the edge of his magical sight? A faint tremble, a slight shiver, had seemed to run through the still bones of the ship. One swift second … and then all was gone.

Old Scratch sighed. Too many e-days in Uttermost Space. Too many spells, too much growling and grousing and drilling of his crew. Rest — that's what he needed most of all.

Then:

Oh! Again that feeling of something just beyond his sight.

Scratch shook his scaly head. Must be that damned Tob. That damned good for nothing Control Brownie!

It was Tob's task to monitor the upper-port PlasmaFeeder but the lazy Brownie was seldom to be found working in its hot jaws. Yet when it came to Really Hot Stories, Tob was an eager champion.

Old Scratch suspected the miserable Brownie had cast a snooperspell on some of the honeymoon suites and was selling his dirty recordings to the dim-witted Goblins.

Scratch didn't blame the Goblins. He felt sorry for them. Their work was the hardest, the dirtiest and the lowest paid. But as for that damned Brownie …

"Tob!" Old Scratch roared. "May the angels and elves roast you to devildust! What are you doing, sneaking around in there?"

There was no answer.

"Tob!"

His Ruling Spell roamed through the ship. An extremely powerful one, filled with real wrath.

Finally, "Yes, Master Scratch!"

A frightened Tob wisped up from the burning throat of the PlasmaFeeder.

"Report!"

"Parameters all normal, Master Scratch. Generating spirits — density twelve megaGhosts per one magic …"

"Never mind," Scratch commanded, cutting Tob off.

And he thought: oddity of all oddities, Tob really *was* at his proper post. So the disturbance couldn't have been caused by him.

His big devil shoulders sagged and he breathed a long sigh, thinking, Old Scratchy, you're just too tired. You need rest, my fiendish one. Rest.

He'd have to be careful. He couldn't let some tyrant of a Supervisor Enchanter know that he, Old Scratch, firm and solid as stone, who never failed to bring a starship to port, suffered from halluces.

Well, so be it.

Nothing had happened. Remember that, Scratchy. Nothing in general or even in particular had happened.

Back to work.

Spell, spell, spells. Casting, whirling, cutting The Way Through. Another spell. Taking the Brownies' reports. Goblin crew hard at it — keeping the plasma hot for the jet-spirits.

Old Scratch's fiendish team was doing its best, but the cold threat persevered.

There — deep, deep in Scratch's memory.

The Void stretching endlessly before the starship was common Uttermost Space, with ruinous streams of many PowerRivers, cold and hot magic torrents, invisible for softskins except for their most powerful Mages.

And then:

It was like a short spasm of pain. Pain running through the ship from rib to rib, from strut to strut.

Dreadful vibrations touched the StarEngine's external circuits. Small, frightened fiends rushed about in blind panic.

The vibration shuddered off the ship's skeleton, stippling the very fabric of space like sand raining on the surface of a still pool.

The disturbance rippled out, stirring the deep Spacefolds where swift scout ships waited, listening, listening. Their tensed antennae bristled in reaction.

Then, before Old Scratch could overmaster his crew, coded signals beamed out.

CHAPTER THREE

The alarm howled at a most inconvenient time.

Katya's uniform skirt was coming up, up, up. And the handsome young Russian officer's trousers were coming down, down, down.

"Damn!" she said.

Not only passion but all her hopes for the future clung to that delicious moment before the alarm sounded. The answer to Katya's dreams was a tall officer with sun-kissed hair and even sunnier prospects.

His name was Igor Dolgov and on his cheek was a dashing combat token — a small, but deep purple scar that whitened when he became upset. And just now as the alarm resounded through the space fortress *Borodino* Katya saw that scar become as white as the driven snow.

Igor's high forehead suddenly glistened with sweat.

"Damn!" she said again.

Katya, assigned to the headquarters' cryptographic team, was a common Frontier Girl. Small, slender, yet her figure was somehow lush. Built for the boat ride, as they say. But all that promise of smooth sailing over gentle swells was being forgotten as that damned alarm hammered away and Igor's scar got whiter and whiter.

Disappointment shone in Katya's big dark eyes. She was thinking, this young busybody seems to be the only one on the whole base thin-witted enough to marry a girl so common. He's my passage off this dismal place.

She'd be swept away to the glamorous life of an officer's wife back in New Russia. With a thick Frontier Officer's spousal credit of LT's to nourish her. Dim as Igor was, he was from a good family and destined for promotion.

And if only Katya could latch on it would be the end of the squalid existence she faced in the poor neighborhoods of her home planet.

Her heart and hopes sank as Igor moved away, clutching at his trousers.

"I'll be damned!" Igor exclaimed. "What's going on? False alarm? A training exercise?"

Katya knew she'd been defeated. But she was game and tried to make that defeat temporary.

"It's all right, Igor, honey," she said, standing on her tiptoes to kiss him. "Never mind. Next time …"

Igor complained, "Those upper echelon arse kissers will never allow us to …"

His voice trailed off and he shook his head at the unfairness of it all.

Then he made a small shrug of apology to Katya, fastened his uniform and pushed open the door of the tiny chamber they'd chosen for their love nest — hidden amongst all the machinery that littered the *Borodino's* powerplant level.

"What's worse," he said, "it's my turn in the chair!"

By this he meant he had the shooting officer's duty watch. When the alarm sounded he was the officer in control of all warsystems on the great space station, with hundreds of men and hundreds of thousands of fiendish creatures waiting to be unleashed at his command.

As he stepped out of the chamber and looked back at Katya, who was adjusting her clothes, he thought, The poor little fool. Is she serious? To consider me such a dolt as to marry *her*? It's just a little fun I want. But she — she …

The corridors of the *Borodino* were suddenly filled with tramping. The boomgrates bellowed, "All hands on deck!"

Igor angrily brushed away all thoughts about Katya. Let the Engine Devils get her! They were crazy about that kind of thing, it was said.

And he rushed on, weaving his way through the throngs to the command center.

*   *   *

It was a wide hall with shields built of the very best armored alloy.

Good plas-metal was accompanied with good spells — eleven mages not less then fifth class and three real Wizards.

Igor took courage from all that strength as he glanced about the command center, moving at a controlled fast walk for his seat. Then he looked up at his problem on the huge vidwall and cursed.

The damned Amers were close, way too close! And suddenly the chamber's armored shielding felt very, very thin.

A huge anatomic chair snatch up his body like a predator. He found himself praying as the heavy bars locked him in place with a clang like prison gates slamming closed. A combat helmet lowered from above, covering his entire head.

Inside, the helmet's display flashed red and blue. White lines shot across and through it.

Igor saw instantly what was happening:

Yeah, coded transmission. On a secret pulse wave, changing its length and frequency each second. Hiding precious information in waves of white noise. He searched, searched, then —

That's it!

And he had it by the guts.

Igor may not have been very bright — he only thought he saw through Katya and in the end he would happily succumb — but he was a genius in the chair.

He feared the device, but once in the chair's clasp he became part of it. Igor was at the top of his class in the training exercises. He played the warboard like a grand musical instrument. Fingers flashing, throat-miked commands singing the song of death.

Deep in the weapons room hundreds of fiendish inhabitants stirred, obeying his orders.

Mentos — mental exchange — is much faster than words or fingers. And so that was what Carvaserin, the human Wizard-In-Chief, used when he received Igor's commands and roused his hordes.

He'd trained his magical crew well and in no time at all his fiendish scouts received their orders.

*　　*　　*

"Uruumph!" belched Chyvaist, the tiny DeathSpirit. He was curled in several smoke rings and he floated up from them to the ready-to-shoot missile. "Hey, guys," he cried, "it's time for a feast! Target in range!"

"Will somebody shut him up!" growled Homula, the great Daughter of Death.

Homula, mother and feeder of the forever hungry DeathSpirits rose from the far corner like an immense black cloud, shapeless and faceless.

She took charge, gulped down the ready time and saw she had five seconds before launch — more than enough time to talk, to consider.

"Maybe we'd better check this further," she cautioned.

Chyvaist turned the color of old blood. "What's to check?" he said. "We've got our orders. If we wait … and I'm caught out … then boom! A big damned boom!"

In the curling wheels of red smoke that formed him there appeared something like an odd, crumbled up and quite evil face. Chyvaist was only an old DeathSpirit, that's all. Waiting out his final moments.

"Let 'em be roasted!" spat Khinvaist, another battle spirit.

None of the supernatural recruits on board the` Russian space fortress cared a bit about the possible massacre of their fiendish kin powering the enemy ship. Those who die are weak and must die, was their motto.

This was one of the cruel, circular laws of the Fiendish World. Some theorized their natural cruelty was the secret of the ancient victories of human wizards over the powerful but primitive Demons and Devils and their lesser kin.

Others dismissed this explanation, hinting darkly of a mysterious cabal, that might, or might not be human. But none of these conspiracy theorists ever spoke openly about their ideas.

Within the spheres of influence of both super powers, it was well understood by all that it was best not to discuss such things.

Homula considered her options and gave a long sigh. "Good luck," she said.

Like a mother, she feared each battleraid. She fed her crew, cared for them, and she knew each launch might be their last.

And she worried, What if those damned shatatniks had a powerful Wizard aboard?

"Well, time to go." This from a column of red smoke that entered the rocket warhead.

Another puff of smoke — "Okay, boss, I'm ready!"

"Good hits," growled Chyvaist, entering the Fiendish Circle — the engagement of all battle spirits' minds. This allowed ghosts and other magical creatures to see what was happening on the battlefield.

Homula whirled the dark veils of her bodysmoke and joined the party.

* * *

The Fiendish Circle transmitted the image from the missile warhead to the central post monitors.

Igor once again requested information from the database.

And then, and then …

* * *

"Wah! To work, to work you miserable horde!" boomed an old bearded dwarf.

He was crouched in the middle of the optics drive inside the base's big main supercomputer.

"Well, well, what are you doing? Don't do that!" This was for Jungde the HellBat, the message bearer and executioner.

Although both dwarves and Jungde were rather small (the HellBat, for instance, was no more than a fingertip in height), the passions burning there were intense.

"How dare you tell me what to do?" shrieked the HellBat.

A long whip snaked in the air.

"Information request! Codes accessed! Read, you fiends, read! Or I'll crack your thick skulls and tear your beards to pieces!"

Mighty spells cut in, accelerating the timeflow.

What seemed like long minutes for the team of OpticsDiskDrive Dwarves was nanoseconds for Igor, who'd just miked the command.

With many curses and much blame-heaping the great force of ODD dwarves rushed to their places. The huge disk began to rotate. Sitting above it in special cradles, dwarves began to spellread the stored information. Another team was busy rotating the drive.

"Well, well," the HellBat said. It seemed pleased and its hideous face reflected a shadow of a smile. "So be it. Continue working!"

*　*　*

That's it!

For Igor there was no mistaking the electronic signature — it was American military code, no doubt about it. You could kiss his ass and call it Father Lenin if it wasn't so.

Woolly-headed Yank bastards, how dare they even think of it? They'd disguised a Class A destroyer, bristling with the latest weapons, as an elderly civilian cruise liner.

And from all the red alert signals on his visor those weapons were moments from firing on the *Borodino*.

Igor took it even more personally than that. They were about to fire on him!

The response was clear. Strike first! To do otherwise risked certain destruction — or a firing squad if you survived long enough to face a court martial.

But Igor didn't have his shooting orders. The authority to take this most final of all actions was not his. He waited, moist breath clouding the vidmask.

He properly kept his mind blank. He was a tense, vibrating weapon ready to be unleashed.

Igor didn't wonder that the long peace in the Frontier Zone had been violated. If asked, he'd say it only figured that those sneaky devil Amers would pull such a trick — violating all laws of warfare, plus the shaky truce that had been in affect for so many years.

It didn't matter to those murderous Amer bastards this was a Danger Declined Zone, declared so by solemn men in sober clothes.

A voice barked, "Dolgov, what's happening?"

Shivers ran up Igor's spine. It was the Wizard-in-Chief!

"An Amer destroyer, Master," Igor replied, "pretending to be a cruise liner."

"Stand by. I'll try to stop him first."

A moment of relief. Mixed with disappointment. He was ready to shoot, dammit! But no, caution first. Let the Wizard-in-Chief deal with it.

The wizard would call upon the Engine Devil. Igor knew those creatures of the cold death of Uttermost Space were protected with the hardest and most solid spells. If any being could stop the Amers it was their Engine Devil.

As the master wizard and the Engine Devil conferred, Igor continued to monitor the enemy destroyer. Now he could see it really was a civilian liner. But it had the armor and weapons and intelligence gear of a Class A destroyer.

The ship's interiors had been gutted to make way for the most modern of hyper engines. And there was a young Engine Devil ready and fresh on first watch.

Igor knew all his observations were being shared by the devils in the weapons room. They'd be outraged at such a long delay. Their fiendish blood would be aboil with the desire to kill, kill, kill.

"Dolgov!" The wizard again.

"Yes, Master."

"No luck."

A breath of hesitation, then:

"You must shoot!"

Igor almost slammed his palm on the fat red fire button. Training held him back. He was the shooting officer. In such circumstances the shooting officer must be certain.

Commander Rusinov's voice crackled in his ears.

"Dolgov! We can't stop it!"

"Give the order, sir. I must have the order."

And they came fast and harsh:

"Shoot, dammit, shoot!"

"Yes, sir. Shooting procedure in operation sir.

"Weapons room. All systems in order. Target in range.

"Launch!"

Igor depressed the firing button and …

" … At last," Chyvaist grumbled, "we get to go."

And in the strange stilled time of the weapons room Igor heard the long hiss of the firing tubes, the sound of it hanging in the air like a slow-burning fuse.

Then the missile slid out, sleepy, just waking up, but waking up grumpy and mean and now it wanted a target.

Searching, searching …

The moment Igor slapped the button he nearly shit his pants.

But then euphoria caught him as all the data rushed in. Raw signals, shouted voices, the smell of magic and the mental echo of fiendish personalities.

It was fantastic!

This was Igor's first real combat launch. All the simulator training and polygon shooting was replaced in a heady rush by real experience.

The missile containing Chyvaist sped toward its target.

A small team of goblins fed the engine, stoking it with hot spells. And Chyvaist himself — curled in a red globe in the very middle of the warhead — was honing in on the enemy ship. His senses penetrated the spells shielding the ship.

Igor flash/caught Chyvaist's observations and was surprised.

The ship seemed too weak for a destroyer.

But was that part of its disguise?

He shuddered as Chyvaist's evil and hissing voice crawled into his mind like a poisonous worm.

"Hey boss! I'm on target! Goblins ejecting! ... Done! ... Yeah, I'm up on 'em! ...

"Okay, now ... now ...

A pause and then Chyvaist's "voice" came, so calm, and so ... cruel ...

"Done, boss."

Then:

"Uh, boss.

"Boss?

"Big fecal OOPS, here."

"What?"

"Uh, I don't know ... but I think we're in some deep ass, Boss. Real deep!"

More static ...

"Uh, Boss? ... Boss?

"You there?"

Igor couldn't answer.

The DeathSpirit's message had come through loud and clear.

Igor was crying.

CHAPTER FOUR

Old Scratch was in big trouble.

Something was happening all around his ship. And those miserable softskins were sleeping. Couldn't they see? Couldn't they hear? Couldn't they feel the sticky web they'd just entered?

A deathly cold web. So cold even he, Old Scratch, was frightened. He continued his work, but … Was that someone calling him?

Nonsense.

Halluces again.

But then …

What?! …

What's this?

The voice of a DeathSpirit? Howling and roaring of a Goblin team? Voices of confusion: The missile! … Turn right! … Right, by damn! Right! No! Too late! … Too late!… And … Damn!, there's civilians aboard that ship!

Tearing his very soul and body, Old Scratch clawed for all his power and hurled the liner to the side.

He roared in pain, already understanding all was lost, but still trying to save those damned softskins!

Frightened dwarves, goblins and brownies cried in panic … and in that same moment the missile reached its target.

In the missile hundreds of thousands of hungry ghosts, tortured with bitter desire, rushed forward, devouring all wizardry, dissolving every bit of magic shielding the ship.

Then the high-explosive heart of the warhead burst through and flame waves roamed the chambers and corridors.

* * *

Billy was asleep.

But his dreams had turned grim and he was uneasy.

A sudden sense of cruelty roughed his senses and he shot up in bed.

He felt It coming for him! A beast rushing down with slavering jaws.

Instinct took over and as he threw up his hands he hurled a hard spell! His first spell.

But potent.

And then … boom!

Billy closed his eyes. Fire scorching and hammering all around.

And he shouted, "Lupe!"

The explosion broke the liner into three parts.

Cold talons ripped at Old Scratch's heart. Black blood covered his sight. Nothing to do … all was lost. His pain and despair made him forget his own approaching death.

Poor Scratch. He couldn't do anything to save his ship. The missile's WarSpell was too strong.

Maybe — if he was given the chance — he'd complain to the Ruling Spirit.

This was intolerable. Too damned much!

First, who in the hells was responsible for that damned DeathSpirit? The whole breed was dangerously irresponsible. Something had to be done about them. Everyone knew DeathSpirits were a race noted for refusing to speak to their enemies until the day of the Great Judgment.

Second, this spirit (with a disgustingly evil name, which could not be said aloud by a well-respected Engine Devil for fear of soiling his tongue) was REALLY, REALLY eager to kill.

It wasn't right, Old Scratch thought.

And then, wham! The explosion reached critical and triggered an ultrafast extrapolation of the PlasmaFeeders. Overheated substances rushed over the fiendish crew.

Tob was the first to die.

Others followed immediately.

Along with all the softskins they despised so much. But it hurt Old Scratch. Hurt him most deeply. It was his duty to protect those despised ones.

Then he felt a small bit of brightness prickle his weary soul. Somewhere out there one of the softskins had survived.

But who? And how?

* * *

Billy couldn't have answered the question himself. How could it be that he was the only human to survive the tragedy of *HolidayOne*?

He had the numb memory of his last actions in the cabin. He'd thrown up his hands like a shield just as the flame waves had reached the door. And in that moment a desperate desire for life made him reach out — a jumble of words, images, thoughts.

He wanted to be safe. To live. To breathe. To hear his heartbeat. Nothing more.

"Lupe!" he shouted, and in his shout he knew she was gone. More terrible still, so were his grandparents.

And he ran, ran, ran …

Ran to a place, ran to a time until he found himself quite whole and unhurt and floating in space over the bursting liner.

* * *

Old Scratch was finally forced to abandon his engines — his ship.

In the final moment, trying to save anybody — never mind if they be fiend or human — he cast a spell of reversion. Pouring the vortex of burning flame into the black hungry mouths of his engines.

He couldn't have done it earlier — he had to wait until the attacking flame was near enough. Unfortunately for his crew "near enough" meant their deaths.

Scratch tried to save them, but in the end he couldn't do it and the "near enough" spell saved his life.

But he didn't want to live!

Shame, bitter shame fouled his soul. His ship, his passengers, his crew, all gone.

If he'd had a choice he would have chosen to die along with his crew and all those wormy softskins.

But, O Mother Destiny! That damned spell saved Old Scratch against his will.

The spell he cast worked quite well without the will of its master. And like Billy, Scratch was thrown into the burning space. Flame tongues licked his red skin — then … suddenly he forgot about the pain.

His senses were overwhelmed by a terrible vision.

But was it halluces?

Or was it real?

He wasn't sure, but it seemed to him that somewhere near — somewhere … quite … near, but not in the same Void — something great, something enormous lurked.

That form, that entity stretched … O Mother Destiny, it stretched beyond the beyond! The entity was all, it was nothing, it was everything, it was … like being able to see Darkness.

What he saw, or imagined he saw, was a creature of intolerable might and power — such might, such power that even Old Scratch had never experienced such a thing.

But here it was at hand. It was … Ah, please, not so near … because Scratch suddenly knew this Thing, this Being could easily tear him to pieces with a single glance of its hoary eyes.

That was enough for him. He tried not to look but those terrible eyes started to turn … he felt the creature's every movement … nearer and nearer … no way to escape …

And then he lost consciousness.

* * *

Igor was tragically conscious.

Between shoot and hit — like thought and action — there is slow-collapsing shadow. There are many Cancel/Abort stops along the way.

But those points pass quickly and then all of a sudden the DeathSpirit is saying "Uh, boss?" and there are no more in betweens.

No place to cancel.

Nowhere to stop but the end of all ends.

In the very last moment he saw it all, saw a vision more savage than any nightmare. He saw the cabins filled with innocent people. Saw their faces, some awake and knowing, some asleep and saved from that final horror.

Although it was impossible, Igor believed he could hear their desperate cries echoing in Uttermost Space.

Then all was cold, silent Void.

Except the mocking voice of Chyvaist, who didn't give a big stooping DeathSpirit fart if it was a mistake or not. The fewer softskins the better.

And if anybody objected they could take it up with his Shop Steward, because this had been a "shoot and no cancel" operation from the beginning.

"Direct hit, boss!" he gloated. "Nice work. Pity it was a wrong'un or there'd be bonuses for everybody."

Then all around him Igor heard a victorious roar sound through the *Borodino's* Command Center.

It rang from chamber to chamber, through the com center, the on watch mess and the lavs and finally into the Hall Of Magic where Carvaserin was smiling his Master Wizard's smile, watching the enemy ship's final blazing gasp, thinking he'd won a great victory over the Amers.

And Igor realized he was the only human in the space fortress who knew what had happened.

He tore off his helmet. The autoreturn swooped the thing up and away, taking all hope with it.

Igor stared blindly at his warboard. His heart was racing, his body poured sweat as if trying to flush away sin.

And he thought:

What have I done?

What have *we* done?
Curse us all. Curse us all forever.

CHAPTER FIVE

The alarm clock roared mercilessly at six-forty. It was an expensive mechanical toy. "Mechanics only," the advert had guaranteed.

It was the only reason she'd bought it. As a clock it was nearly worthless. It gained an hour a day, forcing the owner to do sophisticated calculations when she set the alarm.

A sleepy voice addressed the clock. "Ummm … Just a little bit more … Ummm …"

A thick blanket was immediately yanked over the pretty head of golden hair that spread wildly over the pillow. The space next to the woman was empty and had been so for several years.

The clock roared again. Not "rang", but "roared" with a harsh mechanical voice guaranteed (again according to the advert prose) "to raise the dead from their coffins like the Trumpets Of Judgment Day."

The owner, Tanya Lawson, sometimes thought the sales pitch hadn't been that much of an exaggeration. Now was one such moment.

Damn, damn, and double damn! Gotta get up. On your feet, woman! Up … Up … But, it's such a beautiful dream, and … I don't wanna …

As if sensing the revolt, the clock roared a third time.

Tanya groaned and threw the blanket aside. She untangled the fingers of her lazier but happier twinself, thinking, Can't help it, sister mine. Duty calls. There's worlds to be saved, crime to be hammered to its knees and ferocious bosses to face. Bosses who made their feelings plain to tardy officers of the United Worlds Police.

She reached out, slender fingers uncurling — and clicked on the remote control button. It was labeled "dawn" — the word spelled out in black ink on a small piece of paper and stuck to the button with adhesive tape.

There was a mechanical hum and the curtains drew away. The gray beams of morning crawled into the room, mixing with the light cast by Tanya's lamps.

They were real lamps and the low yellow light they cast came from ancient filaments glowing in vacuum bulbs. The bulbs were powered with good old fashioned electricity. Never mind the electricity came from a PowerGenerator in the basement. And that generator was totally magical.

The point was, Tanya loved those damned lamps and didn't begrudge all the LT's she'd paid for them.

Tanya liked a good breakfast and so as soon as the "dawn" button was pressed a tiny automatic kitchenette went to work for her: Coffee dripping, bacon frying, eggs poaching, toast toasting. Once again, each object was mechanical and electrical, performing its function without use of magic.

It was Tanya's habit to eat well in the morning because it was frequently the last real meal she'd enjoy before the day was done. When a criminal mess hit the fan at United Worlds Police Headquarters the hours got very long indeed.

To the envy of male and female colleagues alike, Tanya had a healthy appetite and could eat when she wanted and how much she wanted with little fear. She was slender and strong and quick and she kept her muscles and stamina trained to their peak. On one wall of her apartment were a pair of rapiers. Below was a set of boxing gloves.

Her entire apartment was filled with primitive electronics, mostly from hundreds of years ago. For that reason everything was very expensive. To hell with the expense! It made Tanya feel ... well, comfortable, dammit.

Actually, it was more than just a matter of comfort. Tanya was border-line phobic when it came to supernatural creatures. The homes and apartments of her friends, relatives, and UWP colleagues were filled with magical servants — Brownies, Dwarves, Goblins, Peaceful Spirits, and on and on. All enslaved in the machinery it took to make a modern, work-free home.

Not Tanya. She'd paid and overpaid for obsolete mechanical devices — and their repair manuals as well — with one purpose in mind. And that was to make her home off limits to all Supernatural Beings.

Most of the mechanical devices supposedly hailed from the last decade or of the Twentieth Century — a little over a thousand years before. A few were dated a little later — the youngest had been manufactured in 2004.

It was during that period that momentous events — whose origins and causes were obscure — changed human kind forever.

Things made by hand, or in factories, were abandoned in favor of a new technology entirely based on sorcery and magical creatures.

And so Tanya was a throwback. A woman out of her time who believed deep in her heart and soul that she would have been more comfortable — and certainly much happier — in that bygone Twentieth Century era. When science and art were limited only by the speed of light and human imagination.

Although Tanya had made her home a refuge from magic, she couldn't avoid such things at her office.

At UWP headquarters there was so much magic buzzing in the air her teeth were always clenched. The place was full of powerful mages casting spells within its walls.

In the modern, sorcery driven world of the 30th Century, Tanya's aversion to magic was a most definite oddity.

Oddity number two was that she was a rather powerful sorceress herself.

Although she hated to admit it, when forced she could cast a spell nearly as fast as a full wizard — humans who could use thought images instead of chants to make their spells.

In a matchup Tanya was strong enough to let that same wizard know he was in a fight. As for the lower ranks — well, let's just say mages and beginning wizards might find themselves in definite trouble if they crossed spells with Tanya Lawson.

Although she was a Master Investigator in the United Worlds Police — the equivalent of a major in the other UWP branches — Tanya rarely used her powers, and then only grudgingly.

It was this little chip in her armor that gave her boss, Harry Cooper, a one star general aching to make it two, a target to attack.

Tanya frowned, thinking of the last time she and Harry had wrestled over the subject.

She remember how furious he'd been, how much his carefully cultured Don Juan act had been shaken …

* * *

"Why, why, why," Harry moaned, "do we have to go through this every damned time?"

Tanya sighed. "It isn't every damn time, Harry. Just *some* times. You of all people ought to know how busy I am. Every time I turn around you throw another case at me."

The situation with her boss was further complicated by Harry's notorious libido. He'd made some very definite moves on her. Moves she'd spurned politely but firmly, knowing as she did so that Harry wouldn't take it well.

He was a Lothario of much low renown and it was said he kept a meticulous record of all his conquests. Regardless of how carefully Tanya spelled out "N … O …" she knew it wouldn't appease Harry.

He'd play hurt, leap on her slightest mistake and jump for any perceived gap at the slightest opportunity.

In between he'd be a generally irritating pain in the ass, looking for any chance he could to criticize her.

That particular day was one of those times.

Tanya spread her hands. "How can I possibly take two weeks off for a seminar?"

"A seminar that happens to be about sorcery," Harry growled. "A seminar aimed at advancement in the magical ranks to full wizardry."

He slammed the desk. "And those are the kind you always turn down, Major Lawson."

Tanya, not one to be alarmed by desk pounding, widened her eyes in surprise. "It's just a coincidence, Harry," she said. "It's got nothing to do with anything."

Harry shook his head in disgust. "Okay. One more chance. But by God I'm going to remember this conversation. You just try calling it a *coincidence* next time around."

The next time would come soon enough and Harry would get mad and Tanya would make excuses. And there was always the complication of Harry's sexual obsession. Although Tanya was beginning to wonder if her boss's obsession might not be playing out in her favor.

There *was* a line which could not be crossed. So Tanya used that edge, made it one of her many weapons in the bureaucratic wars of the UWP. In the end it always came out the same and Tanya would once again sidestep the whole issue of sorcery.

Besides, when you got rock-bottom down to it, what could Harry really say? Tanya was every inch a professional. She was the best investigator on Harry's staff and then some. It was well known by all that the more difficult the mission, the more Tanya would shine.

* * *

Tanya moved through her morning routine: coffee, quick exercises, breakfast, needle shower, more coffee, etc. She disdained the few items of cosmetics she kept on her shelf for "special" occasions.

In her closet, back behind the deep-green UWP uniforms, were a few feminine possessions. A fancy dress or two, accessories and evening wraps. In her bureau there were filmy things for underneath. But the truth was Tanya thought very little of all that frilly business. It was an insult to her identity. She liked her uniform, dammit! And in her civilian hours she dressed casually, like an athlete at rest.

Some of her old school friends said she shouldn't dress so much like a man if she wanted to catch one. Tanya only nodded and smiled when they said this, remembering the days when these same friends argued long and hard in the dormitory about "women who define themselves by the male company they keep."

Tanya just wasn't interested. Men bored her. And they were so spoiled they weren't worth the trouble of getting over the boredom. This is not to say Tanya was attracted to women. Nor was she sexless. She'd had her share of affairs, including a powerful, soul-shattering one that had ended tragically.

But Tanya was older and wiser now and scarred as well, so the ritual of meeting and mating only irritated the hell out of her. Tanya's life consisted of work and friends, with a nice apartment to come home to where all her things — her eccentric things — would be just as she left them.

Best of all there wasn't anyone waiting for her who'd lift a questioning eyebrow at her odd habits.

There was one other thing — one main thing — driving her. Tanya Lawson was determined that one day she would command the United World Police.

Although sometime she had to brush aside a most important question: Why the hell would any sane person want to be UWP chief? At its best it was a thankless job. And at its worst — well, better not think about it.

Now that she was dressed Tanya had time for one more cup of coffee. Sipping at the thick, strong brew, she picked up her trusty antique remote, pressing the button she'd labeled with the letter "N." This stood for NewsNet, America's galaxy-wide information system.

Again, instead of a magically-formed vidcast leaping up in the middle of the room, a good old fashioned TV flat screen winked into view on the wall. The satellite antenna system had cost her a fortune.

Thank God for Aunt Ann's will, which had left Tanya well off enough to afford such things — the UWP not being known for its enlightened salary practices. But freedom had been Aunt Ann's intent, bless her old feminist soul.

In this case the antique television set helped Tanya achieve her most fervent goal, which was: NOT A SINGLE MAGICAL CREATURE in her house!

The screen turned red. Before Tanya realized what was happening she heard the carefully modulated, normally pedantic, tones of a famous news commentator crack into high-pitched hysterics.

It was a rush in her ears, a trip hammer on her senses — words, ugly words, hard words, punishing words; words like rocks fetched for a village stoning. Never mind that America was a village of twenty billion citizens and allies making up twenty billion more. All this spread across a starry empire.

The commentator was saying:

"The Russians have finally shown their true colors, my friends. And that color is blood."

As he railed on, the screen played the StarfunInc advertisement for the tour, showing impossibly beautiful young people boarding the "Honeymoon Special." There were other canned shots of "fun on board," "romantic, starlit nights," etc. All setting the mood for the livecast.

"The fact is, my friends," the commentator said, "in the whole thousand year history of the Cold War there's never been an incident so cruel, so, so ... unconscionable. Hundreds dead, my friends. And no graves for them in space to mark the place where they were martyred in Freedom's Cause."

As the commentator went on an artist's animated rendering of the tragedy filled the screen. The space liner, StarFunInc emblazoned on its side, cruised through wondrous scenes of space. While in clever cutaways a Russian fortress — labeled the *Borodino* — lurked in the shadows.

" ... All innocents," the commentator said. "Honeymoon innocents. Out to start a new life. To create new families. American families. The very heart of our system of checks and balances and freedoms.

"Oh, you'll hear the nay sayers crying in the days to come, my friends. Nay sayers who deny the evidence before their face. And from past history we know those Rooskie dupes in our society — our free society, God Bless America — will say it was only an unfortunate accident.

"They'll say the proof is, there were also a few Russian citizens aboard the *HolidayOne*. But that's all propaganda, my friends. Rooskie propaganda. And I don't apologize for using the word. They're Rooskies, damn them. Cowardly Rooskies!

"And when all is said and done my friends ... When all the investigations are complete ... The facts will be borne out that the Rooskies were willing to kill their own people to get at ours."

On the screen a simulated missile hit the starliner and the TV screen exploded into flames. And over this image the commentator said:

"We're playing with monsters, my friends. No getting around it. I've said it time and again on this broadcast. The Rooskies are Satan's toys. And the only thing they understand is force.

"You either have them at your throat ... or under your boot ..."

The NewsNet livecast was so packed with carefully crafted images and sound that it took Tanya several moments to recover from the shock and horror of it all.

Hate and fear were so strong they even bled through her ancient monitoring system. Then professionalism took over and she grabbed at the few nuggets of real fact offered in the newsfeed.

A cruise liner had been shot down in the neutral Frontier Zone. Mostly young people aboard ... honeymoon couples ... a direct hit so there was no mistake the spaceliner had been the target ... all dead, except one boy … and an engine devil … No denial from the Russians … apologies offered by high officials for the tragic mistake …

After the horror that was *HolidayOne* had sunk in and Tanya got a grip on her emotions, she knew instantly the UWP would be called in to investigate.

She steeled herself to watch the replay of the simulated attack. The screen showed the scheme of *HolidayOne*. Green and red lines, bolstered by animated projections, indicated the Russian fortress and the trajectory of its missile.

Once again she was rocked as the animated missile struck and the screen was filled with fire.

And she wondered, What the hell were those Russians up to?

Her feelings were duplicated — and vastly exaggerated — onscreen as NewsNet sought the reactions of "average" Americans.

What followed was hysteria in the raw.

Weeping people — families and friends of the victims. Clenched fists, angry faces, mouths open in an endless cry for revenge. And there were experts on Russian perfidy. Guys who said, "I told you so" for pay. Shots of Online news heads, reading: "Tragedy In Space," and "Russian Love Killers!" and "Americans Demand Action!"

Just then her antique telephone jangled into life.

Tanya took a breath — she'd been unconsciously expecting the call from the moment she saw the newscast.

She picked up the receiver. "Lawson."

"Tanya! What the hell are you still doing at home?"

Harry's voice was at the edge of panic. Tanya needed to calm him.

"And a helluva good morning to you too, Harry," she said.

"Haven't you heard what's happened?" Harry snarled. "Or is that screwball antique wonder of a TV of yours still warming up?"

"Yeah, I heard," Tanya said. "The Russians have gone and done a bad thing."

"For crying out loud, Tanya," Harry said, "don't be so cool about it. This is a crisis, dammit. A crisis!"

And Tanya thought, patience, patience dear. You didn't take Harry to bed with you, so clench your teeth and recall Mother Lawson's Rule Number Seventy Two for Good Girls: you must not tell Harry he's a complete ass and has no business running your section.

"I'm aware it's a crisis, Harry," Tanya said. "Civilian vacation liners don't get shot down every day, last I heard."

"So why are you still home?" Harry wanted to know.

Tanya choked back the many sharp retorts that immediately sprang to mind. Which would be followed by the entirely satisfying experience of slamming the phone into its cradle, crushing that harsh, foolish voice.

However, if she wanted to keep her job it was best to stifle those feelings.

So she said, smooth as she could, "I'll be at headquarters in half an hour, Harry. Which is as fast as it can be done."

Harry was thrown into a new tizzy.

"You're not going to use that hellish machine of yours, are you? I mean, what if something happened? What if it quit all of a sudden and crashed? Then where would we be?"

Tanya wanted to say, then I'd be dead and the crisis would have to go on without me. Somehow I'm sure the UWP — and the galaxy — would survive.

Instead she said, "There's no other way, Harry. Unless you don't want to see me until tomorrow at this time, assuming the traffic's light."

"But ..."

Tanya cut him short, going formal. "I'll be at the office at seven-twenty, sir. Per usual."

Then in a rush, "Sorry, sir, but if I'm going to be on time I have to leave now."

She hung up. Maybe slamming the phone just a little bit.

Damn that Harry!

CHAPTER SIX

The trouble was he was too hyped for the job.

Here he was two long breaths away from "mission complete." One more breath and he could "confirm kill." It would take only a gasp for "Dustoff!" and then all he had to do was run like hell and dodge the usual barrage of enemy bullets.

Eight breaths — maybe ten, tops — and he'd be a Stealtime hop from the tallest, coldest depthcharger in alcoholic history. He intended to keep several columns of bar'bots busy supplying him for two blissful weeks.

Or maybe he'd get laid first. Screwed, blued and tattooed for two solid weeks. And then a nice drunk weekend before he had to report back for SleepLock at Geronimo Lake.

Okay, fine. Okay, sure, but what about a nice thick T-bone first? Rare with mushrooms and onions and steak fried potatoes. Ketchup. Hot sauce. Apple pie a la mode and black coffee to finish it off and every man a king, boys; every man a king.

All hail Davyd Kells!

But, damntheireyes, a kid was in the way. A wriggler in the beer. A bug under the saucer. A bone in his craw.

Once again Kells considered the target, finger firming on the trigger. He had the latest weapon, a laser bore SeekFinder, tweaked for a thousand yards — his favorite distance. He had a Goblinround primed and anxious. A gorgeous SpectreView of the past/present/future of the shot.

And in his sights was a greasy devil of a third rate Generalisimo. RooskieSymp all the way. Crosshairs fixed on the big obscene gold emblem right in the middle of the thick sweaty pelt matting El Supremo/ Whatso's chest.

This was a guy you dearly *wanted* to kill. Davyd could tell just looking at him that he was a sonofabitch through and through. Flak jacket open to his navel. Cajones of iron, muchacos, cajones of iron!

Big damned voodoo jewel glued to his forehead. Glowing like he was a witch, instead of a fraud with two copper wires stuffed up his arse.

And the gold chains! Davyd really took offense at the gold chains. A cascade of chains, a waterfall of chains, with a big fat emblem right in the middle. The one that made him general.

Kells hated generals with a passion only a major could feel. He'd gladly kill this guy. This El Supremo. Or Generalisimo, or whatever he was.

Side benefit — the Goblinround would also take out the two prissy aides on either side. Damned colonels, from the lightbars on their jackets. Davyd hated colonels almost as much as he hated generals.

Davyd breathed out long and slow, so slow that in hypertime he made less movement than the lizard crouched on the rock beside him.

Each expelled breath cleansed his body of all poisons.

Each intake fueled the high test hormones coursing through his system.

He was keyed. He was stoked. He was ready.

Too goddamned ready!

Was the kid gonna shoot, or what?

Davyd wanted to look across at the opposite hill where the rookie was hidden. But he didn't dare take his eyes off the target.

He'd discussed it with the kid, whose name he couldn't remember — he was just a kid, that's all. Maybe he was nice, maybe he wasn't, who gave a squat?

The point was, Davyd was supervising the hit, backing him up if things went wrong. And he'd discussed the plan thoroughly with the kid, drumming every detail into his head.

There were three hit points in this kill. It could've been two if Davyd had set it up that way, but he'd made it three to put some goose into the kid. Give him confidence.

The first hit point was one breath away. The generalisimo was reviewing his raggedy troops, speaking loudly, throwing back his ammo vest and flak jacket. Hands on hips. Chest bared and aching for the Goblinround Davyd had for him. GhostProgged for his heart.

Boom!

That was hit point number one. Clean, simple and out of here.

Davyd took the breath and … the moment was on him.

His finger curled, adding the weight of a hair. One hair more was all he needed.

But he couldn't shoot. He had to wait for the kid.

Then the moment passed as the kid declined first hit opportunity.

Never fear, Davyd Kells, the next chance was only seconds away.

He eased back. Recounted. Two, maybe three more breaths to go.

His mind reached out to the kid. Sitting on a secure hill opposite him that overlooked the headquarters of the main rebel force.

What rebels? Who cares? There's always rebels and there's always RooskieProp causes to blind them. Davyd wasn't even sure what planet he was on.

It'd be an American ally, of course, or Father Zorza wouldn't have sent him here.

Davyd blinked as the Generalisimo lurched away from his aides. Drunk and staggering across the parade ground to pass out medals and embrace his brave brothers of the cause. Just like Davyd knew he would.

He'd even spiked the Generalisimo's drink to slow him down.

This is when the second hit point reared up.

And Davyd thought, pull easy, kid, but firm. The DeathSpirits are ready and waiting.

Then — shit! — the kid declined again.

Second hit point gone and stinking.

Davyd was pissed. He was keyed for the kill, hypothalamus pumping a flood.

What the hell was wrong with the kid? How had he gotten this far? What lard-arsed deskbound cretin had passed him up the line?

Okay, the kid was a rookie. But he was a two kill rookie looking for one more body bag to make the big three.

Three hits and the kid was solid.

Three hits and he could join all the other men and women who made up America's elite Corps Of Last Resort.

It was called the Odysseus Corps. Named for the first guy in history who kicked ass and gave no names.

And if the kid wanted to get into it he had to pass the Test Of The Three Kills. Stupid name. Davyd had been around enough centuries to know it was nothing more than Zen trash from the Corp's early days of Moral Excuses.

Trash or not, the tradition had lasted. The Three Kills Test. Three sanctioned hits and you were made.

The kid had worked for years to reach this point. Intense study and unpleasant training. Months of surgery endured for the bioplants that gave Davyd and his kin the physical and mental edge over ordinary beings.

Now all the kid had to do was pull the trigger. Boom! No more Generalisimo. Big drunk. Welcome to the fraternity of Hell, kid.

Say hello to us sinners. And goodbye to your soul.

The kid would get a place at the Bar Of The Damned, where every man and woman had sacrificed this life and the afterlife for the good old Red, White and Blue.

He'd even get a place in the Hall Of Peace, where the sleep was long, the dreams kept sweet by strong spells.

Spells no nightmares of murders past or future could penetrate.

All those things, those marvelous things, would become the kid's upon pulling the trigger. He had everything going for him. Mentors willing to coax him along. Powerful men who could wake up Davyd — the best assassin in Odysseus Corps — to supervise and mark this private historic moment.

What more could he want? And why was he hung up? Didn't the kid believe the story?

Old poisons leaked through Davyd's armor.

Shit, did somebody tell him? Did somebody tell the kid sometimes the Ghosts got through?

Hammering on the big glass tubes where the heroes slept standing tall and neon ready, glaring lights swirling all around. Dreams playing out in electrical arcs leaping from crown to groin to toe and then back again. Scores of years passing in each long sleep.

Hospital quiet all around and then the Ghosts would come howling forth. Shrieking, "Murder, murder, murder!"

Like a panther's scream, catching you by the heart and lungs and hauling you down to Hell to meet your Maker and His Opponent.

And then they'd both look at you and shake their heads, saying, "No deal here," and you just goddamn burn, boys, you just goddamn burn.

Sweetjesus, Davyd had suffered that dream too often and now he wondered, every nerve, every muscle and tendon soaked with adrenaline and testosterone, if somebody with a big mouth had maybe dropped this dirty dime on the kid and now he was having second thoughts.

Davyd's gut squirmed as the memory of his own first hit tentacled through.

A Rooskie, natch. Tall and thin with cold KGB eyes set in a hawk's face. Mother Russia's second elected president and all progs indicated that he was a grave danger to America's freedom loving cause.

Least that's what Control'd claimed. Davyd was young then, so what the hell did he know? Except that the quote — fate of the free world — endquote, hung in the balance.

So Davyd had taken him out. Right there in Athens, in the middle of the opening ceremonies of the 2004 Olympics. What the hell was his name. Started with a "P." It was a super symbolic ceremony, with the American president — Bush, was his name, but Davyd couldn't remember which Bush ... there were two of them — standing beside the Rooskie. The two of them opening the games together while the whole world cheered.

Davyd snorted. It was so long ago — a thousand years or more — that he had difficulty remembering all the influences that had led him to that first assassination.

He tried not to bother himself about the details, most of which were propaganda anyway and not to be trusted.

A child of the Twentieth Century, he recalled a time when the Cold War between the U.S. and Russia was only fifty years old. He remembered when it supposedly ended — when the wall came down and Pink Floyd threw a rock concert to celebrate a "new era of peace."

Damned Commiesymps propagandists. The said the Cold War was good and over now that Russia had shed its Soviet empire. Another snort from Davyd. That sure as hell didn't last long.

The symbolic meeting at the Games was crucial to this "new era of peace."

But Davyd's superiors had known better than to be fooled by all that Rooskie-inspired claptrap. They knew very well who was really behind all the so-called terrorist attacks. Exploding jetliners, diseases sprayed from crops dusters, suitcases filled with radioactive medical waste blasting apart at malls and supermarkets.

It sure as hell wasn't the mad mullahs who were behind those attacks. Nor the crazy Christian right-wingers at home.

It was the Rooskies who were doing it, same as they always had all the way back to the days of that bastard Stalin.

Davyd's bosses knew damned well that strong action and severe sacrifices by a few patriotic individuals were required to save America from being destroyed both from within and without.

And so Davyd Kells, a patriot to the core, had been America's first hero in a new world order that would last a thousand years.

To save his country, Davyd had put one round right through that damned Rooskie's heart.

Images from that moment rushed forward to swirl and spark in Davyd's mind.

He'd pulled the trigger.

There was a nearly silent whomp! Followed by the rifle's recoiled kiss against his shoulders.

Screams and shouts and in his scope blood all over the place.

And he'd run, run, run, all the Rooskie hellhounds at his heels.

He'd escaped. How? He couldn't recall … Oh, yeah. Now he remembered. It was the strangest damned thing. After he fired — and the Russian president fell — and Davyd started turning away, there had been another shot. Coming not that far away from his hiding place. And he'd caught a glimpse of the American president tumbling back, his head a bloody pulp.

Someone had killed George Bush. Davyd had no doubt then — and his suspicions had long since been confirmed — that a Russian assassin had taken out the American. So the filthy ones had planned it all along. It was a good thing Davyd had been set to strike as well. Revenge had been delivered for Bush's murder before he'd even been shot.

So that's why the escape had gone so easily. The total confusion caused by the two assassinations had agents and bodyguards falling over each other — even shooting at each other — while Davyd made his escape. Of course, the Russian killer had escaped too. But the world was not a fair place, had been built for villains as a matter of fact, and Davyd had long since learned to accept that fact.

Davyd shuddered as the full memory of that first hit crept. Most of all he recalled how he felt when he depressed the trigger. And had the sudden cold, slimesweat realization he'd just passed the point of no soul's return.

He knew at that moment that he'd crossed some terrible line and there was no going back because the foulest, blackest sin of all now stood in his way — Murder.

Shit!

The images dissolved and he was back on the hill, tensed for yet one more killing.

And Davyd got really, really angry because the third hit point was coming up and he knew the damned kid was going to blow it.

The kid was frozen.

Damnhissoul he was frozen and now Davyd, who was prepped to kill but not for actual murder, felt his whole heart burn with despair.

It was the anguish — never lessened in a thousand years and hundreds of kills since that first time — of the moment between thought and action.

Father Zorza, the wizard priest who had been his Control in these later decades when each murder became harder to bear but easier to accomplish, defined this moment as "Free Will."

A conscious decision. A knowing action. The long shadow between think and do.

"Be at peace, my dear boy," Father Zorza always counseled. "The sin you accept is the ultimate sacrifice for God and Country. And in the end God will forgive you because it was for a just cause."

Davyd played Zorza's speech in his mind and shot the Generalisimo. What else could he do?

The kid was no good, but the mission was still running and the target was important, so Davyd pressed steady as she goes, sir, on the trigger and saw the Generalisimo's chest explode in his sights.

Just like that, pull and it was done.

Got the aides as well, God bless them. Or damn them. Or whatever God wanted, it was no business of Davyd's who had his own problems in that department.

Boom! and then he could hear the jackalspirits released by his rifle squabble over the carcasses of their souls.

CHAPTER SEVEN

"Nice to see you, master. Home at last …" The old wrinkled face of a Brownie presented its most pleasant smile.

Actually, it *was* a pleasant smile as the Brownie understood the term. But to human eyes it was the terrifying mask of a bloody nightmare.

Vlad, however, was very familiar with that ghastly grimace. "Greetings, Brosha." Quite cheery. "How is everything?"

"Everything is all right, master. All in proper order, in its place, and in good condition …"

"Damn it, Brosha, let the Elves have you! Is it too difficult to just say, 'Everything's okay?'"

A grimace made Brosha's face more terrible still. "Oh, master, it is not good to use that filthy Amer word …"

Brosha, an old Brownie who was once in the service of an RGF Army Transport Chief Director, was currently in the employ of Vlad Projogin, a major in the Russian SPETZNAZ commandos — Brown Bears Company. A company where only the best of the best were welcome.

Vlad was the best of *that* best, a "free fire stalker," meaning when on a mission he needed no one's permission to shoot. In fact, few could command Vlad under any circumstances. And those few were among the hierarchy of the mysterious "Church Of The Sword," where he was an acolyte.

"Okay, no okays, old pal, old buddy," Vlad teased his batman, deliberately adding a cacophony of American slang — all terrible obscenities to the sensitive Brosha.

Vlad was standing in the hall of his Moscow flat. Moscow, Belokamennaya, the City of White Stones. Whatever the name, old or new. It was his home. What the hell, home at last!

He threw his bag into the corner and Brosha immediately swept it up.

"A proper place for everything, and everything in its proper place," Brosha said, repeating his favorite motto for the thousandth time.

Vlad tried to ignore this and stepped into the living room. Immediately his Brownie hurled another chastisement.

"Boots! Boots, master!"

"Oh. Sorry."

Another Brownie rule. No one was allowed to cross the threshold in street boots. Even the Lord Emperor himself was required to obey that rule.

Vlad imagined His Royal Majesty, surrounded by a brilliant court, stamping into the hall and Brosha the Brownie, hands spread, a terrible smile scarring his face, barring the way, mumbling:

"Boots! Boots, Sire! Your Majesty, boots! Slippers, please, Your Majesty!"

Vlad had no doubt even the Emperor would not have the nerve to penetrate Brosha's defense.

But Brosha was Brosha and Vlad had grown used to his batman's ways. To the point that nobody other than Brosha would ever dare to speak to him in such a manner. Even that ass Brand Carvaserin, Master Wizard of Special Services.

Brand's younger brother, Daniel, was Wizard-in-Chief, or something, on the *Borodino* battle station in the Frontier Zone. Vlad knew the brothers well and disliked them both.

Never mind the damn wizards!

He was home at last. Home, sweet home. His greatcoat flew away and he slumped into the sofa, running strong fingers through his light brown hair.

Then he sighed a great sigh and rubbed his tired, pale blue eyes. Yes, home at last …

Vlad had just returned from a six-month expedition. One of the most curious missions he'd ever encountered. Never mind that six months was a most unusual length of time for someone with Vlad's talents.

His specialty — the deadliest of all the military arts — usually took no more than a few minutes … once he was in place.

But this latest mission had been rather extraordinary — an expedition into the fiendish Regions Of Reality.

Certainly not a task normally among his common duties …

*　*　*

… The General was uneasy. Strange for a man proudly wearing Russia's highest mark of valor — the St. George Order with the Full Bow. His stone-carved face glistened with sweat. The upper button of his high-collar military jacket was undone.

"Please sit, Major," he said. "Feel free to smoke, if you'd like."

"I don't smoke, General."

"You'll live forever, Vlad." The General lit a Havana. Vlad noted his trembling fingers.

"I have a task for you," the General said. "If you'll agree to it, that is. You're my weapon of last resort, my friend." His smile was bleak.

"Listen, son," he said, "One of those thousandtimesdamned-devils we depend on has taken it into his fool head to escape."

Vlad only stared, waiting. His long chin thrust out. His wide shoulders squared.

"I'm told he was a damned useful fiend and quite clever," the General continued. "The incident has our wizards tearing out the last of their hair. I don't know exactly what the fiend's motives were, or how he did it. But somehow he got away."

The General shrugged. "It's been four months now since he escaped," he said.

Vlad allowed his heavy eyebrows to lift. The General saw and nodded.

"Yes. I completely agree. Those asses from the High Wizardry Corp are all mad. At first they insisted the situation was an internal matter. No one else's business."

The right corner of the General's mouth twitched. "They sent an expedition to the Fiendish Worlds to get him back," he said, shaking his head. "It was a complete failure. Shit! And mind, please, that it was headed by Brand Carvaserin himself!

"Accompanied by two — if you can imagine — *two* Master Wizards. With five of our best Brown Bears to back them up."

Vlad was astounded. "And the Brown Bears failed?"

Some of his steely facade cracked. On the left sleeve of Vlad's jacket there was an emblem — a red circle enclosing the snarling head of a brown bear.

Satan's balls! Brown Bears! His company! Defeated?

The General snorted, disgusted. "Yes. Gottmituns, yes! I couldn't believe it myself! Five men from the Brown Bears is the equal of a damned airborne regiment!"

"Yet they failed," Vlad said, flat.

"Yes, Vlad. They failed."

"Did they survive?"

"According to the last news from the Wizardry Section — yes. But I don't know for how long. This Carvaserin is a maniac, Vlad. He'll kill my boys before he's done with his foolishness. And it'll be for nothing. Stupid deaths."

"You want me to rescue them," Vlad said, quite matter-of-factly, "and get rid of this Carvaserin. Right?"

He didn't wait for an answer. "Sounds easy enough. A Wizard in the fiendish world is somehow like a girl in a perfume shop. He'll be overcome with all that magical scent."

"Alas, no!" the General grinned. "The order is simple. To capture the runaway devil and to deal with those who helped him."

"Helped him?" Vlad was surprised.

Who in the whole Universe, by the Great Buddha's Balls, could help a damned fiend escape from under a wizard's eye? And another thing — a most disturbing thing — this was not his normal job: dealing with naughty fiends.

To send HIM, master of killing — swiftly, shortly and without any traces — to send him to the fiendish world for such a hunt?

Well, one runaway devil is not an Amer's penetration to Beloka-mennaya. And as for those mysterious traitors who helped the foolish devil — that was more of a job for the counter-intelligence staff.

Not Vlad Projogin.

"Are you sure he had help?" Vlad asked.

"Yes. This famed demon was not alone," the general said. "Somehow he recruited some allies … from among us mortals. But that's not the worst of it. When he escaped he managed to steal some piece of shit device that has the wizards running around in a tizzy.

"Our Wizards say this device is more priceless than the Kremlin itself and more powerful than the damned Spell of Creation. They call it the SelfGuard Charm. And they insist that in a month all our devils will flee like rats from a sinking ship."

Vlad was always the doubter. "That doesn't sound possible," he said.

"Well it is," the General said. "Or the wizards say it is, at any rate. Apparently this Charm — and may its creators be roasted in hell — will allow the devils of this race — I cannot say its damned name, only Wizards can pronounce it properly — to flee from our control and to help other fiendish creatures do the same. From ODD dwarves to engine devils."

Vlad's eyes narrowed. He was getting interested.

"Surely this is a dirty trick of those damned Amers," Vlad said.

The General snorted. "I don't suspect it. I know it!" He tapped his chest. "I feel it *here*.

"So, Vlad, you must act immediately. Strike! Strike before all those fiendish shits can even wrinkle!"

Vlad glanced down at the mission folder in front of him. It had a red leather cover. He knew without looking that all its contents were paper.

Not a disk, not a magic crystal, just a thick sheaf of paper. In cases such as this the General would trust only paper and nothing else. When paper was properly shredded and burned not even the strongest Wizard could resurrect a single word from all those top secret paragraphs and pages.

Vlad nodded and took the report. The nod was his acceptance of the mission.

Later, he looked the documents over. They made up a detailed report on the rebellious demon's tricks and traps. It soon became plain to Vlad the General was quite right. The fiend *must* have had the help of mortals to make his escape.

Mortals who had likely fled with him to the Fiendish Worlds, barring all pursuit with strong charms.

Such an escape by a demon was not only rare, but was the stuff of legend. Back in the foggy mystical past — in the days of the Great Spell — it was said that one of the most powerful of the demon breeds escaped.

The ancient tale — which dated back to the early years of the Twenty First Century — claimed the fugitive was a Planetar Demon, a fiend whose duty it was to reform the stuff that made gravity and black holes, worms in the fabric of space, (and who knew what else?) into the stuff of magic.

According to those myths — admittedly nothing more than warning tales to frighten naughty children into submission — that Planetar Demon dwelt at the other end of the galaxy in some never-never nightmare land. Where he was biding his time to return and seize control of the civilized galaxy. Laying waste to all who opposed him.

No adult human believed the stories, of course.

Certainly not Vlad. Certainly not the man who had changed *real* history with a single shot. The moment he'd fired that shot — slaying the Amer President George Bush — the old, primitive world of mechanics had been set on its head. And mortal creatures had rushed forward to seize the power of the demon world, the spiritual world.

Details of that rifle shot rushed into his head like a bloody dream that revolved around and around until it edged into insanity.

Vlad bit back a moan of desperation. The images birthed ghosts who created still more ghosts of all that had followed. Men and woman shot. Teeth bursting through the backs of their skulls. Chests ripped open to expose still beating hearts.

How many more would he have to kill to save Mother Russia?

Then he pushed those thoughts away along with all the terrible images that came with them. He stuffed them back into his mental trunk of unpleasantness. His Pandora's Box of ghastly nightmares.

Nightmares that always ended with one thing: Vlad impaled over an eternal fire, twisting and screaming for all eternity to pay for his murderous sins.

Vlad swallowed a knotty lump. It was some very small consolation that it really hadn't been one shot that had changed history. A dirty Amer assassin had struck that same day — practically the same moment — killing their beloved Vladimir Putin who had struggled so bravely and so vainly against the terrorists the Amers were stirring up against Mother Russia.

Two shots, fired almost simultaneously, at the Olympic stadium in Athens. And everything had been set on its head.

Vlad clamed his shrieking nerves and forced himself into the present. He bent down to study the report …

Yes, yes, the General was right. It was shit from the beginning.

Brand Carvaserin had attempted to penetrate the escaped fiend's defenses, failed, and lost the devil's trail. Then he'd stumbled into one of the fiend's traps, but by some miracle he'd managed to escape without any losses.

"How he could he have been so lucky?" Vlad murmured, looking at the chronicles of Carvaserin's defeats as he persisted in the hunt, each time nearly getting himself and the Brown Bears killed.

There was no doubt about it, Carvaserin had been routed. It was a complete and final failure — marked against the proud name of the Brown Bears team that had pulled the wizard out. And now all traces of the demon and his human allies had been lost.

There was an addendum to the report that was particularly harsh in its judgment of Brand. Vlad could tell from the insider details it had been written by one of Carvaserin's own mages.

Vlad tucked this information away, like a weapon. It was good to know there was a secret, traitorous eye observing Carvaserin. Someone engaged in a petty scheme against his master.

When going against a Master Wizard, even Vlad needed any edge he could get …

*   *   *

… He found the group in a far and quite unpleasant part of the Fiendish Worlds, many EarthDays from the nearest human outpost.

Brand's face turned pale with anger when he saw Vlad. But what could he do? Even a Master Wizard had to obey orders. And Vlad's orders were from the highest of the high. Still, Carvaserin was cold, bordering on surly.

"Greetings, Major." Nothing more.

No offer of help, no further reports, just a "Greetings Major," and then Brand turned away and busied himself with something of pretended importance.

Vlad ignored the implied insult. He didn't need this fool. And wizard or not, Vlad considered Carvaserin a fool.

He'd work alone — as usual.

Vlad was no wizard. As an acolyte of The Church of the Sword he was capable of performing a bit of necessary magic. But how could those small spells help here in the Fiendish Worlds? Especially after all the great wizardly authorities had failed?

He struck out in advance of the others, following the course of a grim fiendish river.

Dark waters rolled from nowhere to nowhere, smooth, black and lifeless.

For a long time he found not one trace, not even the faintest sign of his prey. The horizon was very high — it seemed to Vlad that he was striding along the bottom of a great bowl.

As far as his eye could see there was only gray-upon-gray desert, crossed by a jet-black river.

There was no one, no thing, about. He'd left Carvaserin's group far behind and the ghastly loneliness of the place gnawed at him like rats.

His long legs swiftly ate up the miles, but no matter how far he traveled the land remained bleak and lifeless.

It was a world that seemed completely forsaken. With only ghosts and spirits to flee before the softskin usurper. But Vlad had a strong suspicion his loneliness would not last for long.

When the green sun began its fall, quickly approaching the trembling skyline, he stopped. Rough ground under a gloomy rock became his refuge.

Vlad enclosed his position with three FiendProtectors and crouched down to wait.

... There was night — if that dim half-light could be called so. Deep shadows crept beneath the stony shelf, shrouding Vlad's encampment. The Guard Rings gleamed faintly. Not a single star shimmered in the heavy sky.

The air was hot and dusty, filled with a strange, nauseating stench.

Two pairs of pale green eyes peered into the shadows, studying the man lying under the boulder. Only eyes — nothing more. And those pale eyes crackled with malice as they considered the man.

Was the man dead? Was he sleeping?

"Sleeping indeed," was their conclusion: "A fool. He believes his stupid magic is stronger than ours. Damned softskin, He'll pay ... He'll pay ..."

Now the two devils could hear the man's slow, deep breathing, confirming their view that he was, indeed, asleep. But they were a cautious pair. They investigated further.

Their sharp gaze could pierce his very body and read the signs. Yes, the muscles were relaxed. Not a single tendon under stress. And the man's thoughts were far, far away … dreaming about his mate and offspring.

Quite nasty thoughts from the devils' point of view.

A scout, 'tis plain. With cheeks puffed too much. And too strong a belief in his magic. And — maybe with interesting news for the Rebellion!

"Got him!" was said in an unpronounceable devilish tongue.

Two shadows, both deep-gray, shaped like a wide trembling curtain bearing pale eyes, slowly approached the Guarding Circle. Passing the first ring, one of the shadows cackled in mockery.

The FiendProtectors flashed hopelessly and too late.

In a second both devils were upon their victim. Never mind those useless rings.

But then the sleeping man was moving! Moving at a terrible speed.

Invisible claws scratched near his very soul — but before the demons could act the crossbow sent its first bolt spearing between green burning eyes filled with a hungry hate.

A long shrill wail echoed over the dead rocks. Wailed and died at a distance. The devil was gone.

The crossbow's bolts were suffused with deadly charms, poisonous charms, fatal even to the most powerful devil.

All three rings flashed red. Flame tongues rushed to the sky.

The second devil suddenly found himself imprisoned in a burning jail. He wailed in agony — but it was too late. Now the creature couldn't even escape into death.

"That's it," said a calm voice. A voice that did not sound sleepy at all.

"Who art thou?" howled the demon. The desperate words tumbled out in the strange latin-esperanto argot used in talks between wild fiendish creatures and soft-skins.

"Thou doest not need to know it," Vlad answered in the same argot. "Now thou wilt tell me!"

"I will not speak!" the devil shrieked.

"Indeed thou wilt, dear. I have many questions for thee."

Vlad chanted a hymn of exorcism from the first Litany of The Church of The Sword.

The song was agony to the devil. He twisted and squirmed in pain, his body turning hot like naked iron in a red glowing forge.

Vlad stopped. He studied his victim.

"Well, thou fiend-snake, shalt thou speak?"

"Naught!"

"Eklmn! Another cast on thee?"

"Naught!"

"How impressive. But I need something more substantial from thee."

The devil cursed him long and hard. Saying he was less than a piece of eklmn cast from the bowels of a sewer slug. There was more, but Vlad paid him no mind.

He waited until the cursing became faint and the devil's limbs twitched in fear.

"Thou art weak and old," Vlad said with heavy scorn.

Once again he began to chant the Litany.

The torture continued.

The imprisoned creature twitched and howled in the burning circle. And soon the brightness of his magical armor decreased. New litanies more terrible than the first racked the devil.

"Thou shalt speak!" insisted Vlad. His voice was harsh, fists clenched.

Vlad hated such things, but he pressed on, becoming so completely caught up in the shared agony — victim's body to torturer's soul and back again — that he didn't noticed Carvaserin and the rest of the party approach.

Slowly the fiend weakened. Then, gathering up the last his strength, the demon shouted:

"Death to thee, soft-skin!" And he burst out of his invisible bonds.

The fiend hurled himself at Vlad, raging and desperate to escape. Vlad went down, his head striking against a stone. Any other time, the demon would have been able to finish off this damned softskin, but Vlad was too strong.

The demon knew Vlad would recover at any second, plus he had Carvaserin and the Brown Bears to contend with. And so the devil turned and fled … trying not to shrink against the imagined poisoned crossbow bolts he was certain would be hurled at him.

Vlad jumped up. Swiftly flying away, the devil heard his enemy curse in awful frustration. But the demon fought and won the war against angry instinct and didn't turn to confront Vlad. Instead as he fled the killing ground he swore he'd soon return. Except, this time he'd have help. He'd come back with Ben-Shin's guard. And possibly even Ben-Shin, himself. Vlad smiled as the demon fled from sight.

The first stage of his plan had been accomplished …

CHAPTER EIGHT

It didn't take long for Tanya to get ready.

First she opened the big doors leading out onto the balcony — a balcony whose retaining walls had been removed so it made a smooth — and frightening for dinner guests when it was pointed out — drop off into nothingness.

Her apartment was several hundred floors up in the towering skyscratcher she called home. Far below were the streets of New Washington, the concrete and steel megalopolis that stretched from Greater Quebec to the tip of Old Florida.

She stepped out on her balcony where her flyflapper crouched, wings spread, mechanical heart waiting to be cranked into life. Tanya tightened the belts — sort of like tightening the chain on an old motorcycle. Except there were several, instead of only one, and the belts were made of synthetic muscle operated by mental command.

The muscles drove the craft through the air, flapping like a monstrous bird with Tanya in a kind of saddle protected by a wraparound windscreen. There were a few other rudimentary controls — hand and foot pedals to trim the rudders, or boost or slow the rate and height of travel.

All of which had to be operated at the same time as the mental commands were being issued so the entire thing depended entirely on the skill and quick-wit of the flyer.

Flyflapping was a dangerous enough sport to give anyone pause and certainly not built for a daily commute. Which was why Harry was so worried. But Tanya loved the light machine, which didn't have one magical element in it. It was all mechanics, other than the mental commands, and it looked like a huge dragonfly when it soared through the air.

Tanya's strong hands began their habitual work. She toggled the fuel line on, fired up the hoisting engine and launched off the balcony.

The flyflapper wavered, held nearly a mile over the streets by its little engine. Then Tanya caught the updraft, cut the engine and … flew. Just like a damned bird, flapping for height, then cruising the city's reaches by glide power alone.

She soared between steel towers, past green roof-top terraces and over the gray mist rising from the streets far below.

The traffic was starting to bunch — quickly building into a three-dimensional morning jam of commuters going to work via underground tube, street flits, overhead trams and skyhacks that so filled the air by midmorning they looked like a horde of gnats blackening the sky.

The thought of all the small magical creatures it took to drive those machines — millions upon millions of them — made Tanya shudder. She thought of the spirits as roaches captured in a kitchen and put to some disgusting work.

It was only 7:05 in the morning but many balcony doors and windows were open as Tanya flew by. From them boomed the voices of NewsNet commentators updating the story of the tragedy of *HolidayOne*.

The voices were shriller and even more hate-filled than before — "Heartless Russians …" "Devils From Moscow …" and even, "Rooskie Swine!"

The wrathful shrieks poured from every side, from each window, searing her. She tried not to listen, but suddenly street speakers were added — blasting angry crowd noises from below. Sound waves heavy with rage thundered from the narrow gorges between the glittering needles of the skyscratchers.

They made Tanya's head pulse with pain and she sighed in relief when she finally reached the balcony of her office. She collapsed the flyflapper, covered it against the elements and went inside.

Harry was waiting for her, lounging in a deep visitor's chair, profile turned for best effect. He was in his mid-forties, tall, athletic, and, Tanya grudgingly admitted, handsome.

He had thick brown hair — strange, not a single trace of gray in all that rich brown — and sported an expensive tan no matter what the weather. From burnished boot tips to gleaming general's stars, Harry was every inch the coifed and tailored dandy, which went along with his image as a great lover.

But today, Tanya thought, lover boy looked frazzled. His gray eyes were weary and tinged with red. There was a pallor of worry beneath his artificially tanned skin. His tie was stuffed into his pocket; his shirt had an upper button torn off.

He looked so bad Tanya couldn't resist the dig. "Rotten night, Harry?" she asked, all innocence.

"Rotten isn't the word for it," he snarled. "Listen. We are all in deep, deep shit. Those damned Rooskies have …"

"I know, Harry," Tanya broke in. "We talked about it, remember?"

For the life of her she couldn't figure out how this, this … *guy* … had become such a high official in the UWP. A real nitbrain, nothing more.

"Yeah, yeah, right," said Harry, distracted, fingers playing nervously. "But that was then, this is now. Things are worse and getting grimmer by the second."

He licked dry lips. "You saw the crowds? The protests?"

Tanya nodded. She'd seen … and heard.

"The Russians say it was an accident," she said.

Harry shrugged, impatient. "Who the hell knows? Maybe it was. Maybe it wasn't. The point is, every opinion poll in the whole UGS has jumped past the red zone. People want action. And they want it now."

"What do public opinion polls have to do with us?" Tanya said. "Even though we're both American citizens, we are also representatives of the United Worlds Police. And we're supposed to be neutral, remember?"

"Don't lecture *me*," he protested. "I know who and what we are." But there was no heat, no heart to his snarl, which was quite unlike Harry.

"And that who and what," he continued, "have put us right in the middle."

Like its parent, the United Worlds Organization, the UWP was staffed by citizens from every part of the galaxy. When they joined they forswore all nationalistic feelings and actions. Be they Russian, Russian ally, American, or American ally, it was their duty to act as a buffer between the two ancient enemies.

It was a clumsy system, a badly flawed system, but time after time it had still managed to drag Americans and Russians back from the brink of slaughtering one another.

In short, the United Worlds Organizations oversaw the deadly game that was the forever Cold War and the United Worlds Police was its armed referee.

By treaty the United Galactic States and the Russian Galactic Federation took turns playing host to the peacekeepers. Every ten years UWO headquarters — along with its enforcement arm — moved from the Earth capitol of one empire to the other.

It was Harry's misfortune that there was one year to go before the traditional shift was made. Now a great big political bomb had been tossed into his lap while he was serving on his native American soil. One false move and he could be the proverbial Man Without A Country. He had to juggle and he had to jump.

His first act, quite in character, was to dump as much as he could on Tanya.

"The orders just came in from On High," Harry said. "And those orders are for us to get this thing sorted out immediately.

"They want us to find out if it was an accident, like the Russians claim. Or was it purposeful? And if it was purposeful, who was responsible?"

"They realize, I assume," Tanya said, "that if it wasn't an accident — and we prove it — it might mean war?"

Harry shied away from this. "Let's hope for the best," he said. "A few minutes ago I was handed an official communiqué from the Kremlin. They insist it was an accident. That a civilian ship was mistaken for an attacking American destroyer. And they promise to make restitution to the families of the victims."

Harry sucked in a deep breath, calming himself. "I'd no sooner read that," he said, "then I got another message from the Kremlin. This one warned that any accusations better not go too far.

"And that there might, and I quote, 'be reason to believe,' endquote, that the whole thing was a setup by the Americans to embarrass the Kremlin."

Tanya nodded. She was up to speed now. "Okay, Harry. How do we proceed?"

"Not *we*," Harry corrected. "You!"

"What?" Tanya was confused.

"You'll have complete carte blanche in your investigation," he said, "and broad authority."

As he spoke, he swiped at a vidtablet, legal phrases swirling on its surface.

"I'll be alone?" Tanya asked, brows shooting up in surprise.

This was *very* strange. This was a job for a team, not one person.

"Yeah," Harry said, "you'll be alone." He pushed the vidtablet into her hands. "Two places to sign … here … here … and your thumbprint here."

Tanya ignored his directions. "I don't understand," she said. "This is the kind of situation that calls for governmental commissions — from *both* sides, Harry. Both sides!"

"Sure, there'll be commissions," Harry said. "Ask the Big Boss to explain." He pointed upwards — indicating the penthouse offices of the UWP Commander In Chief, General Hamann.

"Meanwhile, all I've got are these written orders for you." Again he indicated the vidtablet.

At Tanya's glance, the scrolling phrases on the flat screen came to a halt, then leaped to the beginning of the document.

She looked it over. Everything was right. Big red seal and General Hamann's signature.

"I still don't like it," she said. "This makes no sense."

"Okay, I'll tell you this much," Harry said. "But no more. The Russians say they'll only allow one UWP investigator. And that investigator must be no one else but you."

He peered at her, eyes hard. "Why, I don't know," he said. "Can you explain it?"

Tanya snorted. "What? You think I'm an RGF agent? Give me a break, Harry! The fact is, everybody knows I can't be bought, can't be pressured. That's the truth, not a boast, and both the Russians *and* the Americans know it."

"The trouble with you, Tanya," Harry snarled, "is that you have way too high an opinion of yourself."

He jabbed a finger at the vidtablet. "Now sign it, dammit."

Tanya signed.

Harry grabbed it back, rose to his feet and headed for the door. "Well, that's that. Good luck, Tanya."

And he exited. For the first time since they'd met Harry left her company without first pressuring her for a date. What was this? New tactics? Demonstrating his indifference? Or plain old ordinary fear? Funny how guys like Harry shriveled up when their precious parts were really on the line.

Once upon a time in Tanya's life there'd been one man who'd been different from all the rest. There were no games, no jealousies, no man versus woman war between them. But that was long ago, as they say, and besides the man was dead — killed fighting a terrorist gang in the Old Bronx.

She reviewed the document she'd just signed. The order was clear. She was to investigate all circumstances leading to the destruction of *HolidayOne*. She was to gather evidence, form a conclusion, and report those conclusions.

Tanya scrolled down to the expense ledger, whistling when she saw the budget she'd been allotted. The UWP was not noted for such generosity.

A red light flashed at the bottom of the screen. Tanya tapped it and a small card popped from a slot. The card was blue and silver, but otherwise featureless.

Tanya shifted her grip until she held the card by her right thumb and forefinger. A snap of static as the card cast a recognition spell. She felt a tingle as it checked to see if she really was Tanya Lawson, then formed a magical bond with her.

A flash and a full-size image of General Hamann rose up in the center of the room. The image showed a big, burly man wearing the full dress uniform of a two-star general.

Tanya neutralized the spell and the image disappeared. She carefully tucked the card away — it was her authority, her claim to demand help from any agency. She didn't dare lose it. But if she did the elaborate spell that had been cast would make it useless to any other person. Not even a First Class Wizard could break its magical code.

Tanya recognized the rather solemn and formal style of the spells as coming from the UWP's top team of wizards. Someone had gone to a lot of trouble and expense to get this card made so quickly. One more bit of proof the crisis had reached gale force and was quickly rising.

Musing, caught off guard by emotions plunging along the roller coaster of fast moving events, a sudden flush of elation took her.

Well, she thought, this is what you wanted since you were a kid, isn't it? Tanya Lawson, Girl Hero, facing the most difficult of missions. Standing alone before the whole world.

The moment grew stranger still and Tanya found herself leaning on her hands, bending over the table, wild visions floating before her. Tanya Lawson the WorldSaver! Lawson the Great! The woman who stopped the war!

Then a cold peering eye caught her.

It was a terrifying glare, coming from afar, but at the same time she knew the owner was near, terribly near. It felt like some creature lurking in the very depths of the earth, now rising to the surface. No. She was wrong. This was a Being out of nothingness.

And it wasn't in the deep, or in the street, or in the sky. It was everywhere and nowhere at once. Permeating the UWP skyscratcher, inside and out; in this world and all others.

Tanya's senses were scorched in one fleeting second of that glare — as if she were staring at a fierce sun. The glance of that Being was filled with wrath, immeasurable wrath, and Tanya trembled, knowing if it continued she was lost.

No mortal could withstand such anger, such force. She lifted shaking fingers, trying to cast a defending spell; to run, to hide, to shield herself in a cloak of invisibility.

But it was no use.

An icy hand clutched her throat … and then …

All was gone!

There was a gentle knock at the door.

Tanya nearly collapsed. She was weak and her uniform was soaked through with fear's sweat. Her knees trembled.

The knock came again.

Her spine tingled with dread. She just knew it was the Being! Crouching … waiting … beyond her door.

God, God, why didn't it burst through and get her? A wild thought: some said there were a few very evil creatures, like vampires, who couldn't enter a mortal's house against the owner's will.

Maybe that's what was happening.

And the … Thing! … wanted her to open the door!

Again, the knock.

Tanya's hand moved down to her sidearm. Bullets against such a creature were probably no good — but ... but ...

A voice: "Inspector Lawson! Ma'am! Are you there?"

Tanya thought she recognized the voice. It sounded like Kriegworm, the giant Ogre-Mage, one of a very few magical beings who'd managed to enlist in the UWP. He was a very powerful mage, one of the best.

Tanya was too weak to walk the five paces from table to door.

"Open," she commanded and the door swung open.

As much as she disliked Kriegworm she was relieved to see it really was him. To Tanya, Ogres were ugly, nasty things that gave off a powerful odor, made worse by the fact they believed bathing was one of the stupidest of all soft-skin inventions.

Even more — they were MAGICAL BEINGS, and that was enough for Tanya. Still, at the moment she was damned pleased to see him.

"What do you want?" she managed.

The Ogre — eight feet high, four feet at the shoulders, red round eyes, sharp white fangs peering from the upper lip — was elegantly garbed in a gray suit. His tie was perfect and on his wrist he wore an expensive gold Rolex.

Tanya unwittingly sniffed the air. Oh, boy! Eau de Cologne! Seems Kriegworm had prepared well for this visit.

"I have special orders," Kriegworm growled, looking at Lawson with a strange glow in his red, round goggle-eyes. "Very special orders."

Tanya sighed, normalcy setting in. Ogres were rather ceremonial. Sometimes it became boring.

"Report your orders," she said.

"I am to accompany Master Investigator Lawson on her new mission," Kriegworm said.

"But I was told I would be alone," Tanya said.

"Yes, that's so," the ugly head nodded. "The Rooskies allowed only one UWP representative. Very clever of them, I think. Master Investigator Lawson is the appointed person, I was told. But even the Master Investigator must report her activities. I'll put out an active AerialSpell to catch the Master Investigator's thoughts which she will consider suitable to report.

"I was also told that Master Investigator Lawson will go to the Rooskie's space citadel in the Frontier Zone. I've been ordered to accompany you and transmit your reports directly to General Hamann. Is my answer complete, ma'am?"

Indeed it was. And yes, Kriegworm was a master of secret signal transmissions. But Tanya always used her own skills.

In all her years she'd never failed a mission and had never asked for or needed the help of any UWP high-ranked Wizards, to say nothing of Magical Creatures! Strange. But then, this was no ordinary mission.

Still, to send another UWP officer was a clear violation of the guidelines the Russians had insisted upon.

"Do you have written orders?" she demanded. To be formal is to be formal.

The Ogre grinned broadly. "Written, cast and magically implanted," he said.

He bowed, giving Tanya a small black box of polished wood with a ring of gold-encrusted runes on the cover. "Master Investigator Lawson can see everything for herself."

The confirmation looked impressive. The order was written in red ink, the personal seal of the UWP Chief gleaming with gold. Tanya gently touched it and a small image of the UWP Emblem shimmered over the paper.

All of the other documents were also of the highest degree. Headquarters must have been at work all night to prepare the stuff.

"And here's your ticket, ma'am. The lifter to StarKennedy will depart at 8:40. We must hurry. The airport wizards will not delay the start for us."

"Are you joking with me, Second-Class Detective Kriegworm?" said Tanya in a cold voice.

No magical creature ever dared to joke with her. Lawson's fingers crossed. In a moment this Ogre would have big troubles with his belly.

"Please forgive me, Master Investigator Lawson," Kriegworm immediately bowed his huge head. "I beg your pardon, ma'am. I thought …"

"Your humble thoughts are of no interest to me." Tanya cut him off. "I'll be there on time. Now I must work. You may go, Kriegworm."

The Ogre bowed once more and vanished without a word.

Tanya sighed in relief and cast an AirCleaning spell. Then she turned to her workstation. Here it was impossible to avoid magical machines. There wasn't enough money in the galaxy to buy a computer without spiritworld creatures.

However, Tanya pitied them — the miserable OpticDiscDrive Dwarves, enslaved in a prison of timespells, locked in tiny drive chambers.

All information concerning the extermination of the *HolidayOne* was already available. Vidimages rushed in a mad dance — Master Investigator Lawson was at work.

HolidayOne data. Passenger list. One survivor. Billy Ivanov. What a strange name. Now the fiendish crew. Again, one survivor. Scratch, the Engine Devil.

Both the boy and Scratch had been rescued by the RGF space for-tress and were being treated for shock and minor injuries in the Russian infirmary. Very good. She could interview them when she grilled the *Borodino* officers responsible for this incident.

Her shuttle flight from Starport Kennedy would take her directly to a space liner especially chartered for this mission. Its first stop: the *Boro-dino*.

She pored over the data. Well, well, well! Liner course ... Missile course ... Why did they shoot, dammit, why did they shoot? The liner had crossed their path at overlight speed. Which meant it would've been impossible to attack the Russian space fortress.

What did the Russians say? The liner was mistaken for an American destroyer? Maybe for a modified destroyer, suitable for scout missions?

Okay, but what about the magical environment? It must have been clear that it was a civilian ship — clear even to an apprentice enchanter, not just to the True Wizards of insuperable forces and powers!

How could they have made such a mistake? There was no sorcery in the whole Universe that could make such a team blind even for a second.

Well, she would need a whole list of the Russian's citadel crew ...

DirectLink Spell. Uh, that's it. The RGF representative at UWP head-quarters flashed online.

"Master Investigation Lawson here."

"Counselor Sinitsin. Code number 2-5030-341."

"I was appointed ..."

"I know," a deep voice answered.

"I'd like to present my confirmation ..."

"I know," repeated the voice. "No need of confirmations."

"But ..."

"You're in a hurry, Master Investigator. I know what you need. I was waiting for your call. The crew and officer list for the *Borodino* will be at your computer in a second. Anything else?"

"Who should I contact during my investigation? I am supposed to visit your military facilities ..."

Tanya put down the names of the key officers and crew member, plus their codes, and said goodbye to a polite Counselor Sinitsin.

She took a deep breath, settling herself.

Her job was clear. Now she had to go forward. And she could allow nothing to influence her impartiality.

Truth, truth and nothing but the truth, so help me, Tanya Lawson.

But, most important of all, she had to forget she was an American.

CHAPTER NINE

Davyd Kells extracted from the hill, gathered the kid still crouched and frozen/waiting for the shot, and pulled goddamned out.

He dodged the usual return fire, then got unlucky in the draw and was punished with a Puffship for dustoff.

It blackened the jungle all around him with a killing spell so powerful the deathwash left him numb.

Then the bullets were gone and he was safe, but the Puffship spell left him in a mood to take his own life.

A magtech gave him a foul-tasting potion for an antidote and Davyd drank it down, letting it take him, calm him, heal him.

As soon as the shakes stopped he slopped some down the kid's throat and got him chilled out.

The kid steadied himself and said, "I'm sorry."

Then he turned away and wept.

At that moment Davyd remembered the kid's name — Jonz.

First name, who knew? But last name … yeah, it was Jonz.

"Listen, Jonz," he said, "you've got a decision to make."

Davyd pressed a .45 against the kid's temple. The weapon was old fashioned — fat lead, mucho powder, blow the kid's head away and the side of the Puffship to boot. He was too tired to give a damn one way or the other.

Click! and the hammer was thumbed back.

"It's up to you, Jonz," he said.

The kid trembled. Davyd noted, but took no pleasure in the young man's fear.

He said, "You want another go at this? Or do you want to quit?"

"Quit?" the kid asked, surprised.

"Yeah, quit. Sayonara. Goodbye. Calle nictus. So long, it's been good to know you. Call it a day. Junk it all and become a plain old ordinary soldier. Shit, kid, you've got enough schooling to walk in a First Lieutenant in the regular army. Before you knew it, you'd make captain."

The wheels were churning behind the kid's eyes. Davyd could see that he wanted to answer fast and remove the threat, but was undecided on which answer to give.

"If I say the wrong thing," Jonz asked, "I'm dead, right?"

Davyd shrugged. "Seems only fair to me. Hell, I could've killed you back there for freezing."

Jonz thought and thought and thought. But he thought fast: a thousand possibilities swirling through his mind in less than a second.

"I want another chance," he finally said.

Davyd lowered the hammer and put the gun away.

"Right answer, Jonz," he said.

And then he folded his arms across his chest and went to sleep.

Just as he was about to drop off he heard the kid say, "Shit, I got it right!"

And Davyd thought, No kid, you got it wrong. And there's gonna be hell to pay because I didn't tweep you.

This was his last thought when sleep took him.

It was a dreamless sleep, a sleep without sensation. Then there was pressure against his upper arm, a quick sting and then he was coming into hazy consciousness, blearing into the eyes of a frightened young lieutenant.

Behind the lieutenant was the retreating form of the magtech, slipping a hypogun into his little black bag of tricks.

"There's been a change of plans, Sir," the lieutenant said, voice trembling.

He was scared, but in awe at the same time. Stepping back as Davyd unreeled, stretching long, lean limbs. Muscles cabling the tight-fitting cammiesuit. Running blunt-edged fingers through dark hair.

Sleepy eyes getting their focus — hunter's eyes, black as night. They looked old in his young man's face — high cheek bones, aquiline nose, long chin. Brooding lips.

As Davyd groaned awake, the lieutenant memorized everything about him. This was something he could tell his grandchildren. About the time when he met Davyd Kells, the deadliest — and therefor most famous — member of the Odysseus Corps.

Davyd felt terrible, every muscle aching, still deep in the throes of PostMission Stress. But the juice the magtech had pumped into him was starting to work.

The first thing he realized was that he was no longer on the Puffship. The loud roar of its turbos had been replaced by the distant but powerful hum of big SpellEngines hurling a ship through space.

The second thing he noticed was the absence of Jonz.

Shit, oh dear. All bad signs. Apparently the chewing out Davyd had expected was coming sooner than he thought.

"Sir, sir," the lieutenant was saying, "are you listening, sir?"

Davyd scraped away more of the wool. He'd missed whatever the lieutenant had been talking about.

He shook his head. "Sorry, lieutenant," he said. "Repeat your last."

"I said, sir, that I have orders for you to report to CommandStar immediately. At General Link's request."

The last of Davyd's weariness fell away. Now he was up. Now he was alert. Now his greenies were cutting in.

Aw, fuck, General Link! Head of Allied Ops. I'm in bigger trouble then I thought.

Davyd was beginning to regret his act of mercy.

He started framing his excuses, getting his mind set for a locked heels reaming from the foulest tempered four star general this side of Hell.

"Aw, come on, sir," he'd say when the first storm had passed. "So I gave the kid a break. Somebody jumped him too fast, that's all. Think of it this way, sir. Think of Jonz as government equipment. And maybe I saved the taxpayers a little money by sending him back to the motor pool for a tuneup."

Yeah, that's how he'd play it. Old Link was a notoriously tight-fisted bastard. Davyd would appeal to his sense of economy.

"Sir? Uh, excuse me, sir?"

"What!" Davyd jumped at the interruption, then regained control. Sighed.

"Sorry. Didn't mean to shout, lieutenant. Guess I'm still pretty keyed up. Now, what were you saying?"

"I was asking, sir," the lieutenant said, "if the Major wanted me to call up the latest news feed. So you'll be up to date about the incident when you speak to the General."

Davyd swallowed hard. "Incident? What incident, lieutenant?"

The lieutenant was amazed. "Haven't you heard, sir? We're damned near at war. It's the Rooskies, sir! Shot down a passenger ship. Full of innocent —"

Davyd lost the rest.

He was thinking, so that's why I'm wanted. They don't care about Jonz at all. It's the damned Rooskies again.

American blood had been spilled by the bucket and now somebody wanted paybacks big time, so they were calling in the ultimate Paymaster, Davyd Kells.

Then an old ghost crawled out of the sinpit to haunt him. The face of his first victim reared up. Then the name. Shit, he'd almost forgotten the name.

The Rooskie bastard he shot at the Olympics who would have blown the good old U.S. of A. to kingdom come if he'd lived.

Vladimir Putin.

Davyd got the shakes and called for a sleeptab. Washed it down with cold coffee. As he waited for dull oblivion to take effect, other ghosts joined the first. And then everything came back in a mad rush, his heart pumping, adrenalin flooding his veins, muscles twitching like an old dog caught in a nightmare chase to end all nightmare chases.

KGB killers pursuing him through the streets of Athens. Then they had him cornered and all was lost. Oh shit, and damn, damn, damn, you can kiss your ass goodbye, Davyd Kells.

But suddenly they were withdrawing. Davyd in his fragile hiding place staring after them in wonder. What had happened? Why were the wolves being called off?

Then he remembered the flash he'd caught from the corner of his eye. Of George Bush getting tagged. A real pro hit, too. Boom! Smack between the eyes. And the 43rd president of the U.S., was history's meat! Davyd recalled that Bush was some kind of spook, like Putin. Except he was CIA, instead of KGB. No, no. It was Bush's old man who was the spook. George Bush Sr. The 41st President of the Untied States. Bullshit. Spook old man equals spook kid. Father Zorza had taught him that.

The intelligence services kept a tight rein on the families of their operatives and recruited them whenever possible.

Davyd sighed and eased back. Forcing his tense muscles to relax. Sometimes he wondered about the other fellow, the Rooskie who'd shot Bush Jr.

He'd heard the guy had gone on to bigger, bloodier things. The ultimate shooter on the other side.

Some said the Rooskie hitter was almost as good as Davyd. Maybe even his equal. Or better.

For a long time Davyd had dreamed of finding out once and for all. He'd even run into traces of the guy — the faint, yet unmistakable spoor of a Sword Church killer. But nothing more.

Then sleep, warm sleep, stretched out her arms to gather Davyd.

But just before he sank into sleep's embrace he thought:

I wonder where he is now?

Damned Russian!

Maybe, just maybe, if the Hellgods are kind, this time he'd get to meet him.

In his imagination he saw a blurred face through his laser sights.

He centered the cross hairs.

His finger curled around the trigger.

One breath, maybe two, and …

Davyd fell asleep.

CHAPTER TEN

Vlad opened his pale eyes. He was in own apartment. Yes, he thought bitterly, home, sweet damned home!

The memories were painful, almost more than he could bear. Yet it was necessary to remember, no matter how uncomfortable they were. He had to report. And with that report would come forgiveness and relief.

Father Onphim would say the healing words, the words that turned victim into deserving villain. And after all, Father Onphim would say, quoting his favorite quote, "… 'victim' suggests innocence. And innocence suggests guilt."

Another favorite saying of Father Onphim, his mentor and teacher, was, "Never mind what your country is doing. That's your country and that's good enough."

Good old Father Onphim. Once he was a field-priest. Then, wounded in combat with insurgents somewhere in the New Colonies, he retired from the army. Only a few people, Vlad among them, knew that Farther Onphim was the supervisor of Combat Arts for the Brown Bears.

Onphim was only the last, but hardly the least, of many such priestly figures who had long opened a glittering path through the hidden halls of the Church Of The Sword for Vlad.

Then, to his relief, Brosha was at his elbow, handing him a restorative drink. It was a special drink prescribed for Vlad whenever a mission came to a close.

He took one sip and his good mood flew to sweeter heights.

And from those narc-tinted "Lucy In The Sky" vaults he heard his batman say:

"Dinner will be in a minute, master. Maybe you want to have a shower before?"

Vlad chortled with lovely glee.

"Damn it, you woolly-minded Brownie! I don't have your cursed magic. More's the pity. Never to wash and never to stink!"

He sucked down the last of his restorative and was still laughing like a stoned madman as his batman pushed him into the shower.

A moment later Vlad was standing under the hot spurs of washing foam.

And he let go his dreams.

First he'd call Nadya. They'd take a trip somewhere outside. He'd have his rightful leave, by God. No matter what the priest said.

Shit! He still hadn't reported. The damned rules were always in the way. Even in the shower. He slammed it off, jumped out, wrapped a towel around his slender waist and approached the computer. He fumbled around his desk and then fed it a green-and-silver card.

"Hello, dollies," he hummed to himself, still in his heights.

Inside the computer a team of tiny creatures rushed to work. The display flashed. A column of fanciful whirled color beams rose up.

"Hi!" squeaked a small but brave voice from inside the machine. "Hi, master Vlad! Enter your code, please, master!"

"It's always the same, Bick," Vlad teased. "The code. And nothing but the code. How long will you keep asking me that? Ten years? A century?"

"A millennium would not be enough to make me stop, master Vlad," answered the prissy little Operation System-Loading gnome. "Now, enter your code, if you please ..."

Vlad make a face. His computer gnome, Bick, was quite intractable. Well, what was the damned thing? ... 2:5030/318 ... Okay?

"Code's not accessed!" shrieked the triumphant Bick.

Not accessed?

What the hell? Oh, God, really!

"Are you tired, master Vlad, or what? Have you forgotten your own code!"

Vlad shook his head. One more time ... 2:5030/48.

"Code's accessed!" came Bick's triumphant announcement. Then: "My eyes and ears are closed. Let them wither if I only dare to catch ..."

This was a very pompous and solemn pronouncement. Vlad had heard it many times and was bored with it. Bick was swearing not to pick even the slightest piece of Top Secret Information.

If he had, it would have been Master Vlad's duty to notify the proper authorities immediately.

"Stop it, Bick, for God's sake!" Vlad pleaded. "Get back inside the computer! Continue there! I can't stand it! Drop dead, you hear me! Drop dead!"

The Gnome lapsed down. "Drop dead, drop dead," he grumbled in his comic voice. Vlad ignored him.

The computer swallowed the reports like a hungry beast. Unseen messengers carrying the burden of Vlad's report on their thin shoulders were already marching forward to the headquarters of the Brown Bears Task Force — and to the hidden temple of the Church of the Sword.

Father Onphim must have his report at once ... the faster the better. From there, if the good father chose, the report would go to the highest of high. Or maybe not. It was up to the mysterious whims of Father Onphim.

Vlad knew well enough that all of Onphim's orders were confirmed by the Brown Bears commander, but not all of the commander's orders were confirmed by Father Onphim. And the highest SPETZNAZ leaders were always at Vlad's enchanter-supervisor's side.

It didn't matter. The task force was only a cover for Vlad, after all. As a government sanctioned assassin, Vlad's job was to deal with Mother Russia's most important and dangerous enemies — both mortal and fiendish. Rebel leaders, runaway devils, and corrupt politicians.

Although he wore the uniform of the elite SPETZNAZ strike force, Vlad was a force all on his own. A force controlled by Father Onphim and the Church of the Sword. He knew his report would be of great interest to Onphim.

Particularly the story about the runaway devil and the stolen Self-Guard Charm ...

*   *   *

... It was a rather strange place. The yellow river was slowly rolling past banks of rich red stone, covered with black rooted serpents.

Unable to move, the creatures could only hiss at him as he moved by. Nothing special — the common madness of the Fiendish World.

The demon's trail led Vlad onward. Deeper and deeper into the strange land. Once again, he'd left Carvaserin and the others far behind. After a time, Vlad decided to let them catch up.

He crouched down, resting. Finally, they arrived. Brand Carvaserin, grim as if attending his own funeral. The Brown Bears team stood with lowered heads — a single man had succeeded where they had failed.

Brand and the two master wizards said nothing to Vlad. The only thought in their heads was that they must obey a common major. This was intolerable to them.

Vlad smiled. Let the snakes hiss.

He continued onward, the others trailing him. A fat knuckled range confronted him. Vlad crossed it, following the devil's trail.

The fiend's angry thoughts shone red at the edge of Vlad's magical view. Still, even for Vlad, it wasn't easy to stick to his track.

Ignoring Carvaserin, Vlad gave several short, soft-voiced orders. The Brown Bears nodded. Everything was clear. The stormgroup prepared for a chase. They stood still as stone, faces tense, fiery eyes searching the dead banks of the river.

Vlad hefted his crossbow. It had poisoned bolts, powered by WarSpirits. He heard them whisper and bent his head closer to listen:

"Tis a bad smell here," he heard one of them say ...

"Some kind of a rogue?"

"Yeah. A rogue. And I do not like it."

Suddenly Vlad barked — "Target in range!"

The team heard him and reacted. Blue flame whirled around Vlad's hands and then, like a waterfall, rushed down along the sharp slope of the red bank.

"All, switch to Tear-Up and fire at will!"

A common soldier might have asked — "Fire at whom?" But not the Brown Bears Company.

Before Vlad's brain had time to sort the information, his body, reinforced by the contrivances of field surgery, reacted faster than an ordinary man's eyes.

The BattleSpirits howled in bloodlust. The bolt hurled along the red rim of the stony slope and from below came a howl of agony.

"Down!" Vlad shouted.

This was too much for the Brown Bears. They smelled the enemy, they could feel the enemy, they were upon the enemy — and there was no terrain that could stop them now.

They jumped forward as fast as that bolt, moving in Vlad's swift wake.

Vlad leaped over the cliff's edge. There, near the line of yellow water, a strange cloud was swirling — an immense black cloud — but it had already been hit by his crossbow bolts. Fire gouted from one side. The cloud had eyes — huge, burning red holes. And those eyes glared at the commandos with a terrible hatred.

New bolts tore into its black spiritflesh and orange tongues of fire soared over the smoke. An invisible sword smashed the stone near Vlad's feet, but he was swift, too swift for the demon cloud.

The bolt speared through one of the red eyes and with a blood-chilling roar of triumph, the BattleSpirits sank their teeth into the enemy's body. A banshee shriek blasted the soldiers' ears.

And the devil fled, smoke puffs falling like drops of blood. But it was too late. Vlad had him.

He shouted the devil's true name.

"Ben-Shin!"

The creature jerked to a stop, as if it had hit a wall. Vlad rushed over and encircled it with a pentagram.

A moment later Carvaserin came up. He tried to ignore Vlad, pretending he was in full control.

He addressed the demon: "Well, we meet at last. You're a lucky fiend to have made it so far."

"Down with him!" growled one of Carvaserin's wizards. "Down with him!" echoed the others.

"Not only him." The smile on Carvaserin's face was vampire bleak.

"And not too fast," said one of his magical aides.

"Surely," gloated the master wizard. "And we'll slow roast his kin as well." Another death mask grin. "And also the humans who helped him escape. We'll make them pay, by the gods."

"Leave these traitors to me," Vlad said softly.

It was not a request. It was an order.

The wizard's face drained of all blood, making him look even more like a vampire. But he could say or do nothing. There was still the Self-Guard charm to be recovered.

"Squad!" Vlad bellowed to the Brown Bears. "Forward!"

Carvaserin and the other wizards remained behind with the wounded demon as the team moved on.

Vlad knew there was only one way to end this mission. Never mind the SelfGuard charm. The demon had committed the ultimate crime when he fled. Down with him! Let all others tremble! Let their nightmares be filled with him, Major Vlad Projogin.

There was only one way to finish with this kind of resistance — total extermination of the transgressors. Hell, the Amers would do the same. Had done the same. It's a cruel game, nothing more. Shoot first, interrogate later. Or you yourself will be shot.

The choice was simple ...

The yellow water smelled as if it came from a sewer. Vlad and his men crossed the torrent. Another bank. The air was hot and thick. You could hang an ax from it, as the saying went. Unseen eyes were looking at the squad of softskins through the rock.

Vlad ignored them. Let them think we're still blind.

"Up and left!" Vlad commanded.

Without a word the squad responded. It was a good path, narrow but carefully blocked. The wizards were covering the task force from a distance.

Then the first demon force struck. It was a desperate attack. But the hated softskins were too fast. Flame bolts pierced the black smoke which appeared from nowhere to blanket the path. A narrow gorge, cut in the very flesh of the rocks was suddenly filled with a blue fire.

But Brand Carvaserin was alert and cast a searing magical counter attack.

Vlad's magical senses, faint as they were, caught screams of pain, fear and despair. His lighting bolt tore the smoky figure before him — and suddenly all was gone.

Some of the devils fled. How many of them remained, only a Master Wizard could say.

The path ended on a smooth plateau, green as spring grass. Far above the stars were shimmering and the black sky stood in strange contrast to the stony surface below, lit with a magical light.

Vlad turned for a moment and suddenly the yellow river was gone. Gray cliffs rushed to the heights, stubbed by roots all mossy brown picked with the deep green of the forests. In front there was Nothing. A Night of Naught, colorless, shapeless.

Then an icy wind sprang up, stinging their faces.

"Don't let it bother you, boys," Vlad hastened to say to the others. "It's one of those damned devils' tricks."

Then — "On we go!"

There, there, forward, forward, leaping through the hot air, jogging over the hot ground, crossbow alert. Heart pumping the blood through the lungs. And there — Vlad knew — a horde of tiny creatures was busy, enriching his veins with oxygen.

All of the Brown Bears could cover one hundred meters distance in less than nine seconds. But Vlad could do it in six.

He sprinted forward, quickly outdistancing the others.

Suddenly the village leaped into his view. The gray curtain vanished, pierced by fireballs from the Brown Bears' crossbows.

Vlad heard a triumphant growl from one of the BattleSpirits inhabiting his weapons.

"Prey ahead, Master!"

Yes, it *was* prey. Not demons, but human prey!

Vlad saw a village of a dozen small cottages. All wooden, all spell-protected. And damnably well-armed. Human traitors manning those weapons. The cannon tower on the edge of the village spat green fire. The earth was blackened, as if a full scorcher's charge had been emptied.

He fired a bewitched bolt and the hungry host of BattleSpirits savaged the defenders.

The Brown Bears rushed into the village. The humans were firing in vain. The commandos were too fast, too cruel. Swiftly, never losing time, the Bears covered the single street, casting a dead eternal silence on any who tried to fight back.

Vlad wondered who these people were. Allies of the damned Amers, no doubt. So who would care what happened to their dirty souls? Vlad hated all Amers. But he hated the traitors more.

When Brand Carvaserin and his team arrived all was done. Twelve defenders were slain. Others, including women and children, captured. And, most important, the Charm was in the hands of the Brown Bears.

Vlad gave it to Carvaserin. The wizard's eyes narrowed.

"Nice work, major," he grudged.

Vlad looked at him, making no reply.

Carvaserin … Full of powerless wrath. Outwardly he was as always — smooth and impervious. But deep under that cold mask Vlad felt the hate.

Vlad was unmoved. He didn't bother to make a pretense of fear — breaking one of the Church Of The Sword's key Commandments: "Never let those who demand to be strong know you are stronger."

Rule or not, the opinion of a Wizard-in-Chief was of no interest to him.

After the prisoners were escorted to the Ring of Power and magically sent to the nearest RGF outpost, Vlad let the Brown Bears mop up. The village was finished in an instant.

As much as he hated the traitors, Vlad had to steel himself against the villagers' plight. The prisoners wept. Children trembled. But no one pleaded for mercy. Everyone knew quite well there would be no mercy from the Brown Bears. As for what would happen to those people afterward — well, Vlad would never know, although they would haunt his dreams forever.

As for the result, even the poker-faced features of Carvaserin displayed delight. The escaped demon was recaptured. His human allies punished. The stolen SelfGuard Charm returned before the rebels had a chance to use it.

The mission was complete.

But as Vlad left the burning village he caught a strange glance.

It came from nowhere and everywhere and it was filled with hatred. He couldn't tell its source — human, fiendish, some Other Thing?

There was no Force in this glance — only the hatred. Eternal hatred.

It came from the earth, from the black sky filled with strange stars and constellations. From the flame that devoured the wooden houses. And even from the cries of the captured renegades.

The hatred was all around and above. And there was no shelter.

An evil voice hissed in Vlad's ear: "We'll meet soon enough, softs-kin!"

And suddenly all was gone.

Vlad grinned. More fiendish enemies only resulted in more interest in life. And for Vlad, life without enemies was like pork without sauce. A man like Vlad required an enemy, like others require food and air.

How many were there? Who gave a shit? All those ogres, spirits, ghosts, vampires, even devils, who conspired to suck out his soul. To hell with them! They had no reason to be.

And in the end Father Onphim's blessing would reduce them to nothing more than trophies in Vlad's personal Hall of Fame.

Or was it shame? Well, best not to think about that.

Okay, he'd apparently been presented with a new enemy. So be it. Vlad shook his head, throwing the thought away. An enemy who broadcast his threats did not deserve consideration.

The enemy to fear was one who fixed your face in crosshairs, not curses. An enemy to respect was one who spoke only to himself — one, two, three, fire!

The first announcement of hatred should come only when the bullet steals your life.

Like Bush!

Yeah, George Bush.

And may God damn his Amer soul!

Immediately, Vlad's chest muscles clenched as he remembered the hit.

George Herbert Walker Bush. The forty third president of the United States of America. Son of a president. Descendant of a noble American family. Much like Vlad's own family, whose lineage went back to the days of the Czars.

Fear and shame trembled through him. What did you do, Vlad? What did you do?

Never mind that.

Put it away, far away.

But, God, God, God, why in the hell did they pick me? I didn't want to be a hero. And what the hell is the worth of being a hero if you live forever and just keep killing, killing, killing?

Ten thousand men — and yes, even women — in a thousand years. What soul could bear it?

But remember the hate, yes, the justified hate. The Amers wanted nothing more than to eliminate every Russian in the Galaxy.

Some said if they had the chance they'd even kill unborn children who still resided in a Russian woman's womb. They'd rip them out, slicing the mothers' bellies, those fucking Amer's, and hoist the trembling infants on the points of their bayonets.

Past sins collided with present hate and Vlad had to call on all his resources to calm himself.

Never mind that.

Back to the expedition.

Two more months to mop up the fiends. Filthy work, but never mind that.

Vlad was home.

Home, sweet home. With Brosha, Bick and his other fiendish friends.

In his apartment — a personal gift from the Lord Emperor, himself. Near a direct tram line to Nadya … and only a few moments away from the most pleasant of evenings and a much more pleasant night.

Well, he had to finish showering first! Nadya would not be pleased with his sweet smell. Registration was complete.

Now he, Vlad Projogin, could rest for a while. In the shower, beneath the hot streams, Vlad closed his eyes. In his imagination Nadya was standing in front of him in a short girlish checked skirt, looking at him impatiently. And he rushed forward to seize her …

But Brosha's voice was first:

"Urgent message, Master Vlad! Very-very urgent, sir!"

"Heaven and Hell, Brosha!" Vlad growled, again stepping out of the shower and covering his hips with a towel. "What's this? Can't it wait?"

"Do not blame your faithful servant, my son," came a soft, disembodied voice. "He tried his best."

Vlad gaped. The computer screen was shot with color, giving no face to the man who spoke. But he knew who it was.

"Father Onphim!"

"Nice to greet you, my son," came the deep voice, a boom resonating from the speakers and through Vlad's very bones.

"I'm glad you're back again, Vlad. Do not be so anxious. Finish your ablution. I'll wait."

Vlad quickly dried himself and threw the crumpled towel into a corner. While he dressed, Brosha rushed to snatch up the towel. The brownie seized his prey and was off. Urgent messages were urgent messages. No one dared to be near Vlad at such a time.

"I'm ready, Father."

"Ill tidings, my son, ill tidings. An Amer starship was somehow exterminated in The Frontier Zone."

Father Onphim was speaking very soft and calm. But it frightened Vlad much more then a dozen master wizards. A direct contact like this from his mentor could only mean *real* trouble. For Farther Onphim, for the whole Russian Galactic Federation, and for Vlad, himself … But …

"Sorry, Father. But what's so important about this starship? Did the Amers dare to cross our borders!"

"The incident is worse than that, my son," his mentor said. "Much worse. This liner was a civilian ship. Many innocent people were slain. We must investigate immediately. The Sword Church Conclave is quite alarmed by what has happened.

"We need you, my son. I'll take you with me. There you will receive orders."

"I'll be ready in a second," Vlad was already stuffing clothes in a bag. "Where must I be, Father?"

"At our common place, my son," the priest said. "At our common place. The Church is waiting."

"I'll be there as soon as I can, Father!"

"Good for you, my son."

The computer speakers crackled. The screen went back to ordinary fire.

"I'm off, Brosha!" Vlad shouted, rushing toward the door..

"Dinner! What about dinner, sir?" Brosha's faint cry reached Vlad on the stairs.

"No time!" Vlad shouted and then the elevator swallowed him and he was gone.

The Church of The Sword could not wait.

CHAPTER ELEVEN

The great somber hall was dim, scarcely lit by a small chimney fire.

Flame danced madly behind the black iron fender as if trying to escape, to squeeze between the thick rods and rush forward, never mind where, only to … freedom.

The hall corners faded into deep gloom. The dark walls appeared to be covered with a thick soft cloth, like velvet or brocade. Between heavy curtains tall marble columns with carved Doric heads could be seen.

Here and there were the faint contours of huge lamps — now dead, without light, without life. In the center was an immense round table with eight ebony armchairs placed about it — high straight backs inlaid with cunning encrustations, gold upon black.

The great table was empty, the surface marked only by a strange emblem — crossed bolts of white lightning.

The floor was of smooth raven-black stone. Faintly gleaming golden sparks were scattered here and there across its agate surface.

It was in this dank chamber that the Council of Eight had met for many centuries now, plotting their terrible deeds.

There were no doors or windows in that room, so how the man appeared could not be easily explained. He did not enter, he merely popped up near the chimney.

The man was short, bow-legged, and wore a leather vest over bare skin and a Scots kilt.

He stoked the fire with a set of huge bronze tongs, then served himself a flamepiece for his short black pipe, which had a carved fist for a bowl. He puffed the first gray smoke-ring.

"Nice to meet thee, Infeligo," came a soft, menacing voice from behind. "I have heard thy last hunt was a great success. Congratulations."

The bow-legged man called Infeligo did not turn.

"Still joking, Mamri?" he said softly, but it came like the low rumble of a beast.

The man shrugged. "What else do we have to do but jest?"

The newcomer came closer to the fireplace. He was tall, with a thin nervous face cut by several deep furrows. The rest of his face was smooth and healthy, but the deep lines made him seem foreboding.

Mamri was dressed in a gray business suit. The white corner of a handkerchief peeped out of the breast pocket. The suit appeared expensive. The vest pocket was decorated by a thin gold watch-chain. On his middle finger he wore a large platinum ring with a dark polished stone crossed by white lighting.

It was the same emblem that was on the table.

"Jokes," Infeligo complained. "Nothing but jokes. That's what we always do. And what do we have to show for it?"

"We have what we have. Canst thou turn Time itself? Or block the Rooskie's missile? If not, thou hadst best stop that noise generator in thy throat."

"Grrr!" answered Infeligo, making an evil face in mockery.

"What sounds, Mamri! What words! Didst thee swallow too many souls last month, perchance? Launched that pretty raid — and thy precious rebels burned three towns in the Wild Frontier! Thou must have had thy fill! Thy maw — is it satisfied?"

Mamri's sharp face jerked. "That's nothing of thy business, my good and noble Infeligo," he said. "None of thy business at all."

Infeligo shrugged his mighty shoulders. "Thou mayst repeat it over and over," he said. "Thy words are as empty as a coward's skull rolled by waves!"

"The Council hath not gathered in order to discuss my deed!" objected Mamri, nervously twisting the elegant white triangle of a handkerchief in his pocket.

"Perhaps." Infeligo released a thick puff of blue smoke from his pipe.

Mamri lit an expensive cigar with a golden crown and a brown cover.

"The Council will discuss the starliner incident. But there's no reason not to raise another question. And I shalt do this, indeed I shalt."

Mamri's pale lips turned into a thin white line.

"Thou art speaking so because those Free Zone Rulers art under thy protection? And thou hath planned the extermination of those unfortunate rebels? Breaking all guidelines and agreements? Putting flames into those vile places?" Now it was Mamri's turn to mock.

Infeligo's face darkened.

"Well, well, well," came a third voice, a pleasant baritone. "Mamri and Infeligo! Good neighbors quarreling? What is going on, my friends?"

The third man to enter the hall was gigantic. Nearly seven feet high, with broad shoulders and a royal carriage. He was dressed in a strange antique suit — a sleeveless jacket of black velvet with a broad white collar made of fine Venetian lace.

A slender rapier sporting a rich garde decorated with sapphires, gold and diamonds; a belt studded with numerous blue stones; high black jackboots. He looked like a marquise or a noble from the Renaissance.

Both Mamri and Infeligo bowed with great respect.

"Discussing our neighbor's minor deeds, Simionte."

"My legions are ready," the giant newcomer said. He grinned. "If anyone needs help ..."

Simionte let the offer fall, unfinished. After a short, dramatic pause, he nodded and then went to the great ebony table in the center of the hall. Mamri and Infeligo looked after him with hard envy.

"Doest thou see? Simionte!" once again hissed Mamri. "He organized such a nice tyranny on those Chinese colonies in the Frontier! Such a nice, sweet tyranny! Such big donations to the Council Treasury!

"And lo! — look how he's standing now! That vulgar suit. No manners! How can he?"

"Um-hum," Infeligo grumbled. The quarrel with Mamri was already forgotten. "Simionte's behavior is unbearable. We must do something!"

"Good thoughts come simultaneously to good heads." Mamri gave a sugary smile. "Dear neighbor, we must discuss this in more detail ..."

He took Infeligo's arm. They went to a far dim corner and immediately started whispering.

Simionte seemed quite untroubled. He sat in an ebony armchair, stretched his legs and crossed his hands upon his breast. He looked like a man with a lot to do who was being forced to participate in events of little importance.

Soon Mamri and Infeligo joined him. Now three of the eight chairs were occupied. A few moments later the others arrived to fill the empty seats. The men just stepped out of the darkness, as if giant elevators were hidden in the immense shadows.

Five men, already far from youth but not yet close to old age. They were dressed in fantastic suits — leather and furs mixed with up-to-date bright synthetics.

Each had a great platinum ring on the middle finger of his right hand. A ring with a huge black stone, smooth and polished, crossed with white lighting bolts.

"Auerkhan! Pilyardock! Syrr! And — Apollion ..."

The smiles were broad, the greeting warm, the bows polite and low.

But in all eyes there was envy.

Apollion, who looked a little older than the others seemed the most relaxed.

Simionte rose from his armchair to greet the newcomers. He'd been quite arrogant just a minute ago with Mamri and Infeligo, but now he bowed to Apollion with enormous respect. And did not dare to take a seat again in Apollion's presence without permission.

Apollion looked rather common. He was dressed in a black leather jacket and blue jeans. Old-fashioned spectacles, the only spectacles in the whole company, gleamed faintly red from the chimney's fire.

He had the air of an old University lecturer. The great hairless skull and high forehead only enhanced that impression.

He sat, nodded to all the others, as if welcoming them to take their places, and fished a small piece of cloth from a pocket.

Apollion removed the spectacles and began to clean them — quite carefully.

The other members of the company moved the armchairs closer, as if competing for his attention.

The wall behind Apollion bore a strange black-and-red emblem, stretching slowly out of the gloom across the soft velvet waves covering the walls. It was a portrait of a black eagle and a red snake tearing and striking at one another.

The emblem framed Apollion, enclosed him, lifted him, adding to his obvious importance.

Now and again odd shadows crept over the emblem, which seemed partially carved yet also partially woven, so one might take the huge beasts on the wall as living things.

The eagle's eyes were gleaming red. The snake's were translucent, revealing many levels of deadly night.

"Gentlemen!" Apollion finally said. His fingers slowly caressed the carved edge of the table. "You all hath heard the sad tidings. I'm speaking, of course, about the incident which occurred on the border of Sir Auerkhan's and Sir Pilyardock's sectors."

Simionte shrugged his mighty shoulders, interrupting the speaker. The other men stared at him with some astonishment.

"Sorry to speak my mind so rudely, noble Apollion. But I wonder if thou must think we all are blind? And without hearing as well? Canst thou not tell us plainly what thou might require from us?"

Despite this verbal attack, Apollion remained relaxed.

"Noble Simionte, the large donations sent by thee to the Treasurer cannot cancel politeness." This was said in a dry and icy tone, meant to intimidate.

Simionte only grinned.

"We all must be a bit more natural," he said, leaning forward to pierce Apollion with his gaze. "At this particular point I know all there is to know about the incident. So does the rest of the Council, I warrant.

"Noble Sirs Mamri and Infeligo — what wouldst thou say? Noble Sir Syrr? Noble Sir Apollion? And, I daresay once more — why shall I sit and listen to all thy cunning phrases, noble Apollion?

"Answer me, please. Say it and be done!"

Simionte smiled.

Apollion's eyes burned with wrath.

"Gentlemen, gentlemen!" interrupted Syrr, a tall thin man with white hair and strange red eyes, like the eagle's. "Noble Simionte! Noble Apollion!"

"With or without thy agreement, noble Simionte," Apollion said coldly, "I shall proceed."

He took off his spectacles, cleaned them once more, then slowly and even solemnly drew them back on.

"As you all know, the missile was launched …"

The story he told was long and filled with many secret details. The intelligence services of both Russia and America would have been quite upset if they had been able to monitor his speech.

The other seven members of the Council listened carefully; even Simionte, who liked to pretend indifference. The expressions around the table were stony — but tense.

Apollion finished his little talk, then started torturing his poor spectacles with the cloth.

"Well, noble sires. Thy opinions must be spoken. I announced pure facts, nothing more. But the crucial question is, noble sires, what will follow?"

"What will follow!" snorted Infeligo. "War, to speak the truth.

"The Americans and Russians will tear one another in pieces. Thou, Auerkhan! Thou, Pilyardock! Why haven't the two of you kept an eye on this?"

"Yes, yes, why?" broke in Syrr and Mamri.

Simionte and Apollion remained silent.

"Why?" the word hammered heavily, like a great battering ram.

Everyone looked at the two men sitting on opposite sides of the great table. Heads turned to the right and to the left as if the owners were watching a tennis match.

Auerkhan and Pilyardock exchanged grim looks. Each man was a jealous guardian of an enormous fiefdom filled with countless souls to torment and feed upon or to trade for favors with the other members of the council. One man held sway over all that was the Russian Empire. The other kept the Americans in his horny grip.

The first, Auerkhan, was broad-shouldered, even broader shouldered than the giant Simionte. He was short and because of that looked almost square. Deep arched brows leaned above cold, gray, deep-set eyes.

His face was also broad, with thick cheeks and a double chin. He was wearing a black kosovorotka, a Russian shirt with the collar fastening on the side. The collar was decorated with small rivers of pearls. He had huge hands — thick fingers that seemed capable of rolling coins into tubes, or ripping apart iron chains.

"Nonsense," boomed Auerkhan, and clenched his great right fist. "Why do you all look at this noble sneak, Pilyardock? Perhaps that noble sir will answer what the hell an American ship was doing sneaking so close to my Russian base? What doest thou want — to be welcomed there with drums, flowers and a boy's chorus?"

Pilyardock made an evil smile. He was almost a head taller than Auerkhan. Thick black hair fell to his shoulders. He was wearing a dark yellow leather jacket with fringed sleeves. His hair was pierced with a long white eagle feather.

He said, "Noble Auerkhan is blaming me because 'the best defense is offense,' isn't that right? Well, well, well. Much rueth me indeed, as Spencer used to say.

"Look, gentleman, how deep is noble Auerkhan's fall — he did not hesitate to use even the death and last fear of those unhappy creatures from the civilian ship.

"Doest thou, o noble Auerkhan, doest thou know that my Amer liner was coming on a free space path? Didst thou know that it was unarmed and unprotected? Well, didst thou know what reaction there wouldst be? But no, noble Auerkhan's dogs scoured the ship and tore it to pieces!

"And now — Russians and Americans are on the very edge of full-scale war! That's his object, noble ones! To launch a war — and to get filled to the brim with war's juices. To bring large donations of human souls here … to occupy the highest place, which justifiably belongs to our noble Apollion!

"But, never mind all that — doest thou hearken to me, noble Auerkhan? All will be ruined by this war. All humanity! What shalt we do then? Become naked and helpless and hungry whilst he eats his fill?"

His voice sank to a low growl "Before Him, the Planetar Demon!"

"Can the wise Auerkhan explain all this?" Pilyardock's face was almost black because of blind rage. "Well, noble Apollion declared that everyone must speak openly. So do I.

"And here's my word! Noble Sir Auerkhan, the Rooskie's Keeper, must be cast out from our Council of The Eight. He must be banished, at the very least."

Pilyardock paused and Auerkhan immediately rushed into the breach. He was as angry as his opponent. His eyes burned with an wrath.

"Banished?" he rumbled, leaning forward and trying to spear his enemy with his eyes. "I daresay, *someone* here must be banished. But what about thee, o noble Pilyardock, Keeper of the Amers?

"It's a strange incident, isn't it? A liner shot to the dust! Oh, for certain, my Rooskies are very fond of shooting down Amer's liners! They have a dozen ships passing to and fro around their station. Amers and others. Were any of them ever shot down or even stopped?

"And suddenly an experienced soldier opened fire! Can you all imagine that these soldiers could have some reason for this? I mean some other reason than the noble Sir Pilyardock proclaimed here so expressively.

"Why art all listening only to one side? The civilian ship could have been taken as a military one.

"From what I have been told, the battle station *Borodino* reported that the ship appeared to be a military destroyer, camouflaged as a civilian liner. Why must we cast aside this version? This most truthful version.

"And why must we cast aside one simple explanation — that our noble Sir Pilyardock once upon a time sat down, sucked his finger and created a plot. How *he* would launch a war, bring a donation ... etcetera, etcetera, etcetera! And claim that my Rooskies are all murderers! And blame me for all that, as well!

"Nice plan, wasn't it?"

The others broke in. Angry words flew like missiles on a warstruck night. Auerkhan and Pilyardock glared wrathfully at one another.

Apollion raised his hand.

"Silence, noble Council, silence and patience. Our brave comrades must calm themselves. As far as I can judge, not thou, Auerkhan, nor thou, Pilyardock, art ready to answer for this incident?"

The two main opponents nodded grimly.

"That's what I expected." Apollion took off his spectacles. "You are pointing fingers of blame in opposite directions. And, of course, you both hath prepared enough tricks."

Simionte broke in. "We the noble Council must investigate this!" he demanded. "This I, Simionte, the largest donor to our cause, demand!"

The others all turned to stare at this strange creature, who was rising from his seat. Simionte was all wrinkled, crunched, blazed by suns and sins, with dark brown skin and round eyes gleaming with blue. The hooded figure hobbled to the head of the table, bowed low, and whispered to Apollion.

Suddenly Apollion grinned, interrupting Simionte.

"My dear noble Sir Simionte," Apollion began with a malicious glint in his eyes. "I've just received a message. Thy donation caravan was intercepted and destroyed. A trick of the Planetar, I daresay. And thy precious tyranny was overthrown ... the tyrant Kozarra was hanged ... that is the message."

Simionte sat stunned, his eyes wide and staring. Silence fell like death come to rest.

Then Infeligo grinned broadly and winked at Mamri.

"We all grieve with noble Sir Simionte," Apollion said, barely disguising his glee over his enemy's plight. "We shalt discuss this on our next meeting … and now — to return to the subject of this day."

Simionte fell back into his chair. It seemed as if all other issues had vanished for him.

"Let noble Simionte rest for a time." Apollion advised, face much more mournful than his true feelings. "Well, what shalt the others say?"

"Inspection. Close and careful inspection," hurried Mamri. "What were the circumstances? …"

"And if the answer means war?" asked Syrr.

"Gentlemen," Apollion said, "the last thing we all desire is war between the Americans and Russians. We have kept them at each other's throats for more than a thousand years, feasting on their misery. Surely, we cannot allow our differences to ruin such a hearty meal."

His speech mollified no one. Bitter jealousy still reigned in that dark hall.

"I ask again," pressed Syrr, "what if the answer means war?"

"There is still some time to prevent it … a short period, but there just the same," Infeligo broke in. "What if we send …" He searched for a likely candidate …

" … A soldier from our Corp?" Apollion suggested.

"Which man?" Auerkhan roused himself. "From …"

"Odysseus Corp, surely," Pilyardock smiled coldly.

"No!" Auerkhan growled. "I'm not a fool and neither are my noble brothers on this Council. Two investigators! Two men. One from each side! From Odysseus and the Sword Church! If this plan is adopted, all will soon be revealed to us."

"And all thy dirty plots, as well," spat Pilyardock.

"Heaven and hell!" his enemy roared. "That's *thy* plot to be unmasked!"

"Gentleman, gentleman!" Apollion admonished. "I think noble Sir Auerkhan's plan is a wise one to follow. Two investigators — one from each side — is the best course to follow."

"And do not forget about the UWP," Syrr inserted..

"Oh yes. Good of you to remind me, noble one. The United Worlds Police have someone on this …"

"Tanya Lawson," Pilyardock said. "Their best Master Investigator."

"An Amer …" Auerkhan made a face.

"This Amer will fight for the Russians till the last drop of her blood if she finds another Amer is to blame," Apollion said.

"I know that girl. Oh, what a girl!.." he smacked his lips.

"Well, so we must protect her," interrupted Infeligo. "What if she dredged up something ..." he looked first at Pilyardock, then at Auerkhan. Both enemies nodded.

"I'm innocent," proclaimed Auerkhan. "So — not a single hair will fall from Tanya Lawson's head."

"I vow the same," Pilyardock said. "I'll also guard her."

"Very well," concluded Apollion. "But what to do with our men?"

"I'll order them to find out who was responsible for the launch," Auerkhan said. "To learn everything there is to know about the circumstances of this incident.

"And I'll order them to deal appropriately with the traitors!" He threw a stinging glance at his enemy, 'the Amer's Keeper,' adding, "And both our men must report all important information to our officials. We must block any possibility of war."

"Yes, we must," Apollion agreed. "And I think it's clear — the information given to the governments must assure them the accident was indeed only bad luck. I suppose our men can manage this problem well enough. And we must be ready to help!"

"But only after our own investigation is over," Pilyardock insisted. Auerkhan suddenly agreed.

Simionte stirred in his chair.

"Still arguing?" he asked in a tired voice. "Well, well, continue ... what shall you all do without my donations?"

A long pause ... and then:

"We'll discuss that tomorrow, my good and noble Sir Simionte," was Apollion's grave reply.

And the meeting of the Council of Eight was over.

CHAPTER TWELVE

The beetlecraft hissed along the Rio Grande, riding the glowing spirit-rail that hurled Davyd toward his goal.

He shielded his eyes against the New Mexico sun, studying the river traffic shooting along on both sides of him.

It was all military, naturally — nearly the entire Southwest was military. A great Forbidden Zone that had absorbed all of New Mexico and good portions of Texas, Arizona and Colorado.

The river itself — more of a huge canal, really, with plasment walls and bottom — carried only military craft: huge tube-like freighters, flat-bottomed barges, troop transports, etc., all gleaming black-on-black high-tech. Embracing the spirit-rails in their drive slots as they sped along mere inches above the water.

The Rio Grande Courseway was a vital part of America's military might on Earth, carrying top secret goods and people from the fortressed wizard laboratories in the Rocky Mountains all the way to the military spaceport at Old Laredo on the Gulf of Mexico.

Davyd had seen all this before. He'd traveled this route each time he was blessed with a mission for the holy cause of America. So the traffic was nothing unusual to him. However, the *speed* surprised him.

Usually things moved at a somewhat leisurely, although orderly, pace. This *was* Government Work, after all. No need to hurry when you're suckling on the tax teat. But now the barges and transports were moving as if the Hounds Of Hell were baying at their sterns.

There was a sudden windshock and Davyd had to brace himself as the little beetlecraft was rocked by a big freighter booming by — heading in the other direction.

Probably to the spaceport, Davyd mused. Somebody had forgotten to shut one of the freighter's bays and he'd caught a glimpse of a whole battery of evil-looking djinnguns, with worried demon gunners scurrying here and there, tugging at their tie-downs.

It was the kind of weapon used by shock troops spearing an invasion. Yet another sign, Davyd thought, that war was imminent.

Not that he really needed another clue. From the time he'd been plucked off the Puffship to his hurried, almost violent landing at Old Laredo, he'd seen and heard nothing to refute the young lieutenant's breathless declaration that "we're almost at war!"

Davyd rubbed his eyes. Jesus, he was tired. The only thing keeping him awake and moving was the smell of excitement in the air, a heady brew stirred with swagger sticks and spiced with fear.

And he knew damned well that he was about to be thrown into the center of it.

General Link had made that plain in their hurried meeting at CommandStar. Actually it was Link's manner that conveyed the message. The general really had very little to say, except to give him his orders and wish him godspeed. But he'd been so nervous, so much in unseemly (for a general) awe of Davyd, that Kells hardly required a mage's progcasting to read the bones.

And just like the words said in that old Odysseus Corps drinking song, they were, "… my bones, baby/my bones/bound for Rooskieland."

Up in front the little motorfiend shrilled back to him: "Nearing our destination, Master! On time! On time! Godblessamerica, on time!"

Two eyestalks swiveled on top of the creature's bony skull, peering at him to see if he heard.

Grinning, Davyd nodded thanks. There were no beings in the entire United Galactic States who acted more patriotic than one of the spirit world folk. He knew it was a ruse, a shield against their absolute bottom-rung status in modern America.

Davyd didn't mind. In fact, he rather liked most of the devilish breed he'd encountered. In a strange way he even identified with them. He'd heard guys damn their black souls to the hells. Not Davyd, who believed deep in his heart that his own soul was as black as they come and was already damned to spend all eternity in the hellfires.

He slipped the traveling kit from an inside pocket and tidied up for his meeting with Father Zorza.

As he rubbed the disposable depilatory napkin over his tanned face, wiping away his rough beard, he gazed through the plasbubble top of the beetlecraft, enjoying the view.

Davyd had about fifteen minutes to get ready, most of which he intended to use flattening his nerve arcs to dead level calm. So he soaked in all of the exotic New Mexico light he could, letting the clear color waves wash over him. Trying to bathe away the effects of the last mission, which had stubbornly clung to him like cold gritty clay.

He was just north of the Port Of Las Cruces — about seventy five miles from his destination. Shown on even the most secret military maps as Geronimo Springs Proving Grounds.

In fact, there were no proving grounds. Or anything *like* proving grounds. In reality it was Odysseus Corps Headquarters. The most secret place — or so Davyd believed — in all the worlds.

Except for the HQ of the Church Of The Sword, of course. The Rooskies were just as good as hiding things as the Americans. Of that,

Davyd was certain. Underestimating his enemy was definitely not one of his many flaws.

Thinking of the Russians, he wondered what his Sword Church enemies were up to. At this moment a Rooskie just like Davyd might be on his way to a similar meeting somewhere in Old Russia.

Adrenaline glands reflexed into action and in the blink of an eye his whole body started pulsing with killing power, spoiling his whole effort to regain calm.

Davyd quickly cut off that line of thinking. What was the old saying: "Save your juice for the war, kid." Or something like that.

Good advice. Which Davyd took to heart and then got back to admiring the view.

He was cruising along the western edge of the San Andreas Mountains. He'd just passed Fort Hatch and was nearing the Hillsboro Lockstation. The river was about a mile above sea level at this point so he could see in every direction with nothing to impede his vision.

At this point, the high desert looked like the bottom of the sea. A flat empty wilderness, slashed with ravines and littered with strange rock formations — boulders stacked one on top of the other, leaning crazily, like the handiwork of a bored child. Big clumps of sagebrush and mesquite, waving in the wind like sea grasses, fat tumbleweeds bounding through the air.

The ride was exhilarating. He felt like a great magical fish speeding through seas of crystal clear waters.

Then the motorfiend shouted, "Here, master, here! Godblessamerica, we have arrived!"

Davyd's mood darkened when he heard the shout and he turned to see the tall white spire that marked the Las Palomas Dockingstation.

Shit!

A minute later he was shoving a handful of LT's into the motorfiend's claws for a tip — a generous one for luck — and he was tumbling out on the broad white plas platform, duffel over one shoulder, looking around to see who was waiting for him.

The answer was — no one.

In fact, the above ground part of the station was empty — except for a small green gravcar sitting about a hundred yards away. And the only sound was the hiss and rumble of the passing river traffic.

It made Davyd feel better. He had a few minutes more to prepare.

He walked to the car, which he knew was for him. When he reached it he touched a side panel. There was a tingling sensation as his vitals were studied.

Then a gnome's voice squeaked, "Welcome, Master!" And the door hissed aside so he could enter.

Davyd tossed his gear into the opposite seat and climbed in. When he was settled the door closed and the gravcar abruptly and silently sped away. It was so effortless that Davyd rarely thought of the thousands of tiny creatures deep in the car's mechanism casting spells to nullify gravity's effect, as well as all the other myriad details required to make the car go.

But today he did think about them and experienced an odd moment of pity for all the small slaves laboring to do his bidding. Scurrying about like ants under powerful pheromone orders to do this and that and the other thing, with no will of their own.

Once again he felt a close kinship with the spirit world creatures, although he couldn't have said why if pressed for an explanation.

Davyd shifted his thoughts to his greeting — or lack of same — at the dockingstation. Actually, he wasn't surprised or insulted. It was only one more proof that America was preparing for war.

And his mission — should he accept it — was so top secret no one could be trusted to meet him.

Adding further proof was another great absence he'd just noticed. Other than the words of welcome, the gnome had been silent since their departure. They were normally such a talkative breed they had a tendency to annoy people with their squeaking.

Davyd wished he had more time to think.

Then the gravcar was slowing down — just as effortlessly as when it took off — and they were curving over a hilltop. Below was a broad sparkling expanse of water — Geronimo Lake.

The gravcar slipped over a rough embankment and smoothed over the water toward an immense rock, shaped like an elephant. The only mark of beingkind showing on the rock was a large blue eye, rimmed in red.

Odysseus Corps Headquarters.

As he approached the eye vanished and the face of the rock slid away. Without hesitation the gravcar plunged through the opening into darkness.

And Davyd thought, I'm not ready, dammit! I'm not ready!

* * *

Father Zorza had incredible eyes. Dark as a Sicilian conspiracy, deep as a Vatican vault. Once he fixed them on you all your innermost secrets rushed forward, anxious to bare your shame.

Davyd kept his head down, avoiding the eyes.

"I don't want to do this, Father," he said. "Tell them to get somebody else."

"But they asked especially for you, Davyd," Father Zorza replied in his deep, gentle voice.

Davyd didn't answer and he didn't look up. He knew the priest's eyes would be as gentle and understanding as his voice. But there would be pain there as well — a smoky acceptance of suffering from wounds caused by sinners like Davyd Kells.

Zorza let the silence hang just past Davyd's margin of comfort. Then he said, "This mission is of the utmost importance, my son. I thought you'd feel honored. That's why I accepted it on your behalf."

Davyd shrugged. "I've had enough honors, thank you, father," he said, firmly as he could. "Right now, I'd just as soon return to the deep sleep tubes."

Father Zorza sighed. "Why the resistance, my son?" he asked. "What is troubling you?"

Davyd struggled for an answer. "Because," he began, "Because—" He broke off, coughing, as sudden emotion welled up, then congealed into a thick knot. He shook his head, helpless.

He coughed again, trying to break the knot loose, then croaked, "I have a right!"

"Of course, you do, Davyd," Zorza said. "No one is denying your right to refuse any mission at any time."

"And with no explanations required," Davyd pressed.

Another long and painful silence. Then, "Exactly as you say, my son. No explanations required."

Davyd struggled against brainwashed habit to keep everything back. He wanted his privacy, dammit!

"I'm not afraid, father," he said.

"I know you're not, my son," Zorza said.

Then, bolder: "I'm *never* afraid!"

"Never?" A gentle probing.

Davyd shook his head. "Never." Firm.

He'd been trained and medically altered so much that thoughts of pain or death never had time to rouse themselves when he was in action.

With his Jesuit's cunning, Zorza spotted Davyd's weakness and slipped in the knife.

"Not even when you passed the Hall Of Peace and looked inside?" he asked.

Davyd gritted his teeth. Zorza knew him too well. On his way to the chapel for this meeting he had indeed gone by the Hall Of Peace. And he *had* looked inside.

* * *

In the dim, eerie light he could see the iconic holos on the walls of the vaulted room. Each was a portrait of an Odysseus Corps member, one after the other, going all the way back to the very first man — which was Davyd, the Adam of the assassins' corps.

His eyes went to the eight-foot-high glass tubes filled with swirling magical gasses from the spells that kept all the occupants alive and well in SleepLock.

All of the tubes, save one, had a hero in residence. Naked bodies so well formed they seemed like statues sculpted by some ancient genius.

Kells examined the empty tube, which sat in the center — the supreme place of honor. Beneath the tube was a holo showing Davyd's face.

Home.

Davyd's first reaction had been a longing so powerful and so deep he'd nearly wept. He wanted to sleep, by God! He deserved it. He needed it.

A hundred years of sweet dreams to wipe away all the horrid images of the many beings he had killed. With only an occasional nightmare to spoil his sleep.

Davyd's second reaction was fear.

What if the war erupted full force and he'd be required to kill for years without end and never be allowed his peace again?

The thought rocked him to the core.

* * *

Davyd sighed at the memory.

"Yes, father," he confessed. "I looked inside. And I was afraid."

"But, why, my son?" the priest asked. "It seems only natural that instead of fear, you would have experienced much gladness to know what great peace is in store for you when this mission is done."

Davyd bit his tongue. He wanted to snap that he was already supposed to be entering the chamber. That he'd just completed a mission. A messy, bloody mission. Murders on his soul that weren't supposed to be his. They belonged to the kid, dammit! To Jonz!

And now I'm sorry I didn't kill the little sonofabitch for blowing it.

Instead, he said, "I'm not ready, father. I've had enough and now I want to go back to sleep. Wake me in a hundred years. And not before."

It was perfectly within Davyd's rights not only to refuse the mission, but to set the rules on when he should be awakened again. And he was doing fine with his argument — his nerves steady, his resolve hard as steel.

Then he made a mistake.

Instead of stopping, he added: "Unless the war isn't over after a hundred years. Because if it isn't, I want strict orders posted not to disturb me until it's done."

Father Zorza's eyes lit up, which was when Davyd realized he'd blown it.

"Now I understand what is troubling you, my son," the priest said, his gentle smile spreading wider. "You're concerned about all the souls you may be required to release if war should come."

Davyd didn't reply. But that didn't matter one way or the other, because Zorza already had the logic rolled up into a nice neat ball and was running with it.

"I've counseled you many times about this, Davyd," Zorza said. "When you act within the holy laws of America's cause it is impossible for you to sin."

Davyd bit back a groan. But he'd killed so many!

As if reading his thoughts, Zorza said, "No matter how many lives you must take in our cause, your soul will remain as fresh as a newly baptized child. Free of all blemishes.

"And if you should die, you soul will be lifted directly to heaven and into God's glorious sight."

"Yes, father," Davyd said. "Thank you, father. Hearing that again makes me feel much better."

But he didn't mean a word of it.

Zorza knew this too and he leaned forward to make his next point. His final point.

"Here is what troubles me about this situation, my son," he said. "You've already refused. And I hesitate to try to change your mind.

"However, I can't help but feel deep in my heart that in this case your refusal may turn out to be the blackest of all sins. One that no amount of time in Hell could burn away."

Davyd was jolted. "What sin?" he asked. "How can I sin when I'm asleep?"

"By refusing to help stop this war, my son," Zorza said. "Think of all the thousands, nay millions, of lives that will be saved if you are successful."

The priest's eyes narrowed, "Why … To reject this mission might very well result in mass murder. No. Greater still. A holocaust. And you would be responsible."

Davyd trembled. There would be no sleep.

Zorza caught his reaction and twisted the psychic knife to make sure.

"This assignment," he said, "may be the crowning glory to your already illustrious career. You changed history once, my son. For the betterment of all. And now we are forced to ask you — nay, beg you — to change the course of history once again."

Davyd drew in a ragged breath.

Then he nodded. "All right, father," he said quietly. "What do they want me to do?"

The priest abruptly rose to his feet, long golden rosary beads clacking against his black robes.

"Come with me," he said. "You will receive your orders directly from on high."

And he walked swiftly out of the chapel.

Davyd followed, shivering.

What now, he wondered? What now?

CHAPTER THIRTEEN

The Church of The Sword cannot wait. This was the first and capital rule of the Order and Vlad knew it perfectly well.

Just as he knew that if Father Onphim had taken the time to call him personally, it meant that Great Annoyances were being stirred up.

Vlad rushed from the elevator. People in the hall dashed aside: if a major with a bear's head on his left sleeve tab was running wildly it was better not to find yourself blocking his path.

A small group waiting for a taxi gave way to Vlad without a word. One glance at him was sufficient.

If Nadya had witnessed him pushing people around to get his way she'd have been furious.

His girlfriend was a rather punctilious person: "Hah, you, a stout guy! All hail the mighty Vlad, The Hero! What the hell are you thinking about? That all people must kneel before you, or what?"

She was always angry if he used his rank and privileges in her presence. Most of their altercations had their roots in this subject.

But hell! He was *not* like all the others, by damn! And a major's rank in the Brown Bears Company was not a Christmas gift.

Vlad secured a belt, inserted his card and entered the address. Let all the world go the fiendish Chaos! The Church of the Sword cannot wait.

He was far above the city. The new RGF capital, with an exact copy of the old Kremlin in its very midst, was floating under him: a huge conglomerate of sky-piercing towers, steel-and-glass pyramids belted with the green strings of pendent gardens. Heavy transport tubes snaked across the bottom of this hand crafted sea.

A peaceful town, but Vlad knew how many anti-space and aircraft complexes were hiding in the near and far suburbs. How many carriers and launchers, camouflaged as civilian vehicles, were circulating around the city, ready to shoot.

How much hard soil was excavated for deep underground war stores, secret communications, civilian refuges. How many eyes and ears, whether human, fiendish or electronic, were searching the sky.

The Enemy is near! Psst! The Enemy is listening! A gas-bag is a gift for a spy!

Vidposters were everywhere. A large hairy ear, catching all careless phrases. An evil-looking crouched man, crawling behind the back of a lazy and sleepy sentinel. The whole country, the whole galactic conglomeration was still at war. Or in a condition very much like war.

Vlad was standing near a small church at the very edge of town. The temple was hidden between two ultra-high skyscratchers and the only thing to mark it was a tiny icon-lamp that glowed above the entrance.

An ordinary church. Like many others in the city. But, above all, one of the meeting-points of The Sword Acolytes.

Vlad crossed himself and entered.

The temple was practically empty: only two or three figures were standing before the icons, busy with tapers.

Now step aside. One, two, three … four!

"Name'n'code!" growled an evil voice.

He gave it. A sudden gloom descended over him. And then an unknown force was dragging him into immense darkness. Then the cold grip of a fiendish creature seized Vlad.

Father Onphim's disembodied servants never lost a chance to play with softskins. Ghosts had to obey, but that was not to say there couldn't be small deviations from exact orders.

Vlad clenched his teeth. "Does that make you proud?" he barked. "Can't you think of anything new?"

The unseen creature growled in anger, but in the end it loosened its magical grip.

"Enter, my son," said a soft voice just in front of Vlad.

The darkness was smashed and torn by a sudden light. A tiny room with carved stone walls was revealed, lit by several antique lamps. If Tanya Lawson had seen those electrical lamps she would have immediately classed their owner as a Magic-Hater like herself.

She would have been mistaken, for fiendish creatures by the millions — nay the billions — were hard at work in the Church Of The Sword. And it took an enormous amount of energy and cunning effort to create all those powerful spells and to hide them from the damned Amers.

However, in the secret chamber Vlad entered, not a single magical device was allowed. The demands of super secrecy forbade it. Thus, the ancient electrical lamps.

The only furniture was a small black table which sat in the middle of the room. Black polished wood, very old and carved on the sides with runes. The glittering surface was empty except for one sheet of paper, pressed by thin pale fingers.

Father Onphim was the owner of those fingers. He was clad in the common cassock of a field warpriest, with a dark silver cross — badly dented — resting on his bosom.

This cross, Brown Bears' legends said, had saved Father Onphim's life when the bullet of a rebel sniper had found the old man many years before.

"Nice to see you, my son, nice to see you." A deep voice, filled with Force.

Father Onphim raised his head. A high and noble forehead, stern eyes of gray steel, thin colorless lips and a strong massive chin. Several old scars near his right temple, slightly covered with silver-stained hair. No medals. Only that dented cross.

"Time to earn our pay, my son, time to work," said the old man. "The whole Conclave is waiting. I'll show you the way. But first read this order. Signed by His Majesty Lord Emperor."

The Russian Galactic Federation was a Constitutional Monarchy. That was the pretense of the generals, at least.

Vlad took the paper. Not a vidtablet, not a magic scroll; a common, ancient paper, with the watermark of an Imperial Two-Headed Eagle.

The paper was most official. Cold words marched along the smooth surface of the page, nominating and confirming someone's crash, exile, imprisonment or even death.

Armed with this document, Major Vlad would become a local God. All military and civil staff would have to obey him without a word. He would be able to enter classified X-zones, never mind how high the classification.

He could interrogate anyone he chose, no matter how important their rank. He could wear and transport any weapon he liked, fiendish or non-fiendish.

"Only God himself could be higher, Father," Vlad said.

"Yes, my son. But there will be one small step between you and Heaven — your humble servant," the priest bowed.

"Report only to me. No exceptions. Not even to the Lord Emperor, prime minister or chairman of The Duma. Not even to anyone from The Conclave. You understand, I know. Other instructions will be coming from The Conclave.

"I don't have the most up-to-date information, so we'll have to go see for ourselves what is happening."

Father Onphim rose. His head was only a little bit higher than Vlad's shoulder.

His hand glided over the wall and the stones moved aside, giving way. Behind the door was Nothing. A many-colored glittering Nothing, the inner side of the Fiendish Worlds. The Conclave of the Church of the Sword was hidden with cunning.

Vlad took a step. Something like fear stirred slightly somewhere deep, deep in his soul and then was gone. The Brown Bears Never Retreat, Surrender or Fear.

If this was a fiendish world, then it was a very special one. Most worlds have both solid surface, air and sky above, and something pretending to be a sun. Here was nothing but a grim, everlasting night.

"Follow me, my son," came Father Onphim's voice.

Under Vlad's feet was a surface that felt something like resilient jam. Nothing more. No sounds, nor smells — nothing. Only the voice of the old war-priest.

Then light suddenly rushed in from all directions — oceans of bright flame. It was hard not to raise a hand to cover one's eyes.

But Vlad only narrowed his eyelids. It was clear that Judgment Day was at hand. Well, he was ready.

"That's thy man, Onphim?" growled a Rather Unpleasant Voice. "Art thou sure?"

This voice … it was filled with pure Force and Might. A great master, thought Vlad. A great master of magic. Maybe he was facing one of those fabulous enchanters who could shut down stars like people switch off lamps, giving rest to the tiny devils working there.

A cold shiver ran down his back. Vlad, Vlad, remember the Rule of the Brown Bears!..

But it was very hard to follow all the guidelines. Vlad still could not see anything in the surrounding flame. All his senses gave up, unable to penetrate the thick magic border around him.

"Yes, noble Conclave," came Father Onphim's answer.

To Vlad, Onphim sounded as if he were addressing a whole chamber, instead of a single entity.

"Here's *my* man," the priest continued. "The best warrior we have. As all know, he's been a loyal soldier of our Church for more than a thousand years. In the Church Of The Sword he is our greatest hero. This is why I have chosen him to assist us now in this mortal crisis. Of course, the Amers could still play tricks, so …"

"The UWP claims it is sending its best as well," broke in another voice. "A Major Tanya Lawson. She is in charge of the investigation. We just learned this news. And it is somewhat disturbing, since Investigator Lawson is an Amer and her final decision could be influenced to go against us."

"Then it is even more important, noble Conclave," Father Onphim said, seizing the moment, "that we send this man to represent us." He tapped Vlad on the shoulder.

Vlad heard murmurs of assent. For some reason this made him feel most uncomfortable — as if a sharp-edged knife had just been placed at his throat.

Still, he knew his duty and he stiffened to attention, clicking his heels together and snapping a salute.

"What are my orders, sirs?" he asked.

"They are quite simple, Major," the Unpleasant Voice boomed in reply. "We claim the incident with the Amer cruise ship was an unfortunate accident. A chance shot.

"It is thy duty to make certain this is so! However, if it proves otherwise, eradicate all traces that lead back to us. Never mind how. Just do it!"

"Yessir," Vlad replied.

"There is one more, most important thing, major," the Unpleasant Voice went on. "It is possible this 'chance' shot was the work of an Amer spy. And the incident was a conspiracy to cast blame on us."

Vlad shivered. Yes, that was it. Surely. How could an experienced crew, well-trained officers of high rank, make such a mistake? It must have been the result of Amer trickery.

"This possibility thou must keep in mind," said the voice. "And, if so — eradicate the traces of this, too. Remember, Tanya Lawson must proclaim that it was a complete and awful mistake. The version of an Amer spy is not allowed. Otherwise war will follow, and war we must prevent. If there really was a spy, we'll deal with it ourselves. Is this clear to thee, Major?"

"Yes sir," Vlad said. "Quite clear."

"Very well then. Father Onphim, thou mayst depart."

"Thank you, noble Conclave," said Vlad's godfather.

*　　*　　*

"Are you certain you are willing to undertake this mission, my son?" Father Onphim asked.

He and Vlad were standing in a small chamber beneath the church. "I know you have just returned from a most difficult assignment. No matter how important this new mission is, you still have the right to refuse it and choose the long sleep, instead."

"No!" Vlad said. Quite adamant.

How could he refuse with the lifeblood of Mother Russia at stake?

Father Onphim smiled. "No? Good for you, my son, good for you," he said.

"But do you understand about the spy? To tell the truth, I was astonished. Look, if this scum still lurks somewhere at the station … imagine, he could falsify the records in the *Borodino* computers! And what about this Inspector Lawson? What will she do?"

"Can she … er … be influenced by us?" asked Vlad.

Father Onphim shook his head. "Alas, no. Not by us, I'd say. As for the Amers … the boys must be busy sniffing through her files, looking for a weakness. Each man or woman my son, has a weakness. I'll do my best to find her weakness myself, but I don't have much hope, to tell the truth."

Vlad was astonished at this admission of failure before his mentor even started.

"Why, father?" he asked.

"Lawson is an Amer, my son. Maybe the best of all that clumsy nation, but still an Amer. Can you trust an Amer? Just tell me that."

Vlad bowed his head. Never trust an Amer, boy — a child, an old man or a girl. A girl, especially. Father Onphim was right. As always.

"I'm considering all the possibilities, my son," the priest went on. "First, what if Lawson reveals a plot? I cannot exclude some maniac on the *Borodino* …"

"The Amers will strike," Vlad said.

"Yes, my son," the priest said. "And this would throw the whole galaxy into a Holocaust. The Great Judgment before its time, an Apocalypse. Millions upon millions would be slain on both sides.

"How many planets would become radioactive dust, or became part of the Chaotic Fiendish Domains? A war-ghost attack can suck off the very souls of the defenders. The borders and outposts would tremble. And then what?

"I'm a war-priest, my son, I've waved the last good-bye to hundreds of boys — and my hands still remember their blood."

Onphim shook his head, his face grim. "Our superiors no doubt understand this perfectly well," he went on.

"Otherwise, we and the Amers would have destroyed one another long ago. It is the wisdom of our leaders that has kept the balance from tipping over the edge into full scale war for more than ten centuries."

"But, this time …" anguished, he let his voice trail off.

"Yes, Father?" Vlad dared to press.

The war-priest sighed heavily. "Our leaders have sent apologies to the Amers," he said. "They have also offered to pay reparations to the families of the people who were killed in the incident. Perhaps this might help prevent war."

Another heavy sigh. "Except …" again his voice tailed off in despair.

"Except what, father?" Vlad asked.

Father Onphim was too mysterious today. Vlad liked his orders plain — shoot, or don't shoot. On the whole, he preferred to shoot. The Amers and their allies were his enemies.

Vlad was trained to hate all enemies without fear or favor and he killed them whenever he could.

"Except it's not so simple, my son," the priest said. "What if as a result of this tragic liner incident the Amers fire on a ship from our fleet? And then tell us it was a grievous mistake, just like *HolidayOne*?"

"Then we fight back!" Vlad said firmly.

"That's easy to say," Father Onphim replied. "But it is my suspicion the real war has already begun. I think the destruction of *HolidayOne* might have been a real provocation.

"It looks very much like the dirty work of the Amers, doesn't it? Beware a spy, my son. Beware a spy!"

Father Onphim took a swift glance at his watch, "Now it is time for you to go, my son. And all our prayers are with you.

"You must reach the *Borodino* and interview the officers and crew before Inspector Lawson arrives. Other than that, I will not give you further direct instructions. I will not think for you — make your decision on who is responsible by yourself."

Suddenly his fists clenched and his lips twisted. "Get this spy scum for me, Vlad!" he growled. "Get him! And then you may rest."

The priest's intensity shocked Vlad into silence. Onphim misunderstood his reaction and rushed to reassure him.

"I promise you," he said, quite seriously, "that this time your rest will be long enough to sweep away all the bad memories. I swear this by all that is holy to us."

Vlad had never seen Father Onphim so solemn and somber. "Well," he said, "perhaps I had better go, Father."

"Yes, my son," the priest said. "Let me bless you. And … please, come back to us. I beg you."

With strange feelings, astonishment and even a little fear, Vlad took his leave.

He was on his way to the StarPort where an interceptor waited to carry him to the *Borodino*. It would be a stripped down ship, with no comforts for a weary soldier home from the wars, only to be rushed off again.

But Vlad didn't mind this. He needed to think deeply and without distractions of any sort. And it wasn't only the mission that he wanted to think about.

There was something else. Something quite new and mysterious he wanted to ponder:

Who was the owner of that deadly voice who had given Father Onphim his orders?

CHAPTER FOURTEEN

It was said that Engine Devils could only swear.

It was said they could not really be sad, or really grieve or suffer despair.

Softskins believed their powerful slaves to be nothing more than emotionless spell-casting machines.

Let them vapor off their hatred in the "Three Hanged Monks" and that's enough, said the softskins.

It was true that Old Scratch really was a great swearer. And yes, Engine Devils Local 666 often met at their favorite inn to gossip about their weak softskinned masters.

And yes, yes, yes, Old Scratch knew many Engine Devils who would praise the extermination of the arrogant "softers."

As for the many grand fiends and lesser fiendish creatures slain aboard *HolidayOne* — well, a la guerre com a la guerre, as it's said. Many creatures both great and small will perish in this endless and unseen war, Engine Devils often grumbled. We could be next!

Must we weep because of it? Definitely not! Let's drink and laugh and mock the softskins!

Maybe Old Scratch would have said those things himself. Maybe. If some other devil's ship had been destroyed by a missile with a horde of DeathSpirits in its warhead.

After the explosion Old Scratch was located by Daniel Carvaserin's SearchSpell. The *Borodino's* chief wizard had immediately ordered him to be picked up.

And Scratchy had suddenly found himself in a vast chamber deep within the Rooskie battlestation. The softskinned mage's stern face and malice-filled eyes were the first things Old Scratch had seen.

However, the magician did not ask any questions.

"You are wounded!" Old Scratch heard a terrifying exclamation and pain suddenly arose in him. A bitter and evil pain from both his wounded fiendish flesh and soul. And then he knew no more.

Later, when he came to, he was in a great Fiendish Hall. An immense black cloud was near. Covering him, nursing him, struggling with his remaining pain …

"I'm Homula," Scratch heard. "Keep quiet. Do not move, brother. I'm keeping the chant."

Scratch was surrounded by hundreds of different fiendish creatures, most of warlike origin. The Hall itself looked very much like an Inner

Hell. Hand-crafted plas-steel was hidden behind floating clouds of hot yellow smoke.

Flame flickered here and there. Lightning streaked like golden snakes and the heavy odor of boiling sulfur caressed Old Scratch's nostrils.

Pain released its cold jaws, but even so he could only float slowly and helplessly beside one of the thick clouds.

"Ha! Behold, he's here!"

One of the tiny DeathSpirits approached him. This little one also looked as if it came from the Softskins' Bonecrusher, but it was still filled with much conceit.

"Back, back, Chyvaist!" Homula halted him. "This Devil cannot speak yet."

"Oops, Mother," rebuked the DeathSpirit insolently. "I've come from that very explosion. I must know what softskin's luck brings this Devil here? I must, Mother! My goblins are all ash. Unsuccessful ejection."

"What was there on the ship to burst into flame with such power? Listen, you, big claws! It was me in the warhead. Me, Chyvaist the DeathSpirit, from the Greater Abyss! Answer me! Answer me, now!"

DeathSpirits were rather daring creatures.

"Peace, Chyvaist," sighed Homula. "What happened was not thy fault."

"To the softskins with all faults! The less of them, the better. Why was this Devil sneaking around? And why was he mimicking a destroyer? It's me, Chyvaist, speaking! I felt this! I'm not a blindfolded softskin.

"We took aim. We chased the target. I myself cut through the interference! War interference, I daresay! And then — lo! — a peaceful liner! Civilians!"

Chyvaist hissed the last word with great disgust.

"And I made — a great BOOM! And a great fecal oops. And now they can say anything, those softskins high above, even that I was working for the Amers! No, Mother, this Engine Devil must reply!"

"Chy ..." started Homula, but Old Scratch interrupted.

"Hey, lad, thou asked for my answer? Well, I'll speak. It *was* a civilian ship, I swear. No war devices aboard. Not a single one. Doest thou understand? I can swear on any holy thing thou likes. And there was no interference about. Thou must be wrong ..."

"Wrong? Wrong?!" came the shrill shriek. "Listen thou Space-in-the-ass-Pusher, I am never wrong! I'm ..."

"Peace everyone," came a cold voice from above. "Scratch, the Engine Devil, Local 666, I must speak with thee. That's me, Daniel Carvaserin, Wizard-in-Chief of *Borodino* station. Prepare to meet thy master!"

Carvaserin was a real Power. Scratch felt the cold strings of the soft-skin's might separating the main chamber from his personal cloud. The lightning vanished, plas-steel and armor lifted, giving way to reveal a tall, ascetic softskin with dark gray eyes. Powerful eyes.

Daniel Carvaserin's forehead was crossed with three deep purple scars, unmistakably of magical origin. The wizard was clad not in an ordinary Rooskie space uniform but in a pure black cloak, as if he were an ancient druid. And he was quite alone.

Not even a fifth-class mage would dare enter the Hall of Battle Fiends. But Carvaserin dared and all the WarFiends, DeathSpirits, legions of lesser creatures and even Homula bowed before their Master.

There was no humiliation in such a bow. Carvaserin was the strongest.

"Take seven steps back," commanded the Wizard coldly. "All of you!"

Everyone obeyed. The Power they feared filled the Wizard's voice.

"And now, my noble Devil, we'll talk."

Old Scratch shivered. He had faced many perils. He had slipped through the spreading flame from dying planets; he had avoided meteor attacks; he had raised research ships from the living swamps. But real fear now reached into him with its cold grip.

From the steely eyes of the softskin mage a shrilling fear was crawling, seizing the very soul of the Engine Devil. Carvaserin's face loomed above, emotionless.

"Why didst thou not answer my call?" the Wizard demanded.

"What call?" Scratch asked in astonishment.

"Thou insisteth thou didst not hear it?" boomed the Wizard. "Thou hadst to hear it! But thou didst not reply! The order — from whence came this order?"

"The order?" muttered the Engine Devil, shocked.

Carvaserin's eyes narrowed. Now he looked exactly like the "evil interrogator" in a pulp police story.

"Thy Amer masters art now blaming my crew and my country for the bloody extermination of innocent civilians," hissed Carvaserin. "Very clever plan, very clever. Those Rooskies, bloody bastards, et cetera. But they hadn't counted on me!"

"I do not know how to answer thee," said Old Scratch.

The wave of hatred coming from the Wizard overwhelmed him, pain-fully pressing in on his own thoughts, trembling his very soul. What did this softskin …

"Do not speak to me so!" growled the wizard, eyes glowing, lips pale as he read Scratchy's thoughts. "Keep the nickname of my race for thy accomplices! For thy favorite inn! This is the *Borodino*, thou miserable fiend. So cast aside thy pride and reply! Who gave thee the order?"

The mind pressure increased. Flame was boiling in Carvaserin's eyes — the pure white flame of Power — and poor Scratch had no weapon to withstand it. Tortured, he groaned. It's hard to make an Engine Devil groan, but the wizard knew the ways.

"I … I wish to know …" Scratch forced out. "But … sire … I really *do* not know. There is nothing I can tell thee, sire."

"Doest thou want me to turn over thy whole memory?" threatened the wizard. "I'll do it. It's not at all interesting to dig into thy dirty fiendish dreams, but I'll do it!"

His voice softened, becoming more reasonable. "Listen, Scratch," he said. "This is too serious for jokes. I have to uncover the truth about this conspiracy. How can it be that to all our sensors thy ship looked like a heavy destroyer of the 'Perry' class, eh?

"How can it be that all communications were blocked, blocked even from me, Daniel Carvaserin, the Wizard? I called upon thee, trying to stop thee, and I failed. How can it be? It looked like heavy magiarmour surrounding thy vessel. Very strange for a civilian liner!

"So tell me, unhappy being, how all these things could have occurred?"

"I know nothing of what thou hast said, sire," Scratch replied. "It was a civilian liner. I was responsible for the pathfinding spells. I controlled nearly all the magic aboard. We were unprepared. I was casting common chants and nothing …"

"Doest thou understand what my spell will do to thee, unhappy one?" Carvaserin said, head rising high.

"Aye, sire," sighed Scratch.

He could not withstand the wizard's evil will. And he was helpless against his growing wrath.

"And thou still insisteth that nothing …"

"Aye, sire," said Scratch once again.

Carvaserin nodded. "Well, well, well. Thou hast spoken. I'll return soon, Scratch. I do not know whom thou art serving so faithfully. And it's a pity that thou hast declared thyself an enemy of my country."

Before Scratch could protest, the wizard vanished.

All the fiendish horde rushed to Scratch, squeaking, howling and shrieking only four words:

"What doest he say? What doest he say?"

Old Scratch didn't answer.

Vlad was in an extremely bad mood. Damned Amers, damned Rooskies, damned fiends, gods, heavens and the several hells. All were against him. All.

He entered the huge battlestation clad in the ordinary naval uniform of a one-star Major. In Space Navy terms, a third rank Captain without ribbons: just another officer among several thousand from *Borodino's* crew.

Only two men aboard knew about his mission: Rear-Admiral Peter Amiriani and Wizard-in-Chief Daniel Carvaserin, brother of Vlad's old enemy, Brand.

When Vlad entered the Admiral's saloon he caught two glances. In the first, fear was camouflaged by the Admiral's everyday confidence. In the second, cold magical ice barely hid naked hatred.

Obviously, Brand Carvaserin had told his brother much. Vlad didn't care. He had survived Brand's wrath, so surely he'd survive Daniel's.

Vlad disliked and distrusted lofty gestures, such as displaying official vidtablets with the signatures of Very Important Men. It was something he did not ordinarily do.

After all, his authority didn't depend on such men. He was simply the best the Church Of The Sword had to offer and that was all. So what use were high words, stern glances and all those foolish things?

Unfortunately, Daniel Carvaserin, the stupid ass, had forced him to do what he disliked. Perhaps Vlad could have managed things more easily if he only had to deal with the Rear Admiral.

But the Chief Wizard, filled with paranoia and false ego ... well, that was something else.

Carvaserin at once proclaimed that Vlad must confirm what he, the chief wizard, had already determined.

"Your job, here," he announced, "is to support my findings. All must believe that this incident was not our fault, but was due to an Amer conspiracy. I do not doubt this conclusion, so ..."

They spent an hour or so, arguing. The poor Admiral kept silent — what else could he do?

At last Vlad — with a faint gleam of wrath — took out his wallet. Between the thick leather there was a single sheet of paper. With an Imperial Two-Headed Eagle and the Emperor's signature.

Daniel Carvaserin's pale face purpled as he studied Vlad's authority.

"Well." A deep sigh.

The wizard sat very stern, very haughty, hiding his wounded pride under a gray cloak of indifference.

"Do as you want," the wizard said. Then he suddenly stood up. "But rest assured I'll contact my superiors as well. My report has already been filed, and I ..."

"Haven't you read this?" Vlad insisted, once again displaying the document. "It's my obligation to carry out all investigations, Master Chief Wizard. So my advice to you, sir, is to piss off!"

Pure insult, to be sure. But such men as the Carvaserin brothers only understood forceful words.

"Pardon, Admiral," the wizard said, refusing to look Vlad in the eyes. "I have my duties."

Then he whirled and stalked out of the room without another word. The paper in Vlad's wallet had trumped the wizard's magic. The furious mage was helpless before it.

As for Admiral Amiriani, he immediately agreed to all of Vlad's demands.

He had to work quickly and carefully. Major Tanya Lawson from the United Worlds Police would be arriving soon. The liner bearing the beautiful investigator — Vlad had seen her picture when he went through her dossier — had already been spotted approaching the *Borodino's* Forbidden Zone.

According to the terms of the UWO agreement between Russia and America, Lawson was to be given complete access to all evidence and witnesses. It was Vlad's job to get to them before she did, plus to leave no trace of his presence.

The first thing he did was order up all the records from the ship's black boxes. There were no security seals on any of the battlegraphs, but surely no one would dare alter those records. It would be very easy to catch such a deed.

Many times and from many different viewpoints, Vlad watched the tragedy of the *HolidayOne* unfold.

A dot on a vidscreen. Endless legions of magical creatures peering into the depths of space spotted danger. It always began with the glowing trace of the *HolidayOne's* Engine Devil at work. Then a faint gleam of black armor shimmered into life. And then — the trembling pulse of a mysterious transmission.

Immediately, another legion of fiends would come into the chamber, sniffing, soothing, snorting as they uncovered the trace of a powerful code contained within that transmission.

Yes, that was it. A code. They couldn't decipher the message, but it had the "fingerprints" of an Amer military code all over it.

And next, the ship entered *Borodino's* optical range. It was clearly a destroyer: one of the *Perry* series. All its parameters were from the

Jane's edition. A classical destroyer. Class A. And it was disguised as a civilian ship.

Vlad listened in to the conversation that followed:

"Dolgov, what's happening?" came Carvaserin's voice.

"An Amer destroyer, sir, pretending to be a cruise liner," the voice of Igor Dolgov, the shooting officer. The calm but tensed voice of a professional.

"Stand by. I'll try to spot him first."

As much as he disliked the wizard, Vlad was pleased to hear him say this. When that Amer bitch, Tanya Lawson, reviewed these same tapes she'd see that all had been thoroughly checked out before the firing order was given.

Vlad resumed listening:

The *Borodino* issued warnings to the approaching ship. But there was no reply.

Then all the *Borodino's* alarms went off as the Amer ship painted it with its magical target sensors and prepared to launch a missile …

"Dolgov!"

"Yes, Sir."

"No luck … You must shoot!"

The wizard's decision had been a correct one, Vlad thought. Disguised like a civilian ship, but with weapons and gear like a Class A destroyer. And no one replied to the *Borodino's* warnings. Plus the Amers had been clearly getting ready to fire on the Russian warship.

By why? Why had this happened?

Vlad traced the Russian missile. And he felt real shock, when — lo! — all visions of the mighty destroyer vanished and the stunned *Borodino* staff realized they were shooting into innocence.

The remaining questions were too numerous to contemplate.

All vidscreens displayed a common civilian ship. All the rest "the ether traces of weapons," etc. were also present, but … those could be imitated. Hard to do, but not impossible.

Daniel Carvaserin's words about spies and Father Onphim's warning about provocation echoed in Vlad's mind.

But Major Lawson would surely argue, "Why the hell did you have to shoot? Are you saying you couldn't intercept and destroy a single missile? Why was it necessary to shoot when it was still unclear what this ship's particulars were?"

And she would be right.

The *Borodino* is done, Vlad thought. Time is short, but to make certain of my findings I still have several more witnesses to interrogate.

Billy Ivanov, the Russian child, and Old Scratch, the Amer Engine Devil. And also Igor Dolgov, the *Borodino* shooting officer.

Vlad was doubtful that Dolgov was a spy. The young officer had no access to the external surveying systems. He could not have influenced them. And their work had been double-checked by Carvaserin himself.

Someone from the tech team?.. Maybe. But such a man would have to be suicidal. He would have had no chance to leave the station. And surely, the first suspicion would have fallen on that part of the crew. The military prosecutors would have been after them at all hours.

Also, the incident didn't seem to be the work of the Odysseus Corps — the Amer version of the Church Of The Sword. As much as he hated them, Vlad had a healthy respect for his Amer opposites and had a fairly good idea what they would and would not do.

Not that they'd shrink from killing so many innocents if they felt it necessary. It was just that such grand scale actions weren't their style. Just as it wasn't the style of the Church of The Sword.

We both prefer to work in the shadows, Vlad thought. This is what we have in common.

But it could be some other Amer intelligence service. And if the Odysseus Corps got involved at all it would be to cover up the evil deed committed by their colleagues.

Vlad wondered if Lawson might be working for this group, whatever it was. Maybe she would try to rescue the spy while she was aboard the *Borodino*. Or even kill him so he couldn't talk.

Not a single possibility must be missed, Vlad thought. Not one!

He called Admiral Amiriani. "Set a triple guard around the bay," he commanded. "No one must leave the station, Admiral. It is critical, dammit."

"This was done in the first minutes — nay, seconds — after the disaster," came Amiriani's resentful answer. "Those same security precautions are still in effect. Until that Amer bitch arrives not a single ship will have been allowed approach since the incident."

"Not a single ship?" Vlad demanded.

"Not a single one except your *sturmovik*," Amiriani admitted. Then, "Lawson will be on the *Stardove*. No other ship will be allowed to approach us."

Vlad thanked him and hung up.

So it is. Not a single ship.

Which meant the spy — if there was a spy — must still be here!

However, since arriving aboard the *Borodino*, Vlad had not experienced the sensations that crawled up the back of his neck when his prey was near.

This was quite unlike him. Father Onphim used to say that Vlad could "smell" the enemy. But now there was no such spoor for him to trace.

Vlad made a face. Maybe Father Onphim was wrong; or maybe the spy was much more cunning than even the priest could imagine.

Well, enough.

Time to grill the witnesses.

CHAPTER FIFTEEN

After the ghastly Wizard was gone, Old Scratch collapsed. Trembling, he rolled into a black ball, nursing his feverish flesh.

Carvaserin's wrath was still hot within him; the flame claws were tearing the unhappy devil from inside — it was dangerous to cause such an angry mood in a softskin wizard.

Damn! Their spells were too powerful to withstand. And no amount of courage or strength could help. A single cast and you were lying on your belly before the victorious enemy. A coward and a hero — both are equal.

"Thou, Chyvaist, and all of you — cease! It is I, Homula, speaking! Abate! Lie down! Pass off!!! What other words must I speak?! The Engine Devil is dying. Come on. Give me space! Cease thy shouts! I must cure him."

The black cloud of an immense darkness wrapped the collapsed soul, draining out the pain. All the fiends in the great hall were frozen.

Even the most rambunctious and violent spirits obeyed, for Homula in her wrath could be nearly as deadly as the most evil softskin wizard.

Old Scratch recovered after a long, long time. Homula's magic was vanishing and a unnumbered chorus, led by Chyvaist, was already urging:

"What did the mage say?"

Scratchy forced himself awake. Homula had whipped out the pain but much weakness still remained. However, he had to speak.

"The human mage demanded to know if my ship was military or not," Scratch said.

"And was she?" interrupted Chyvaist. The impatient DeathSpirit was in the first ranks.

"No, she was not," replied Scratch. Evil fire blinked into Chyvaist's eyeholes.

"Thou hast a coward's spirit," hissed the DeathSpirit. "Now thou art protesting like a franion in sight of a gelding knife! How it can be? I myself ..."

"Shut up, Chyvaist," growled Homula. "And speak with a normal tongue. I'm sure our guest will tell us all in time. Now he must rest. You all have heard him say his ship was not a destroyer. 'Tis well known that Engine Devils do not lie. And that is enough for now. To work, all, to work!"

The Daughter of Darkness could easily master any budding fiendish revolt.

Old Scratch was left alone. And he had time to think. What had the DeathSpirit said? A warship? An Amer's destroyer on a missile run? The softskin wizard had said the same thing.

Rubbish. Complete nonsense.

But … they seemed so certain. Chyvaist was not lying. He really believed his target had been a huge, Class A capital ship.

Could all the softskins be mad? And their fiendish slaves as well? All at the same time?

In principle, a really strong spell could turn mad not just a single battlestation, but a whole planet or Fiendish World.

Long ago several such spells had been cast by the great softskin warrior-mages — in the time of the fierce wars between Flesh and Spirit. A thousand years had passed since that time, but not even the human wizards of this era could chant such words, much less explain how those castings had been made.

No. This could not be the cause.

Also, Scratchy thought, the Russian installation was too well defended. And Carvaserin was too strong to be overwhelmed so easily. The wizard stated his true name without hesitation — he was that certain no one among his fiendish servants would dare trespass against his might.

Carvaserin had no fear. Old Scratch sensed this. But he sensed something else as well. A grim and too-proud will hid behind the wizard's brow. A will that was the real master of its own bearer. A will filled with bloodlust.

Old Scratch shivered, appalled at a sudden horrible vision: Carvaserin, grim and tensed, casting a cloaking chant above the unhappy honeymoon liner.

And with a maniacal and terrible smile he was watched a flamewave shattering the *HolidayOne* into pieces. Smiling in supreme joy at the agony of the victims … Yes, the wizard could have done this.

But had he really done so? How could he cast blame on the human mage simply because he was morally capable of doing such a thing?

Then Scratch remembered that strange glance from innermost space just before the ship met its fate.

It didn't seem possible that it could have originated with Carvaserin. No, it had been the glance of an inhuman being. But it was non-fiendish as well.

A glance — and a missile struck the starboard side of the *HolidayOne*.

What kind of glance could have caused such a tragedy?

Old Scratch was thinking. And the more he pondered, the more grim he became.

As Vlad approached the Fiendish Hall he considered how to handle the Engine Devil. It was a pity Daniel Carvaserin had already interviewed him. It was difficult to make an Engine Devil speak against his will — to speak openly and unambiguously ...

"Scratchy, awake. Awake, Scratch!"Homula's frightened voice penetrated the dark protection spell around the resting devil. "Here's a man for thee, Scratchy."

She was really frightened, Scratch noticed. But by the name of the Great Hell, what in the whole Universe and in the endless Stair of the Fiendish Worlds, what could frighten the Daughter of the Darkness?

Carvaserin returned, perhaps?

Frightened, Scratch opened his eyes. And immediately screwed them up.

Before him was standing a tall and slender man with a single major's star on his shoulder-straps. He was very much unlike Carvaserin. Yet at the same time very much like him — because this major could also control the power.

And there was some force behind him ... much more terrible than the force that had supported the wizard.

However — although the man's eyes were keen, there was no malice or scorn in them. None at all. Could it be that this softskin was cunning in hiding such things?

"I need to speak with thee," said the major. "Canst thou feel that we must speak or wouldst thou prefer to see my identification?" He smiled. He had a good smile.

"We shalt speak," sighed Old Scratch. "No need for identification."

In his bones he knew this man had the right to interrogate him.

"It will not be an interrogation, Scratch," said the man. "Carvaserin has already done this ... or failed, to tell the truth. He pressed thee ... pressed thee hard, I suppose ... suspecting, complaining and threatening. Do not say anything, I know I'm right."

Who is this man, thought Old Scratch? Who is he to confront the Wizard Carvaserin? The Engine Devil had spent enough time with the softskin race to know what the True Wizard meant. And this restrained major — how can he?...

"I can," said the man patiently, as if reading his thoughts. "Listen, Scratch, I'm here to investigate, not to execute. 'Tis no good to torture. We must find who is to be blamed for this massacre, Scratch, or two great Powers will be involved in the most terrible war in all of history.

"And do not think, Scratch, that thy kin will remain intact. There will be no winners nor survivors. I hope thou canst see the problem with clarity. Help us, Scratch. I, a human, am seeking thy aid. Understand? Seeking *thy* aid, Scratch.

"Help us, and millions of thy race will remain alive. Say 'nay' and a war of annihilation will be waged upon hill and plow, upon the strange flesh of the Fiendish Worlds ... Well, 'tis said. What shalt thou reply?"

Suddenly, Old Scratch realized the space around them was empty. The fiendish horde had vanished, hiding themselves in deep and far corners. Even Homula had whooshed to the top of the chamber and had covered herself with her immense black cloak.

They feared this man even more than Carvaserin, the Engine Devil suddenly thought. Damned fate! It had been all right ... a good job, a good vessel, a good contract, good flaming ale on promise in the "Monks." For what sins was he being punished?

The terrible man before him was waiting — solemn, somber, calm and silent.

Scratch started to speak.

*   *   *

Sometimes it was better to hide your pride, thought Vlad, as he left the chamber.

Of course, there was little sense to Scratch's story. A civilian vessel ... unarmed ... without armor ... no combat casters abroad ... All these things Vlad had heard before.

Also, of course, Vlad was checking not only Scratch's tale, but his own suspicions. And he was checking Father Onphim's and a mysterious person from the Conclave's opinions concerning possible provocation.

The liner was now no more than spacedust so not even the cleverest forensic engineer could check to see if there had been any cloaking devices aboard. However, if there had been provocation and Old Scratch was lying Vlad would have to kill the Engine Devil.

After all, Scratch had been the real master of *HolidayOne* and knew every nut, bolt and screw on the whole vessel.

And right now, Vlad believed the Engine Devil was lying. He must be either more faithful to the Amers than their own President, or ...

But then it occurred to Vlad how odd it was that Scratch was even here for him to kill. Surely, if Scratch had been responsible, the Odysseus Corps would have assassinated him to keep the Amers' dirty secret hidden.

Instead, he had miraculously survived. Not only that, but he had been picked up by the Russians. Something the Odysseus Corps would have avoided at all cost.

Which led to the next logical step. Scratch might be telling the truth and there had been no cloaking device aboard *HolidayOne*.

If that was so, then it was quite possible an Amer spy was still aboard the *Borodino*. And the Amers would either attempt to save their man (or men) now, or try to hide him here as long as they could until an escape could be made later on.

If Vlad were the head of Odysseus, he would prefer the second variant.

Wait, he said to himself suddenly. What had the Engine Devil said about the strange glance from innermost space? It seems Scratch had been really frightened. Also, he had not reported the incident to Carvaserin.

What was it Scratch had said?.. "Thou canst understand … An evil look from … from outside. Not from the Fiendish part of the Being. From … I do not know. But it was terrible," — and Vlad recalled the trembling of true fear in Scratch's voice.

"It was terrible … terrible! I … I cannot imagine what it could have been. Not a fiend at all. A great power … no, not 'great' … irrepressible, irresistible, invincible! There's no such power in the fiendish worlds. Or in the human ones, either …"

Scratch had not added anything more.

The power? Was this a cunningly prepared lie? No, Vlad was ready to believe Scratch if other evidence was forthcoming.

And some instinct suddenly prompted him — keep it in mind, major.

Cast aside all other versions and what will remain is the truth, never mind how fantastical it looks at first glance.

Once again Vlad called Admiral Amiriani. Time to check the tech team, then talk to the other witnesses.

CHAPTER SIXTEEN

A woman's voice, sounding so silky calm that Tanya wanted to hunt her down and claw her eyes out, purred over the ship's com:

"The *Stardove* is now approaching the *Borodino*, ladies and gentlemen. In a moment, our ship will move through the first security checkpoint. You may experience a slight discomfort while the *Stardove* is scanned, but please don't be alarmed.

"This routine scan is entirely harmless and the sensation will soon pass."

Tanya bit back a groan and gripped the arms of her seat. Fighting nausea, she concentrated on the unseen woman. First mate or not, she was clearly a gum-brained fool.

Didn't she know they were entirely surrounded by magic? Didn't she realize that during the journey all their lives had been in the claws of spirit world creatures?

That the very bubble surrounding the *Stardove* — allowing it to plunge through uttermost space at overlight speeds — was controlled by these creatures?

A bubble that could have been purposely burst by an Engine Devil any time during the course of the trip from Earth to this godforsaken military outpost at the very edge of the known Universe?

The first wave of the *Borodino*'s magical snoopers tingled over Tanya's body and her flesh pebbled in fear. She imagined the woman strangling in space, then bursting apart in many pieces, and felt a little better.

Another wave followed, then another, and to get through them Tanya conjured new tortures for the woman with the silky voice.

And then it came again: "The *Stardove* has passed the first security check successfully, ladies and gentlemen. We will now proceed on to the *Borodino*."

Control regained, Tanya reflexively leaned forward in her lounge chair to peer through the big main viewing port at the front of the passenger's observation deck. But only a flat black screen presented itself.

She snorted in disgust. Security, again! The *Stardove*'s captain had obviously been forbidden to display a view of the mighty Russian battlestation.

Well, be damned to their security! She had an investigation to conduct and she wasn't about to start off blindfolded. Under the UWO charter for her mission the Russians were required to show her anything she asked to see.

She knew from past experience that they'd fight her all the way. In the end she'd win, but it wouldn't be easy. Harder still would be to know exactly what to ask for. No one would volunteer any information to help her, that was for sure. So she'd have to go by instinct and wise guesses.

The mission had hardly begun and Tanya already felt like she was swimming in mud provided in river-like quantities by *both* sides.

Hell, the Americans and Russians had even fought over how she would be transported to the *Borodino*. Not one starliner company could be trusted!

In the end a private charter arrangement was made with Sigmund Hammer Inc. — a company whose family had acted as trading go-betweens for the Russian and American empires for centuries.

Of course, there were spies among the officers and crew. Spies for both sides and double agents as well all looking for a fast bundle of LT's to fatten their credit accounts. That went without saying.

But everyone seemed to be satisfied some kind of spying parity had been achieved, so the decision was made to hire an entire liner.

At first the journey aboard the empty liner had been surreal — cabins and game rooms, dining rooms, ballrooms, libraries, theaters, casinos, all sitting vacant. And the crew avoided her except when necessary to tend to her needs, so it was like being on a ghost ship.

Only the officers had the courage to address this strange UWP Major who was under such secret orders for a mission so important that an entire starliner had been put at her disposal.

Tanya's only companion — which was too strong a word for what she was stuck with — was Kriegworm, the eight-foot Ogre-Mage, who had been assigned to play Watson to Tanya's Sherlock Holmes. In this case "Sherlock" studiously avoided "Watson," leaving her almost completely alone.

A few days into the journey, however, the attitude began to change among the *Stardove* officers. The men gave her knowing looks, openly admiring her figure and golden hair. The women started casting jealous eyes in her direction.

This was obviously a company with an employee problem, Tanya thought. They were so used to having malleable civilians under their control that they had very little respect for anyone.

Tanya didn't trouble herself putting the captain and the others into their places. She couldn't be bothered and so she simply ignored them.

She sighed and glanced at the blank screen again. Suddenly she knew where to start. A small portion of revenge on the captain and his officers would be a side benefit to her plan.

Tanya lifted her head and spoke to the air: "Captain!" she barked. "This is Major Lawson!"

A second later there was a faint buzz, then a voice: "Yes, Major? How may we help you?"

It was that woman again! The First Mate with the hateful voice.

"I asked for the captain!" Tanya demanded.

"Captain Lasky is busy with the approach right now, Major," the woman said. "A very difficult maneuver, I'm sure you can appreciate."

Then the woman had the temerity to giggle.

"I'm happy you find my communication so amusing," Tanya said coldly. "Now tell the captain I *will* speak with him immediately. I have new orders for him!"

There was a long embarrassed silence. Finally, Tanya heard a muffled curse and Lasky got on the com.

"What is it, Major?" he demanded. "I'm in the middle of —"

Tanya cut him off. "I'm ordering you to stop the ship immediately, captain. And prepare to abandon the mission!"

Lasky made surprised noises. Then: "You can't do that!"

"I can, and I am!" Tanya said. "My orders are to be obeyed precisely and without question. You were informed of my authority when I boarded this ship. Were you not?"

"Yes, yes, but the Russians! They'll wonder! It could be dangerous."

"They won't have to wonder long," Tanya said. "Because my next order is for you to contact the *Borodino* Command. Tell them I will proceed no further until I speak to Rear-Admiral Amiriani."

Silence.

"There seems to be something wrong with the ship's com, Captain Lasky," Tanya said. "I didn't hear your answer."

Lasky chewed at something gritty in his throat, then: "Aye, aye, Major!" Very military brusque.

Satisfied, Tanya leaned into the soft-backed chair to wait. This might take a while — the Russian command would need time to jabber among themselves, trying to figure out what she had on her mind. Double and triple thinking her actions.

Finally, they would realize there was nothing else to do but put the big boss on, Admiral Amiriani, and find out what was happening. Tanya smiled to herself. Brass was the same the Universe over. They hated surprises!

To kill time, Tanya slipped her "Angel" from the inside pocket of her tunic. Angel was a small hand-held device from the 21st Century. And one of the last non-magical devices that was mass produced.

In its heyday two thirds of the Earth's population carried one around. All business, all entertainment, all files, records, note-taking and communications could be performed with the Angel.

And much better, Tanya thought, than any currently available magical device could perform. Which meant no little fiends swarming around inside like roaches in a tenement kitchen.

She pressed a stud on the side and the device's cover snapped open, revealing a screen with little icon buttons. She tapped the "Review" icon with a stylus and a series of images started swirling on the screen.

Tanya bent closer to look. A man's face swam up at her. At the moment President Sean Garcia was making an appeal to his "fellow Americans all across the shining galaxy" to remain calm while the "tragic incident" concerning "innocent civilians" aboard a resort liner was fully investigated.

This was good, Tanya thought as she half-listened to the taped speech given by President Garcia some days before. Obviously, the pleas of many high-level UWO diplomats had met with some success.

That, and the promise of a tough, impartial investigation by the United Worlds Police, had somewhat quieted the dogs of war. It made Tanya feel better about her mission. There was *some* hope.

Tanya's head snapped up.

Someone was watching her.

* * *

Davyd cursed himself as he closed down the gremlin box. He shouldn't have lingered on Lawson so long.

He'd been monitoring her actions since he'd slipped aboard the *Stardove*, but only in quick snatches to avoid rousing suspicion.

Most military personnel had "sixth sense" training to make them sensitive to watching eyes and Davyd had sensibly assumed the UWP had provided Tanya with the same education. So he'd been extra cautious whenever he hooked the gremlin box into the ship's sensory banks to check her out.

But today, as he neared his objective, the fighting juices started boiling in his belly. All his senses were moving into overdrive and so when he'd gremlined into the Passengers' Lounge to see what she was up to, he'd become suddenly, helplessly, moonstruck.

Before that moment Tanya had merely been someone to be wary of. Someone whose motives must remain in doubt until her actions proved otherwise. He'd grown to admire her evident professionalism, but that'd only made him more wary.

Then for the first time he'd noticed just how beautiful she was, golden hair spilling over her uniformed shoulders, the pleasing shape she gave to her crisp tunic, the lovely line of her profile when she'd tilted her head to hear the ship's announcement.

So he'd lingered too long, seeing first her beauty; then, feeling lonely himself, her own loneliness, her all-too-human vulnerability hiding beneath that frosty mask.

Get your head out, bud, Davyd chided himself. No time for romance. And sure as hell no opportunity!

Then a little voice hissed, "Psst, boss! How 'bout a rest?" Davyd glanced down at the small box glowing in his palm.

It was the ultimate, high-mage snooping device, powered by a team of small fiends who could creep into any connection unseen and without leaving a trace of their presence.

Designed specifically for the Odysseus Corps, Davyd doubted there were more than six such devices in the known Universe.

Even so, this one was extra special. It had been juiced up with added features that allowed him to remain unnoticed even when faced with the most powerful and sophisticated Russian snooper.

"Psst! Boss?" came the voice again. "The boys say they're pretty tired."

"Go ahead," Davyd said. "Get some sack time."

"Thanks, boss," the gremlin said and the box became cold and dead.

Davyd put it away, thinking just how hard he'd worked the little fiends during the past days. From the second he'd gotten the idea of how to get aboard the *Borodino* to this moment, he'd kept them in nearly constant action.

Yeah, let them rest. There was a long, long way to go before this job was done.

Davyd closed the lid on all the spaghetti wiring in the ship's main comboard, then ducked down to slither into the vent opening that led back to the ship's hold.

He had to hurry.

It was his last chance to do something about the dead guy.

*　*　*

Tanya shook her head. The feeling was gone. Or maybe it had never been there, she thought. Maybe she was being paranoid — imagining things again.

Or maybe not.

Even so, *if* someone had been watching her, she didn't think there was any danger. The feeling hadn't been like the time before — assuming the worst case and that too was real.

That definitely had been an evil presence, a dark and forbidding thing, lurking in the ethers.

This time the watcher — if he existed, and *he* was definitely a *he* — had seemed coldly neutral at first. But then the watcher had suddenly become very warm, and certainly not neutral. The gaze was sensual, but unthreateningly so.

She wasn't being ogled, however. And the feelings aroused in her had not been wholly unpleasant. For a moment, Tanya had felt an incipient girlish blush coming on and would not have been opposed to meeting whoever was behind that gaze.

Time to enter the real world, woman, Tanya scolded herself. There is no dreamboat waiting in the wings for you. It was your imagination! The result of wishful thinking and the empty bed blues.

Lasky's voice blared over the com: "We're receiving a transmission from the *Borodino*, Major. Shall I link it through?"

"That *was* my intention, Captain," Tanya said, deliberately maintaining her chilly attitude.

If something went wrong, these people would have to jump when she said frog, no questions or hesitations permitted.

"Aye, aye, Major," Lasky said. "I'll patch it through."

There was a splash of light and Tanya turned to see the main port flicker into life.

A handsome, middle-aged Russian admiral with silver hair, craggy features and moody eyes was peering out at her. Tanya made a special note that he was smiling.

Good! She had them damned worried.

"Greetings, Major Lawson," the admiral said in barely accented English. "I am Rear-Admiral Amiriani, commander of the *Borodino*."

Tanya nodded but said nothing, letting him get on with his little speech. She knew very well who he was. More than the good admiral, whose first name was Peter, would probably like. Her briefing had been *quite* thorough.

"I bid you welcome, Major Lawson," the admiral continued, smile growing wider. "I have been anxious to meet you. Your reputation is known to us all."

I'll bet it is, Tanya thought. But she kept her face blank. The admiral hesitated a beat, giving her a chance to speak. Tanya only narrowed her eyes, gazing at him steadily. She wanted him to sweat.

The admiral coughed to cover the hesitation, saying, "I should mention that your honored visit is much anticipated by my officers as well. We have many recreations and tours planned for you. I think you will have a most enjoyable time during your stay with us."

He wagged a finger, chuckling, "All work and no play … as you Amer — I mean, Americans say."

He wiped his suddenly moist brow, forcing Tanya to bury a smile of victory.

Instead she gave him a stern look. "I'll be sure to report that to my superiors, Sir," she said. "I suspect they'll be quite interested in your ideas concerning the proper way to greet a UWP master investigator."

The admiral fingered his collar. "We were only trying to be hospitable," he said. "The recreational activities I mentioned should in no way infer a callous attitude on my part. Or on the part of my officers.

"We are as shocked and saddened as the rest of the galaxy at the innocent lives that were lost."

He frowned, thinking he might have gone too far. "Not that we accept responsibility for the incident!" he added.

At that moment Tanya sensed a familiar presence and smelled a foul, familiar odor. She glanced behind her and saw that Kriegworm had entered. From his red goggle-eyed look of horror, she could tell he'd been listening in and didn't approve.

Tanya ignored him, concentrating on the admiral who was saying, "*HolidayOne* was clearly the result of a conspiracy. No one knows who is responsible, of course, but we on the *Borodino* have our ideas!"

"So noted, Sir," Tanya said. "But I don't see what any of this has to do with my problem. The problem that may force me to abort the mission immediately and return to headquarters to report your interference with my investigation."

The admiral's jaw dropped. A most amusing sight, Tanya thought.

"Abort the …" he gobbled "… interference … return to headquarters … I… uh …" and then he straightened it all out, showing how he had made rear admiral in the first place, drawing himself up and saying, "What seems to be the trouble, Major Lawson?"

"Why was I *personally* scanned by your security, Sir?" she said, making it sound like an accusation, rather than a question.

Tanya shot a look at Kriegworm, who had his big fiendish head down, examining his Rolex. He didn't want any part of this.

Meanwhile, on the port screen, Rear Admiral Amiriani had the wisdom to frown, as if considering deeply.

Then: "But … but … That was purely routine, Major. The *Borodino* is a top-secret military post. Everything must be scanned before it enters or departs our zone."

"Except for me, Sir," Tanya said.

"What?" Amiriani was startled.

To Kriegworm's horror, Tanya threw the book at the admiral: "Sir," she said, "it is expressly forbidden by the charter your government has signed with the United Worlds Organization to in any way search, touch or interfere with an official representative's person or belongings in any manner, including the use of magical surveillance techniques."

"Pardon?" Amiriani had the look of a stunned bull.

"If you review the charter item in question, Sir," she said, "… which, I'm sure you have posted in all appropriate places aboard the *Borodino* as is required by the terms of that very same charter …" she tilted one corner of her lips for a small smile, stealing breath to go on … "you will see that my memory is quite accurate. And that I quoted correctly."

Amiriani waved at her. "Quite correct, I am certain, Major," he said. "No need to look it up. However, it should be noted that the *Borodino* is a special case. A *very* special —"

"If that's how you want to view the situation, Sir," Tanya said, cutting him off. She shrugged. "I'll make note of your 'special case' plea when I report to my superiors."

She started to turn away. "Excuse me, Sir," she said, "but I must give the captain my orders for an immediate return to Earth."

Kriegworm waved at her frantically, hissing in alarm. He clearly thought she'd gone mad to risk this break with the Russians. Tanya, fearing he was giving her game away, prayed Amiriani hadn't noticed the dissension on her little team.

Evidently he hadn't, because the next thing she heard was:

"Please, please, Major! Don't be so hasty!"

Tanya turned back to see Amiriani turn on all the charm at his command — which was considerable. "Can't we discuss this further?" he urged.

"I'm convinced that the unforgivable intrusion on your person was accidental. Surely, some young lieutenant, eager to do his duty, failed to key you out of the security sweep.

"Why don't we put this unfortunate incident behind us so you can proceed with the *Borodino's* full and eager cooperation. We want to get to the bottom of this tragedy at once.

"And it would be cruel to deny the families of the innocent victims an answer to what became of their loved ones, and why."

Tanya pretended to hesitate, mulling over his appeal.

The admiral placed a hand of insincerity across his broad chest. "Let us make peace, Major," he said. "For the good of all."

Tanya rewarded him with a smile. "Very well, Sir," she said. "I'll overlook the incident."

Amiriani had to struggle manfully to keep from sagging in relief. His own superiors would have skinned him alive for making such a mistake with this stubborn and dangerous woman.

He'd heard from "certain sources" that she was a bitch. He didn't doubt the description then — and he certainly didn't now that he'd met her.

Tanya knew exactly what he was thinking, so she gave him a parting shot.

"I'll ignore it, Sir," she said, "but I should warn you that there will still be a reference to the incident in my raw notes. Which, I suspect, will be subpoenaed by all parties when I report."

She shrugged, saying, "They can't be erased, you know. Once entered in a Master Investigator's raw notes, they become a matter of legal record."

After an exchange of a few pleasantries, a much chastened rear-admiral signed off. The port screen flickered and suddenly there was a view of the massive *Borodino* battlestation, in all its deadly glory.

Tanya smiled, chalking up another victory.

"Pardon, ma'am," Kriegworm said, spoiling her mood, "but I think we maybe made a mistake with the admiral. If you don't mind me saying so."

Tanya gave him her full attention. Kriegworm's bulky, eight foot form was draped in the usual gray suit, decorated by the Rolex on his scaly wrist. The heavy scent of eau de cologne thickening the air.

"How so?" she asked, fighting revulsion.

In her heart she knew Kriegworm was one of God's creatures who must struggle to live out his span. Once again she thought of a roach. An eight-foot roach. And wondered what the hell had been on God's mind!

Meanwhile, Kriegworm was saying, "The exchange was rather rude, don't you think, ma'am?"

Tanya snorted. "Not any ruder than the missile he fired that killed all those people on the *HolidayOne*!"

An hour later she was being piped aboard the *Borodino* with full military honors.

A much chastened rear-admiral at her elbow. A very worried Kriegworm at her heels.

And she thought, Boy, wouldn't Harry be surprised to see me now!

CHAPTER SEVENTEEN

To Vlad it was as if the very size of the immense battleship had slowed time to a crawl.

And through the tough armor, through the uncounted combat chambers, through all that combined massif of decks, guntowers, missile batteries, radar outposts, fiendish pens, et cetera, no one in the whole galaxy — not even the greatest Wizards of old — could quicken that lack of movement.

For Vlad, it was as if the small drops of time were falling in slow-motion from an ancient Chinese water torture machine. And they were gradually driving him mad.

He was only a few hours away from the arrival of Tanya Lawson and he was still at a complete loss.

Not a single trace of a diversion or sabotage. Moreover, all the battle records of that unhappy launch were ambiguous.

His first impression had been false. Now he was beginning to wonder if the crew had indeed fired too hastily, paying no heed to minor clues which should have stayed their hands until they had time to investigate more closely.

Such as the discrepancy between the size of the "attacking" vessel and her magical innards. Of course, there were no traces of criminal laxity.

It was beginning to look like the entire crew — from Daniel Carvaserin down to the lowest member — had suddenly turned mad.

Vlad gritted his teeth. He was sitting in a small cabin on the middle officers' lounge deck. Despite all his talents, he didn't dare manipulate the combat records to cover the *Borodino's* actions.

An experienced investigator like Lawson would surely trace him. Father Onphim had sent an imperative "NYET!" to Vlad's coded inquiry to do so. And Vlad had been vastly relieved to receive that negative response.

But what could he do further? The boy, Billy Ivanov, was still in such shock that he refused to talk to Vlad, or anyone else.

The tech team interrogation had also resulted in nothing. No traces of any manipulation, by hand or by magic, with the inner connection systems.

Vlad had even investigated the Optic Disc Drive Dwarves Team, but that had also been a useless effort.

Patiently he'd studied all the paths of the magical signals, talking with tiny dwarves and little gargoyles — different kinds of fairies, who worked as information transmitters.

He'd interrogated the fiendish crew of vidpallets and vidscreens. And the radar-wave bearers, grim creatures, whose food was a Vacuum — nothing. Not a single trace of a plot or anything like one.

However, there was SOMETHING. Practically all the fiends aboard *Borodino* were both frightened and astonished.

Surely, no one could confirm Old Scratch's words about a great power, but no one considered the missile firing a common incident. The battlestation had made many such shots during training — but this was different.

Why? — no one could explain.

Chyvaist, the DeathSpirit, had been extremely grim and ungracious. Vlad had forced the battle fiend to speak, but even his deadly power had been unable to make Chyvaist a single bit more hospitable.

"Yea, boss," hissed Chyvaist. "I was there, in the warhead. And it was a damnably good blinding field around that little beauty we punched. I was sure …"

"But when thou penetrated the field," Vlad was very patient and calm, "thou saw a civilian ship, didn't thee?"

"'Twas too late to abort," Chyvaist said grimly. "That fiendish explosive … thou must know."

"Of course. But what didst thou feel in the last moments before execution?"

Vlad hated such questions. Questions must be clear and plain, especially when talking with fiends. However, Chyvaist balled himself up in a globe of wrath.

"What didst I feel? Listen, softskin, thou art the first to ask me 'bout it, and I'll tell thee. I felt someone's mockery."

"What?" — Vlad was astonished.

"Mockery. A faint laugh. It sounded like one of my goblins chuckled." Goblins never chuckle. Not in all the long millenniums of slavery.

"And thou?"

"My balls were burnin,' like you softskins used to say, I expect. And there was nothing more. But, I repeat my last — I think that one of my poor fellows really chuckled before he was taken by the flame …"

And that had been that.

As Vlad reviewed his notes, the loudspeakers suddenly blared into life, announcing that the *Stardove*, the liner bearing Master Investigator Tanya Lawson, was preparing to dock.

Vlad was out of time.

He made a grim face. So it is. Nice to meet you, Ma'am.

At first Vlad decided to monitor everything from a distance. That way he could avoid any physical contact with the woman.

He felt as if he were standing on the very rim of a great defeat. Possibly the greatest defeat in all his long life.

Oh, there were ways to get around it. Such as declaring someone from the crew — for example, that miserable wretch of a firing officer, Dolgov — an Amer spy.

And he could make Dolgov an offer, promising him life in exchange for his "true" testimony. And then Dolgov could be hidden away where no one would ever find him while the official announcements were made.

Obviously, both Daniel and Brand Carvaserin would prefer that way. Both Wizards would — but not Vlad.

He felt as if he'd been stricken with a black fever. He wanted to take that scum — what scum? Who knew? — by the throat.

Vlad steeled himself. By damn, he would not retreat!

But how could he turn his defense into an offense? Where, by god, did the cotton string end?

Oh yes, he suspected Daniel Carvaserin. But suspicion was nothing but suspicion and this one was pretty naked. Nothing to confirm the accusation. Nothing!.. Nothing except faint visions and the imagination of two fiends who could not be called as witnesses in a human court.

Vlad forced himself to cast aside such thoughts.

Lawson — let's keep an eye on her …

He flicked the vidscreen into life and saw her for the first time and his eyes became chained to the screen in a single moment.

And he thought, Oh yes, vot eto da, this is a woman!

He'd never considered himself a lady-killer. And he rarely was so rude as to ogle girls, even if they weren't looking.

But this woman was marvelous! A beauty unlike any he'd seen before.

Vlad's senses were rocked by the sight of her.

The blonde in a UWP Major's uniform reminded him of a tigress — a tense and fearful grace in each movement. Proud head raised, unruly golden curls forced under a UWP forage cap. A woman's glance, keen and professional, swiftly and tenaciously running to and fro.

And for a moment Vlad's eyes met Investigator Lawson's gaze and never mind he was looking through a vidcamera. Through the eyeholes of numerous fiends, carrying, sorting and exposing the signal.

For Vlad Projogin got his second big surprise as he felt a swift touch of inner fire.

The woman before him was a mage — and a rather powerful one!

But there was something else in her eyes. Something he couldn't describe. He sensed that beneath Tanya Lawson's cold iron and invisible armor was a living heart, tempered and hardened by years of loneliness.

This woman could be everything, Vlad thought in sudden confusion. A fierce enemy and a seductive lover. A cold-handed sniper and a friend like no other.

To Vlad all her firm curves cried out to him like trumpets of doom.

It took him long minutes to recover from the shock of his reaction to her. He forced himself to take note of her assistant — a huge Ogre-Mage in an expensive suit.

Then he sighed, shaking his head. Well, she's here. She's here and this means I must work like hell.

He forced his senses to come to order. Haven't you ever seen blondies? Both dressed and undressed? What's going on, man? Father Onphim would be very displeased and disappointed, if he only knew.

Suddenly Vlad realized he felt like a student facing a difficult exam. In feverish haste he checked all his steps aboard *Borodino*. All his actions had been in plain disobedience to the guidelines both sides had agreed upon.

He'd interrogated Dolgov. Had talks with all the men from the crew involved in the incident. All those things were strictly forbidden under the UWO agreement.

And now he trembled before that woman, who might trace his work and maybe — if he failed — would be his judge and executioner.

Yes, she looked very much unlike all the ordinary pretties, to whom Vlad could easily say "dinner tonight, baby?"

In fact, he could hardly imagine a male who would dare to do so. And he certainly wouldn't attempt to break through Tanya Lawson's armor without an entire heavy tank regiment behind him.

After a short time Admiral Amiriani appeared on the vidscreen, red as a boiled beet. Vlad listened patiently as he complained about their guest from the UWP.

"You see, Major? You see?" — The Admiral looked like he was pissing his trousers. "Such a damned bitch! Major, I urge you to stop her. It's clear she's here to place the blame on us, on me, on us all!!"

"Be calm, admiral," Vlad said coldly. "If things turn to the worst, I'll deal with her. Be sure of that."

"I can be sure? You promise?" asked the Admiral, sounding like a small boy.

"I promise," Vlad said, nodding grimly — and thought that for the first time in his career he might be making an intentionally false promise.

The vidscreen turned pale and Amiriani was gone.

Vlad pressed his fingers to his temples. He felt uneasy and he hated himself for succumbing to such weakness.

Miserable fool! You looked at a cute face and were overwhelmed. Caked, by damn, caked! No, no, he would not give up, he would not …

He sat down. Calmed himself. His breathing slowed. His eyelids drooped. Vlad tried to cast himself into a soothing trance. But something suddenly broke through his concentration.

A small, practically unnoticeable thing in the shadows. It was? … movement? Or something else? A faint tremble of alarm. What could it be?

He felt as if something was lurking somewhere near — on *Borodino* itself.

And this Thing was strangely chained to him.

Vlad was stunned by this strange sensation, which was accompanied by an acute feeling of despair. All was lost. All was lost.

He clenched his teeth and the sensation vanished as quickly as it had come.

Hastily, he rose and exited the cabin. He decided he'd better get closer to Tanya Lawson and watch her every movement.

At first glance she'd seemed to be a worthy and most capable enemy. Assuming she was an enemy, that is. If so, she'd be someone to test him before his ultimate victory.

Now he was worried that if such a contest came that victory would not necessarily be assured.

And he'd have only his own weaknesses to blame.

CHAPTER EIGHTEEN

Davyd dropped off the catwalk into the ship's cargo hold. It was supposed to be not only empty, but sealed — that was the deal when the UWP charted the liner for Lawson.

However, stacked against one corner of the hold was a neat pile of large crates marked:

BORODINO
MEDICAL SUPPLIES
URGENT

Of course, the crates actually contained many forbidden luxuries for the *Borodino's* high ranking officers: American food, drink and gifts for their wives from elegant Amer shops.

This was the sort of routine violation of security that Sigmund Hammer — the *Stardove's* owner — was notorious for. And it was not only known by all but encouraged. How else would the brass on both sides receive such perks as Russian caviar or American whiskey?

Soon, a lighter would show up from the *Borodino* and the *Stardove's* crewmen would help those on board unload the "medical supplies."

LT's would exchange hands and everyone concerned would be happy, since the lighter's Russian crew would expect a portion of the urgently needed "supplies" for their troubles.

For Davyd's purpose this small violation offered a very large hole in the *Borodino's* security.

He walked to the rear of the stack and found the large crate he'd once called home.

Davyd pressed his thumb against the fourth bolt head from the bottom. A little red light beamed on, examined his thumbprint, then blinked off. There was a whir and the front of the crate swung open.

And the corpse of the naked, tattooed man tumbled out.

Davyd wrinkled his nose. The body was getting kind of ripe.

He stared at the corpse, remembering:

*   *   *

At first, Davyd thought it was the rats.

All spaceships of any size were infected by rodents. There was nothing that could be done about them. Over the centuries rats had become immune to anything — magical or otherwise — aimed at their slaughter.

So when Davyd heard the scratches and scurrying noises somewhere off in the hold, he thought it was the rats.

He'd heard the sound of rat-like movement shortly after he'd exited the crate — when the *Stardove* was well underway and no one would enter the hold to discover him.

Davyd was setting up temporary quarters — consisting of an inflatable mattress, a few rations, and a little generator to keep him warm — when he suddenly noticed the ferret-like scratching coming from the vent above.

He checked, climbing up on crates to examine the vent with a pinlight, but found nothing. Just rats, he thought again. And that was that.

It went on like that for a time, the sounds becoming particularly active when he was eating, which seemed reasonable considering he had rats fixed in his mind.

The image had been shattered the day before they entered the *Borodino's* sector.

Davyd was crouching over his ghost-flitter, getting prepared well in advance for the insertion. The flitter was contained in a large, torpedo-shaped tube that took up most of the space in Davyd's crate.

It was about eight feet long and its color was a smoky gray. A hatch opened on one side, revealing just enough room for a man Davyd's size.

This was where'd he'd hidden when the crate was put on board with the rest of the "medical supplies." The ruse had taken only a small bribe and since there was no true ship's manifest no one would be the wiser that there was an extra crate.

When the time came, Davyd would climb inside again and launch the flitter. The moment he entered cold space the flitter would automatically unfold and unfurl until it took on its true form — a small craft built to literally sail through space.

With Davyd safe in the torpedo-like hull he could operate the enormous sail, catching the space winds to close the distance between the *Stardove* and the *Borodino* with relative ease.

Best of all, the flitter was made of special material, bolstered by powerful camospells, that would make him invisible to all the *Borodino's* instruments. Still better, the flitter was so disguised it would even be difficult to see with the naked eye.

Davyd was using the gremlin box for a final check of the flitter's circuits when he sensed a sudden change in air pressure behind him.

He didn't think, only reacted. Twisting to meet his opponent, but clumsily, cursing himself for being caught in such an awkward position.

Davyd had time to see a broad-bladed knife slash at him, a quick glimpse of swirling colors, and he dropped to one knee, catching a wrist and breaking it, hearing the knife clatter to the floor.

Then he was coming up and under, fist powering in for the killing chest blow. But then he saw a second knife thrusting toward him.

Shit!

Two knives!

The man had two knives!

And injured or not, he was driving the second blade with such force that he would beat Davyd's blow by a hair.

Davyd hurled himself backward, skittering across the smooth plas deck on his shoulders, arms and legs all akimbo.

He knew he was wide open, but there wasn't anything he could do about it except pray that his enemy was too hurt to follow up.

And then God must have had a good laugh at his prayers, because the next thing he saw was a huge man, naked to the waist, torso glowing with garish tattoos, hurling himself at Davyd. Knife gripped in a mighty fist that was swinging down, down, down.

Davyd let him come.

Everything was in slow motion battle-time now. The big body floated toward him. Wide-bladed knife plunging for Davyd's heart.

Davyd reached out with both hands, catching the blade between his palms. Then turning it.

A harsh scream brought time back to normal and the man slammed down on Davyd. There was a gasp. Then a gush of warm blood soaking Davyd's clothes.

A final twitch and then the man was still.

Davyd pushed the body away and came to his knees. His head swiveled slowly, senses on full alert, checking the cargo bay for another threat.

Nothing.

Davyd sighed relief, then looked down at the man, wondering who he was. The guy was barefooted, wearing only ragged shorts. Davyd checked them closer and saw they were old uniform trousers cut down to trunks. The uniform was Russian.

Then his eyes went to the guy's face, noting the rough but good-looking features. He was thirty, maybe thirty five. His face was tanned the deep color that came from working many years in space. And swollen. From drink?

He saw two or three broken blood-vessels on the man's nose and confirmed his hunch. Yes, drink.

Okay, fine, okay sure. Now the tattoos.

Actually it was one tattoo. But it was so large, so magnificently elaborate, that it seemed like many. The tattoo was an enormous portrait of a Russian battlestation. It covered the man's chest and spread out onto his arms, going all the way to the wrists, including the poor bent thing Davyd had broken.

Then it went all the way around to cover the guy's back so the whole portrait was like a three dimensional view of the battlestation.

If you looked close you could even see scores of small vehicles standing off the battleship and the face of miniature men peering out through portholes.

Near where the left shoulder joined the trunk was the ship's name, written in Cyrillic:

It was the *Borodino*!

For Davyd this was an even greater puzzle. What was a hand from the *Borodino* doing hiding aboard the *Stardove*?

He went through the guy's pockets, finding nothing. Then he searched the entire bay until he located the man's shoulder pack hidden deep within a vent.

Inside was a set of civilian clothes — rough, spaceport bar wear — and a crisp Russian naval uniform. Rank? Davyd checked the tabs, deciphering. A warrant rating of some sort. Or its equivalent. But low, he guessed.

He checked further, noting that the awards on the tunic included none for combat. As good as the guy was with his two damned knives, he wasn't a professional fighter.

Then Davyd spotted the faded spot where a patch had once been sewn. He clawed through the pack until he found that patch. He was surprised. It was for the medical corps. The guy was some kind of medical tech.

Hells, bells, what was going on here?

More delving and he came up with a wallet. A military wallet built to withstand the elements. Davyd pressed a tab and it came open.

Inside he found the man's documents. All revealing that Davyd's guesses about rank and job description had been right on target.

He also found a wallet holo that made things a little clearer.

There were two men in the holo — Davyd's dead friend plus a younger man with fine features. They were both in uniform, but a little drunk, caps askew, Russian spaceport bar in the background. They had their arms around one another and were beaming into the camera.

Davyd squeezed the holo slightly and a message in Cyrillic started running across its surface.

It said: "Friends to the death! Alex and Dmitri forever!"

Davyd shrugged. What did he care? To each sinner his sin and all that.

He unfolded a final document, quite battered and stained, and the mystery was solved.

Alex, which was the dead guy's name, had been cashiered from the Russian navy. It didn't say what his offense had been, but Davyd guessed it probably involved drinking or drugs — maybe both.

And considering Alex's skills with a knife, he'd been wise to the ways of tough space port bars and streets.

He glanced at the holo again, the two drunken friends embracing one another. Alex, it seemed, had been so distraught, so foolishly in love with young Dmitri, that he had stowed away on the *Stardove* to return to his lover's arms.

Risking certain capture and imprisonment — possibly even death by firing squad — to accomplish his purpose.

Davyd glanced over at the body again. Very well, so that's what he was up to, he thought. But why did he try to kill me?

The answer was so simple that it occurred to him immediately. Once a military man, always a military man. Even one who had been cashiered.

To Alex, Davyd had obviously been an enemy up to no good. It was Alex's duty to stop Davyd. To kill him. And so he'd tried.

Ah, well, it hadn't worked and it had cost him his life. But what was grim news for Alex was good news for Davyd. The medical papers and other documents in the wallet had given him definite ideas about how to do his job on the *Borodino* …

*   *   *

Davyd blinked, coming back to the present. Alex's dead eyes stared up at him — accusing.

"Sorry, friend," he said, "but I'm short on time and burial space."

Davyd lugged the body to the hatch leading to the cargo bay's shredder, which was used to get rid of packing materials and crates too battered to be recycled.

He dumped poor Alex through the hatch, locked it, and punched a button. He tried not to listen to the grinding noises of Alex's body being turned into molecular-sized bits.

Then he returned to the flitter. Stripped off his clothes and changed into Alex's med-tech uniform, which he'd cut down to fit. He stowed his gear in the flitter, then man-handled the tube over to the garbage locker.

Got it open, shoved the flitter inside with all the filth that had gathered during the journey — now including Alex — then slipped into position.

The hatch automatically hissed down on him and soft lights came on. Not that there was much to see except the simple retinal screen which was operated by the movement of his eyes. He was on his stomach, arms at his side, feet brushing against his gear.

Davyd blanked his mind as he waited.

A few minutes later the *Stardove's* First Mate got clearance for a routine dump. She touched a palm switch and there was a slight rumble, like gastric juices roiling in a giant's belly, and the trash was expelled into space.

In the flitter, Davyd examined the *Borodino* as his small craft unfolded around him. After memorizing Alex's tattoo, he knew the ship quite well.

Then he gave the command to set sail.

And the flitter soared toward the massive battlestation, tacking on the hot spell winds.

CHAPTER NINETEEN

Davyd had once read of a small spiny fish that hunted the Amazon River. Large mammals, including humans, were its favorite prey — not as food, but as nests for its eggs.

Unlike its larger cousin, the piranha, this fish worked alone, slipping up to its huge victim while it bathed in the shallows.

Big as the fish's prey might be there was one vulnerability it could always exploit — the rectum. The details of what the fish did once it spotted its target were not amusing.

Even so, as Davyd approached the *Borodino's* Recycling Section he thought of that fish and laughed aloud.

Rupturing from one side of the battlestation was an immense tube, flanged at the end like an exposed rectum. The tube was excreting large squares of compacted organic material into space.

Robot garbage scows swooped in and out of the steady stream, gathering up the space-frozen hunks of matter to transport them to the main recycler, where billions of magical microbes would turn the waste into food and drink and air.

It was the perfect cover.

Using the scows as a shield, Davyd sailed the flitter right up to the aperture, which was many times larger than his tiny craft.

He hovered there in the dense roar and clack of machinery until the there was a pause for the machines to gulp up another load. Then he put on full power and shot forward into the guts of the *Borodino*.

At this point the Amazon fish would have spread its spines. Davyd, however, collapsed his — folding up the sails until the flitter was a smooth torpedo again.

He studied the small, curved panel in front of him, which gave him a colorful gremlin-box view of the interior of the tube. He passed several gate locks — red on the panel — but they were all too small.

Then the recycling machines belched back into life and he started getting worried. Just in time he saw a lock large enough for his purposes.

Davyd whispered a few quick commands to the gremlin-box and moments later the flitter skittered to a halt within inches of the lock, gluing itself to the plas surface of the recycling tube like a barnacle on a great gray whale.

At the same time big blocks of compacted filth — all the size of grav-buses — tumbled past him. He whooshed relief. Another second or two and he might have met with a rather disgusting fate.

Hardly a fitting end for a hero of Odysseus Corps.

The interior of the flitter shivered light and the underskin started to fold around him. He stretched out his legs and arms, splaying his fingers, and a skin-tight space suit formed around him.

When the process was complete he pulled the glowing panel toward him, twisting left, then right, until it came loose, revealing itself to be a helmet shaped like an old fashioned goldfish bowl.

He slipped it over his head and the helmet automatically fixed itself to the suit, making a perfect seal. Finally, he tucked the gremlin-box into a kit pocket.

And Davyd was ready.

He opened the flitter and got out, moving in the weightless environment with practiced ease as he retrieved his gear sack.

The suit offered only a rebreather, with air enough for ten minutes tops. It made up for this lack by being less cumbersome than a bulky full suit.

Besides, ten minutes was plenty of time to get in. The tricky part would be cutting that time in half so he could get out again.

Assuming I live that long, he thought. He snorted laughter, wasting precious breath. Davyd couldn't help it — in his mission-hyped state his humor button was on hair trigger.

He worked the lock mechanism. There was a blast of foggy air that instantly turned to snow and the lock came open. He slipped inside, sealing the hatch behind him.

Davyd made it in well under four minutes — moving through several hatches, tight-rope walking over clanking machinery and wriggling through a series of vents until he came to a storage bay where the atmosphere was breathable.

It was a dark warren of crates and supplies stacked all the way to the high ceiling.

He scanned the interior with the gremlin-box. No one there. Good. Luck holding.

A few minutes later he was checking the pockets of the Russian uniform to make sure he had everything he needed — spacesuit and gear bag already hidden among the crates.

Things didn't go quite so quickly after that. Even with the gremlin-box it took him a good fifteen minutes to locate the wiring terminal, which was hidden behind a column of crates next to the entrance; and another half hour to uncover it.

Still another hour was lost after he patched in as the little fiends in the gremlin-box crept through the ship's optical links, ducking and dodging small Russian devils as they went — leaving a private trail behind them like magical snail tracks.

The process was slow, but at the end of the hour Davyd was plugged into several key sectors of the *Borodino* — all of them low security areas like bookkeeping, personnel, billeting, etc.

This way he could avoid detection, but still manipulate nearly anything he needed — like the location of the battlestation's hospital. Where he could find the records and whereabouts of a *Borodino* medical tech named Dmitri Aizenberg.

He had a list of other names after that — starting with Billy Ivanov and ending with Igor Dolgov.

Oh, yes. One another person — Tanya Lawson.

Then the door beside him suddenly creaked open.

Davyd whirled to see a grizzled Russian sailor gaping at him in surprise — eyes darting to the mess of wires hanging from the open terminal box, then back to Davyd.

The gape became a red flush of anger and the sailor bellowed in Russian: "Kakogo cherta?"

Which Davyd instantly translated as, "What the hell?"

Those became the sailor's last words as Davyd's fingers pincered into his throat, crushing the larynx. He caught the toppling body and lowered it to the floor.

As he finished off the still-twitching sailor, he thought: Shit! Another dead guy to get rid of!

This job was getting grim and he'd hardly even started yet.

* * *

Dmitri Aizenberg would never know how close he came to being corpse number three.

It was drink that saved him.

Pining for his lover, Alex, he had lingered too long in the NCO Club after he got off duty. His friends had tried to cheer him up, but it was no use. Brandy seemed the only cure and so he'd absorbed great quantities of it.

Now, as he approached his quarters, he was so sick he could barely stand. He fumbled the door open, supporting himself against the frame.

As he stumbled into the dark cabin his stomach lurched toward his throat and he flung himself across the room into the little lavatory.

There he crouched on his knees, an acolyte of excess, and gasped and heaved for many long minutes. Muttering to himself, he came up off the floor, wiped his face on his sleeve, then fell across his cot.

A moment later a loud snore rattled the room and Davyd slid out of the closet and approached the bed.

Another loud snore erupted from Dmitri and Davyd smiled.

"Lucky bastard," he said aloud.

But just to make sure he hit Dmitri with the hypo gun, injecting a mild sedative into the med tech's veins. Other than keeping him asleep for a good eight hours, the only effect the drug would have was that his hangover would probably be worse.

Not much of a price for Dmitri to pay, Davyd thought, for not being murdered the moment he'd stepped into the cabin.

Davyd flipped on the light and got busy. First he scanned Dmitri's vitals — prints, optic nerves, blood and saliva. With this data he could move at will through any physical security checks.

Another loud snore came from the cot. Davyd laughed. Except for the snore, he thought, for all intents and purposes he was now Dmitri Aizenberg.

Feeling like the most merciful of men, he exited the cabin, young Alex buzzing away in innocent sleep

Davyd's elation was short-lived.

He sensed the danger the moment he stepped off the gravlift. Just ahead of him was the great sprawling complex that was the *Borodino's* Hospital Section.

This was the sleep period for the patients so only the medtechs' stations were lit, making puddles of light in a lake of darkened wards. There were very few nurses or medtechs about and there were certainly no doctors present.

But as he observed this silent, peaceful scene he felt a sudden sense of danger. His nostrils flared as if picking up a scent — a scent that made his spine tingle and nerve ends burn.

He turned his head, eyes sweeping all around, body coiling like a spring under great pressure. Needing only the flare of a single neuron to trigger him into action.

All his hunter's senses probed here and there, searching for the source of danger. The first thing he made certain of was that no one was watching him from some dark hiding place.

Then he whispered commands to the gremlin-box and quickly eliminated the possibility that he had set off some invisible alarm and that monitors were now being tuned in his direction.

Still, the viper's buzz of danger persisted. He had a feeling that a very deadly someone had passed this way not long ago. A grim Reaper on his way to harvest someone's soul.

More puzzling still — the spoor was vaguely familiar. Had he encountered it before?

Davyd gave himself a mental shake, thinking, Don't be stupid, Kells! You've never met *this* sonofabitch. Cause if you had, either you would've killed him, or he would've killed you! No other way about it.

At this point he had three choices. Lift on the mission and get the hell out of there before the guy noticed Davyd had invaded his turf.

Or, screw that — no way am I gonna run — track the asshole down and turkey gobble stomp him to hell. Which I like a lot, but that would blow the mission just a surely as option number one.

Only Option Number Three remained.

Davyd uncoiled and proceeded into the hospital.

He moved casually, acting as if from old routine. When he passed a medtechs' station no one bothered to look up at the tall, slender tech who strode past — tray of medications in one hand, a report board in the other.

And even if somebody *had* noticed him and asked his business there would still be no reason for suspicion. Davyd had gremlined into the staff roster and made a small change in the shift schedule, posting Alex for Billy Ivanov's regular 02:00 Vitals and Pharmacological check.

Davyd was a fine actor. In his business you had to be. But tonight he thought he was putting on a performance worthy of a Galactic Drama Award for it was increasingly difficult to maintain the pose with the smell of his enemy all around him. Before long, however, he became convinced the man had come and gone — retracing his steps like a prowling tiger returning from a kill.

Finally, Davyd came to Billy's room. He hesitated a moment before entering. It was clear from the signs that his enemy had entered this same room. He was no longer present but Davyd wondered if he'd return.

A part of him relished the thought and licked wolfish chops. To kill this man, he thought, would be no sin. In fact, it would be cleansing — washing away some of the deepest stains on his soul. But duty — ridged duty — called and he turned away from the trail and entered the boy's room.

He was in for a surprise.

CHAPTER TWENTY

The *Borodino's* interrogation room was like interrogation rooms everywhere: stark. Three bare walls, a two-way mirrored fourth, one long steel-gray plas table with two steel-gray chairs on opposite sides.

Tanya's victim was standing stiffly at attention beside one of the chairs. He was like all men who waited to be grilled by a Master Investigator: frightened.

However, behind his fear there was something more: the wounded but still living pride of a doomed gladiator.

"You may sit, Igor Dolgov," Tanya commanded, purposely using English instead of Russian.

Igor's eyes widened at the mention of his name. But he didn't move. Good, Tanya thought. He doesn't speak English.

She gestured at the chair and Igor quickly took her meaning and sat. Then she turned to Kriegworm, her only companion in the room.

"You have duties to attend to, I believe," she said.

Kriegworm puzzled at her — at least she thought the he was puzzling. Who could tell for sure on such an ugly face?

"But, ma'am," the ogre protested, "I thought I was to be included in the interrogation."

Tanya shook her head. "Not necessary," she replied. "And inefficient as well. We have many other examinations to conduct before we leave.

"They'll go much faster if you get everyone ready and the records in order."

Kriegworm started to object again, but lost his nerve under her steady gaze.

"Yes, ma'am," he said.

Tanya waited until the door hissed shut behind him, then fished out her Angel. Keyed it on.

"Admiral?" she said to the air.

Immediately Amiriani responded, voice crackling across the com: "Yes, Major? How may we assist you?"

"Until advised further, sir," she said, "I would prefer all communications between us to be conducted through my own com unit." She raised Angel to demonstrate.

"I see no difficulty in that, Major Lawson," Amiriani said.

She heard muffled orders, then the interrogation room com let out a pigsqueal and died.

"There," Amiriani said — voice now coming through the little speaker in Angel. "Is that to your wishes, Major?"

"Thank you, sir," Tanya said. "One other thing, sir?"

"Yes, Major?"

She waved around the room. "Please turn off the bugs."

A long silence as Amiriani and his aides realized that Tanya had once again caught them out. She hadn't needed to look at the glowing pea-bulb on Angel to know many listening and viewing devices would be scattered all over the room. It was only natural.

Finally, "Forgive me, Major," Amiriani said. "Apparently someone missed my explicit orders concerning monitoring devices. They will be shut off at once."

True to his word the pea-bulb blinked once, twice, then went out. A green light bloomed into life: All clear.

Tanya turned to Igor. She studied him for a moment, using the old cop's trick of taking much longer than necessary for the examination. It did wonders to weaken a stiff spine.

Not that she expected trouble from the young man before her. He was already quivering. She suspected he was looking into the deep, deep abyss of his own writhing conscience. Fighting to maintain a poker face, but losing that struggle mightily.

Igor Dolgov was all military. A build like a Greek god's draped in a carefully tailored uniform. Made of a far better quality material, Tanya noted, than was normal for officers of his rank and pay.

His face had a noble bearing to it: finely etched structure, skin nearly translucent, intelligent eyes framed by Spanish fan lashes. In short, a fast-rising young officer whose family members were, as the Russians said: "men of the old court."

Tanya scraped her chair back, carefully watching the way Igor jerked as if stung by the sound.

She sat, back stiff, feet flat, a portrait of cold authority. Then she slowly and deliberately placed her briefcase on the table, snapped it open and drew out several official-looking forms and objects.

Tanya carefully laid an old-fashioned notebook on the table, flipped it open, took out an antique pen, uncapped it and laid it next to the notepad.

Finally, she raised Angel to her lips, thumbed "record," and said in English: "This is Major Tanya Lawson, UWP Master Investigator. I am aboard the Russian battlestation, *Borodino*, continuing my inquiries into the matter of *HolidayOne*."

She brandished the Angel before Igor's face. His eyes widened and he licked dry lips thinking he was being called on to speak.

Instead, Tanya switched to Russian — and to Igor's immense surprise her accent was flawless — and continued:

"I am presently in the *Borodino's* interrogation room. All monitoring by the command has been neutralized. The conversation between myself and the subject, one Igor Dolgov, will be completely private."

She laid Angel down between Igor and herself. He eyed it, licking his lips once more.

"State your name, rank and military identification number for the record, please," she said.

Igor cleared his throat: "Igor Dolgov. Senior Lieutenant. My number is 2-5054-10."

Tanya nodded. A Russian senior lieutenant was the equivalent of a low-level captain in the American military.

"What was your position on the *Borodino* at the time of the *Holiday-One* incident?" she asked.

Igor paled. Eyes misting slightly, he croaked, "I was the firing officer."

He started to go on, but Tanya shook her head — Stop.

"And what is your position now?"

Igor hung his head. "I have no position," he said, low. "I have been suspended from duty."

"For what period?"

Igor was surprised. "What do you mean?"

"What is the length of your suspension?"

Igor shrugged fatalistically. "Until it is decided, Ma'am."

"Until what is decided, Igor Dolgov?"

Igor was confused. He waved a hand, taking in the interrogation room. "Why … all this!"

Suddenly he broke, face turning swiftly red: "All this! All! They want you to roast my ass! I know this! I'm not fooled!"

Then his shoulders fell and his voice dropped to a whisper as he continued, "They want to make me the scapegoat. Am I right?"

"Calm yourself, Dolgov," Tanya said coldly. "You're still an officer and not a young monk-girl caught in bed with a shepherd. So … Are you saying your suspension will end when my questioning is completed?"

Igor shook his head, hard. "No. I'm sorry, ma'am. I wasn't being clear. When the blame is fairly fixed, then my suspension will be complete."

He grinned harshly. "Of course, we both know where that blame is going to fall. I am the one responsible, no one else."

Tanya shied away from the obvious next question. She didn't want this young man to condemn himself from his own mouth. Perhaps he *was* ultimately responsible. But if a confession was forthcoming, she wanted it untainted by outside influences.

Instead she said, "You have been questioned before, correct?"

Igor flinched. Very unusual, Tanya thought.

"Yes," he said. "I have, ma'am."

"Who? Name them for the record."

Igor started to protest. "But it is only natural my superiors would —"

"I didn't ask what was natural, Lieutenant Dolgov," she said. "It is not for one such as you to decide what Galactic Law deems proper or improper. I asked for names. Nothing more."

Igor drew in a ragged breath, then answered. Listing his immediate superiors, all the way up the chain of command to Rear Admiral Amiriani. Then the names of the *Borodino's* internal Incident Investigation Unit. And finally Daniel Carvaserin, the ship's Chief Wizard.

It made quite a list and confirmed her concern that a quick confession from Dolgov would be tainted. After so many interrogation teams and individuals had gone at him, he'd be so dazed and confused he'd be willing to admit anything.

If she were investigating a ghastly sex murder on the other side of the galaxy, he might even confess to that.

Plus there was one other thing she sensed. Not in the list, but the delivery of that list. There'd been a slight hesitation when he'd ended. And he'd bitten his lip, as if to shut off further reply.

"Who else questioned you?" she demanded. "After Daniel Carvaserin, who else?"

He shook his head. "No one, ma'am. The wizard was the last."

A red bulb winked on Angel.

"Why do you lie to me, Igor Dolgov?" she demanded. "You needn't fear your superiors' reactions. Your answers are private.

"And even so, it is forbidden by UWO law for you to be punished because you cooperated with us to the best of your ability."

"I swear to you, Ma'am," Igor said, eyes stark with fear. "No one else."

His voice rose nearly to a shout, "I SWEAR IT!"

"Calm yourself, Lieutenant!" Tanya said once again. "You are not a child to make such an outburst!"

Shaking with emotion, Igor visibly strained to regain control. He said, voice quivering, "It is as I said, ma'am. The list of names you asked for is complete."

"Very well, then," Tanya said, as if accepting his statement. Even though the red light on Angel still indicated he was lying.

"We'll move on to the incident. Describe it please. And leave out no detail, no matter how insignificant."

She got what she asked for — a microbe by microbe account of what had happened from the moment Igor took his seat in the firing chair to the instant the missile impacted with *HolidayOne*. The information was delivered dully and by rote.

He'd either been coached, Tanya thought, or had gone over the same ground so many times he had it memorized. Probably a little of both, she decided.

Tanya only half-listened to him, relying on Angel to give her a thorough playback later, complete with a veracity report showing when he'd lied and when he'd told the truth.

Instead Tanya was concentrating on her surroundings. She'd caught the whiff of a strange spoor in the room. A dim presence picked up by her magical side that she hadn't noticed before.

A spoor that until this moment had been obscured by the powerful magical scent of the wizard, Carvaserin.

It's the missing interrogator, she thought. The one Dolgov was so frightened of that he wouldn't speak his name.

She made a strong mental note of it, then went on. The unnamed man may or may not have anything to do with her investigation. However, this was also a mystery that could easily lead her down a false trail and away from her main objective.

But she must keep in mind the possibility that this mystery man might be the one ultimately responsible for the incident.

When Igor ended his recitation, she asked, "What about prior to the incident? What were you doing immediately before you were called to your station?"

Igor turned fiery red. He mumbled something she couldn't hear.

"What was that, please? You must speak clearly for the record."

"I was … uh … with someone, ma'am," he said, still low, but loud enough to hear.

Angel winked green. He was telling the truth.

"Name her," Tanya commanded, easily guessing it was a "she."

Igor raised a hand. "She had nothing to do with it, ma'am. She played no part in the incident."

Tanya merely stared at him. A moment later, he sagged. "I was with Katya, ma'am," he admitted. "Katya Popova. She's a junior cryptographer with the Headquarters Cryptographic Team."

Tanya thought a moment. Popova was a very common Russian name. Putting that together with the young woman's position — a junior cryptographer — she sensed a definite class difference between the two lovers.

She pressed a stud on Angel. Amiriani's voice immediately blared through the unit's small speakers. "Yes, Major Lawson?"

"I require the presence of Katya Popova. Sir," she said in English.

After a moment of surprised silence, Amiriani said, "She'll be with you presently, Major."

Tanya clicked "off," ostentatiously scribbled a note on her pad, then put the pen down. Igor was staring at her, eyes bulging slightly from worry. Although he hadn't understood exactly what she'd said to Amiriani, he'd caught Katya's name.

"Please, ma'am," he said. "Katya is completely innocent. She knows nothing."

Tanya merely raised an eyebrow at him, then picked up a document from her briefcase and pretended to find its contents extremely absorbing.

Other than to wring his hands, there was nothing Igor could do but wait.

CHAPTER TWENTY ONE

Billy knew Davyd was on his way long before he reached the corridor.

He didn't know Davyd's name, of course, or who he was, but he had a damned good idea what he wanted. Which was more of the same old questions, questions, questions.

It made Billy mad. When would they get it through their stupid heads that he wasn't going to answer *any* of their dumb questions?

Billy Ivanov had gone through many stages of severe emotion since he'd escaped the *HolidayOne*. First, he'd mourned his grandparents. Then Lupe.

Then the shock of the entire disaster had gushed through the haze of anesthesia the doctors had pumped into him while he was stabilizing in the intensive care ward.

The horror of what had happened and what he'd witnessed was almost too much for such a small boy.

He'd wept uncontrollably for hours. Then somehow he'd realized he was at some sort of brink and pulled back, retreating into anger at what had happened to the *HolidayOne*.

Billy was too young to know what "insane" really meant, but old enough to be aware he was skirting the edges of a terrifying abyss.

Ultimately, it was the boy's determination and marked differences from so-called normal people that had saved him.

He was an orphan and alone. So be it!

He was a hated half-breed, part Rooskie, part Amer. So be it!

And he was also a wizard. Damn, but now he knew it for certain.

So be it!

Sure he was a child mage, sure he was weak, but it was still him, Billy Ivanov, who had conjured up a spell so powerful that he'd been able to rescue himself from the space disaster.

Who else could do something like that?

That pompous little man named Daniel Carvaserin? Powerful wizard though he was, Billy hadn't been impressed when he'd met him.

He didn't think Carvaserin would have been able to escape a space-liner that had just been blown up. Much less be capable of staying alive in Uttermost Space.

Billy had done that.

He wasn't sure how. Desperation had apparently uncovered strengths he hadn't known he'd possessed. Not that he could duplicate the magical effort, although he'd secretly tried several times.

Still, he had a deep awareness, growing daily, there were powers within that wanted to get out.

And with that growing awareness had come the realization that one other had escaped the *HolidayOne*: Old Scratch, the Engine Devil, whose presence he'd only dimly noted when he'd been aboard the liner.

Sometimes when he slept his dreams took him to the strange, fiery demon world where Scratch was housed with the other odd spirits enslaved to the *Borodino*.

He'd seen Scratchy in those dreams — which Billy was beginning to think of as "real," so maybe they were visions or something.

He was also certain that Old Scratch had seen him.

That very night Billy had experienced another of those dreams. Scratch had opened the huge maw that demons call a mouth as if to speak.

But Billy never got a chance to hear what the Engine Devil was going to say, because just then he'd sensed the approach of the strange man and had come awake. Heart bumping against his chest, anger flooding through his veins.

The anger was so extreme, Billy had the sudden, unreasoning desire to form some sort of killing spell that would shrivel the guy to a crisp.

Well, maybe he wouldn't really *kill* him. Billy couldn't imagine doing such a thing.

But something that would hurt him. Hurt him bad.

Except, no matter how hard he tried, he couldn't come up with anything.

Then the man came into his room and the moment passed.

"Who are you?" Billy said in English, his tone accusatory.

Davyd hid his surprise. He shrugged, pretending not to understand. "I'm here with your medicine," he said in Russian.

"If you can't talk English, go away," Billy demanded. "I told them all that. I hate Russians! Russians killed my grandmother and grandfather. And Lupe, too. And … and … everybody else.

"So I won't talk Russian. 'Cause from now on I'm an American. So put that in your report and go away."

Billy flopped over, turning a stubborn back to Davyd.

"Okay, no problem," Davyd said in English. "No more Russian."

Despite himself, Billy was curious. He turned back, sitting upright.

"Hey, that's a pretty good accent," he said. "Real American! You don't sound hardly Russian at all."

Davyd shrugged, putting the medicine tray down and busying himself with the record. "I used to watch a lot of old American movies."

"Weren't you worried about getting thrown in jail?" Billy asked. "Amer movies are forbidden."

Another shrug. "I was just a kid," Davyd said. "I didn't know any better."

Billy laughed. "So am I," he said. "A kid, I mean. And *I* know better."

Davyd grinned. "I guess you're smarter than I was," he said. "But you sure missed a lot of good movies just the same."

Billy didn't like that. Did this guy think he was dumb, or what?

"You can't fool me," he said. "You're not a medtech."

Davyd froze. Shit, he thought. Now I might have to kill the kid. He glanced at the tray. Among the medicines and devices was a small hypo gun. It was Davyd's.

The gun had two settings: one would shoot a deadly poison into the child's veins, killing him instantly. The other was a special Odysseus Corps drug that would wipe the boy's memory of this visit.

The only thing was, he'd been warned the drug wasn't always completely effective. When in doubt, his orders said, always trust the kill.

Davyd's head came up and he looked at Billy, misery churning in his guts.

CHAPTER TWENTY TWO

It made a tender sight: Two lovers facing the cold fates together; Katya sobbing, Igor embracing her in strong arms, face a mask of anguish.

As charming a scene, Tanya thought, as one of the "weepies" currently cluttering the entertainment bandwidths.

She had a secret fondness for them herself when she was sick and stuck at home. Nothing like a good old-fashioned tin of chocolates and a good cry at a fantasy person's expense to cure what ails you.

Unfortunately, she couldn't see Katya and Igor without also seeing the *HolidayOne* exploding on her screen and hundreds of innocent lives being snuffed out.

That was no "weepy." That was bloody reality.

"Let me get this straight," Tanya said in her most sarcastic tones. "The two of you were in a closet enjoying a little knee trembler when the alarm went off."

She curled a lip at Igor. "And you — your mind stuck in your zipper — stiff-walked into the firing room and finish the deed by blowing a tourist ship off the map.

"Is that how it was? If so, congratulations! You've just made history in the sexology books. A classic example of the evils of coitus interruptus if I ever saw one."

"But we did nothing!" Katya wailed. "Nothing!"

"I believe that was my point," Tanya sneered.

"We were off duty, ma'am," Igor protested.

"But you were on call," Tanya accused.

Igor hung his head. "Yes."

Katya's tears turned to fury. "You are making everything sound so … so … dirty!" she shouted. "But it wasn't like that. We were … we were …"

She stomped her foot. "We are engaged to be married, damn you!"

Instead of Tanya putting Katya in her place for insubordination, she merely shrugged. "And the hundreds of people he killed," she pointed at Igor, "were already married couples on their honeymoons. Lot of interruptus there, don't you think?"

Katya's jaw snapped shut and the blood drained from her face. Then she heard Igor's groan of agony and she turned to embrace him. Quickly, she pulled herself together. It was her turn to be strong.

"Please, ma'am," she begged Tanya. "Can't you see what this is doing to him? He suffers every second for each and every one of those people. He's nearly been driven mad with horrible nightmares. I hold him every night like a child so he can catch a few moment's peace.

"Let him be, ma'am! Let him be! Can't you see your questions are killing him? Every single one a new wound in his poor heart? Mercy, ma'am. Mercy! He only pressed the stupid button, ma'am. And it was not his decision to do so!"

Tanya listened intently to her every word. Making notes now and then. Her face blank during the entire speech. When Katya was done, Tanya scribbled a few more notes, then raised her head.

"Tell me, Igor Dolgov," she said, "if this woman's claim is true. For the record: Are you engaged to marry Katya Popova."

Igor shrugged. "Why, yes. It's exactly as Katya says, ma'am."

Angel blinked green. He was telling the truth.

"You are engaged *now*," Tanya persisted. "But were you engaged at the time of the incident?"

Again Katya stamped her foot. "Absolutely!" she shouted. "Absolutely!"

Angel blinked red. Actually, truth or lie, it made no difference to Tanya. The answer wasn't all that important. Other than for filling in the necessary record, this whole line of questioning was of small value. Her purpose was much more calculated than that.

To get at the truth of *HolidayOne* she desperately needed a break. The faster the better. In any investigation, truth is available for only a few moments after the event. Then it sinks along with all the evidence into an oily swamp of half truths and lies.

The only thing different from this case and most others was the stakes were higher and the price of failure bottomless.

Unfortunately for Igor and Katya, she'd found a hammer to use on them and now she was going to wield it. She hated herself for it. They were innocents, of this she was now certain.

But what could she do except still her heart, grit her teeth and commit the high sin of duty?

Tanya picked up Angel, glanced at the winking red light, then sighed with infinite weariness and placed it on the table again.

"You beg my mercy," she said to the two — ignoring that it was only Katya who'd begged — "but even as you beg you tell me lies."

She shook her head. "Lies, lies. Nothing but lies."

Then she exploded. She slammed to her feet, knocking the chair back with a crash. In a fury worthy of the greatest actress, she stabbed her finger at Igor.

"Is that your intention, Igor Dolgov?" she demanded. "To lie and keep telling lies until you bury all those poor souls with your prevarications?

"Is that right? Is that fitting? Lies for their graves? Lies for their tombstones? Lies to choke on in the hereafter for all eternity?"

Igor shattered. He collapsed on the floor, shouting, "I know it! I know it! I killed them all! I know it! Even God can't forgive me for what I've done!"

Then he hid his face in his palms. His shoulders shuddered and he sobbed soundlessly.

Katya stood over him, so shocked by the force of his grief that she was frozen in place.

Tanya lifted Angel. "Admiral?"

Slight pause, then: "Yes, Major?"

"Please remove the woman, sir. I have no further need of her."

Katya remained frozen over her sobbing lover until the guards came to usher her away.

Then she came unstuck, shouting at Tanya: "I swear to the heavens that if any harm should come to my Igor, I will hold you responsible. You, and only you — the bitchwoman with a heart of stone will be to blame!

"And by the name of Heaven and Hell, I'll be after you. You only want to condemn him and to receive a ribbon. A medal! But —"

And Katya suddenly burst into tears, crying, "I swear, I swear, I swear ..."

She railed on, but her words collapsed into ravings as the guards dragged her away, spitting and screaming threats.

Although stony-faced, Tanya was not unaffected. She'd been threatened many times in her career and by far more deadly people than this poor little girl.

But Katya's wrath had been so intense — like a fire out of the earth — that it had seared her. Given her reason to reflect once more on what she was doing and to despise herself for it.

Tanya shook off the feeling and strode over to Igor's collapsed form.

Sensing her presence, he moaned, "What more do you want of me?"

"Tell me what happened again, Igor Dolgov!" Tanya demanded. "But this time I want no lies."

Then she helped him to his feet, sat him down, let him compose himself and then clicked Angel back on.

"Begin," she said to Igor.

And so he began, telling the tale much as before. But this time it was no dull recitation. This time he was there! This time he was reliving the events ...

... The commander's voice crackled in his ears. "Shoot, dammit, shoot!"

"Yes, sir. Shooting procedure in operation sir.

"Weapons room. All systems in order. Target in range."

"Launch!"

Igor depressed the firing button and ... and ... and the missile containing Chyvaist sped toward its target, his senses penetrating the spells shielding the ship.

With a jolt, Igor flash/caught Chyvaist's observations. The ship seemed too weak for a destroyer! But was that part of its disguise?

Then he shuddered as Chyvaist's evil and hissing voice crawled into his mind like a poison ...

"Hey boss! I'm on target! Goblins ejecting! ... Done! ... Yeah, I'm up on 'em! ...

"Okay, now ... now ..."

And then in the very last moment Igor saw it all. He saw the ship, only a tourist liner and not a destroyer at all. He saw the cabins filled with sleeping people. Innocent people.

Then he heard Chyvaist's mocking voice: "Direct hit, boss! Nice work. Pity it was a wrong'un or there'd be bonuses for everybody!"

"Stop!" Tanya commanded.

Igor stopped in mid-flow, lips bloodless, eyes wild from the images crawling through his brain.

"Go back, lieutenant," she said. "Return to the point where you first realized it was an American ship."

Igor shook his head. "Please, no more. I see ... I see ... damn, but I see all their faces! Don't make me look again!"

"One more time," Tanya insisted. "Only one ... I promise."

But this time she went with him. She let her senses flow into his ... and ... and ...

Tanya was a missile hurtling toward an Amer destroyer. And she hated the Amers like Igor hated them ... like a true Russian ... centuries of inbred hate erupting ... wanting to kill ... to evaporate the Amers with this powerful missile!

And then her blood turned to ice as the destroyer suddenly became an ordinary spaceliner. A weak and innocent thing, filled with weak and innocent people.

And emblazoned on the ship's side was the legend: *HolidayOne*!

But it was too late, she couldn't stop. Chyvaist was shouting at his devils, urging them on and she couldn't stop ...

The force of the imagined blast was so realistic that Tanya's head snapped back in reaction.

She opened her eyes — although she hadn't realized they were shut. Her heart was pounding at a furious rate and she could taste blood in her mouth.

Igor was staring at her, eyes bright with madness. "Did you see it?" he asked.

Tanya nodded. "I saw."

Igor laughed, a touch of hysteria in his laughter. "Then you know I am the guilty one," he said. "No need for any others to suffer. It was my fault. My mistake. An accident due to my incompetence."

Tanya shook her head. "It was no accident, Igor Dolgov," she said.

She wanted to add that it wasn't his fault. But suddenly a strange feeling of lethargy came over her. What had only a moment before seemed quite clear, now appeared hazy and confused.

Maybe it *was* an accident. Maybe she was leaping to conclusions. Still, she thought, she should tell Igor that he wasn't at fault. Why, she'd known that almost from the beginning.

Tanya opened her mouth to speak, but she was so weary that dealing with poor Igor's guilt seemed too vast an effort.

It could wait. She'd talk to him later when she had her wits about her.

Tanya picked up Angel. "Admiral Amiriani?"

"Yes, Major Lawson?"

"I'm done with Lt. Dolgov, sir," she said. "For the time being, that is. I'd like to talk to him again later. So if you could keep him available, please?"

"Very well, Major," Amiriani said.

Tanya keyed out and leaned back in her chair. Every bone seemed to ache as if she were coming down with an old-fashioned case of the flu.

"What of your promise?" Igor asked, voice quivering. "You said it would be over now."

At that moment the doors of the interrogation room hissed open and two guards entered to escort Igor away.

"Don't worry, Lieutenant," Tanya said. "I'm done with you. Just one more little chat so I can complete my report. Nothing more."

Her soothing words didn't seem to have any effect on Igor. He was suspicious — not that she blamed him. But never mind, she'd put his guilt to rest before the day was out.

To avoid Igor's accusing eyes, she kept her head down as the guards led him away, concentrating on putting her things back into the briefcase.

The door hissed closed and she had a sudden sense of dread so powerful that the lethargy was shattered.

"Wait!" Tanya shouted, crashing to her feet.

She ran to the door, which obediently came open. "Wait!" she shouted again as she ran into the corridor.

The corridor was vacant, but she could hear bootsteps coming from around a nearby corner.

Tanya sprinted for the bootsteps but then she heard loud shouts and the sounds of a wild struggle.

As she around the corner she saw both guards sprawled on the floor, Igor standing over them.

And dammit he had a gun!

"Igor!" she shouted. "Don't!"

He turned to her, weapon turning with him until the barrel was pointed at her face.

Igor smiled at her. "This time it's over when I say so," he said.

Then he turned the gun around and shot himself through the mouth.

CHAPTER TWENTY THREE

Oh yes, Lawson was really good, Vlad thought as he followed her around the ship, observing her as she questioned key people. She even made Daniel Carvaserin hop and wriggle like crazy.

To tell the truth, Vlad had felt much vindictive joy as he monitored that conversation. Miss Lawson had been clever enough to command the admiral to "shut off the bugs!" She couldn't have expected that Vlad was listening in. Oh yes, she had made things very difficult for him. But it wasn't anything he couldn't solve.

Once again Vlad said a silent thanks to Brosha — his old batman Brownie — who had taught Vlad a lot about minor fiendish creatures.

It was easy to shut down a fiendish device, but it was very difficult to detect a small eavesdropping thing lurking somewhere between the plas-steel plates of a floor or wall.

In those circumstances a collapsed fiend, lying like the dead, was the best spying device. However, it was very difficult to make a fiend behave like this. But Brosha had instructed him on how to get around that problem.

The tiny spirit, smaller then a needle's head, hid himself in an unseen fissure. He was not a psychonic, not a telepathic creature. He was only listening, listening, listening, lying in a deep trance. Even Miss Lawson's talents failed to detect such a "bug".

However, for some reason Vlad wasn't able to intercept and decrypt the coded messages sent by Miss Lawson's assistant, the ugly Ogre-Mage Kriegworm. It made him quite uneasy, but there was nothing he could do about it at the moment.

Analyzing Lawson's questions and tactics during her interrogations he started worrying that she was going to come to "Option Two" — which, in Fathers Onphim's tongue meant, "She's going to blame our side."

That damned Amer, thought Vlad, looking through Lawson's questions over and over again. That damned cunning Amer bitch, weaving her spiderwebs, eager to report: "Yes, I've got them!"

But at the same time his original opinion about her was strongly supported: she was not just a pretty face. Several times Vlad caught himself thinking, How good is she at shooting, I wonder? Instead of, How good is she in bed?

And yes, he really wanted to meet her. Just to meet her. To lock eyes with her. To hold her gaze for a space of time, giving freedom to the burning flame inside, allowing a small amount of Sword Church power to float through.

Oh yes, it would be a real delight, pleasure, enjoyment — choose any word you like. To cross swords with such a seductive enemy. There was something in this thinking that set his blood boiling, making him silly, making him forget the Rule: "The best enemy is a dead enemy, so shoot from afar."

There was no heroism, only foolishness in close combat. Vlad understood this rule perfectly well. But now there was something strange scenting the air, something unnatural and rather unfamiliar to the Sword Church acolyte: Temptation. A challenge.

During the now swiftly moving hours sometimes Vlad was sure Lawson had discovered his presence and was searching for him — spreading the force field of her mind all over the battlestation.

The fact that he couldn't armor himself against his beautiful enemy made him angry — not with Lawson, but with himself. He should have been better prepared to face her.

But there was something worse, much worse. And it may or may not have anything to do with Lawson.

He was becoming increasingly convinced there was someone else on board. Someone like him!

A vague shadow crawling on the very edge of his mind and sight. Someone powerful, diligently making his way — to what aim? Vlad didn't know.

He felt the enemy, he smelled him, he was ready to rush after him — but that enemy was also cunning and careful. A tiny movement of Vlad's mind and searching gaze — and the faint shadow faded into a darkness.

Oh yes, there was a decision to be made. A fast and simple one — inform Amiriani and launch a thorough hunt. A round-up. A swoop. And take this miserable thing by its throat and force him (or her, or it) to crawl on his knees.

Yes, this would be sweet. And yet it was not suitable. The Odysseus Corps and the Church Of The Sword had been at war for many years. But those long years had somehow melded those old enemies into partners in a dangerous and most secret game.

There was another Special Rule for such things. If he encountered an Odysseus assassin he must deal with him in person. A knight's courtesy, so to speak. Strange? Yes. But it *was* so and Vlad was too good a knight to change the rules of honor.

He waited. His enemy would be active, but Vlad wasn't too worried. After all, what could the Amer do about the spy Vlad suspected was on board? Automatically, he'd separated the two in his mind. The Odysseus

Corps warrior and the spy had to be two separate individuals. There was no other possibility.

Never mind the spy. If there even was a spy. The main thing was the recent arrival of the Odysseus Corps killer.

The fellow was not only surrounded by Russian forces, but also he didn't dare alert Tanya Lawson to his presence for fear of giving himself away to Vlad. Of course there was the nagging possibility Vlad's enemy had been in league with Lawson from the start and they had conspired together before she'd docked with the *Borodino* ...

Vlad took precautions. The mysterious person would most certainly attempt to infiltrate *Borodino* security. Let him do it. Vlad would keep an eye out. A close eye.

The trap would slam shut very soon.

One of the things that came to Vlad's attention was a simple little fellow from the medtech team. Why had he displayed a sudden and quite strange interest in certain restricted zones? It was not forbidden, but this simple lad had never before shown such interests. His prior history showed that he mostly enjoyed X-rated computer modeling. But now ...

Vlad came to the conclusion that the poor medtech was already gone. And that the man from Odysseus Corps had taken his place.

In his mind Vlad even applauded his unknown enemy. To penetrate the *Borodino's* security was a damned good trick. The guy was practically equal to Vlad himself. Very good. When they finally met the duel would be most pleasurable.

From the very beginning Vlad had thought about the coming fight with his Odysseus enemy as a "duel," — nothing else. Not bloody, clumsy fighting but a graceful ritual.

Meanwhile, Miss Lawson had at last confronted the unhappy Dolgov. Very swiftly she had checked up on Igor's girlfriend, that Popova woman. The golden-haired Amer was like a bulldog.

But ... what was that buzz?

What was happening?

Vlad rushed from his lair. The dreadful aura of approaching death made him run like mad for he felt the terrible lust for death and extermination start to overwhelm the mind of poor Igor.

He hadn't gone ten steps when the gun fired.

And then Vlad looked up and found himself staring into the wild-looking eyes of Miss Tanya Lawson.

When Tanya's eyes met Vlad's there was a long frozen moment. The horror of Igor's death retreated before a shock of magical awareness.

This was the man whose scent she had caught in the interrogation room! The man whose name Igor dared not speak when she asked the young lieutenant to list the names of those who had questioned him.

Vlad's aura was so powerful that at first she thought he was a wizard. Tanya quickly corrected that mistake.

She thought, he's no magician, but there's magic in his making. On the surface this reasoning made no sense, but on a visceral level the realization cut through her like a knife.

The air around him was super-charged with his strength. Other men seemed small and weak-willed in comparison. He was also the deadliest man she'd ever met.

Not evil, though. Somehow his deadliness had an inner purity to it. He'd seen much, done much, suffered much. But he believed his cause was sacred and so was able rise above the common crimes of his actions.

There was still one more thing about the strange man with the pale blue eyes. And it was most disturbing. She felt a sudden attraction to him — like two powerful magnets had been placed near each other, opposite poles whipping up a storm of electrons whirling toward a sub-atomic embrace.

Then a double thrill of realization pebbled her spine. She turned her head slightly — still not breaking the gaze between herself and Vlad.

Another scent called to her — magical pheromones carried on ether-ous winds.

The world swirled about her with a sudden sense of deja vu.

And then she knew!

Somewhere on the *Borodino* was another man like the one standing before her! Someone with the same powerful purpose and deadly skills.

The same man who had watched her through the monitors when she'd been in the ship's lounge preparing to board the *Borodino*.

She clearly remembered the oddly pleasant feelings that had stolen over her while the man had watched. Feelings quite similar to the animal attraction she felt toward the one now standing across from her now.

What was happening here?

Who were these two men?

Blood rushed in her ears and she felt like she was on a bullet-train speeding through the night.

She closed her eyes to steady herself.

When she opened them again the strange young man was gone!

But she could still feel his presence quite strongly.

And the other one. He was still near!

Tanya's heart trip-hammered against her chest. She had to find them both, and quickly. There was the stink of murder in the air.

She raced down the corridor, tracking the spoor of the two mysterious men.

CHAPTER TWENTY FOUR

Damn, damn, damn, Davyd thought. The last thing I want to do is kill this kid.

Then, suddenly he realized that Billy hadn't stopped talking. And what he was talking about might just be winning him a reprieve.

"You only want to ask some more stupid questions," the boy was saying. "Like that other guy who was here before. Did you talk to him?"

Davyd was a little dazed as he drew back from his agony.

"Talk to whom?"

"The other guy. Vlad."

"Never heard of him," Davyd said, a broad smile spreading across his face.

He was much relieved. The boy's suspicions were so far off the mark that Davyd would be able to spare him. For the time being, that is. The interview wasn't over yet.

"At least Vlad didn't pretend to be somebody else," Billy said. "So I guess that makes you a big liar."

Davyd set the tray down. "How did you know I wasn't a tech?" he asked.

The boy gave him a crooked grin. "That's a secret," he said with some pride. "My secret!"

It was then that Davyd sensed the small trickle of magical power emanating from Billy. He blinked in sudden realization, thinking, *Now* I understand! The boy's a little wizard. *That's* how he'd survived!

Laughing, Davyd sat on the edge of Billy's bed.

"Okay, you got me," he said. "I'm not really a tech. And like you guessed, I was sent here to ask you some more questions."

Billy was delighted at this confession. "Who sent you?" he demanded.

Davyd pretended to look this way and that to see if anyone was about. "Promise you won't tell?" he said.

Billy crossed his heart. "Promise," he said.

Davyd pointed upwards, as if at the heavens. "My bosses," he said. "Real big shots." He sighed. "The thing is, if I don't come back with any answers I'm going to be in really big trouble."

Billy frowned. "That's not right," he said. "Why should you get in trouble because I won't talk?"

"That's how big shots are," Davyd said.

"I'm sorry," Billy said. "You shouldn't have to get in trouble because of me."

"That's all right," Davyd said. "I understand."

Then, pretending he had an idea, Davyd let his eyes widen. "I know," he said. "Why don't we just pretend?"

"Pretend what?"

"That I asked you some questions and you answered them. I'll make something up. Then I won't get into trouble."

He looked at Billy, as if worried. "If I do, you won't tell, will you?"

"Wouldn't that be a lie?" Billy said.

Davyd thought a moment, then let his shoulders fall, as if in defeat. "Yeah, it would," he said. "I hate lying. I wouldn't have done it this time, except they made me."

He rose and started packing up his tray. "Never mind," he said. "I'll think of something."

Davyd was about to walk out the door when Billy stopped him. "Wait a minute," the boy said.

He turned back, a shy smile on his face. "You mean, you've changed your mind? You'll help me make something up?"

Billy shook his head. "No. We'll give them the real thing." He settled back into his pillows.

"Go ahead," he said. "Ask your questions. And I'll answer every single one."

Davyd sat back down. "Thanks," he said. "You've probably saved my job. But let's make it simple. Just tell me what happened. I'll put it in my report and tell them not to bother you anymore."

Billy nodded, then started relating the tale. He left out a few little bits that might be embarrassing — such as the beautiful Lupe who'd captured his boyish fancy. He tried to tell it straight, without emotion, but the deeper he got into the story the more he had to fight back tears.

Suddenly, the awful memory overwhelmed him and he found himself flung back into that night of terror, reliving the events …

…He was asleep. But his dreams had turned grim and he was uneasy. A sudden sense of cruelty roughed his senses and he shot up in bed.

He felt It coming for him!

A beast rushing down with slavering jaws.

Instinct took over and as he threw up his hands he hurled a hard spell!

His first spell.

But potent.

And then … boom! Billy closed his eyes. Fire scorching and hammering all around.

And he shouted … Lupe! Lupe!"

Then he was back in his room, sobbing and ashamed of the tears.

Davyd leaned close, wanting to comfort Billy, but not making that mistake. Instinctively he knew the child would feel humiliated if he treated him as anything less than an adult.

Billy shook free of the memory. Davyd unzipped a package of stim-cloths and the boy wiped his face, the sharp scent of the astringent-soaked material gently shocking him into composure.

He laughed, a little giddy. "That was stupid," he said. "Sorry."

"Not as stupid as the guys who are making me ask you this stuff," Davyd said, keeping his voice light.

Billy's eyes brightened, his pupils narrowed from the mild pep drug contained in the cloths.

"What happened after that?" Davyd asked.

Billy giggled. "The next thing I knew I was sort of like, you know … floating in space. Like a fish."

He wriggled his body, giggling some more. Then he became serious. "Then everything went sort of blank. I was unconscious, I guess. When I came to I was in this stupid hospital. And everybody else was … dead."

His voice thickened and he stopped.

A long silence followed. Billy stared at his hands, pulling the net tight on his emotions. Davyd studied him, seeing his own self in the child.

A thousand years or more ago he'd been like this very same boy — an orphan at six when his parents died in a plane crash. Only Davyd's special talents had kept him from disappearing into the warrens of the poor. His sharp mind and extraordinary physical abilities had saved him.

A star athlete from an early age, he'd easily won a posting to West Point. There he'd shone both in his studies and on the field, winning many medals for his country in the both the decathlon and military pentathlon.

He'd been headed for the Olympics when he was recruited for the Odysseus Corps.

A sudden feeling of depression overcame Davyd. All the old regrets came rushing in, along with the bloody nightmares of the people he'd killed.

Grisly scenes: blood, so much blood; people on their knees, begging for mercy, and no mercy in him, just hate and the mission the to take out the target at all costs.

In his pocket the gremlin-box grew warm and vibrated in alarm.

Something was wrong!

Davyd was under attack!

Battle drugs were pumped into his body and his thought process sped up. Where was the enemy? He looked at the boy — who was staring at him strangely.

Davyd thought, No, not from there.

But where? Where?

"What's wrong?" Billy asked. "Are you okay?"

Davyd forced himself back into the role. "Sure," he said. "Everything's fine. But tell me … when you were still on the liner … you said something about an animal. A monster that woke you up."

"It was my imagination," Billy said. "There wasn't any monster." He signed. "Only the missiles."

"But you didn't, uh, sense the missiles, right?"

Billy's eyes widened, realizing Davyd had figured out he had magical powers.

"Don't worry about the magic stuff," Davyd said, as if reading his mind. "I won't mention it to anyone."

Billy grinned, accepting the bargain. Then, very seriously, "I was dreaming about some kind of … beast," he said. "Not missiles." He shrugged. "Maybe I got mixed up."

"That's most likely," Davyd said. "It was a coincidence."

He didn't believe that at all. If there was one thing Davyd knew, it was that there no such thing as coincidence. Just like his talking to Billy and the sudden attack of severe depression was no coincidence.

Davyd shivered. There *was* something there!

Something dark. Something fierce. Waiting …

But what?

What?

"Somebody's coming," Billy said.

Davyd's head jerked back. He turned toward the door and caught a familiar scent. His nerves thrilled. Finally, a legitimate kill.

"It's Vlad," Billy announced. "The guy who was here before."

Davyd nodded, "I know," he said, flat.

Billy suddenly caught what was happening.

"Are you going to kill him?" His voice was very small.

Davyd pulled himself together. As badly as he wanted to face this man — this delicious, hateful equal — to do so would blow the mission.

No one must know he'd been aboard the *Borodino*.

"Not now," he said and at the same time he leaned forward, sweeping the hypo gun off the tray.

The boy's eyes were huge as Davyd took his arm pressed the gun against his bare flesh.

"Are you going to kill me?" Billy asked.

Davyd pressed the trigger, shooting the fluids into the boy's arm.

The child fell back on his pillow. Pale and silent as death.

Davyd turned away, looking for an avenue of escape.

And he thought, Screw 'em! Screw Father Zorza! Screw all the rest! No way am I gonna kill this kid.

CHAPTER TWENTY FIVE

"He's coming, Master!" the gremlin squeaked. "Hurry!"

Davyd didn't waste his breath cursing the gremlin, telling him to shut up! That he knew damned well the guy was coming.

As for hurrying, he was going as fast as he could, but the vent cover was resisting him.

The bolts holding the grill in place were old, some of the heads nearly stripped, slipping the grip of his little pneumowrench. The wrench made no sound, other than a faint purr, like a cat.

Behind him, Billy moaned in his drugged sleep, whispering "Lupe, Lupe," with so much pain in his voice that Davyd knew the child was in the grip of a nightmare.

Poor kid, he thought. Wish I could tell you it'll get better, but it won't.

And then another bolt fell into his palm and he was almost there! Two more to go. Then through the vent and away to the storage room where his gear was stored.

He'd be off the *Borodino* and on his way to the rendezvous point in no time flat.

Too bad he didn't have everything he needed. The report would be pretty damned slim. But it was a good start. Nothing to bitch about. Father Zorza wouldn't be ecstatic, but he wouldn't be disappointed either.

Davyd pressed the pencil-shaped wrench against the next bolt. He triggered it and the tool jumped in his hand, biting into the bolthead. The bolt came half-free, then jammed.

Davyd gave the wrench more power, muttering, "come on, baby, come on ..." The bolt snapped, but no matter, he could bend the vent back. But then:

"He's here, master!"

And Davyd sighed, dropping the wrench and coming to his feet to face his enemy.

He turned toward the door, drawing his weapon, already thinking how the guy might come, worried because Billy was on the bed and would be between them.

But if Davyd angled to the right, getting the kid out of the line of fire, he'd be in a lousy position — field of fire drastically reduced.

And from his sleep Billy cried, "Lupe!"

Davyd moved to the right.

Vlad came down the dark corridor like a wolf on the stalk, feet gliding silently, muscles working smoothly like powerful machines bathed in warm oil.

He was in a crouch, the corridor wall on his left, ahead dim yellow light from Billy's room spilling through the open doorway to puddle on the floor.

Vlad could feel the presence of his Odysseus Corps enemy in the hot marrow of his bones. His heart ached for this kill — and kill it would be.

He had been fairly certain who his enemy was well before he entered the hospital. Any niggling doubts were swept away by the scent of cold darkness.

Pheromones of death — of kind knowing kind — drifting on the air.

Obviously, the proper course would be to capture the man and question him. Torture him until he confessed all he knew about the filthy Amer plot to humiliate Mother Russia.

Vlad's methods in such things had never failed to get the desired answers.

If the enemy had been an ordinary man, that's what Vlad would've done. Backed by a squad of the *Borodino's* best, he'd have rushed the room, easily disarmed the guy, then bundled him up for a leisurely session of pain threshold testing.

But this was no ordinary man waiting for him in that room. And yes, he was waiting … Vlad had no doubt about that.

His enemy had thought about escaping, but he'd caught Vlad's spoor as well and now he was getting into position to fight.

Vlad had to do this alone and not just because of The Rule. Against someone from Odysseus Corps, added men — no matter how good — would be in Vlad's way.

His enemy would use them as a shield, dodging at super speed, trying for a lucky shot at Vlad as he killed everyone else.

Capture would not be a possibility.

The enemy would escape or die. It was the only choice open to him. Just as it would be Vlad's only choice if he were in the same situation.

He was nearing the doorway now, and he slowed.

Creeping softly, softly, *so* softly. And thinking, "Come to me, enemy mine, come to me …"

*　*　*

Davyd was in full battle-mode, nerve endings on fire, a strange joy singing in his veins as he waited for his enemy.

It'd been a long time since he'd faced an equal. Only twice in a thousand years had he pitted his skills against the Russian assassins of the Church Of The Sword.

That he'd come away victorious, albeit wounded, in both incidents made a large part of the Davyd Kells legend in the Odysseus Corps' Hall Of Heroes.

Now I'll make it three, lucky three, Davyd thought, senses so finely tuned that he caught the soft fall of a shoe whiskering across a plas floor.

His enemy was only a few feet away, coming in from his blind side, but Davyd could feel his presence through the wall that divided Billy's room from the hospital corridor.

Davyd lifted his weapon and considered putting a burst through the wall.

*　*　*

Vlad hesitated, thinking the best thing to do would be to simply toss a pin grenade into the room and blow the man into charred hunks of flesh.

But that would also kill the boy. Like Davyd, Vlad had no desire to kill children, especially that poor, soul-wounded little thing who had already suffered so much.

If there was no other choice, well, he'd have to accept that sin and the boy would die.

Even so — even if there were no child — Vlad wouldn't have used a grenade.

Oh, no. This must be one on one. Mano-a-mano, as they said. The greatest thrill would be to kill him with his own hands, although that was unlikely to happen.

It would be over quickly.

One shot.

At the most, two.

Vlad paused inches away from the doorway.

He crouched lower, getting to ready to move.

*　*　*

Davyd dismissed the wall shot. If the guy was only wounded the return fire might hit the kid.

Okay, fine, you Rooskie son-of-a-bitch, show yourself!

And then we can play.

Come on … Come on …

Without warning a dark shape flew across the doorway.

Davyd fired.

*　*　*

Vlad launched himself into the air. He was on his side, presenting only a fast-moving, horizontal target.

As his head passed the doorway he saw Billy on the bed, then a man crouched in the corner, weapon at the ready.

There was a harsh cough as the man fired, but Vlad managed to get off a shot at the same moment.

A heavy blow struck his heel, then he was past the doorway and tuck-rolling to his feet.

Whirling around for the counter, feeling no pain in his foot … just a little clumsiness … smiling to himself as he realized only his bootheel had been shot off.

And his enemy had missed!

But so had he.

Vlad prayed he'd have better luck with his next shot.

*　*　*

Davyd felt the round pluck at his sleeve and laughed in hot glee at his enemy's misfortune.

True, Davyd had missed as well — although for a second there he'd thought he'd blasted the guy's foot off.

But from the sound of his enemy's acrobatic recovery, he was unhurt. Still, now he was no longer on Davyd's blind side. No wall to hide his attack until the last possible moment.

From Davyd's position he could see a short distance down the corridor to where the light from Billy's room faded into darkness.

Best of all, Billy was well out of the line of fire.

Just then he felt another presence!

It was moving down the corridor from his blind side.

Shit! Were there two of them?

*　*　*

Vlad sensed the second presence as well.

Surprised, he turned his weapon slightly to cover the darkness where he thought the figure would emerge.

Probably some damned security officer who hadn't received the order to stay clear of this area. It might very well prove to be a fatal mistake for both of them.

Then he caught the scent of familiar perfume.

Tanya Lawson!

Vlad hissed silent curses. He could only draw one conclusion: Lawson, as he suspected, was working with the Odysseus Corps.

There could be no other explanation for her presence.

He felt a wrench of deep regret when he realized he'd have to kill her.

The emotion surprised him.

*　*　*

"It's Major Lawson, master," the gremlin whisper-squeaked.

And Davyd thought, Damn, damn, double-damn! What the hell is she doing here?

Then it suddenly occurred to him that she might be working for the Russians.

A turncoat?

Tanya Lawson?

Davyd was suddenly very sad.

And then he heard her voice:

"This is Major Tanya Lawson of the United Worlds Police. I order you both to cease your hostilities at once!"

CHAPTER TWENTY SIX

Tanya had never felt more stupid. As soon as she'd blurted the command she regretted it, but she couldn't think of anything else to say.

It was plain that she'd just walked into the middle of a duel. She also had no doubt the duel had everything to do with her current investigation. She had to stop it, or valuable information might be lost.

But there was more to it than that. Her magical side — curse it — was buzzing with conflicting signals and sensory information.

Even as shadow figures, the two men were unlike any others she'd ever encountered.

Who were they?

She had to know, she just had to!

Realizing she could die in the next instant, Tanya stepped into plain view, saying: "I'm unarmed, so I'm no threat to either of you."

Then, going by gut instinct, she added, "Be warned. If any harm comes to me, I promise you, neither of your governments will be pleased."

She saw Vlad first. He was coiled on the far side of the doorway, weapon pointed directly at her. His eyes were glittering, frightening. For a moment she thought he was going to shoot.

But Tanya kept walking forward, dipping deep into her hated magical side, fumbling for a spell. She imagined a serene glade in a quiet forest with a smooth-surfaced pool in the center of that glade. All was calm. All was peace.

Tanya formed the image and cast the spell.

At the same time she was saying, "You, in the room! I'm going to walk to the center of the doorway where you can see me. Again, I warn you — don't shoot!"

As she came forward she saw the surprise on Vlad's face. The fires in his eyes were burning less intensely now.

Tanya held up empty hands, turning them this way and that. "You see, I'm unarmed. Just as I said."

She came to the center of the doorway and stopped.

"Now I'm between you both," she said. "If either of you catch me in a lie, I'll be an easy target."

Vlad started to speak, then shook his head. One word would give his position away.

Tanya strengthened the spell of peace. Vlad relaxed ever so slightly.

She turned her head slowly so she could see into the room. The sight of the sleeping boy gave her a jolt. For a few minutes she'd forgotten about him.

Christ, the stakes just went up! If she was unsuccessful the child might very well be killed.

Then she saw Davyd. Black Irish handsome, with curly hair and amused eyes.

He was crouched in a corner grinning a crazy grin, weapon aimed a few inches past her — covering the gap against an attack from Vlad.

"Hello, Tanya," he said huskily.

An electrical thrill ran in the air between them. A small, bemused part of Tanya noted that the spark of mutual interest was identical to the one she'd experienced when she'd seen Vlad.

At the same time she caught Vlad's twitch of surprise at the sound of Davyd's voice. The Russian took one pace forward, pale blue eyes narrowed and gleaming like a Siamese cat on the stalk.

"Hey, you out there," Davyd called out, freezing Vlad in place. "I don't mind talking first, because you already know where I am."

He barked laughter. "Hell, there's not many places I could be in a room this size."

Vlad didn't reply. Despite Tanya's spell, the sound of his enemy's voice roused the serpent of hate in his breast.

Tanya bore down, drawing on her reserves to make the spell more powerful.

"He probably knows where you are as well," she said to Vlad. "Why don't you answer? What's the harm?"

Vlad hesitated a moment, then nodded. He could see her logic.

"What do you want?" he called out to Davyd.

"A short truce," Davyd said. "That's all."

Vlad grinned. "I don't see where you're in any position to ask for anything, my friend," he said, voice heavy with irony.

"Depends on your point of view," Davyd said. "Personally, I think I have a pretty good shot at tweeping you within the next few minutes. Problem is, we've got a kid in the way, plus Major Lawson. No sense taking them both with us."

"He's got a good point," Tanya said to Vlad. "The boy is a complete innocent. And I've already warned you about harming me."

She saw Vlad's eyes cloud and she sensed he was looking within himself. When his eyes cleared they widened in amazement.

"I have no wish to … harm you, Tanya," he said, voice thick with emotion.

Tanya felt an odd tug at her heart as somehow a bond was formed between them.

Before she could speak, Davyd called out, "So we get the truce then, right?"

"What makes you think I've agreed?" Vlad asked.

Davyd shrugged. "Simple. Right now both of us are violating orders. Just by not killing her. She's seen us … spoken to us … and can guess who — and what — we are.

"Unless you guys at the Church Of The Sword have changed the rules, that means she's a required kill. No exceptions. Am I right?"

Vlad nodded. "Of course," he said. "Our rules are the same as the Odysseus Corps."

Tanya was bewildered. "Church Of The Sword?" she said. "Odysseus Corps? Who the hell are you guys?"

"It would be best if you didn't press for any further details, Tanya," Vlad said. "To hear the names is reason enough for a death warrant."

"Even though you're a UWP cop," Davyd added. "Our bosses don't give a damn one way or the other."

"So, why am I still alive?" Tanya demanded.

Davyd started to answer, then his jaw snapped shut. He shook his head. "For very unprofessional reasons," he replied.

He looked at her with unshielded eyes, his troubled soul naked, his deep attraction to her plain.

Tanya sighed. "I understand," she said.

She meant it. She could feel the attraction just as strongly.

And Vlad said, "Apparently you have two admirers, Tanya. I'd be jealous of my enemy, except it seems his feelings for you have kept you alive."

Tanya was rocked by these twin declarations. Everything had suddenly become unreal. It was as if she'd stepped into another world where only three people existed: these two men and … Tanya.

She gave herself a mental shake, coming back to reality. Thinking, it must have something to do with my spell. Maybe I'm caught up in it myself.

Although she suspected her logic was wrong, she didn't want to delve any deeper into the matter at the moment. There was an opportunity here. She should grab for it no matter what the reasons.

Billions of lives were at stake.

"I have a proposal for you both," she said. "Starting with — why don't we extend this truce we've managed to work out? I'm sure your missions are essentially the same as mine. Which is to find out what happened to the *HolidayOne*.

"We should talk together. Combine our information. And get to the truth."

"It is not within the power of either of us to grant what you ask," Vlad said.

He waved his weapon at the doorway. "My Odysseus Corps friend in there knows this as well as I."

"He's right," Davyd said. "In a few minutes, one of us has to die. That's the way things are. And don't think that I regret it for a minute. In fact, I'm going to take great pleasure in snuffing out his lights."

Vlad smiled sadly. "You see how it is?" he said to Tanya. "We are sworn enemies. Have no doubts about that fact."

Tanya snorted in disgust. "That's ridiculous!" she snapped. "What's more important, your missions or killing each other?"

The question surprised both men into silence.

"Here's how I see it," Tanya said. "We have a unique opportunity here to solve this incident. And I have to say this is the strangest case in my career. Things aren't what they seem.

"Nothing so simple as the Russians did this, or the Americans did that. There's more to it. Much more. And unless you two are dim-witted fools you're already coming to the same conclusion.

"Am I right?"

No answer from either of the men.

Tanya stamped her foot. "Am I right!?" she demanded.

Slowly Vlad nodded. "Yes," he said. "You are."

And Davyd said, "Keep going, Tanya. Makes sense to me so far."

"Good!" Tanya said. "I was hoping you guys wouldn't disappoint me and reveal yourselves as complete numskulls."

Davyd laughed. "Does that mean you're thinking of liking me?"

Vlad also chuckled. "Dare I dream the same, Tanya?"

Tanya definitely didn't want to get into that subject with either man.

"Never mind," she replied to both. "Let's stick to the subject. Which is my suggestion for an extended truce. The three of us can meet in some neutral place. Like aboard the ship that brought me here. The *Stardove*. That's official UWP territory, under UWP jurisdiction. No one can bother us there."

"I like that idea," Davyd said without hesitation.

"Why am I not surprised to hear that?" Vlad called out to the unseen Davyd. "If I were so stupid as to agree, I'd have to allow you to leave the *Borodino*. Russian territory. Under Russian law. Which would make me a traitor.

"Besides, I know you are lying to Tanya. As soon as you're away, you'll either flee to some prearranged rendezvous point, or turn back and try to kill me."

Tanya looked at Davyd. "Are you lying?" she asked.

Davyd started to give a smart answer and lie through his teeth.

Tanya held up a hand. "Please say you're not! And mean it."

Davyd hesitated a long moment, then, solemn, "I swear," he said. Then, "On my … feelings … for you."

Tanya knew he spoke the truth. "Thank you," she said.

Davyd smiled gently. "My name's Davyd, by the way."

Tanya blushed, although she didn't know why. "Thank you, Davyd," she murmured.

Then to Vlad, "You see. He's not lying."

"He's not lying, Vlad," the Russian corrected with a grin.

"What?" Tanya was puzzled.

Vlad tapped his chest. "Vlad. That's me."

Tanya was tormented by another unwanted blush. She nodded to cover embarrassment.

"Vlad," she said softly. "Vlad."

He smiled, loving the sound of her voice saying his name. Then he frowned. "We still have a great problem," he said. "I can't allow … Davyd … to escape the *Borodino*. That would be in violation of all orders. Gross negligence of the worst kind.

"At the very least they'd courtmartial me. More likely, they wouldn't wait for such official pleasantries. I'd be executed on the spot."

He sighed. "So you see, I can't allow him to escape."

Tanya laughed, a most pleasant sound, Vlad thought. "He already has," she said.

The Russian's eyes widened in realization. He bolted toward the room, a blur of motion, brushing past her with ease.

He gaped about the room — empty, except for the sleeping Billy. Then he saw the open vent cover that Davyd had slipped through.

Vlad turned to rush out and track him down but was brought up short by Tanya, who barred the way with outstretched arms.

"Let him go!" she pleaded.

Vlad took her arm, meaning to pull her aside. But the feel of her soft flesh and smell of her sweet perfume made him hesitate.

"Please," Tanya begged. "For me."

His hand dropped away. "He's lying," Vlad said, hoarse. "I'm sure of it."

"I don't think so," Tanya said, firm.

Now it was her turn to take Vlad's arm. He flinched at her touch. Startled anew at the intensity of his feelings for her.

"Let's go to the *Stardove*," she said. "Davyd will be waiting for us. You'll see."

She tugged gently at his arm and after a long moment Vlad said, "All right, Tanya. I'll go."

CHAPTER TWENTY SEVEN

When Davyd and Vlad finally met face-to-face the blast of recognition rocked them to the core. Their super-charged instinct to kill — already partly disarmed by Tanya's spell — vanished entirely as each gaped at the other.

"You're Bush!" Davyd blurted.

Vlad nodded. "And you're Putin!" he marveled.

"Guilty!" Davyd said.

"I thought you were dead," Vlad said.

"Same here," Davyd said. Then he laughed. "Guess we're not."

An amazed Tanya was desperately trying to follow the exchange, head going back-and-forth as if it were a tennis match. She hadn't known what to expect when she'd led Vlad into the *Stardove's* passenger lounge where Davyd had been waiting.

Feeling as if at any moment she could be caught in the middle of a fire-fight, she'd gingerly entered the lounge — Vlad a few steps behind her.

Tanya could sense Vlad coiling like a razorwire spring as Davyd came to his feet, then the tension eased somewhat when Davyd raised his hands to show he was weaponless. Vlad did the same. It was then that the two men had truly looked at each other.

Their reactions plunged Tanya into confusion.

"Putin?" she broke in. "Bush? I thought you were Vlad and Davyd!"

Davyd and Vlad exchanged secretive looks.

"We are," Davyd said.

"Then let me in on the joke, guys!" Tanya demanded.

Vlad sighed. "It really isn't much of a joke, Tanya," he said. "And it would be better if you didn't know more."

"You *said* that before!" Tanya snapped. She was getting irritated by what she thought of as small boy games.

"Okay, I'll bite," she continued. "What do the names Bush and Putin have in common? First, there were two famous political leaders with those names about a thousand years ago. One was president of America. The other the Russia. Right, so far?"

Neither man said anything.

"Won't talk, huh?" Tanya said. "Fine, we'll go into the second similarity. Which is that both of those men were assassinated."

Becoming interested in her own train of thought, Tanya scratched her tawny head. "On the same day, if I recall."

Another head scratch. Eyes widening. "Now, I remember! For a minute there I thought I was going to shame my old history professor. They were both killed at some kind of big ceremony.

"At the opening ceremonies for the Olympic Games in Athens. In the year 2004 — of that I'm certain. August 13, 2004. The day the whole world changed forever. And also the last time the Olympics were ever held.

"My professor said that Bush and Putin wanted to present a united front against all the terrorism that was going on all over the world. Gruesome attacks on New York and Moscow and other places as well. All aimed at destabilizing the peace between the U.S. and Russia.

"So they made a joint appearance at the Games. But then they were both assassinated. Nobody knows why, but there sure wasn't any chance for peace after that."

She frowned in thought. Then said, "Hell, now that I think of it, my old professor said the assassinations were the main cause of the Second Cold War. The one we still seem stuck in after a thousand years."

A long pause, then Davyd cleared his throat. "Thanks for the history lesson, Tanya," he said.

Vlad grimaced. "Quite enlightening," he said.

"It's more than just a damned history lesson!" Tanya snapped. "From that day forward, magic started taking the place of natural physics. And as far as I'm concerned the whole world went straight to Hell!"

Tanya flushed, as she realized she'd lost her temper. Her only excuse was her extreme sensitivity to the subject of magic versus natural physics. Damn, but it was the real reason she'd remembered such details of an event that had taken place so long ago, never mind her revered "old professor."

Calming herself, she examined the two men. Their faces were blank. Giving nothing away.

"You're still not talking?" Tanya said. "Even though you both know I'm on the right track?" Neither man answered. Stone faced to the end. She sighed, accepting momentary defeat. "Answer this, then. Obviously the two of you have met before. Right?"

"That we have," Davyd said, suddenly brightening.

"At a sporting engagement," Vlad added, a mischievous smile tugging at his lips.

"Why do I find that hard to believe?" Tanya said sarcastically.

"But it's true," Davyd insisted.

Another uncomfortable silence — broken by Tanya. "Well? Tell me the rest. Or, at least flesh out the story a little more."

"It was a draw," Davyd said. "The athletic contest, I mean. We were supposed to compete against each other again … but things … just didn't work out."

Tanya made motions for more. "And? *And*?"

"I don't think it would be wise to go into any more detail, Tanya," Vlad said. "We've both stretched the rules as far as we can. Well past that point, actually."

"I should have killed him on the *Borodino*," Davyd said, pointing at Vlad. "I broke that rule entirely."

Vlad's face darkened. "You'll have your chance soon enough," he said to Davyd. "The moment this truce ends."

"Which is when I say it ends, correct?" Tanya said. A long hesitation. She gritted her teeth in frustration. "Correct?"

Finally, both men nodded. Davyd sank back into his seat. Vlad settled into a lounge chair across from him.

"Tell us your proposal, please," Vlad said to Tanya.

"Damn, this had better be good!" Davyd said. "Or there is going to be a whole lot of hell to pay."

Tanya snorted. "Hell would be a Walk On The Mild Side, compared to what's going to happen if we don't get to the bottom of this business."

"If that were not the case, Tanya," Vlad said, "there would be no reason for this truce."

Davyd laughed. "Speak for yourself, friend!" he said.

He cast glowing eyes on Tanya. "No offense, Tanya," he said, "but I'd be a liar if I didn't admit up front that I when I saw you, professionalism flew out the window.

"This is personal. Real personal."

Vlad grimaced. "Moving rather quickly, aren't you, my friend?" he said to Davyd. "But then Amers always did lack style."

Davyd shrugged. "I didn't think there'd be another chance to say it," he replied.

He gave Tanya a sad look. "At least you know my mind," he said.

"In that case," Vlad broke in, "perhaps I should also tell you, Tanya, that —"

"Enough!" Tanya commanded, cutting him off. "Are you two crazy? Have we suddenly taken a time trip back to high school? Two murderous boys trying to impress the girl.

"My female friends would never believe it. The ultimate illustration of Guydom. Brain eaten through by rampant testosterone.

"I mean, Jesus Christ, they are about to blow up the damned galaxy and you two are fighting over who gets to take me to the dance!"

Davyd chuckled. "What can I say? I guess I don't get out much!"

"Is the reason so important, Tanya?" Vlad asked. "You have our attention. Our serious attention. Does it matter so much that being a most remarkable woman didn't hurt?"

Tanya bit back an angry retort. Now was not the time to give these men a lesson in women's equality. At the same time a part of her could not deny that she was powerfully attracted to both of them.

My God! she thought. You must be losing your mind, Tanya Lawson!

She said, "I'll take what I can get. And the first thing I want is to continue this truce indefinitely."

"Impossible," Vlad said.

"Why don't we wait and hear her out?" Davyd said. "Then decide."

Vlad thought for a moment, then said, "All right, Tanya. We've come this far. I'll listen."

Tanya started pacing between them, the two men in rapt attention, following her with their eyes.

"Here's how I see it," Tanya said. "When I started on this case, I thought there could only be four explanations for what had happened.

"First: the *HolidayOne* really was a military ship disguised as a liner."

"Not a chance," Davyd said. "My investigation has already eliminated that possibility."

"You view things more strongly, perhaps," Vlad said, "but essentially I agree."

"Good start!" Tanya said. "The three of us agree on at least one thing. Now, let's go on.

"The second explanation was that the *Borodino* purposely fired on a civilian liner."

"Absolutely not!" Vlad said, firm. "Mother Russia does not make war on civilians."

"Give me a break," Davyd said. "You hit civilians all the time. So do we. Just not a whole damned space liner. He shook his head. "Honeymoon Special! Jesus Christ, how low can you go?"

Tanya fixed Davyd with a penetrating look. "Do you really believe that?" she said. "Do you really think the Russians want to be cursed in every outpost of the Galaxy?"

Davyd shook his head. "Who can say what possesses the Devil?"

"We both know all about devils, don't we, Davyd?" Vlad murmured. "Hmm?"

Davyd gave a weary sigh. "Okay. Gotcha, pal. And maybe you're right and it didn't happen that way. From the information I've already gathered it's becoming a dimmer possibility."

Then his head bulled forward. "But that doesn't mean there wasn't gross incompetence," he snarled. "Criminal stupidity!"

Before Vlad could respond in kind, Tanya said, "We're getting ahead of ourselves. Let's stick to taking this point by point."

She didn't wait for agreement but went on. "I don't think the *Borodino* purposefully fired on the ship, knowing it was a liner. The tapes pretty well prove that. But it still could have been an accident, due to incompetence."

Vlad gave a grudging nod. "I have yet to eliminate that possibility," he said. "Although it will be more difficult to rule it out completely now that Igor Dolgov is dead."

The name stopped Tanya in her tracks. Her face paled, remembering the incident.

Davyd frowned, suspicious. "The firing officer's dead?" he growled. "That'd kind of handy, isn't it."

"Suicide," Vlad said.

Davyd gave a cynical laugh. "Sure it was," he said. "Probably shot himself four or five times in the back of the head."

"It wasn't like that!" Tanya snapped.

Davyd looked up at her, startled at the anguish in her face.

"I saw him do it!" she said.

She paused, getting herself together. "The fact is," she continued, voice calm and professional, "I probably caused it. Drove him to suicide, as it were, by my interrogation techniques. There's always a danger of that. And I went too far."

"You can't blame yourself, Tanya," Vlad said softly. "Dolgov was on the edge. I saw that for myself when I spoke to him."

Tanya bit her lip. "Right!" she said. "And I pushed him over it."

"This is not the usual case, Tanya," Vlad said. "There are other forces at work."

He meant the Church Of The Sword and The Odysseus Corps so he was startled when Tanya said:

"And that's the explanation that I never considered when I started on this case. That some other force, a third force, is responsible."

"You mean terrorists?" Davyd said, doing a bad job of hiding scorn. "There isn't a terrorist group in the galaxy that doesn't operate for one side or the other."

"No, not terrorists," Tanya said. "Something else. Something I can't quite explain. Only feel."

She glared at them. "And I don't want to hear any sexist cracks about 'women's intuition,' damn you!" she said.

"The boy ..." Davyd said quietly, musing aloud. "He was talking about that too."

"How could you have spoken to the boy?" Vlad demanded. "He told me nothing. He refuses to speak to anyone. Why would he suddenly bare his innermost soul to an Amer!"

Davyd grinned at him. "It's my bedside manner," he said. "Doctors come from the ends of the Universe to study my methods."

"Never mind that," Tanya said. "What did the boy tell you?"

Davyd summed up his conversation with Billy. When he was done, he added, "I didn't think much of it at first. Figured the kid was still too shook up to know real from fevered imagination.

"The thing is, the boy's a wizard. A baby one, to be sure, but he's still a wizard. Which is the only explanation for how he got off the ship in time.

"And how he could be unaffected by being in space with no protection whatsoever. So, maybe he really did pick up on something weird."

He looked at Tanya. "Your third force, for example," he said.

Then he slapped his knee in frustration. "Hell, I'm not even sure what I'm talking about. When you say it out loud it sounds even stupider than it thinks!"

"Just the same," Vlad murmured, "I have the testimony of Old Scratch, the Engine Devil, that also points to mysterious things."

He held up two fingers. "That's from two separate points of view, mind you. Coming from two individuals who have never met, or spoken together."

Davyd shook his head. "Not enough," he said. "They're off the same ship. Could be the same hysterical reaction."

"It's possible," Tanya admitted. "But I'm not sure that's what happened."

She drew in a long, ragged breath. Tanya hated what she needed to say next, but she couldn't see any way to avoid it.

"You're going to think I'm crazy," she told the men. "But I had an unnerving experience not long ago. In fact, it happened twice. Once at the beginning of this mission. And the second time while I was ... talking to ... Dolgov."

Vlad and Davyd leaned forward, intensely interested.

CHAPTER TWENTY EIGHT

In a hidden place deep in the bowels of the *Stardove* another being listened in with equal interest and growing alarm.

He fidgeted with his gold Rolex as Tanya told the two men about the "cold peering eye" that had observed her.

Kriegworm strengthened the eavesdropping spell so Tanya's voice boomed into his hiding place.

"You can't imagine how terrifying that look was," he heard her say. "It seemed to come from afar, but at the same time the ... watcher ... was near ... terribly near."

She suspects! Kriegworm thought, fear flooding his fiendish veins. Oh, Master, he silently begged, do not fault this undeserving devil. Thou knowest I gave no hint, no sign to the softskin Lawson of thy existence.

"At first I thought my imagination was running wild because I was tired, or over-excited by what was happening," he heard her continue.

"Hell, that still might be so. However, when I was with Dolgov the same thing happened again. This ... feeling ... of something very powerful, very — damn, but I hate to use such an unprofessional description — but it was by God, evil!

"And powerful beyond thinking. A conclave of a thousand wizards couldn't possess such power."

Kriegworm twisted his watch band until it nearly broke. She doesn't just suspect, he thought, she knows! It took all his effort to fight off the growing hysteria in his horny breast.

Then to his horror he heard Vlad say, "Hmm. I experienced a similar situation not long ago. I wonder. Could it be the same ... umm ... Watcher?"

The Rolex band snapped. Kriegworm was so upset he didn't notice his prize possession drop from his wrist and fall to the floor.

His fangs chattered in fear as a baleful eye turned on him. A fierce pain gripped his heart — like a taloned fist squeezing, squeezing ...

"Mercy, master!" he shouted. "Mercy!"

* * *

Vlad paced the floor, thinking of his first encounter with the mysterious ... Watcher ... during his expedition to the Fiendish Worlds.

Of course, he couldn't tell the others the details of what had happened. The mission, after all, had been of the highest secrecy.

It takes much to make a Church Of The Sword acolyte shiver, but that's what Vlad did when he remembered the evil voice hissing in his ear: *"We'll meet soon, softskin!"*

His respect for Tanya's abilities as a detective soared. She was not only beautiful, she was brilliant.

"Well," Tanya said, a little impatient, "aren't you going to tell us what happened?"

"He can't," Davyd said. Vlad was surprised to hear the sympathy in his enemy's voice. "Secret stuff, I'm sure."

Davyd caught Vlad's eyes with his own. "Isn't that right?" he said.

A moment passed between them. They were enemies, but still one of an extremely rare kind. Each understood the other's deepest feelings without a word being spoken.

Vlad grinned. "Right," he replied.

He turned to Tanya. "Would it anger you too much if I pleaded state secrets and let it go at that?"

Tanya chuckled. Vlad loved the sound of her laugh. It was low and throaty … from the earth, as they say.

"How could I be angry with you, Vlad?" she murmured. "Now that we have this … understanding … is that the word? Understanding?"

Vlad's mouth parched. His tongue felt thick. He nodded, swept up by the perfume of her presence. "Yes," he said. "An … understanding!"

To his immense disappointment Tanya broke the gaze — reluctantly, he prayed — and turned to Davyd.

"And you, Davyd?" she said. "Did you share such an experience?"

Davyd thought a minute. "Maybe," he said. "Maybe …. When I was talking to the boy, I felt …" He shook himself. Squared his shoulders.

"I'm not the sensitive type," he said. "So maybe I missed something."

Tanya gave him a gentle smile. "Not sensitive, are we?" she said. Then, low, "I think otherwise, Davyd."

Davyd flushed, heat rising, feeling as if only he and Tanya existed.

Vlad made a discreet cough, shattering the moment. At first Davyd was irritated. The guy was butting into his game. Then he saw the confusion on Vlad's face and jealousy vanished. Davyd could tell that Vlad was as mystified by Tanya's effect on him as Davyd was.

Tanya said, "I don't know what's happening, here."

Her voice was anguished and the men looked at her and saw she was trembling. Her face was pale as she struggled with something within.

"Why don't we just … you know … let it be?" she said, almost pleading.

"Sure," Davyd said.

"Of course," Vlad said.

But as they spoke all three knew no one would just "let it be."

Davyd felt as if the three them had climbed onto a high-speed railed vehicle that was charging ferociously toward some dark destination.

Tanya recovered, straightening her uniform, back to business.

"So, are we agreed? This matter demands the fullest investigation, am I right?"

Both men nodded.

"Then the truce is extended?"

Davyd and Vlad exchanged glances.

"It's extended," Vlad said for both of them.

"Does that mean we'll work on this … together?" Tanya said. "That we can combine forces, so to speak?"

"Combined forces," Davyd nodded. "Best way to go."

"We'll have to consult our superiors, of course," Vlad put in.

"Naturally," Tanya said. "I've got my bosses too. Beats the hell out of me how I'll explain it. But I'll think of something. I always do."

She grinned wide. "Meanwhile," she said, "peace?"

"Yes, peace," Vlad said.

Davyd shrugged. "Never tried it before, but what the hell, peace it is!"

"One thing," Tanya said. "Can you two give me any hint at all about yourselves? So I can explain it to my bosses, you understand."

"We're sin eaters," Davyd said.

"Sin eaters?" Tanya puzzled. "I don't understand."

"A long time ago," Davyd said, "when a guy died, his family and friends would prepare a big funeral feast. All the goodies they could afford were set out on a table. The food represented the sins of the dead guy.

"Then they'd hire a Sin Eater who'd sit down at the table and eat all the food. Consuming the guy's sins along with the feast. Taking them on his own soul.

"That's what Vlad and I do. Take on the sins of the galaxy so the innocent don't have to suffer."

Davyd looked at Vlad. "Close enough?" he asked.

"Sin eater," Vlad said thoughtfully. Then he smiled. "Yes, that would describe it exactly."

Tanya stared at them. What had she gotten herself into?

She said, "After we've talked to our bosses we'll need to set up a way of contacting to each other."

"Never fear, my Tanya," Vlad said. "At the appropriate time, we'll find you."

"We're experts at that sort of thing," Davyd added. "It goes with sin eating."

*　*　*

Kriegworm remained cowering on the deck long after his master withdrew. He found his Rolex and absently picked it up and examined the broken band.

It would be easy to fix. If only the mess he was in could be so easily attended to.

But it was plain that his orders were impossible to carry out.

Well … perhaps they were possible, but if he acted as commanded Kriegworm was doomed. They'd catch him. That was certain.

Once he acted he would not escape the dogs put on him by the United World Police. The thought that hurt him most was that his action would be a betrayal of the organization he was so proud to be a member of.

Kriegworm hated all softskins, just like any normal fiend. But when he wore the suit that was his UWP uniform, gold Rolex strapped about his wrist, he almost felt like a softskin himself. And that made him feel sinfully good.

He suspected his master knew this shameful secret, which made Kriegworm even more vulnerable.

The fiend thumped his head on the floor, crying aloud, "What shall I do? What shall I do?"

Then light dawned and his weeping ceased. There was a way to accomplish what had been commanded with no danger to himself. He scrambled upright, laughing gleefully.

His mission was to kill Tanya Lawson.

And he knew just the person to do it.

CHAPTER TWENTY NINE

It was once again the same hall and the same light and the grim man in the leather vest was once again in his place before the fire.

If some poor softskin had dared enter this room he'd soon have learned to his infinite horror that this was no man, but the fiend — Infeligo — in mortal disguise.

Like his seven colleagues — the members of the fiendish Council Of Eight — Infeligo was more deadly, and certainly more evil, than any mere human could imagine.

But at the moment all was not well with the noble Infeligo. Although his movements might easily be mistaken as leisurely, even peaceful, his inner turmoil was revealed by the shaking firebrand in his hand as lifted it to light his pipe.

When Infeligo's face was momentarily lit by the pipe's soft flow, his wrinkles looked like deep, bottomless crevices.

A nasty voice hissed from behind him. "Shizdetcs, as Auerkhan's Rooskies used to say, isn't it, noble Infeligo?"

Once again it was the scoffer, Mamri. But his mockery lacked the strength it had held before. He too was deeply troubled. Mamri took a seat next to his colleague.

"Thou bug in the rug," grumbled Infeligo. "What's going on? What happened to thy marvelous —" he almost sang it "— to thy marvelous suit?"

Mamri was in a full Japanese commando's field uniform — but it was disheveled and marked by several burned holes. The old fiend's face was covered with a web of green, orange and purple lines, signs of the decadent spells he was wont to cast for his dark pleasures.

"This is not a really good time for joking," Mamri snapped. "Heavens and Hells, Infeligo, I think we're all in a big rusty pod in the very middle of the storm. Time to declare peace and to cease fire. We both have returned from perilous journeys, have we not? I'm sure we both have a lot to tell.

"Why should we sit here in our main hall, tossing insulting jokes at one another? We must not be fools, Infeligo, if we still want to live and to rule."

"Such a noble thing!" grinned Infeligo.

However, his grin was rather pale, as if he were preserving hope that ill tidings were his own self torment and his colleagues might have something more optimistic to report.

"Good thoughts are coming to good heads simultaneously, aren't they?" he said. "Well, Mamri, a bargain, right? Thy news for mine. Some small exchange, before all our friends have arrived. Our sweethearts, Auerkhan and Pilyardock, thou knowest ..."

After a long hesitation, Mamri nodded agreement. "The Green Hordes are uneasy," he said.

"Art thou sure, Mamri?" Infeligo asked. "Do they really plan to overcome the softskin outposts on the Border?"

Mamri's thin mouth jerked. "They had good practice with me!" he said, indicating the burned holes in his costume.

Infeligo sniffed the air, then caught the magical scent of the ice lightning the wild demons used when defending their borders at the edge of the galaxy. One cheek twitched in alarm.

Mamri caught his reaction and grimaced. "Yea, noble Infeligo. The Green Hordes, the Flesh Eaters, the Bone Shadows, the Gliding Crushers ..."

"Do the wild fiends plan an invasion?" Infeligo asked, astounded.

"No doubt," Mamri sighed.

"But they don't have a chance!" Infeligo said. "The softskin mages ..."

"Will be busy tearing one another in pieces!" Mamri broke in with a snarl.

Infeligo lapsed into silence, thinking dark thoughts. Then: "Art thou quite certain thy information is correct, noble Mamri?"

"Correct?!" exploded Mamri. "How darest thou doubt my word!"

"Easy, my noble colleague, easy please," Infeligo said, making a wry face. "I do not doubt a single word. The Amers and Rooskies are overcome by thoughts of war. Arms clashing, reserves called up, hasty graduations at all the military-mage universities. And much more."

"It seems that all our brave warriors art nothing but dull handsuckers," Mamri growled.

Then he calmed himself, hoping against hope that Infeligo had better news to report.

"Perhaps there is still time to stop this foolishness," he said. "Tell me, what news of our much vaunted investigation, my noble friend? And what of the famous Major Lawson? What is happening with her? Is there any word on the Mageweb?"

Infeligo shook his head. "The Mageweb is filled with hysteria," he said. "Everyone is speculating on *what* Lawson is saying to her superiors. But not one reliable scrap of information has been revealed. The UWP security is so tight, I doubt even the Amer president or the Rooskie monarch has clearance."

Mamri was stunned. "Doest thou claim that not even *we* know the truth?" he wailed. "How can that be?! Never in a thousand years have we —"

"Sorry to interrupt you, gentlemen," came a third voice. Jolted, the two demons whirled about to see Apollion. Apparently the formal chieftain of the Council had abandoned his old habit of arriving late, surprising them both.

"I've only caught the last words, noble ones," he said. "And Mamri is quite right in his concerns. But I'll speak about that a bit later."

Mamri and Infeligo looked at one another with real fear.

*   *   *

The members of the Council were listening to Apollion's report in dead silence.

"...Thus, noble colleagues," Apollion was saying, "we still have a great lack of information. What we have received from Auerkhan's and Pilyardock's scouts amounts to nothing but wild charges with nothing to support them.

"At the same time the situation between the Amers and Rooskies grows more difficult as each e-day passes.

"Thy Amer wards, Pilyardock, are screaming for revenge. And thy Rooskies, Auerkhan, are like stupid and stubborn cattle, claiming about 'Amer provocation' and so on.

"I fear we've lost any control of the crisis, noble ones, and if we do not act soon we may permanently lose our rule over all the softskins. And the donations that have fed us and made our lives so pleasant for a thousand years will cease to pour in!

"What art thy Odysseus Corps doing, noble Pilyardock? And thy Church of the Sword, Auerkhan? What art thy infamous assassins doing?

"Despite the peril we are in, both of you have refused to allow your assassins to declare a truce so they can join forces with Major Lawson to get to the bottom of this most unfortunate incident.

"I personally intervened, but both of you continue to fight me most bitterly about this wise proposal. I can't understand why such noble ones are making things so difficult for us all?"

Pilyardock and Auerkhan said nothing, but only glowered at one other with intense hatred.

Apollion sighed, then turned to the others. "Gentlemen," he said, "Somehow we must block this war. But in doing so we must not reveal our existence to the softskins. That is of the utmost importance, as you all know."

There was a deep and gloomy silence as the last words sunk in.

Then Infeligo spoke up. "Could we not we cast a Great Spell?" he asked. "Such as the one we used in the Old Days, when the feasting on the softskins began?"

"Impossible," Simionte objected. "The hatred between the Amers and Rooskies is too hot for even us to overcome."

Pilyardock turned an evil glance on Auerkhan. "Doest thou see what thou hast done?" he growled. "One missile shot and now all is imperiled!"

The Fiendish Keeper of the Russians looked at the Keeper of the Americans through narrowed eyes.

"Thou art a flaming liar, noble Pilyardock," he said.

He turned to the others at the table "And that Amer bitch whom my noble colleagues have praised so highly is nothing but an Odysseus whore. She'll say whatever our noble Pilyardock requires."

"Shut up!" Apollion roared. "Enough of this foolish talk. Noble Pilyardock, do not answer! Noble Auerkhan, take back thy words. We all understand they were said in rage and cannot be taken seriously."

Then, to the entire gathering, he said, "Gentlemen, I intend to exterminate all disagreement in the womb. Yes, we have a serious problem with this Amer-Rooskie crisis. But is that all? Is it, noble ones?

"We have heard the reports of noble Mamri and the no less noble Infeligo. What means that stirring across the softskins' border? What means that tremendous shadow above Lawson and her reports?

"Noble Sir Pilyardock! Can thy Amer lads create anything like this?"

"No," sneered Pilyardock. "I hath no doubt this is from my dearest friend, the noble gentleman Auerk …"

"Please desist, noble Sir Pilyardock," Apollion broke in, speaking softly.

But it was a silky softness hinting of many dread things and it brought a dead silence into the hall. Apollion looked into Pilyardock's face and his eyes were like an old owl's contemplating a tasty mouse.

Pilyardock gulped. "I beg thy pardon, colleagues," he murmured.

"Thank thee, noble one," Apollion said.

Then he scanned the faces of his colleagues. "Let's start from the very beginning. Noble Sir Mamri?"

"The noble Apollion is quite correct, gentlemen," Mamri said. "More things are stirring than just this impending war. As was said, I've wandered far beyond the uttermost human outposts.

"I've received distress signals from my watchers in the Fiendish Wilderness. I've crossed the Human Continuum and then over the Great Fracture — through the Inner Hell and other conquered dominions …"

"What doest thou want us to do to repay thee for all this travel?" Syrr said sarcastically. "We know these places well. Do not tire us with a lengthy list. What we want to know is what thou didst see!"

"I saw nothing," answered Mamri coldly, but rather calmly. "But I heard much. And it was all ill tidings, noble Syrr. Those long-enslaved creatures, — whom thou art smashing into dust without notice — were whispering about the Wild Hordes, moving from spell-conquered but uncharted regions near to the softskin's outposts."

Syrr laughed. It was a ghastly sound. "And thou believed those weaklings?"

Mamri shrugged. "I always believe dark news, my noble friend. For Truth always hides in Evil shadows."

He turned to the others. "Am I right, noble sires?" he asked sardonically.

No one answered.

Mamri grinned. "I thought as much," he said. Then he continued his tale. "After that, I crossed the Inner and the Outer Hells and I passed over The Eight Circles. In Limbo and Kocyte the rumors became more detailed.

"It was said that the Green Hordes ripped down the collapsed globules of their space and, so to say, raised the war-banners. I've met the Flesh Eaters, the Gliding Crushers and the Bone Shadows myself."

He indicated his burned clothing. "The result thou canst all see, noble sires. I daresay — this means a greater war than even that between the Amers and Rooskies!

"A fiendish uprising, to tell the truth."

Simionte clenched his huge fists. "Fools!" he roared. "Damned fools! How much blood and death — and no donations of mortal souls to the Council's storehouses! And with such a great lack of souls, we would be threatened with starvation and the loss of our powers."

Pilyardock nodded. "Well reasoned, noble sir."

Auerkhan broke in. "But for what reason?" he demanded. "These wild fiends cannot win."

"Maybe they believe they can," said Apollion, removing his spectacles to polish them. "Or maybe they were assured by someone that they can."

"Treason!" Infeligo hissed.

Then, glaring at Mamri all the while, he said, "I daresay, noble ones — there is treason and there is a traitor sitting here among us!"

Mamri turned pale. "Art thou blaming anyone in particular, noble Infeligo?" he demanded.

"Easy, gentleman, easy," Apollion, cautioned. "Noble sir Infeligo, I beg thee — there's no need for harsh words. Noble Mamri has passed through real peril, even to a person of his stature, might and chivalry. Look at the signs on his face. It was combat, wasn't it?"

"Oh yes," Mamri replied with a grim smile. "Of course, they did not recognize me. I was disguised as a human warrior-mage. They attacked immediately and without hesitation. I cast down several of the most outraged. And then delineated as if I'd fled in panic.

"I remained in the region as long as possible — the Green Hordes have a rather good flair for real Power. All Boiling Planes art moving, gentleman. And it seems to me that they art all crazy with lust for revenge.

"Let's agree, gentlemen, that if anyone really was standing behind all this tumult, he has chosen a damned good moment. Isn't it strange, noble colleagues? And who in the whole Universe could create such a plot?"

Mamri stopped for a moment, then gave a long sigh. "Alas, but I must agree with noble sir Infeligo," he said reluctantly. "There is treason inside our council. But I cannot understand the aim of such a conspiracy."

"All of us thank thee for thy bravery in bringing us this news, noble Mamri," Apollion said.

Then he scanned the faces of the others, letting a long silence build.

Finally he said, "Gentlemen, I suggest we do not discuss this possibility of treason just now. More things must be learned before we can hurl such accusations.

"Now, let us listen closely to the noble Infeligo. Thy main conclusion, colleague, please!"

"My main conclusion ..." Infeligo grumbled. "Yes, yes, my main conclusion."

His eyes were flickering red, but he mastered himself with an effort.

"I've met some Force or Power hiding a large part of Major Lawson's information. I played several roles, but all ways were blocked.

"Also, I've seen great war preparations in both the Amer and Rooskie sectors, noble sirs. I had considered proposing a mass simultaneous strike on all their war installations ... but the result would destroy our reign over the softskins as well.

"Meanwhile, as you all know, a full scale war may soon break out that would accomplish the same thing — and, as you said, my noble friend, that would leave us starving for lack of donations from the softskins.

"Moreover, I've noticed dangerous signs of irreversible mass hyperhysteria. For our own purposes, we have kept the Amers and Rooskies on the very edge of war for a thousand years. From the time when we cast the Great Spell, with the assistance of the Planetar Demon, curse his soul!

"How else can we rule these softskins or our cousin fiends? How else can we feed? However, now that a real war threatens between the softskin empires, there seems to be little we can do to stop them.

"Unless … unless …"

"Unless what, noble one?" Apollion urged. "Tell us thy thinking."

"To say more, I fear I must return to the subject of the traitor," Infeligo said. "If such a bastard exists among us, we must find him and make him eat his own shit!

"Either that, or we must go to the arsenal and cast another Great Spell. To do so would likely reveal our presence to the human wizards. If that happens we would find ourselves contending with a revolt from both the mortal *and* the fiendish worlds!"

Infeligo wiped his brow. "Sorry, noble sirs," he said, "but what other options do we have? I daresay, none, gentlemen."

"Easy to say, noble sir Infeligo, but hard to do," Syrr replied. "How can we reveal that mysterious plot, assuming it even exists? We are short of time. In fact, we have no time."

He took a breath and then said, "But, gentlemen, what if we create not a war-smashing Spell, but one aimed at mass information? At brainwashing? What if we make both sides think this incident with the *HolidayOne* was an unfortunate accident, no matter if it was or not?"

"That would be a grave error!" Auerkhan protested. "Believe me, noble Syrr, I am a master of information-bending chants. Brainwashing spells are my specialty. But thou must keep such spells small so the softskin mages aren't alerted. A Great Brainwashing Spell is simply too dangerous for us to attempt. Why, we would have to blanket the whole galaxy!"

"Noble Sir Infeligo is right," Apollion said, polishing his glasses. "The risk is too high."

"But what else can we do?" Syrr demanded. "Either we risk exposure by using one of the Great Spells from our Armory, or sit and watch the self-destruction of our dominion!"

"Even the most terrible war between Rooskies and Amers will leave *something* left," Simionte pointed out. "For example, we have my far dominions …"

"Thank thee, noble Simionte," Apollion said a little coldly, dismissing this idea. "If the situation requires it, we'll be forced to fall back on other resources.

"However, the Head of this council has not forgotten the bitter fighting in past over those same resources. We must look forward, not back.

"Unfortunately, this means we now must examine the idea of finding the true villain behind these incidents. The *HolidayOne* incident and the rising of the Green Hordes at the same time could not be a coincidence. And so, gentlemen, I ask you what we should do to end this crisis?"

"Good rhetorical question," Simionte boomed angrily. "May Hell save us, our noble sire Apollion is once again on his favorite steed. Go on, chairman, tell us more! What art we to do, at last?"

"First," said Apollion calmly and coldly, "we must stop the Green Demons. Second, we must advance our most powerful pawns to soften the sound of the war drums. This will give us some time to seek out the villain.

"Moreover, to do this we must grant the request of our Odysseus Corp and Church Of The Sword pawns to forge a temporary truce and join forces with Major Lawson."

He glared at the two Keepers of the Americans and Russians, saying, "Is that clear, noble sirs Auerkhan and Pilyardock?"

"And I warn you both, if you do not agree, I fear the Council surely will vote to excommunicate he who refuses. I will call upon the ancient Runes to do so. Even if this Chant shakes the Human Universe and the whole Continuum."

As the two fiends quaked at these words, he turned to the others.

"I have spoken, gentlemen," he said. "Now it is your turn to choose. You can even vote to excommunicate me, if you decide my actions to be extremely irritating."

Suddenly, he grinned, letting his power radiate over them all.

A great silence crept into the hall. Even Auerkhan and Pilyardock stopped exchanging looks of hatred.

Apollion nodded. "Good," he said. "We progress. Now, to the Green Hordes. We must send scouts to their domain. Do you remember, gentlemen, the magical artifact that was stolen by the runaway demon? Thy man, noble sir Auerkhan, recovered part of it.

"Now I'm sure there must be a connection with this artifact and what is happening among the Green Hordes. To find this connection our scouts must search the very edge of the Continuum.

"It is time for strong action, gentlemen! Time to let our Force flow!"

He looked about the hall. "Does anyone object?"

Silence.

"Excellent!"

"Now, my last proposal. We must send someone to talk with Old Scratch. The Engine Devil, according to Vlad Projogin's report, noticed something strange during the *HolidayOne* incident. We must understand the nature of this 'strangeness.' It may lead us to the villain — the traitor among us — who is causing all these things.

"Now, who among us should go to the *Borodino*? The candidates for this mission, alas, must exclude two of us. I dislike this solution, for it tastes of unfairness.

"However, the noble sires Auerkhan and Pilyardock must logically agree that it would be unseemly for them to participate — for reasons elementary enough not to be presented here."

"I will go," Infeligo growled.

"I am also willing," Mamri said.

Syrr and Simionte also demanded that one of them be chosen to interrogate Old Scratch.

Auerkhan grinned. "Thou art presented with The Dilemma of Choice, noble sire Apollion," he said.

"What? Oh yes, dear colleague," Apollion replied sarcastically.

"Thank thee for pointing that out to me. The Dilemma of Choice in the unwieldy number we have been blessed with in this Council Of Eight. Not a good choice, I'd say … but better than nothing."

He turned to Auerkhan and Pilyardock, saying, "The Dilemma Of Choice means only the three of us together can determine who shall be chosen. So let us test Fate, gentleman. And see who shall go."

Apollion drew his magical knife — a long silver dagger — and the other two did the same.

"Time to earn our pay, noble ones," Apollion said.

And immediately the three knives glowed hotly, piercing the gloom.

Three spurs of flaming red rushed over the table, crossing, seething, sparkling.

The three streams of fire met in the very middle and a burning fountain rushed into the air, then shattered into red snow drifting downward.

"The fate is mine," Infeligo boomed.

A red crystal burned on his forehead.

"I will not say thou art lucky, my friend," Mamri murmured.

And for a change he was not making a sarcastic jest at Infeligo's expense.

CHAPTER THIRTY

The light was dying. Caught in a net of heavy gravitation, it was doomed to circle the dark center before being completely swallowed by an immense Naught. It was shapeless, sizeless, colorless. There was only pure power.

And — hatred.

A tiny spirit, riding on the head of a lightwave, looked in fear and despair at the impending doom. Born in the overheated depths of a star, he had flown billions of miles, had passed countless stars and planets, had seen the domains of both the softskins and their fiendish slaves.

And now he was in a trap. Where this trap was, he could not say. Everywhere — and nowhere. It looked like a black hole, yet it was not the grim corpse of a dying star. It was far, far more fearful.

The spirit knew that even in the grips of a collapsar there should have been hope for him. The vacuum of a collapsar was a great sleeping beast, pregnant with countless Beings.

Heavy grav made the collapsar produce particles and over much time these particles might have escaped.

The spirit, who was essentially immortal, would have had an infinite amount of time to wait his chance to escape aboard one of those particles

But this great Naught he approached would never allow such an escape. For here was the Lair of The Final Death that could not even be overpowered by the Horns of Judgment Day.

Finally, the little spirit gave up his hopeless struggle. Hypnotized, he looked into a yawning blackness that contained no stars, planets or voids.

He wept. What else could he do?

For the great power lurking in the spacefolds was merciless. A myriad of LightSpirits had vanished in its ever-hungry maw. And once consumed, there was no way out.

The poor spirit raised his head. Above him the gates of gravitational collapse were closing in. Soon, he would learn what it meant to die. He bowed his head and closed his eyes.

His only hope was that the end would be swift and painless.

*　*　*

Immense muscles moved slowly in the warm darkness. The Planetar Demon, which possessed wings, could move where it willed without them.

If the spirit had lived and had dared approach the Planetar Demon, he might have asked why he kept the wings if they were of so little use to him.

And the Demon, had he chosen to answer, would have said it was because he liked to have a mortal reminder that the things he loved to kill suffered pain — and death.

The Planetar Demon thought all was quite right as far as he could see — which was very far, indeed.

He'd set the trap for the Council Of Eight and they'd swallowed the ledger-bait. However, a final stroke was still required before his plan was complete. And then there would be a fierce howling, biting and tearing.

Easy work.

Thinking about it, he wondered: Why have I delayed it for so long?

Promises were made by the Council Of Eight, when he'd added his power to theirs to cast the Great Spell. Which had changed the course of softskin and fiendish history forever.

But those promises had never been kept. They'd fed well and fully. While he'd been tossed off to an empty place, a hungry place, at the very edge of the Galaxy.

A few million souls had been presented to him now and then to appease his hunger. Meanwhile, the Council Of Eight had grown fat on the souls of billions!

Patience, they'd always said. Be patient while we organize the realm. And soon offerings will be poured out to thee in such quantities that thou wilt be satisfied throughout eternity.

I have been patient long enough, the Planetar Demon thought. I have granted more than enough time to the miserable fiendish scum who compose the Council Of Eight.

I am hungry. I must eat, or soon I will have not have enough power to press my cause.

And then he thought it must be the Council Of Eight's desire to reduce him to such a weakened state that he could not forcefully oppose them.

This conclusion, which he'd come to slowly, was quite correct.

They have played me like a cosmic fool, he thought.

His hate was deep. His hate was intense. And it had gradually broadened to include all softskin and fiendish kind.

But he'd come to hate the softskins most of all.

They've missed all my warnings, he thought. Drunk with their lives, they'd came under the rule of those pompous wretches who've named themselves The Council of the Eight.

They present the COE with plenty and deny me my rightful feeding. Hah!

As I weave the doom of hate for all beingkind, I'll deal with those greedy wretches on the COE as well.

Now to the plan. The most recent reports the Planetar Demon had monitored were filled with panic. Those fools — even the best of them — were weak, weak, weak, possessing only empty hearts.

However, there were signs of trouble from those three raindrops of organic slime with the softskin names of Davyd, Tanya and Vlad.

They had uncovered too much.

Even so, the Planetar Demon considered their efforts as pitiful as the plans currently being hatched by their secret masters — The Council of Eight.

This only made him angrier. How dare any of them think they could withstand him?!

But to be prudent — and the Planetar Demon was a master of prudence — it was time for him to proceed to the second stage.

The forces were already moving. Good! The humans were primed to destroy themselves. The Council Of Eight's pet armies were in full readiness. Their toy magicians were hastily chanting the most dreadful spells.

That was also good.

The softskin and fiendish races were cowering beneath a great mountain of doom. A small final effort would bring down the avalanche upon them. Billions would be slain.

Well, that was the price that must be paid to remove the Council Of Eight and put himself in direct charge.

Then all the donations of spirit and flesh would flow to him and him alone.

To work, the Planetar Demon thought.

Far away — at the borders of common space where time floated lazily and the inhabited planets obediently rotated around their stars — unseen legions started moving at his command.

Despite all his power, ancient rules required that the Planetar Demon could not act alone. He had to operate through other creatures but this was no difficulty because his influence was vast.

Hiding in the deepest folds of space, a myriad of the great creature's slaves rushed to a distant yellow star.

Their target, all green and blue in the common spectrums, was the planet in the third orbit about the yellow star.

Shapeless and invisible, like their terrible Master, the creatures approached the first guarding circle.

Frightened, the fiends in the warheads and the missile control consoles let them pass without dispute.

The fiends penetrated the upper surface of the atmosphere and the dwellers of the thin air layers spurted away, blinded by tremendous fear and panic.

Lower, lower was their course. They pierced the clouds and saw the ground not far below. But its beauty remained hidden from their empty eyes.

The fiends smelled their target and felt the evil glowing above it — the angry red glower of armies in wait.

And this was the end of their long road.

All those installations filled with softskins and their fiendish slaves. Along with their dull machinery and weak magic.

The watch dogs howled in fear when the legion from the sky reached the ground, but the Planetar Demon's messengers silenced them with little difficulty.

The Earth's stratums were also not a barrier to them. Deeper and deeper they were penetrated, approaching the planet's hot core.

Then they suddenly stopped, obeying the voice of their Master.

There, far under the earth — near the tensed stone strings of the plain — they stayed. Gnawing and gnashing the firm rock.

Transforming the flame rivers of hot magma in the uttermost depths of the Earth.

Waiting for the Call.

And it was a dead night on the ground.

CHAPTER THIRTY ONE

"Give a man who is not made
To his trade
Swords to fling and catch again,
Coins to ring and snatch again,
Men to harm and cure again,
Snakes to charm and lure again —
He'll be hurt by his own blade ..."

From *Kim*, by Rudyard Kipling

Old Scratch was in the deepest of depressions — so miserable he could hardly muster strength enough to swear.

Nothing consoled him, not even Homula the great mother of the death spirits. Her charges danced and sang in the flames of the *Borodino's* Fiendish Hall, beseeching Scratchy to join them in the soothing fires of the Inner Hell.

But all he could think of was Uttermost Space, the shimmer of uncounted stars and hard x-ray storms and the voices of distant friends he longed to hear again. And the engine spells, ah the spells — the "spells-spells-spells movin' up an' down again!"

Old Scratchy despaired that they'd ever let him leave this awful place, where the war devils danced and sang their songs of blood and terror. That he'd ever be permitted to once again ply his honest trade as an Engine Devil, guiding great starships to distant ports. Or any of the other wondrous things that were the very sense of an Engine Devil's life.

Even Kipling offered small comfort. In Scratchy's depression the only poems he could think of were dark compositions. Like the one about the "man who is not made to his trade and ..."

"He'll be hurt by his own blade,
By his serpents disobeyed,
By his clumsiness betrayed,
By the people mocked to scorn —
So 'tis not with juggler born.
Pinch of dust or withered flower,
Chance-flung fruit or borrowed staff,
Serve his need and shore his power,
Bind the spell, or loose the laugh!"

It seemed to Scratchy that he was doomed to remain in this place forever. No more to see the stars, much less dear Avalon.

Although everyone agreed he was innocent, he'd become convinced they'd never let him go. Each time he'd raised the issue of leaving, excuses were made.

By the fires of all the burning levels of Hell, the masters of the *Borodino* were the greatest manufacturers of lying excuses Scratch had ever met!

And now the boy was constantly on his mind ... nay, *in his mind*!

Sending stream upon pleading mentos' stream to come away with him.

Waugh! Billy was a most powerful young mage, "speaking" to Old Scratch from a guarded hospital room somewhere aboard the Russian space fortress.

He'd grown quite fond of Billy, giving him the nickname of "Little Friend of the World," which was from Scratch's favorite Kipling book.

Even now the boy was whispering from afar, saying, "We have to get out of here, Scratchy! We must escape! They're not gonna to let us go!"

"But, how, Little Friend of the World?" the Engine Devil asked. "How can we escape? They have us in their power! Waugh! Hast thou seen the mage, Carvaserin? Who could escape *his* clutches?"

"Sure, I've seen him," Billy said, his mentos *voice* sounding unimpressed. "So what? I call him Danny just to make him mad!"

"Oh, thou must be careful, Little Friend of the World!" Scratch said, although he couldn't help a grin at the child's boldness.

"Master Carvaserin comes from a family of mighty wizards! And that is very rare, indeed. Why his brother, the Master Brand Carvaserin, is known as a wizard above all wizards!

"Even now, I am told, this Brand Carvaserin rules the weapons' mages in a mighty Russian fortress set on old Earth itself!"

"Oh, they're big shots, all right," Billy said scornfully. "Old Danny is always bragging about that. But that's even better, don't you see? We're not important enough for guys like that.

"Once we're gone, they'll look around some, then forget about us because they have so many other things to do. Big shot stuff for big shot mages!"

Scratch thought of the grim-faced wizard and couldn't help shuddering. "He'll be angry!" he said. "He'll grind poor Scratchy's old bones to dust!"

"Never mind him!" Billy said, mentos so strong it was almost a shout. "There's *something* worse. Can't you feel it, Scratchy? Something really bad is gonna happen!"

Cold dread raced up and down Old Scratch's spine: the foreboding that kept creeping in of late, making his big devil's heart twitch in fear.

"Yes, Little Friend of the World," Scratch admitted. "I can feel it!"

"Somebody's coming to see us, Scratch!" the boy said. "He's big and he's mean and he's thinking about us a lot. I don't like that! I don't like how he's thinking!"

Scratch shuddered. Now that the boy mentioned it, he could see the shape of his enemy more clearly: a huge black cloud, all shot with lightning, sweeping through Uttermost Space.

He had a sudden vision of a cruel-visaged creature with a blood-red crystal on his forehead. The creature was coming for him and Billy! This dark truth burned in Old Scratch's chest with hot certainty.

"How do we flee, O Little Friend of the World?" he asked. "Hast thou pondered this weighty matter?"

"We did it before, Scratchy!" Billy said, mentos sparking with hope. "We got off the *HolidayOne*, didn't we? And damn if we can't do it again!"

Scratch thought, growing hot with excitement. Yes, it could be done! Especially if he and the young mage joined sorcerous forces!

"There's only one thing wrong," Billy broke in, worry creeping in now that he could sense Scratch was on his side.

"I don't know where to go. Or where we can hide. It's easy for you, Scratchy. You're an Engine Devil. Now, that's really something! You can make starships go.

"But I can't do anything. I'm just a kid. And a half-breed bastard to boot!"

"Do not call dishonor on thy blood, Little Friend of the World," Scratch said. "The stars shine brighter because of thee. This is the only way to think of thy life."

"But where can we hide, Scratchy?" the boy pleaded. "Do you know of a place?"

Old Scratch picked at a thick talon, pondering. This was indeed a question of much difficulty. One worthy of several pots of fiery punch, like they served at the favorite inn of Engine Devil's Local 666.

An honest devil could think at that inn, fumes and flame rising all around. Yes, if only he were in …

"I know of just such a place, Little Friend of the World," he said suddenly, cares falling away and hope glowing in his chest.

"A place where we can be safe among friends for a time. Wise friends, who can advise us."

"Where is it, Scratchy?" Billy asked, mentos images bright and full of happiness. "What's the name of this place?"

"Ah, but it bears a name above all names, Little Friend of the World," Scratch replied.

"'Tis in a place known to me as … Avalon!"

CHAPTER THIRTY TWO

"The dogs are still uneasy, sir," the young Russian soldier said to his sergeant, a massively built veteran with a permanent frown hammered into his features by foolish young men making foolish statements.

"So what, private?" came the angry reply. "Do you think you can trouble me because of that? Shit on your uneasy dogs! It's two hours before dawn and I've enough work left to do without wasting my time on whining arse lickers."

"Yes, sir! But, sir ..."

"Still here, lad? Put yourself on report so I can remember to kick your ass when I have more time."

"Sir," the soldier pleaded with true despair. "Sir, the Manual ..."

"Manual, manual ... thrust it up your ass. There's no manual at this god-forsaken hour! Put yourself on report twice, so I can kick your ass twice. Now, off with you, private!"

The unhappy young soldier, whose name was Gregor, exited the door of the guardroom. The chewing out he'd received from the sergeant was of little consequence to him. He was too worried about his dogs, by damn!

As a dog master he only cared about his four-legged charges. And they'd been decidedly unhappy for some hours, although they hadn't given him a hint about what was bothering them.

He was especially worried about his personal charge — the great Alsatian he'd been partnered with since his training. Gregor called him "Fang" after one of the dogs in Jack London's books. And Fang had been acting up ever since they entered the guard shack.

Gregor sighed. Well, no more of that. Like the sergeant, he had other duties to attend to before his long shift was done.

At the moment, it was his job to join the patrol of the inner rim of the razor wire fence that surrounded the military installation.

As bases went, this was one of the most important in the entire Russian empire. It was the home of the very best airborne troops: Twelve Red-Banner Kenigsberg-Pskov Airborne Guards Divisions — fourteen thousand men in all; approximately twenty thousand fiends in war machines; special strike airwings with MiG-229 and Su-327 heavy tactical fighters; plus a whole battalion of anti-ballistic missile batteries.

The enormous base was laid out in a strategic circle of Anti-Rocket Defense around Old Moscow. Besides the troops and other defenses, it was also the home of many powerful war-mages and wizards of all classes and ranks.

Most of the mages and many of the higher ranking soldiers had their families living with them. This was to provide stability in an atmosphere that was always burning with many emergencies.

The young soldier and his dog, of course, didn't know — nor would they have found it remarkable — that among the wizards residing on the base was Brand Carvaserin, brother of Daniel Carvaserin, chief mage of the *Borodino*.

Brand's family lived on the base with him and it was the duty of the soldiers to guard his family at all costs, just as they were charged to protect the wizard.

That was the law.

Gregor strode slowly along the guard-path. As they patrolled, Fang crowded close to his master's right leg, whimpering dolefully. The dog was really frightened, but without any reason the soldier could see.

The night was warm and calm. The sky, deep, clear and covered with innumerable stars. The Milky Way … Orion … the Great Bear …

A dismal chorus of howls from many dog-throats burst up from the distance. Despite all the magical security systems woven about the base, dogs were still one of the best instruments. There were hundreds of them assigned to all the main bases.

"Easy, Fang, easy," the young soldier tapped his comrade slightly. "What's wrong, pal?"

Two big brown eyes looked at the human with terrifying anguish. Fang whined softly, jumped and licked Gregor's cheek.

This was considered "unsuitable" behavior for a war-dog, according to the young soldier's instructors. And Gregor hadn't witnessed it since Fang's puppy days.

"Goodness …" Gregor whispered.

He seized his friend by his thick ruff, pulling him close. The dog was trembling, his ears were pressed close to his head and the fur all along his spine was stiff with alarm.

Then he began howling again, a howl filled with untold despair and fear — becoming louder and louder.

* * *

Young Gregor, along with his woolly-minded praporshick (sergeant) and many others — airborne commandos, pilots, junior mages, lesser fiends, techs, guards and cooks — knew nothing about the true purpose of the base.

Beneath all the barracks and laboratories, beneath the armories and fiends' dungeons, beneath the command center, there was a level that contained the most terrifying secrets.

The entrance was thoroughly camouflaged by both magical and physical means and was guarded by tongueless and eyeless DeathSpirits of an especially evil breed. Creatures filled with black malice, spiced with a terrible blood lust to kill. DeathSpirits of that nature could not be bribed or, if captured, interrogated with any chance of success.

The secret level was buried deep under ground — so deep that even the special corps of Tecktonic Wizards, specialists in searches for underground caverns, would not be able to find.

There were many things to hide.

Brand Carvaserin was among the exalted few who had clearance high enough to enter the facility. The wizard's face was grim as he passed the last post of human guards, striding forward, right into the immense darkness.

For three months he had been working here, in this top secret underground facility of magic. Along with several other Fifth-Class Wizards, he was creating a powerful series of magical weapons, never seen before, plus the all important means of delivery.

Good old spells that caused fires, floods, tornadoes, plague, mass madness, or epidemics of suicides had lost their effectiveness.

Effective counters to these spells had been created long ago and now both sides were working hard on new, super-destructive spells.

Day after day, night after night, the Russian wizards at the base labored over new monsters of magic, hiding their work in spell-bound containers.

They were charged with seeking "Something Really New," which had resulted in the name for the crash program: Project SRN.

And so it was — despite the lateness of the hour — that as the uneasy dogs plagued the young sentry, Brand Carvaserin was on already on his way to the lab.

The darkness surrounding him was thick, hot and sticky. There were no walls or floor in the passageway he moved through — the wizard floated on a pillowy force — like clouds in a child's dreams.

As he moved, streams of encapsulated power played around his fingers, which identified him to the silent guardians who watched the secret entrance to the laboratories and shops.

The Wizard was uneasy. Project SRN was still far from completion and might not be ready in time if Mother Russia had to fight the Amer bastards. And before he'd descended into the lab level he'd heard the howling dogs.

Brand hated dogs. Also cats, birds, beasts and other living creatures. His old master had told him long ago that this was the price of True Power.

However, Brand was not a fool. Something was wrong, he thought, as he passed the two gray globes that marked the facility's entrance.

Did it have something to do with the Amers? Would they dare attack?

No, Brand told himself after several seconds of thought. Bastards though they may be, the Amers were not suicidal maniacs. Major Lawson's investigation was still in progress. Before she announced her verdict the Amers would be forced to wait. Content to shout curses at the Russians.

However, we can shout back, Brand thought, and delay as long as possible until Project SRN is ready.

Therefore, whatever was bothering the dogs couldn't be the Amers.

But why were the damned animals howling?

Brand became so lost in thought over the matter that he almost forgot to show his clearances at the last check point.

Then the darkness was gone and Brand found himself in a tiny room with several lockers along the walls. He changed clothes.

A door led out of the area into the main facility. It was decorated with all the known runes that protected against evil. There was even a Christian Cross. Brand palmed a switch and the door hissed open.

There was a long corridor with many doors on both sides. Brand opened one of them.

"Privet, Brand. What's going on outside?"

An old man was standing before a long table covered with a thick slab of the best Italian marble. On the stone Brand saw several rat-sized black creatures scampering beneath a glowing web-curtain.

"Nothing special, Alex. Except I see that your experiment was successful. Congratulations."

"Thank you, sir," Brand's fellow wizard replied. "All parameters are stable. And the any up-scaling will only strengthen the spell, Brand."

"Excellent work," Brand said. "So the mimicking portion of the experiment is nearly complete. Pray for the same success in the warheads division, Alex, and our girl will be ready to dance at the ball."

Alex grinned evilly in his beard. "They'll love it," he said. "Fabulous monsters terrorizing the Amer cities. Diving from the Naught! Jamming all communications! Ripping the Amers apart body and soul! What a panic there's going to be. And then we ..."

"Shut up!" Brand Carvaserin commanded. "These things can't be discussed even here, you old ..."

Alex straightened. "So sorry, sir," he whined. "I was overwhelmed with joy. I'll never do it again! Please forgive me, sir!"

"Let it be," Brand said. Then: "Well, Alex, put your little ratty demons away and see what's wrong with the dogs outside. They are howling so much it's driving everyone mad. You are the Beast-Master, Alex. Prove your worth!"

"Yes, Brand, I'll attend to it immediately," the old wizard said. "The dogs are upset, you say? Interesting …"

Nodding absently as he thought about the possible causes, Alex swiftly exited the room.

Brand looked after him, considering. Despite his unpleasant nature, he was an excellent wizard. Swift in action and possessing a rich intuition. Something was really wrong! If asked, he would have taken an oath that he smelled danger.

And the odor was evil to the core — the rotting smell of total decay.

Brand shook off the feeling. It was nonsense, he decided. A feeling caused, no doubt, by the powerful magical waves given off by Project SRN.

Meanwhile, there was a mountain of work that needed his full attention. Brand straightened his shoulders and strode out of the room.

It was an error the whole Galaxy would soon regret.

CHAPTER THIRTY THREE

Tanya stared up at the stars winking through the transparent dome. She was floating on warm perfumed waters, with wisps of steam — tinted a rosy gold by hidden lights — flowing deliciously around her.

Although she was dressed in a retro-modest one-piece bathing suit, she felt a little naughty knowing two handsome men were watching her from opposite sides of the private grotto.

She smiled, thinking, this was *definitely* the way to do detective work!

Her old college girlfriends certainly wouldn't be shaking their heads at her choice of careers if they could see her now: basking in the waters of luxury, with not one, but *two!* good-looking men at her beck and call.

Plus it was all in the line of duty. Of course, it was quite unprofessional of her to be actually enjoying herself. But for crying out loud, she wasn't made of steel!

She was a normal woman, with normal thoughts and it had been a damned long time since she'd allowed herself *those* kind of feelings.

Tanya had blown a large part of her expense account on three connecting VIP suites at the *Library Of The Universe*, where she was ensconced with Davyd and Vlad trying to unravel the mystery of who was behind the attack on *HolidayOne*.

She supposed she ought to feel guilty wallowing in luxury while the whole galaxy teetered on the edge of war, but it wasn't her fault their hunt had taken them to such commodious surroundings.

Just as it wasn't her fault the three suites let into this splendid little warm-spring grotto where they could take their ease while busy servants of knowledge scurried about fetching the data they required to narrow their search.

A favorite vacation resort of wealthy literati, the *Library Of The Universe* boasted some of the finest hotel accommodations in the galaxy.

The library — which was really an entire artificial world — was the ultimate source of all information, past and present. And if you were really smart, even into the near future.

Set in orbit about Mars, the library was a vast above- and underground repository of electronic and magical databases. Even better were its millions of real books that could be swept into your presence with a single spoken command.

Much effort and several billion LT's had been lavished on the *Library Of The Universe*. It was a cultural paradise, with concert halls, nightclubs, galleries, theaters, restaurants and film palaces where history's best music, art, cuisine and stage and screen dramas were available around the clock in perfectly recreated settings.

Tanya and her two new colleagues had spent a week sampling these pleasures in between long brainstorming sessions which frequently ran into the small hours of the morning.

The grotto was the ideal cure for the exhaustion that typically overcame them after one of these sessions and they'd made a regular habit of visiting it. And the intimacy of their surroundings added greatly to the bonds that had begun to form since their first meeting.

After a week Tanya no longer needed the calming spell that kept Vlad and Davyd from each other's throats. Her mere presence seemed to accomplish the same thing.

She was acutely aware of them now. Each man drifting on his side of the pool, their attention on the woman between them. Eyes caressing the lush form that defied her costume's attempt at severity.

Tanya didn't have to wonder what they were thinking — *she was thinking the same thing*. Only it was very sweet and very lazy, with no feeling of pressure from either of the men to make a choice.

Even if that choice was not to choose at all.

Just then a comline buzzed and Tanya slipped over on her belly and swam to the edge of the grotto to answer.

Davyd studied her graceful motions appreciatively, delighted by the way her long golden hair trailed in the water like the tail of some mythical beauty of the deeps.

He turned his head and saw Vlad's gaze returning from the same path.

Their eyes met.

Both men smiled.

And Davyd thought, too bad I'll have to kill him when this is done.

And Vlad thought, if it weren't for my orders I might possibly allow this Amer to remain alive.

The men's smiles broadened.

Both of them looked over at Tanya who was talking to someone on the comline. Then their eyes swept back to meet once again.

The smiles were smaller … and sad.

And Davyd thought, when I kill him I'll have lost any chance with Tanya.

And Vlad thought, there *will* be no spoils for the victor. Tanya would hate the one left standing with a bloody knife.

And Davyd thought, Father Zorza gave me his orders. I *must* carry them out.

And Vlad thought, the Church Of The Sword *cannot* be denied. The greatest killer in Odysseus Corps could never be allowed to go free.

Meanwhile, Tanya was having difficulties of her own with an order giver.

"Listen, Harry," she said, "I can't help it if the brass made you the go-between. I know you didn't want anything to do with this mission. But they've tossed the ball back into your lap and you're just going to have to live with it."

Harry said, "Getting a little above ourselves, aren't we, Major!" His voice was harsh, underscoring the difference in their ranks.

Tanya didn't care. Although she was grateful Harry couldn't see the look of scorn on her face. The magical encryption web that shielded their conversation from any attempts at eavesdropping had taken a team of wizards many days to construct. However, only voices could be carried, not pictures.

Tanya kept to the firm high road in her response. "Look, Harry, the brass is going to do what the brass is going to do," she said.

"And they aren't going to listen to the complaints of a lowly major. I asked for a policeman's brain on this mission and they picked you."

The highest officials of the United Worlds Organization were mostly men and women with diplomatic backgrounds. But this was a police hunt Tanya was conducting. And she badly needed a ranking police official to cut through the red tape at United Worlds Police headquarters.

To her immense disgust, Harry was the only one she could turn to.

Her boss sighed the sigh of a long-suffering man who had been forced into a position where his future was on the line.

"All right, Tanya," he said. "What do you need?"

"Thanks, Harry, it's good to have you on my side," Tanya lied.

"Actually, my request is fairly simple. I just need somebody to put the whip to some bureaucratic bodies to retrieve some UWP reports for me."

"And those reports are?"

She read off six series of letters and numbers.

Harry whistled, the comline crackling from the shrillness of his surprise.

"I can see why you're having so much trouble," he said. "From the coding it's obvious they're all top-top secret!"

"Yeah, but there's no reason for them to be," Tanya said. "All six terrorist incidents were very public emergencies. Covered by the media in Galaxy-wide broadcasts.

"Yet the UWP reports on those incidents have been buried under enough secrecy seals to make a small, red mountain."

"What's to hide, then?" Harry asked.

"The eye-witness reports," Tanya said. "That's my suspicion, anyway. In each of these incidents the on-scene UWP investigators did extensive eye-witness interrogations.

"And I think somebody doesn't want anyone to give those reports a second glance."

There was a long silence. From experience Tanya knew that on the other side of the line Harry was having a heart attack.

No way did he want to go up against anyone with clout enough to bury evidence so deeply.

Finally, he said, "Exactly what do these … ah, incidents … have to do with your mission?"

Forgetting Harry couldn't see her, Tanya shrugged. "All six of them," she said, "have definite things in common with *HolidayOne*.

"First, they involved attacks on either Russian or American civilian facilities.

"In one case a biobomb was set off at the largest New Ukraine wheat-processing complex. Ten employees dead. Two hundred injured. The entire output of the plant poisoned.

"There was quite a panic, because in normal times about fifty million people depend on that plant to eat. Fortunately, the timing of the attack was off. Most of the harvest had already been processed.

"Even so, despite some pretty heavy-duty investigating the case remains unsolved to this day."

"I remember that case!" Now Harry sounded surprised. "It was five or six years ago. There was some backchannel grumbling from the Russians that they thought the Americans were to blame. Which we absolutely disproved. It a terrorist attack, no doubt about it. Although no particular group ever made any claims."

"Same thing with the other five, Harry," Tanya said. "For instance, two years ago an American spacemall was hit by a rather large meteor.

"Turned out the meteor was man-made and man-directed. The complex was destroyed. More poor timing by the bad guys. The mall wasn't completed, so only a few constructions workers were killed.

"Again, there were backchannel charges that the Russians did it. Also disproved by us. However, the case is still unsolved … With no suspects … or claimants …

"I could go on, but take my word for it, Harry. They're all too similar to be ignored."

Another long pause. Which Tanya correctly assumed was because Harry was considering how much he wanted to get involved in this. How to accomplish his orders, but still keep her at arm's length to maintain deniability.

Finally, he spoke — "As you suggested, Tanya … I'll take your word for it."

Then, trying to sound tough and in charge — "Let me kick some serious ass around here, Tanya. I'll get those reports to you within twenty four hours."

"Thanks, Harry," Tanya said, and despite her feelings about Harry, she meant it.

Even if he acted out of bluster and wounded pride, she could count on him to make the lives of several petty bureaucrats as miserable as possible.

She was about to sign off, when Harry suddenly said — "Wait, Tanya! I almost forgot!"

"What's that, Harry?"

"I just had a report from the *Borodino*," he said. "Apparently that Engine Devil you talked to … and the kid … Billy Ivanov … have gone missing."

Tanya was shocked. "What do you mean … 'gone missing?'"

"I know this sounds strange," Harry said, "but they can't be found anywhere. Not one trace of them."

"How could that be?" Tanya asked, confounded. "The *Borodino* is in the middle of … well, space, dammit! How could they get off without someone knowing?"

"I can't answer that," Harry said, and there was a note of satisfaction in his tone. He'd passed the responsibility to her and was swiftly fleeing the scene. "But I have complete faith in you, Tanya," he continued. "You'll figure it out."

Then the comline went dead and Harry was gone.

CHAPTER THIRTY FOUR

Brand Carvaserin was standing in the very midst of a huge underground installation, surrounded by an enormous machine.

At first glance it could've been mistaken for an huge gas-generator, but it was in fact the body, heart and soul of Project SRN.

As Carvaserin examined it with some pride and satisfaction his only real worry was that the Amers would come up with such a doomsday device first. Surely they were engaged in a similar project. Of this, he had no doubts.

"All posts, report to central point," he commanded.

"Post one — checkup cleaned," came the first answer.

It was Old Fisagava-san, the descendent of rebellious Japanese war-mages who had long ago had fled to Mother Russia when their plot to overthrow the government had failed. Fisagava was nearly as powerful a mage as Carvaserin.

"Post two — all in order," came another voice.

Also aged. And also belonging to a powerful wizard. This was no place for apprentices or minor sorcerers.

Like an echo, the reports continued followed: "Post three ... four ... five ... six ... ," and finally — "Seventh!"

The sacred count was complete. Seven points to control the ultimate magic, which was ready to rush from other dimensions and worlds to be bound, bent and put into service.

And even Brand Carvaserin himself did not dare ponder too long on just how much killing power Project SRN would unleash.

"Very good!" Brand congratulated his colleagues. "Horosho!"

There were murmurs of appreciation from the others. Praise from Brand Carvaserin was quite rare.

When the murmurs had died out, Brand said, "Gentleman, now we must all concentrate on ..."

But before he could continue his heart suddenly heaved inside his chest. Brand clutched his breast, doubling over from the intense pain.

A moment's relief and he straightened, gasping for breath. Then it struck once more, tearing at his heart!

Though he was in caught in the throes of intense pain, Brand realized he wasn't suffering a heart attack. For each time the sensation ripped at him he smelled the odor of wild magic.

The pain subsided and Brand swiftly raised a hand to warn the others that there was an intruder among them. He wasn't afraid. A wizard of Brand's experience and strength was primed for any magical emergency.

Then the terrible sensation tore through him again and he moaned in agony.

Fisagava shouted to the others. "Hurry, comrades. Brand needs our help!"

Fighting to remain conscious, Carvaserin heard his colleagues running to his side.

He only hoped they were in time.

*   *   *

The young soldier slowly made his rounds, a feeling of dread stalking his heels. The moon was high. And there were few lights in the windows of the distant settlement.

The air seemed heavy and filled with a strange odor. Gregor wondered, what could it be?

Then he shivered as he suddenly remembered what a corpse in a morgue smelled like.

Gregor forced himself onward, continuing his patrol. As he walked it seemed to him that a black cavern was opening under his feet.

It was only his imagination, of course. But the tremendous depths he saw in his mind were like a magnet — stretching out invisible hands, calling the soldier.

Promising untold wonders.

Far away the other guard dogs were howling. And behind the young soldier, Fang crept along in Gregor's shadow, whimpering and almost crawling.

Oh, if the dog could only speak!

*   *   *

The wave of pain loosened its grip and Carvaserin sagged in relief.

"I'm all right," he protested to his colleagues, who were holding him so he wouldn't collapse.

Fisagava looked at Brand's bloodless face and trembling hands.

"You don't look all right to me, comrade," he said. "In fact, you look like just escaped the jaws of ..."

Before he could finish, Carvaserin jerked forward, tearing himself away from all those supporting hands.

And he cried, "The jaws! The jaws!"

Then he gave a shriek of horror and fell to the floor, where he remained quite motionless.

The magicians looked at one another in helpless bewilderment.

* * *

In a far place deep under the very roots of the earth, the servants of the Beast heard their master's call.

The terrible voice, inaudible to any mortal or spirit world creature, reached the ears of his legions and put them into motion.

Millions of gnashing teeth gnawed through the earth. Millions of claws tore at the barriers that held back the molten rivers of magma.

The frightened creatures who had dwelled beneath the Earth for eons fled in terror when they saw the Beast's invaders.

Flaming streams rushed forward, then up, up, bursting through old pathways that led to the surface.

As it hit cooler stones the overheated magma shrieked defiance like a mortally wounded animal in final assault.

* * *

When the Beast unleashed its fury upon the Russian base it was as if thousands of DeathSpirits had been released at once.

They shrieked wild, soul-shattering spells full of malice and hatred.

A dark-crimson fountain rushed into the frightened night sky.

And the earth sighed, as if grieving for all those doomed creatures. Then its surface burst, like spring-ice giving way before the pressure of waiting waters.

Then the black abyss opened its filthy maw and hungry red flames shot out to eat the very clouds that obscured the moon.

Fang howled his dog's terror, but despite his fear, the faithful animal did not flee his master's side. The dog's teeth clutched Gregor's sleeves, trying to pull him away to safety.

But the young soldier remained frozen in fear and amazement. He couldn't move, he couldn't shout, he couldn't think.

Then he saw a spiderweb of burning cracks race up the walls of a five-story barracks. The walls folded inward liked melted wax, and then the barracks exploded into flame. Never mind that the barracks were made of the best bomb-proof plas-steel and would not burn even during an mage-nuke attack.

It happened anyway — fire racing here and there. Exposed men and women screaming and beating at flames.

All before Gregor's horrified young eyes.

One explosion followed another. Then the entire plain the base sat upon seemed to be transformed into ground zero of an enormous artillery training range.

To Gregor it was as if heavy shells were exploding one by one, smashing everything above ground. At the same time the shells tore deep craters into the earth, swiftly bursting through the hardened roofs of the underground levels.

He saw the flaming beast swallow whole buildings and installations. Cars, armored pillboxes, tanks, guns and the humans and fiends who manned them — all destroyed.

Soon the entire base was consumed by a great crimson sea of flame. In the center, the ground sank more than two hundred feet under the weight of the overheated magma. Poisonous vapors filled the air, killing those few who still remained.

Miraculously, the young soldier was untouched by all this destruction. It was as if he was standing at the edge of a flaming abyss, looking down on all that horror.

Desperate, Fang bit deeply into Gregor's leg.

Shocked by sudden pain, the young soldier clawed his way out of the trance that had pinned his feet to the ground.

But he still felt barely conscious. And as he jerked forward, it was like being held back by thick mud.

Fang grabbed his sleeve again, pulling, pulling.

And the young soldier finally broke free.

Led by his faithful friend, Gregor fled into a nearby forest.

He was the only survivor of the thousands who were struck that day.

*　*　*

Brand Carvaserin was not unconscious, as old Fisagava thought.

When the wizard saw the terrible jaws leaping out of Nothingness to savage him, he cast a great spell that temporarily saved his life. And his soul as well, for he could see that those jaws were hungry for mortal spirits.

But Carvaserin had no intention of giving up his soul that easily. Project SRN had many magical resources. All of which he could command and turn against the mysterious invader.

The first thing he had to do was report the attack. He had no doubt that the Amers had developed their own doomsday machine and this was what had been unleashed upon his base.

Lying motionless on the floor, the wizard cast spell after powerful spell. First, to notify his superiors. Then to fight the Amer machine he believed responsible for this attack.

He acted just in time, because the walls of the underground fortress shook and then cracked as he chanted his spells. But Carvaserin's still strong will struck back, re-uniting the girders and cross-beams.

Then, gathering the remnants of his might, he fired one last counter-blast.

Brand knew it was over. Finis. Even so, he kept up his desperate fight, drawing the full wrath of the mysterious enemy upon himself.

Giving his comrades one faint chance of escape. And perhaps Brand's mighty struggle was the reason the young soldier and his dog managed to survive.

In the end, it was no use. The Beast's minions ripped through Brand's magical barriers, destroying the great magical doomsday machine the Russian wizards had labored on for so long.

Some of the mages tried to flee, but it was a pitiful attempt. There was no way out: the corridors were cut off by collapsed ceilings and flames danced madly over the flotsam and jetsam of ruined men's lives.

With a last terrible cry Brand Carvaserin tore out his own throat before the Beast's fiends could get him. But before he did, he cast one last spell. A vortex of cold blue flame smashed the attacking hordes, making them quiver and fall back.

It was too late. For at that moment the roof collapsed and whole rivers of magma poured inside to destroy everything and everyone within.

*   *   *

The base obliterated, the Beast sent out the call to his hordes. It was time to cover his tracks and retreat before the softskins discovered any traces of him.

To the Beast's surprise, the losses among his fiendish army were quite heavy.

Apparently the softskins had not been as weak as he'd believed.

CHAPTER THIRTY FIVE

Mind working feverishly as she pondered Harry's startling news, Tanya hauled herself out of the pool and started toweling off.

To her surprise she found Vlad and Davyd had beat her out of the grotto and were already dragging on robes.

"We overheard the transmission," Vlad said in a rush. "We'd better return to the *Borodino* immediately and find out what happened to Old Scratch and little Billy."

"Probably a waste of time," Davyd said, manner languid, belying the fire dancing in his eyes. "But it'd be stupid to take anybody's word about what happened."

Spurred by the prospect of action, Vlad started getting angry. "By that, I assume you mean a Rooskie's word!" he snarled.

Davyd turned on Vlad, adrenaline pumping. "Now that you mention it —"

"Gentlemen, gentlemen!" Tanya broke in.

She was a little frightened at how fast their moods had changed. From peace to fighting mode in the blink of an eye.

"Let's not spoil all our efforts to make this a real team!" she said.

Then, while casting her calming spell, she added, "I've seen this kind of thing happen before. And every single damned time that egos go to war, the bad guy is the one who ends up winning because he gets away while the fools are arguing."

Her spell plus her words had an instant affect. Both men ducked their heads, mumbling, yes, yes, of course you're right, Tanya.

Her quick victory puzzled her at first. Then she realized if the men hadn't been such willing victims the spell wouldn't have worked so well.

Love was the master here, she thought. As soon as this thought leaped up she flushed in embarrassment.

What a thing to presume! That they might … love her? And she might … love them?

Was it possible?

And then, the chill thought: but, my god, they're both assassins! How could I-

At that moment a cultured loud-speaker voice broke through: "Attention! Attention all guests!"

Startled, Tanya and the two men turned toward the sound — which came from a wall fixture mounted high above the grotto. It was the *Library Of The Universe's* central address system.

"Ladies and gentlemen, we beg your urgent attention," said the voice. "We have just received grave news from our sister library on Earth.

"A Russian military installation has just been attacked! Early reports indicate that the death toll is in the tens of thousands!"

Tanya heard Vlad groan.

The voice continued: "We repeat … An Earth-based Russian military installation has just been attacked, with possibly tens of thousands of lives lost!"

A slight hesitation, then: "Your pardon ladies and gentleman. We have received further details … Oh, this is most disturbing indeed.

"According to sources at our sister library, Russian authorities charge there is no question that the attack emanated from the United Galactic States … Wait … still more … your patience, please …

"Ah! Here it is! The Russian High Council Of War has called an emergency session. No details as yet on the subject of that meeting."

Vlad muttered, "It can only be one thing — War!"

Tanya and Davyd looked at him, faces pale.

"We didn't attack!" Davyd said. "You must believe it wasn't us!"

"It doesn't matter what I believe," Vlad said.

He was having difficulty breathing. Hate for the Amers and all things American crept up from his belly. He couldn't control it. All his nerves were burning with organic messages demanding violent action.

He grated, "War is certain!"

"We must speak to them!" Tanya said, struggling, but losing the battle to maintain her calming spell. "We must stop them from going to war!"

"Why?" came Vlad's harsh response. "It's clear to me that this has been an Amer plot all along. *HolidayOne* was caused by them so they would have an excuse to retaliate!"

As he spoke she saw his right hand come up, fingers arcing like a snake ready to strike.

At the same moment Davyd's left foot shifted slightly, readying to launch him forward like a human missile.

Tanya stepped between them.

As soon as she moved Tanya realized she might very well die in the next few seconds. Both men were so overcome by mutual hate her life could be swatted away like that of an annoying insect.

She swayed a moment, both men leaning in with her motion. Then she recovered, spine becoming steel.

"Stop this!" she shouted.

The men hesitated.

Tanya seized that slight moment. Replaying that first scene aboard the *Borodino*. But this time she was afraid it wouldn't work!

"If you want to kill each other, you'll have to kill me first!" she said in deliberate echo of that first meeting. "And be damned to you both!"

Then she looked straight into Vlad's eyes, daring him to act. "Well, Vlad," she said. "Is it you who is going to kill me?"

The Russian's hand slowly fell.

Tanya whirled on Davyd. "Or possibly it's going to be you, Davyd! Maybe you're faster than he is. And you'll be my assassin!"

Davyd eased back.

Tanya kept going. "Think, dammit! Think of all the evidence we've gathered! Only last night we talked and talked until we were all blue in the face, but no matter how we looked at it there was only one reasonable answer —

"That there was a conspiracy to start an intergalactic war. A conspiracy that was neither Russian — or American.

"But a third party with its own dirty plans."

"A theory, only," Vlad protested.

"We don't have hard evidence," Davyd agreed.

"But we will if we can continue the investigation," Tanya said.

"Once we get those reports from Harry I just know we'll find the common thread we're looking for. Why, I'm already starting to get a picture. Think of those errors in the six incidents. There's something about those mistakes that's not quite ..."

Her words trailed off as she had a sudden realization. Damn! The mall wasn't open when it was hit. Damn! And the harvest was long over when the biobomb went off. Damn and double damn!

"Listen to me," she said, excited. "I think I know how to go! What kind of *person* would —"

The address system blared into life: "Ladies and gentlemen, there have been further developments. It's official! War has been declared!

"We repeat, war has been declared!

"All guests are kindly requested to make immediate arrangements to return to their home planets. The *Library Of The Universe* will be closed until this emergency has passed. We repeat, the Library will be closed in twelve e-hours. All guests must depart by that time! Our travel staff is standing by to ..."

Numb, Tanya turned back to the men.

Davyd shrugged. "We're too late," he said.

And Vlad said, "I'm sorry, Tanya, but I have to go."

Then, giving her no time to feel surprise, he stepped close, took her in his arms and gave her a long, sad kiss.

He stepped back. Eyes moist. "Farewell, Tanya," he said.

And he left.

Dazed, she looked at Davyd. "What's happening?" she asked.

Davyd sighed. "It's war. So, he's got to report back to his boss for further orders." He shrugged. "Same as me."

He smiled. "He's gonna have a lot of explaining to do. Like, how come he left me here alive.

"Once again — same as me."

Another sigh. "I think I have a pretty good idea what our next mission will be."

Tanya didn't have to ask him what he meant. It was clear that Davyd and Vlad would meet again very soon. And this time one of them would not walk away.

Suddenly, she found herself in Davyd's arms. His kiss was as long and deep as Vlad's. And filled with as much sadness.

Then he broke the embrace, saying, "I'll never forget you, Tanya."

And he was gone — vanished like a shadow.

At that moment Tanya drew on all her strength and all her courage to make the decision. She would stop this damn war in its tracks, or die in the trying.

And she knew just where to start: Billy and Old Scratch.

CHAPTER THIRTY SIX

As the entire galaxy held its breath the two great empires of America and Russia lumbered over the brink into full-scale war.

But instead of the instant mutual annihilation everyone had expected, events moved at a glacial pace. The thousand-year Cold War had forged military cultures in both empires more suited to defense than offense.

In the past blood had only been spilled by surrogates. The main battles were fought with words delivered by skilled propagandists, rather than by missiles.

To be sure, the armories of both empires were filled to the overflowing with sophisticated weapons of destruction. However, those weapons had never been tested in real combat. Plus they had been developed and built more for arms race propaganda purposes than for actual use.

So when the combatants finally climbed into the ring to settle their differences once and for all, they were like two aging heavy-weight boxers, shuffling in slow circles as each measured the other with rheumy eyes, flexing enormous biceps more swollen with fat than muscle.

The generals on both sides were also exceedingly cautious. They were looking for a single knock out blow. Reasoning if their enemy survived the first punch it was unlikely there'd be a chance for a second.

And that the enemy's counter punch might very well win the war.

Massive battle computers, operated by billions of tiny, sweating demons, worked overtime figuring the odds of one scenario after another. But as each plan was conceived, it was just as swiftly dismissed when fatal flaws were uncovered by the prog machines.

Both empires were ringed with gigantic magical defensive systems that would not only disintegrate anything hurled against them but would automatically trigger an even greater assault on the attacker.

American and Russian diplomats converged on the United World Organization by the hundreds, shouting angry charges and counter charges.

The Americans denied attacking the Russian base. The Russians scoffed at their denials. Saying, who else could have done such a thing?

It couldn't have been the work of terrorists, they said. Only a super power had the capability to mount such a sophisticated operation. And there were only two super powers.

Obviously, the Russians railed, the Americans were responsible and they were using the excuse of the destruction of *HolidayOne* to retaliate. Once again, the Russians claimed the *HolidayOne* tragedy was an American plot aimed at excusing the assault on the Russian base.

The Americans replied in kind. The "Evil Empire," they charged, was the cause of everything. Including the attack on the base, which they said might never have actually happened, but was probably sheer propaganda.

It was a manufactured "Wag The Dog" event, they claimed. And they demanded on-site inspections to prove their point.

The Russians saw this charge as a diplomatic error and immediately leaped at the chance to take advantage of it. They claimed they had mountains of visual documentation and eye-witness accounts of the attack.

And they urged that a task force of "neutral scholars" be assembled to tour the area.

Immediately, the diplomats on both sides began arguing over the make-up of the task force. Many days passed without agreement. Cynics quietly remarked that it was unlikely such a task force would ever come into being.

The sole purpose of the verbal quarrel, the cynics said, was that the American and Russian diplomats were playing a sophisticated waiting game.

The diplomats' main purpose, the cynics claimed, was to obscure and delay while each empire massed its forces and ran combat progs to find the perfect plan.

The cynics were quite correct.

But as the hot talk raged, blood *was* spilled.

For in the first days of the war both sides noted that the frontier areas and some of the weaker allies were vulnerable to attack. And it was in was in those places that the Russians and Americans let loose their terrible wrath.

Troops and weapons were rushed here and there, attacking or defending. Thousands of innocent civilians were slaughtered in a series of bloody skirmishes.

Several sparsely populated frontier zone worlds were destroyed as the Russian and American combat wizards tested planet-busters armed with new breeds of ferocious DeathSpirits.

But these actions also exposed key officers and wizards to the fortunes of war. Even in the Thirtieth Century the person who directed any crucial military operation had to travel to the battle zone and step out into the killing light.

Immediately, the Church Of The Sword and Odysseus Corps rushed their assassins to those battle zones to reap a deadly harvest.

Among them were the "best of the best" — Davyd Kells and Vlad Projogin.

Within weeks Davyd and Vlad had each slain a hundred high-ranking military officials. Easily double what any operative on either side had managed.

Word soon leaked out to the mass media on both sides that two unusually skilled combat aces were taking a terrible toll on Russia's and America's most important combat officers and wizards.

Well-oiled and funded propaganda machines went into instant action, boasting of these mysterious sniper heroes who worked alone for the greater good of their nation states.

At first the Odysseus Corps and Church Of The Sword worked mightily to withhold the identities of Davyd and Vlad.

Fathers Zorza and Onphim, as well as other high officials, worried that if Vlad and Davyd were exposed, so too would be the existence of their top secret organizations.

The Council Of Eight was of the same mind. For if the trails leading from Davyd and Vlad were followed to their logical end, all beingkind would learn of the COE's insidious conspiracy.

As Apollion pointed out, "We will be viewed as parasites, gentlemen. And to be fair, this is what we are.

"Except we are parasites who have manipulated our hosts for more than a thousand years."

After several e-days had passed, Apollion had an idea that forced him to reverse his thinking. It involved an extreme measure, but Apollion reasoned that only something extreme could stop this war and put things back the way they were.

He called an emergency meeting of the Council Of Eight. All attended — except Infeligo, who was still pursuing the elusive Scratch and Billy Ivanov.

"Gentlemen," he announced, "I have a plan that may give us the time we need to expose the traitor among us and stop this foolish war before it destroys us."

His fiendish colleagues listened intently as he spelled out his proposal. At first there was much bitter argument, but in the end the vote of approval was unanimous.

And thus was launched the most famous duel in history.

The combatants: Davyd Kells and Vlad Projogin.

CHAPTER THIRTY SEVEN

As Tanya approached "The Three Hanged Monks" she could hear Old Scratchy singing at the top of his demon lungs:

> *"... On the road to Mandalay*
> *Where the flyin'-fishes play,*
> *An' the dawn comes up like thunder outter China*
> *'Crost the Baayyyy ..."*

"Obviously, we've found the right place," she said to Kriegworm. "Boozing and singing as if he hadn't a care in the world. What a fool this one is."

Kriegworm pulled a face, making his ogre's countenance even more horrible to behold.

"Possibly so, ma'am," he replied. "However ..."

And he waved a mighty claw that took in the begrimed tenements and shabby business fronts that made up the Rayal spaceport's Devil District.

"... the Engine Devil could hardly have expected that a human would attempt to follow him to this place."

The whole scene was lit by the eerie green light of the Rayal moon. The atmosphere was thick with danger.

Strange fires burned in the tenement windows, odd smells carried by poisonous red smoke rose from the cracked-girder street.

Even more intimidating was "The Three Hanged Monks" — the favored retreat of Engine Devils Local 666. The proprietors had chopped off the ugly end of an old space transport and stuck it on a vacant lot.

Scarred and rusted, it presented a face that Tanya thought made Kriegworm's look handsome. There were dark steaming holes like monster's eyes, a glowing red protrusion that might be a nose.

No one had bothered to cut the cables, which were still alive and crackling with magical power, so they trailed off the front like a beard, sparking and waving in time to Scratch's high-volume performance.

There was a sign on the front door to the inn which read:
Softskins Beware!
Enter At Your Own Risk!

Meanwhile, Scratch was singing:

> *"...Ship me somewheres east Of Suez,*

Where the best is like the worst;
Where there ain't no Ten Commandments
An' a man can raise a thirst;
For the temple-bells are callin',
An' it's there that I would be ...
By the old Moulmein Pagoda,
Looking lazy at the sea ...

Tanya shook off the feeling of being the helpless heroine of a gothic novel.

"Don't think much of his singing," she said, "but I do like his choice of songs. Kipling, hmm?"

"I do not know of this Kipling, ma'am," Kriegworm said, ogre eyes glowing with disapproval. "But it isn't right for a mere devil to sing a human song."

He shook his scaly head. "Most disturbing. When we catch him, I shall give Scratch a good thrashing for his impertinence."

Tanya glanced at the ogre. Eight feet in height and four at the shoulder, any thrashing he administered would be most severe.

"Not while under my command you won't," she said. "The UWP strictly forbids mistreatment of prisoners."

Kriegworm chuckled — it was the first time Tanya had ever heard him do such a thing.

"Some policies are worse than others, ma'am," he said, thrusting out a stubborn chin. "The one you cite is my least favorite."

Like the chuckle, Tanya thought Kriegworm's words and manner were rather odd. Normally, the ogre was a by-the-book stickler, who treated UWP policies as if they were holy gospel. Which was probably why he'd been admitted into the department — something very few other fiends had ever been allowed to do.

However, for some time now, Tanya thought his attitude seemed to be undergoing a change. Ever since the *Borodino* he'd been outspoken to the point of insubordination.

Tanya wondered what was going on beneath that thick skull. Why the change? Then she thought, maybe it was the war. These days everyone seemed to be teetering on the edge of hysteria.

"I'm not concerned with your likes or dislikes," Tanya growled, putting him in his place. "Do what you're told!"

Suddenly humble as of old, Kriegworm bobbed his head. "Yes, Master Investigator! Whatever you say, Master Investigator! Forgive my rudeness."

Although his manner was contrite, Tanya heard sarcasm in his tone. She decided to ignore it.

"Circle around to the back of the inn," she ordered. "When I give the signal, we'll both go in."

"Yes, ma'am!" Kriegworm said. "We'll catch 'em in a crossfire."

"Dammit!" Tanya said. "No shooting. I need to question these witnesses. Besides, I don't want to see the boy hurt!"

Kriegworm smiled. "Oh, yes, the *human* child. We mustn't harm him … at any cost!" Very sarcastic.

"Remember that!" Tanya gritted. "Now go! And signal me when you're in position."

Kriegworm snapped a regulation salute and departed. Tanya watched his huge bulk shamble off into the darkness. There was an arrogant hitch in his massive shoulders, a swagger to his walk.

And she thought, What in the hell is going on with him?

Just out of sight, Kriegworm paused near a dark jumble of crates and barrels. "Are you ready?" he whispered into the shadow.

"Yes, Master!" was the hissed reply.

"Wait until we have them in custody," Kriegworm ordered. "Then strike!"

Tanya's killer smiled.

Revenge was near!

* * *

Inside the "Three Hanged Monks," the hellfires were burning brightly and many jugs of steaming Fiendish punch were hoisted high as Scratch sang the last notes of his song …

"…An' the dawn comes up like thunder,
Outter China.
'Crost the Baayyyy!"

Thunderous roars of applause greeted Scratchy's bow, then he lumbered off the swirling flame wheel that was the stage.

Tanya was wrong about Old Scratch's sobriety. The whole night he'd sipped sparingly from his punch. To be sure, he wanted more than anything to drink until his insides were afloat.

Just as he ached to enter the special room in the back to bask in the healing fires of the True Flame, where all time ceased and an old demon's sore bones would be warmed through and through.

But he'd resisted these temptations with all his strength and was only pretending to be drunk so as not to worry his old friends and shipmates.

Scratchy had received a hero's greeting when he'd shown up at the tavern's back door, Billy in tow. His miraculous escape from *Holiday-One* was known to Engine Devils everywhere. Just as the reports of his equally miraculous flight from the *Borodino* had doubly thrilled them.

Of all the beings in the galaxy, Engine Devils were the most experienced in the vagaries of cruel fate. Ships could mysteriously stall near a black hole. Spell engines could suddenly go cold.

Deep gravity could reach through uttermost space itself, throwing sucking tendrils around the ship, dragging everyone to their doom.

And the after-reports always blamed the disaster on "Engine Devil's Error."

As Scratch moved through the curtains of marvelous smoke that filled the inn, ducking around the floating black stones that gave off blissful warmth, he returned the shouted greetings from the many well-wishers who had gathered to pay their respects to a fiend all declared one of the "best of the best ... an engine devil supreme!"

In the far corner he found Billy being regaled by Scratch's best friend, Ashgaroth — an Engine Devil known far and wide for his tall tales.

Billy was floating at eye-level to the big gnarly fiend, comfortably ensconced within a glowing bubble of protective magic.

Although humans could bear the atmosphere of the "Hanged Monks" for short periods of time, without the bubble it would definitely have been an unpleasant — if not downright painful — experience.

"... and then Old Scratchy let out such a curse," Ashgaroth was saying, "that he peeled the suit right off that port master's back!

"It was the great king of all curses, starting with the bassad's mother and running all the way back in evolutionary time to the first speck of DNA that made him."

Billy laughed, clapping his hands in delight. "What did Scratchy say?" he demanded. "What was the curse?"

Scratch wanted to smile, but he forced a frown. "Don't listen to this great twister of truth, young friend of the world," he warned Billy.

"His father was a charm-seller, his mother a foul wisp from the garden of lies. And the result was an egg of such low character no fiendish priest would come near enough to bless it. Fearing all truth would run out their toes if Ashgaroth's egg cracked before they could flee."

Ashgaroth coughed amusement. "Doest thou see what I mean, Billy?" he said. "Is not Scratchy a swearer above all others?"

Billy laughed agreement. Since their flight from the *Borodino*, he'd heard some masterful swearing from his new mentor. Although he still mourned the loss of his grandparents — and Lupe — his new adventures as a fugitive had pushed most of the tragedy to the back of his mind.

In some ways, he thought, these had been the happiest days of his short life.

"Nobody, but nobody swears better than Scratchy," he said.

Scratch harumphed, as if insulted. But secretly he was pleased. The human child was a most enjoyable companion, full of pranks and jokes that made him feel young again.

The Engine Devil was also much impressed with Billy's magical powers. Without him Scratch would never have been able to cast a spell strong enough to slip the clutches of the mysterious and evil creature who had tracked them to the *Borodino*.

He shuddered at this thought, then pushed the memory away.

Scratch leaned closer to Ashgaroth. "Hast thou made contact with thy friends?" he asked.

"Verily, and I have met with much success," Ashgaroth said in a low voice. "In fact, they should arrive here at any moment and whisk thee and Billy away to the Fiendish Worlds.

"There both of you will be safe until the crisis passes."

Scratch frowned sadly. "With this war between the Amers and the Rooskies," he said, "it may be many years before we can resume a normal life."

"Never mind, Scratchy," Billy said. "We'll be all right. And think of the fun we're gonna have! You'll be visiting the place of your ancestors. And I'll be making all kinds of new friends."

He turned to Ashgaroth. "Are they really coming for us tonight?" he asked, excited at the prospect of a daring journey through the fiendish underground — something he had never known existed before.

"And are there really humans living there too?" he asked. "Rebels, you called them! That's me! Billy Ivanov, leader of the rebels!"

At that moment twin explosions shook the tavern.

The heavy doors — front and back — burst inward, crashing to the floor.

Then, amidst Engine Devil roars of angry alarm and confusion, two figures stepped through the blasted openings, wicked-looking sidearms leveled.

One was Tanya, the other Kriegworm.

"United Worlds Police!" Tanya shouted, waving the UWP shield with her free hand. "Nobody move!"

At the same time, she cast her most powerful spell, immobilizing everyone in the place.

Everyone, that is, except for Billy.

* * *

Outside the "Three Hanged Monks" Tanya's killer waited patiently — almost serenely — as the two fugitives were led from the inn at
blaster-point.

Katya hoisted the heavy weapon Kriegworm had given her. It was set
on "full shatter."

At the proper moment she'd fire and Igor — poor, dear Igor — would
have his revenge.

Never mind that the weapon would release hundreds of tiny death
sprites who would destroy not only Tanya but everyone within a twenty-
foot radius.

Never mind that it would be a most painful death — innards bursting,
brains melting, bones and sinews turned to dust.

Never mind that many innocents, such as the boy and the Engine
Devil at the edge of Katya's sights, would be caught in the sorcerous
explosion.

Katya centered on Tanya, finger heavy on the trigger. She took a
breath, letting the hate flow through her, firing her courage. It was a hate
that was not only inbred but stoked by years of sophisticated propaganda.

A hate so intense only Tanya's death could release it.

She lowered the weapon slightly, noting Kriegworm moving away
from the police grav-van Tanya had borrowed to receive the prisoners.

Slowly, secretly, he was distancing himself from "ground zero."

Finally, the giant ogre was in a safe position. He looked over at
Katya's hiding place. A claw came up, getting ready to signal.

Once again she put Tanya in the center of her sights.

Finger tightening … tightening … tightening …

* * *

Billy was waiting his chance, despairing that it might never come as
Tanya led him and Scratch to the yawning doors of the police van.

He kept hoping Ashgaroth's friends would show up and create a diversion so he and Scratch could escape into the fiendish underground. He
stretched his senses, trying to see if they were there.

Then he caught it!

Around the back of the inn … the now familiar spell scent of Engine
Devils approaching … Rescue was near!

He glanced at Tanya, praying she wouldn't notice.

"I only want to ask you two some questions," Tanya was saying. "You're not suspected of anything. And I promise I'll put you in protective custody so no one can harm you."

"Protective custody?" Scratch said. "Bah! I defecate great mounds of devilish waste upon thy protection. Too many evil ones want us. There's no such thing as a safe place among softskins. Especially not with this war going on!"

Billy was starting to wonder why Tanya hadn't picked up the scent of the rescue party. From the moment he'd seen her he knew she was a most powerful mage.

So powerful that she'd been able to storm the "Hanged Monks" with nothing but spells to keep her safe from the poisonous atmosphere.

Was she pretending? Was this a trick to capture the rescuers as well?

Billy prepared to send a warning blast of mentos to the rebel fiends. Then he caught another spoor ... And the outlines of a spell meant to block Tanya's senses.

At first his heart leaped in joy. It must be the work of the rescue team! Then he picked up something else that made his blood run cold.

Danger! Severe danger! Aimed at Tanya, but more than sufficient to kill Scratch and himself.

Frightened, he scorched Scratch with a mental blast. "Look out, Scratchy!" he mentos shouted. "Look out!"

Kriegworm signaled and Katya clamped down on the trigger.

Night turned to day as white-hot light blossomed from the muzzle of her weapon. Thousands of tiny death sprites rushed forward, eager for the kill.

But at the same moment Billy hurled a counter-spell. He thought of it as a huge shield — red like the shield of Justiceman, his favorite comic-vid hero.

The death sprites shrieked as they punched into it. The shield held for a moment, then they started gnawing through.

"Help me, Scratchy! Help!" Billy mentos shrieked.

Scratch leaped in with a spell of his own — firming the shield. But he didn't have enough strength and the spellshield started to crumble.

Then Tanya, who had been momentarily stunned by the sorcerous blast, recovered and cast her most powerful spell. At the same time she fired her sidearm — aiming beyond the hot white light.

In less than a heartbeat the death sprites were overcome by the combined assault and all was darkness again.

Tanya paced forward, still blinded, but her weapon at the ready. Then her sight returned and she saw the horror collapsed on the ground.

Although the body was charred beyond recognition, she could tell it was a woman.

"Kriegworm!" she shouted. "Search the area! See if there's any more of them."

There was no response.

Surprised, Tanya turned in time to see Kriegworm's huge form disappearing into the night.

That was the first shock of realization: Kriegworm had betrayed her!

The second shock was the absence of her prisoners. Billy and Scratch were gone.

From behind the inn, she heard the sound of grav-engines firing up. She sprinted toward the sound, leaping over rubble and trash.

But by the time she rounded the corner the grav-flit was powering over a tenement roof. Then it was gone.

Tanya sagged against the building's edge, too shocked to even curse. Wondering — Who do I chase? Kriegworm? Or Billy and Scratch?

Finally she pulled herself together and headed back to the police van. Her steps were slow at first, as if dragging through the mud of defeat.

Then the idea struck and her pace quickened.

She knew exactly what to do next.

CHAPTER THIRTY EIGHT

"You have done well, my son."

Father Onphim was sitting on a hard wooden armchair deep in the gloomy mission room of the Church Of The Sword.

Major Vlad Projogin, code number 2:5030/48, stood before the priest, a cold sweat drenching his uniform. He shrugged, pretending indifference.

"Thank you, father," he said. "But I've only done my sworn duty."

"A hundred kills in such a short time is far beyond normal duty, my son," Onphim replied. "It is a record unmatched in the Church's whole history."

Another shrug. "Davyd Kells has done as well for Odysseus," he said. "At least I assume he's the mystery assassin all the Amer news feeds are boasting about.

"I don't know another man on either side who could have managed those deeds."

Onphim studied him a moment through narrowed eyes, then he asked, "Why are you so certain the Amers aren't lying, my son? It seems logical, doesn't it, that their propagandists might concoct such stories so your feats would be diminished?"

Vlad sighed. "It's possible, father," he said. "The Amers are past masters of the Big Lie."

"But in this case," Onphim pressed, "you don't think so."

"No I don't, father," Vlad replied. "If I could slay a hundred men, so could Kells. We were the first holy assassins. I killed George W. Bush. He killed Vladimir Putin. And we've had a thousand years to perfect our craft since that day.

"No other man or woman in either the Odysseus Corps or the Church Of The Sword can even come close to making that claim."

Vlad felt a terrible bitterness coming over him. He was so tired, so soul weary, that he wished he could die and end this never-ending killing spree that love of Mother Country had condemned him to.

He also wished Father Onphim would come to the point. Vlad knew very well the priest hadn't summoned him to praise his bloody record.

As if reading his thoughts, Onphim said, "You are quite correct, my son. The Amers are not lying. Exactly one hundred of our best generals and combat wizards have been assassinated by that rabid dog, Davyd Kells."

A small part of Vlad's back brain murmured that if Davyd could be called a rabid dog for what he'd done, that what did that make Vlad?

Then his mind hurled him back to that moment in the warm waters of the grotto when he and Davyd had watched the beautiful Tanya Lawson floating in the pool. And then their eyes had moved from her lush figure to meet. A spark of friendship leaping from one man to the other. Momentarily arcing over their shared hatred.

Recalling that scene, Vlad felt a sudden sense of loss. And then a chilling thought struck him.

"Is Davyd Kells the reason you sent for me father?" he asked.

"Yes, my son," Onphim replied.

And Vlad thought, God, help me. I've lost Tanya forever!

*   *   *

"Godblessamerica!" the motor sprite said. "We're gonna kick those Rooskie butts from here to Betelgeuse. They'll be sorry they ever messed with us."

Davyd turned away from the little chatterbox, wishing mightily that he could pray. But what self-respecting deity would ever listen to the pleas of a sinner like Davyd Kells?

Behind him, the huge elephant shaped rock that hid the Odysseus Corps headquarters was swiftly receding. Ahead of him, military barges hooted and honked as they maneuvered out of the path of the beetlecraft.

The Rio Grande throughway was practically the personal property of Davyd Kells that day. He had top priority clearance all the way to the El Paso Spaceport — and beyond.

As he traveled, urgent, coded messages were being beamed out for all military or civilian personnel and vehicles to either give Kells every possible assistance without question, or to get the Hell out of his way.

Moments before, as Davyd had prepared to leave Odysseus Corps headquarters, Father Zorza had made certain that his orders were quite clear:

"My son, you are to expend every effort, spare no expense and dare any odds, until you can return to me with Vlad Projogin's head on a serving dish."

Davyd's reply had been to snap his most crisp salute, saying, "Yessir!" And doing his damnedest to mean it from the bottom of his spit-shined boots to the flat crown of his black beret.

But at the same time he'd felt lost. What the hell were they doing to him? Didn't he have enough black marks on his soul without adding a man who could have been a friend?

And what of Tanya? What would she say when she heard Davyd had ripped Vlad apart with explosive bullets?

Thinking of Tanya, Davyd's heart raced out of control, trip-hammering against his chest. In all his long life, Davyd had never known what it was like to love a woman. But now that he did, he was being denied this most human of necessities.

And then he thought, What does it matter, Kells? Who the hell said you were human, anyway?

Davyd reached deep into himself and pulled up the comforting cloak of hate he'd worn for over a thousand years. Bitter juices boiled up and over. Nerves crackled with arcing fires. A red haze colored his view.

And by damn, he felt good! He was gonna kill that Rooskie son of a bitch! Blow his goddamned heart out of his chest! Put his teeth right through the back of his skull!

Pumped up with positive energy, Davyd reviewed his mission.

As bewildering as Father Zorza's words had first seemed, they were beginning to make sense. What was it the Jesuit had said? Oh, yes. Now he remembered. He replayed the scene in his head. Once again Father Zorza was sitting across from him, his face solemn ...

"... In ancient days, my son," the priest was saying, "warring kingdoms sometimes chose champions to represent them in battle. And as those heroes advanced on the field to fight hand-to-hand, they carried the hopes and dreams of all their people upon their shoulders.

"And whichever gladiator won the contest, also won the war."

"Are you saying that when I kill Projogin the war will be over?" Davyd asked. "And America will have won?"

Father Zorza smiled gently. "Not exactly, Davyd," he said. "But you will have gone a long way to winning the war. Think of how the newscasters will portray this duel, my son.

"It will be painted as a contest between the two greatest warriors on either side. And whichever one wins will prove, once and for all, who is right — and who is wrong."

"I assume the Rooskies will do the same thing with Vlad," Davyd said.

"They already have, my son," Zorza said, much to Davyd's surprise.

He gestured and a vidsprite rushed to bring the latest newsfeed to life. It played out against the chapel wall in living color.

Davyd saw a red-headed Rooskie newswoman interviewing a high Soviet official.

"We are throwing down the gauntlet," the general was saying in Russian. "We challenge the Amers to send their very best soldier to fight our nation's greatest hero, Vlad Projogin."

A picture of Vlad appeared in the background. It was a helluva pose, Davyd thought as he saw Vlad standing there in his Brown Bear's uniform. Looking like a Thirtieth Century knight.

"What if the Amer dogs refuse the challenge?" the Russian newswoman asked the general.

"Then they will prove what cowards they truly are," the general replied, slamming his fist against the desk.

Then the general turned to look straight into the camera, saying, "Come out and fight, Davyd Kells. The whole galaxy is waiting for you to show what kind of a man you are!"

Zorza made another gesture and the picture vanished.

He turned to look at a stunned Davyd. "You see how it is, my son," he said. "They have already issued the challenge.

"Now, the question is, do you accept?"

There was nothing else Davyd could do but say yes ...

Kells shook off the stern image of Father Zorza and settled back into his seat.

Up ahead a troop transport was frantically trying to maneuver out of Davyd's way. As his beetlecraft passed, he looked out the window and saw hundreds of young men lined up against the transport's rails.

They were cheering him.

Damn, Davyd thought. The news of my acceptance must already be out.

Damn, damn, damn!

* * *

"Now listen to me, lad," Father Onphim was saying. "You must find this Amer dog, Davyd Kells. And you must kill him."

Vlad kept his features expressionless. But inside he was burning up. Part of him thought Davyd was ... well, something more than just a cursed enemy. While another part recalled that Davyd was the only person he'd ever failed to best in single combat. And Tanya ... Yes, Tanya!

Vlad was rocked by a sudden burst of anger. Yes, yes, yes! We must settle this, Davyd and I. And if I must lose Tanya, well, it would be good to know that his enemy, Davyd Kells, would lose her as well.

But what about their interrupted investigation? Oh yes, that really hurt. To solve that great mystery would have been better than fame or wealth. For the true warrior pleads for mysteries to test his strength.

Except now Father Onphim had given him something beyond personal aims and delights to defend. His country was at war. The enemy was mighty. Now he, Major Vlad Projogin, must earn his pay.

"Yes, Father," he said, accepting the mission.

"A simple yes is not enough," Onphim said sternly. "You must know something else, Vlad. Those Amer dogs have already announced that their greatest hero, Davyd Kells, has challenged you to a duel. This very duel we are discussing."

"Announced?" Vlad said, stunned anew.

"Yes, my son. Announced. Advertised. Propaganda bulletins issued without cease. Do you realize how serious this is?"

Vlad nodded. He understood all right. And he burned with renewed anger, feeling — unreasonably perhaps — that Davyd had betrayed him.

"Excellent," Father Onphim said. "Now we'll make an announcement of our own, accepting the challenge.

"This duel will be like the great warriors of old, Peresvet and Chelubei at the battle of Kulikovski. And remember well, my son, how we won that battle!"

Again, Vlad nodded. But he couldn't help thinking that both of those ancient warriors had been killed.

Father Onphim smiled, reading Vlad's thoughts. "The Tatar Chelubei was a trained swordsman and spearman. But Peresvet was but a lay brother. Remember that, my son, before dwelling on their mutual doom."

"I will, Father," Vlad promised.

Then he asked, "Where can I find Kells? Do we have any intelligence reports?"

"Not yet," Onphim replied. "Most of our wizards are now corking that damned Carvaserin's hole. You must act yourself.

"But keep in mind that Kells will also seek you. The men of the Odysseus Corps are hardly stupid. They know everything about you, Vlad. And I'm sure they'll expect your appearance. So be ready."

Vlad saluted smartly. "The next time you see me, Father," he said, "I swear by all that is holy I'll have the corpse of Davyd Kells hanging from my shield."

* * *

Just before he reached the El Paso Spaceport, Davyd got the lead he needed.

A news bulletin playing on the beetlecraft's system, announced that Major Vlad Projogin, of the Russian SpetzNaz Commandos, had just increased his score by one.

He'd assassinated an American general on a frontier world outpost.

The Russians were boasting that their ace now had one hundred and one kills to his credit, whereas Davyd had only one hundred even.

Again, they made a mocking challenge for Davyd to come out and fight Vlad.

Immediately, the screen dissolved and fiery letters spelled out the words "Special War Bulletin." A woman with a big voice, backed by a brass band, started singing the "Star Spangled Banner."

Then the President of the United Galactic States appeared on the screen. Davyd's jaw dropped as he heard the President declare that America had taken up the challenge and at this moment the great UGS hero, David Kells, was hunting down Vlad Projogin.

Davyd shook his head. He'd only left Father Zorza's side an hour ago and already the President was announcing Davyd's mission.

Man, they work fast, he thought.

He sighed. So be it. Come out, come out, Vlad Projogin wherever you are. Little Davyd Kells wants to play.

An idea suddenly jumped up to present itself. A simple, but elegant trap he could lure Vlad into.

All I have to do, he thought, is prime the pump with a few more kills. And then he'll know where to look for me. But *I'll* be waiting when gets there.

Before considering who and where those new targets might be, Davyd thought he'd better visit the Odysseus Corps armory. There were many secret weapons rooms scattered all over the galaxy.

Some were better than others, but after a thousand years of killing for the corps, Davyd knew which were the best.

Also, for this mission he'd need some very special gear. Davyd ran a wish list of deadly things through his mind, then decided which armory he ought to visit.

Time's a wasting, he thought. Then he plucked the com unit from his jacket pocket and ordered up a ship. As an afterthought he told his contact to be sure to stock some thick steaks and a case of cold beer.

Then he swallowed two pills from his stym-pack and kicked his killer's system into overdrive.

Godblessamerica, he thought. Godblessamerica, indeed!

CHAPTER THIRTY NINE

Harry was talking but Tanya didn't hear a word he was saying. Her total concentration had been kidnapped by the glowing magecube sitting on the desk in front of him.

Although it was quite small, the magecube muscled all other sensations to the side. Its color was active — a slow-throbbing green. The scent was palpable — the faint ozone stink of sorcery. The cube's presence was commanding — a wizardly contract that would bind her forevermore.

On top of the cube there was a slight depression in the shape of a thumb. Tanya's own thumb tingled.

She felt oddly compelled to press it into the depression, but at the same time was repelled by the thought.

Harry raised his voice, breaking through. "I don't think you realize, Tanya," he said, "it's my ass that's at risk, here! I've got generals, admirals, diplomats — you name it — all lined up to plant their size 12's into my lily white.

"And you come running in here with some wild, unrelated tale about a UWP officer who went bananas and tried to kill you!"

Tanya tore her gaze away from the magecube. "It isn't a wild tale, Harry," Tanya said, biting back anger. Jesus, her boss was thick.

"And what happened isn't unrelated. Kriegworm was trying to stop me from getting to the bottom of this mess."

"Now, why would a UWP officer do a thing like that?" Harry demanded. "You must have done something to offend him. Everyone knows you don't get along with Spiritworld folk."

He shook his head. "Tell the truth, sometimes I don't blame you. They can be a prickly lot. But the point is, you obviously did something that drove him over the edge. Only someone insane would risk what your are accusing Kriegworm of doing."

Harry toyed with the cube "I mean, he'd lose his pension and everything!"

Once again, Tanya's attention was snared by the magecube. She knew damned well what Harry was after, but she kept fighting it. Tanya curled her fingers into a fist, nails biting into her palm. Pain loosening the cube's sorcerous grip.

"I don't think he was worrying about his pension, Harry," she said dryly. "We're talking about a pretty elaborate conspiracy, here. Somehow Kriegworm got to Katya and poisoned her mind against me. Then he ran her like she was a double agent. Compelling her to desert the *Borodino*.

"For Christ's sake, Harry, desertion during war time is a death penalty offense in the Russian army. Hell, it's a death penalty offense in *every* army!

"And then somehow he managed to position her so she'd be outside the 'Three Hanged Monks' waiting for me when I exited with my prisoners."

Tanya sighed. "That's certainly not the description of a guy — fiend or otherwise — who's counting his future benefits! And he sure as hell isn't helpless."

"Okay, okay," Harry said. "I guess I see your point. Besides, I've put out a Galaxy-wide APB for him. He'll be picked up by and by."

"I doubt it," Tanya said. "Where he's gone, they don't give a damn about APB's."

Harry's eyebrows shot up. "Where would that be?" he asked.

Tanya told him.

Harry whistled in surprise. "How sure are you?" he asked.

"Sure enough," Tanya said, "to put my own lily white, as you so colorfully described that area of the human anatomy, in harm's way."

"And you really think you'll find evidence that will stop this war?" Harry asked.

"If I didn't," Tanya said, "I wouldn't waste my time. Kriegworm's conspiracy is obviously related. Otherwise, why would he try to stop me?

"Also obviously, whoever is running him — call him, Mr. Big — will continue to try to block me. Mr. Big knows where I have to go next. And that's where Kriegworm will be."

Harry tapped the cube. "I suppose you want my help on this," he said. Then he grinned. "If so, you're going to have to do something for me in return."

Tanya grimaced. "Conditions! Jesus!" She shook her head. "What's the matter, Harry," she asked, "don't you want to save the world too?"

Harry's grin widened. "Never mind that," he said. Then he pushed the cube forward. "If you want my help, Master Investigator Lawson," he said, "You're going to have to finally make a commitment to the magical wing of the UWP."

The cube glowed brighter, the ozone stink thickened. Instinctively, Tanya drew back.

"What's the big deal, Tanya?" Harry said. "All you have to do is put your thumb into the depression and you'll be able to add Wizard First Class to your rank? Hells, bells, you'll even get a raise."

"I don't want to do this, Harry!" Tanya said.

"Do it!" Harry growled, "Or you'll get no help from me!"

Tanya's shoulders sagged. The son of a bitch had her. Only Harry Cooper would hold a whole galaxy hostage to get his way.

She pushed her thumb into the depression. There was a slight stinging sensation, a flash of green light, then the cube went dead.

"Congratulations, Wizard First Class Tanya Lawson," Harry said with a sneer of victory.

Tanya shook off the defeat. "Screw you, Harry," she said. "Now you'll do what I say, or I'll go right to the top and make sure you never get those stars you've been longing for all these years."

"Oh, come on, Tanya," Harry said. "It was all in fun."

Tanya just stared at him.

After a long uncomfortable moment, Harry shrugged. "Okay, what do you need?" he asked.

Then, trying to make a weak joke. "Besides six or seven UWP Marines, that is?"

"That's exactly what I need, Harry," Tanya said, flat. "Six Marines, a fast ship … no make that two. And a dozen Marines. Plus as many Big Freakin' Guns as they'll hold."

Harry gasped at her audacity. The UWP's naval forces were used sparingly. There were too many political toes that could be stepped on.

The same with the Marines, which was a super elite corps of fighters. Harry would have to stretch out his coward's neck big time to get commandeer six of them.

He tried to argue. Tried to offer other alternatives. Tanya swatted his protests aside like so many flies.

The next morning she gave the order and the two little ships blasted off for Uttermost Space. And there were six combat-hardened Marines stuffed in each ship along with the crew.

*   *   *

It was hands down the most dangerous journey Tanya had ever attempted. It was also the most depressing.

The whole Galaxy either seemed to be girding for war or fleeing the war.

Tanya's route took her right through the middle of the gathering storm — with flashes of missile lightning on every side from preliminary firefights as the two superpowers jockeyed for position and tested the mettle of their foe.

Even more depressing were the constant news accounts of the coming duel between Davyd and Vlad. The men had yet to meet in battle, but the newscasters were crowing about what a fight it'd be. The galaxy's two greatest warriors going at it man to man.

Tanya was feeling desperate around the edges. If only she could uncover the conspiracy before they killed each other.

For embarrassingly selfish reasons she didn't quite understand, Tanya was more troubled by the threat to Vlad and Davyd than she was about the brewing war.

Her first goal was a planet in the Frontier Zone, so small and undistinguished that it went by the rather drab moniker of Gray Sector One. GS-1 for short. Meaning, the settlers hadn't even got their acts together enough to file for a territorial name.

Tanya's purpose: According to intelligence, GS-1 was a key smuggling and money-laundering outpost. And she was sure she could pick up the trail of Billy Ivanov and Old Scratch there.

As she'd mentioned to Harry, there was even a far-off chance she might run across Kriegworm's spoor at GS-1 — assuming Kriegworm was looking for Billy and Scratch as well.

This was only a guess on her part, but she'd learned to pay attention to such guesses long ago.

Although distant in normal star map bytes, GS-1 sat on the edge of an anomaly in the fabric of space that ought to have cut the trip down to an e-week max.

Just off Jupiter there was a jump point big enough to allow the two little Thunderbolt 220' Class scout ships that had been assigned to her to squeeze through. In theory, they'd grab a fast spectral wind ride through Uttermost Space to GSO.

"Ordinarily, this would be no problem, Major,"   Lt. Commander Sean Moon told her during the pre-takeoff briefing. "But if it's anything like the patrol I just got back from, we'll be lucky if we can make it in an e-month!"

"I don't have that long," Tanya said. "Hell, a week is seven days too many!"

Moon shrugged. A former American Coast Guardsman, he'd distinguished himself early in his career thwarting terrorists, arms smugglers and pirates.

Recruited by the naval arm of the UWP, Moon was known as much for his cunning as he was for bravery under fire. And he also spoke his mind, as Tanya quickly found out.

"You'd better start practicing holding your breath, then, Major," Moon said, "because you damned well aren't going to get what you want."

He pointed with unconcealed pride at the two small ships waiting on the tarmac. Last minute supplies and ammo were being jammed into every nook and cranny of the command ship — the *Hamilton*.

While a fuel 'bot strained to force every spark of power it could into the big ion-batteries of its sister vessel — the *Rubin*.

"We wouldn't make it at all without these babies," he said. "Either some Russian or the American warship would spot us. And there's no questions being asked, these days.

"Even a UWO mission isn't safe. Those boys fire first and look to see who they hit later."

Tanya couldn't help but cast an admiring eye over the sleek lines of the ships. She'd been impressed when she'd boned up on the specs last night. But in the titanium "flesh," the ships were mechanical works of art.

They were the ultimate in stealth. Based entirely on ancient laws of physics technology, there was not one magical particle in either ship. Which meant they were almost impossible to spot using conventional military radar spells.

Originally designed as American military special forces support platforms, each ship was a remarkably slender two hundred and fifty feet long.

This was chunked into thirds: one third engine, one third weapons, one third fuel and supplies. The crew got whatever space was left over, so it was damned crowded.

Later, when Tanya saw what was laughingly called the crew quarters she was glad her aunt was no prude and had stomped on any signs of false modesty during her upbringing. Because there was no privacy at all on the little ships.

Even more impressive: Tanya had asked for some Big Freaking Guns and the UWP naval wing had delivered in spades.

Since the stealth design rejected the use of all magic, there was an assortment of old-fashioned missiles. But the piece-de-resistance were the two Bushmaster XXI automatic cannons mounted in the main weapons stations.

According to her copy of Jane's, the parallel physics technology had overcome the old problem of barrel wear that ancient weapons had suffered from.

A ceramic-like material was used to line the chainguns' barrels so they could fire high explosive ammunition at a satisfying rate of 200 rounds per minute.

There was no shielding spell Tanya knew of capable of standing up under that shattering fire, especially with the special canister rounds the guns fired.

She was anxious to talk to the weapons expert, Lt. Robert Rhodes, who also commanded the *Rubin*. Antique weapons had always fascinated Tanya and she was intrigued by Lt. Rhodes' nickname — "Bullet Bob." Now, this was a guy to know!

She heard someone curse and glanced over at the *Hamilton*. Two crewmen were trying to shove a rectangular trunk through the cargo door. The trunk contained her collapsed fly-flapper, which Tanya had decided to take along at the last minute.

Lt. Moon winced. "I hope that's an absolutely necessary piece of gear, Major," he said. "We're light on rations as it is and that's not making anything easier."

"It's necessary all right," Tanya said firmly.

She wanted to make certain that non-magical transportation was available to her once she reached GS-1. And the fly-flapper not only fit that requirement, but was totally silent as well.

"It might make the difference between the success or failure of this mission," Tanya added.

Moon laughed. He was a handsome, amiable young man. "Okay, but when the crew starts bitching about the grub, don't expect me to save you from the lynching party."

Tanya grimaced. "And I won't blame them, either," she said. "One thing you ought to know about me, is that I like to eat!"

Moon looked her over. It was a casual look, but admiring in an inoffensive way.

"You'd never know that from your superstructure, Major," he said. "Pretty trim lines for a big eater."

Then he winked. "We're going to get along just fine," he said. "You like to eat and I just purely love to cook."

Tanya was puzzled. Since when did skippers of fighting ship start pulling down galley duty?

Two e-days out — to her intense delight — Tanya learned the answer.

Delicious smells drew her from her bunk to the tiny galley where the crew cooked and ate all their meals.

Moon, wrapped in a food-spattered apron, was standing over a big pot, ladle in one hand, a battered antique paperback book in the other.

"That smells heavenly," Tanya said. "What is it?"

Moon grinned. "Only the best damned chili in the entire galaxy," he said, stirring the contents of the pot.

Even more fabulous smells were released by this action and Tanya's belly gave an unladylike growl.

"You've convinced me, commander," Tanya said, "and I haven't even tasted it yet."

She glanced at the book, frowning when she saw a picture of a strange looking space vehicle on the greasy cover.

"What kind of cookbook is that?" she asked.

Moon laughed. "Actually, it's an old science fiction novel written back in the Twentieth Century. A couple of guys wrote a whole series of them, called the 'Sten Chronicles.'

"Great action, fantastic stories, but best of all they put two killer recipes in each novel."

He gave the pot another vigorous stir. "This dish comes from one of those books. It's called 'The Eternal Emperor's Chili,' after one of the major characters."

Tanya shook her head. "Amazing!" was all she could say.

Moon chortled. "You should see the faces of the recruits when they see their Old Man standing over a pot, spoon in one hand and a greasy science fiction novel in the other.

"They think I'm suffering from a bad case of space bends and start wondering how they hell they can swing a transfer."

Moon put his cooking tools aside and ripped a big hunk of bread off a fresh loaf of sourdough — also a recipe from the Sten novels, he later told her.

He dipped the fragrant hunk into the pot and held it out for Tanya. The bread was soaked with a thick red sauce.

"Tell me what you think," he said.

Tanya took a bite. And, wow! she thought her head was going to come off. The chili was that peppery. Then the taste came through, coating her tongue with the most delicious and complex flavors.

She groaned in pleasure. "Fabulous!" she said. "Simply fabulous."

Then, "When do we eat?"

"Right now, major," Moon said.

He scooped up a huge bowl of chili and beans for her. She went through two more before calling it quits.

Moon's grin grew wider and wider as he watched her enjoy the food.

He tried out some of his other Sten recipes on her during the journey. Each more delicious than the other.

By the time they reached GS-1 Tanya was so stuffed with good food that for the first time in her life she began to fear for her waistline.

CHAPTER FORTY

Millions of miles away from Tanya and her quest, Vlad's fiendish servants were gathered before their absent master's vid system.

Even that grumbler Brosha was so taken by the events playing out on the screen he didn't notice that many of the little fiends wore shoes — which was completely forbidden by the obsessively tidy Brosha.

On the vidscreen, a silver-haired Russian official was saying:

"And now, comrades, as we all face the great perils of the coming thunder together, let us reflect on the valor and heroism of those who guard the motherlands from those Amer dogs. I speak of brave men, such as Major Vlad Projogin, of the SpetzNaz Commandos.

"Major Projogin, as all know, is the greatest of our heroes. And even now he is stalking that treacherous Amer assassin, David Kells.

"The entire galaxy awaits the outcome of that coming duel, which will surely go down in our glorious history as another marvelous victory for our Russian fighting forces.

"I promise you that once Major Projogin has slain the Amer, he won't be satisfied. He'll shoulder even more burdens in our defense. He'll move swiftly to intercept the treacherous enemy hordes.

"He will hunt down and bring to swift justice spies and saboteurs, who are even now slipping into our dominions. Intent on destroying our most important military facilities and civilian life-supporting systems.

"Brave as he is, Major Projogin is only one of many heroes of Mother Russia. Perhaps you will someday join that band of valorous warriors.

"Come, comrades. Do not be shy. Mother Russia has need of you. Join the SpetzNaz now and be one of them.

"Be a real man. A real soldier!"

Brosha wiped an unaccustomed tear from one of his fiendish eyes.

"Our poor master," he said. "I wonder what he's doing now?"

* * *

"Yes? Who is there?" growled an inhuman voice.

Vlad stood before a small door in a quiet block of offices, minor temples, craft shops and family-owned restaurants.

Behind the door, he guessed from the timbre of the voice, was an ogre. A rare occupant in a middle-class human neighborhood.

"Speak up!" came the voice again. "Who is it that seeks entry?"

"Vlad."

The single word was sufficient. There was no password. The fiendish Church Of The Sword guardians didn't require such things. They had their own magical ways to confirm identities.

The door opened, revealing a thick cloud of mist floating just beyond the threshold. The place was protected by mighty spells and Vlad had to click on a special Church Of The Sword device to pierce the sorcerous haze.

"Enter, softskin," said the ogre.

The fiendish creatures who served the Church of the Sword suffered a rare disease: the lack of ordinary courtesy.

Vlad shrugged. The rudeness was a small but pleasant perk the fiends enjoyed. Well, let the kids alone, as the saying goes.

He passed through the thick cloud, which was filled with hundreds of unseen eyes all studying him intently.

Vlad soon found himself in a narrow corridor whose walls were covered with runes and other mysterious symbols.

He sensed the presence of something huge and rather hungry lurking beneath the floor. A demon of some sort who was ready to defend the others from any unwelcome strangers.

"Advance, softskin," came another unpleasant voice.

Vlad looked up and saw an enormous female ogre. Green scales formed her hide. And two sharp white fangs peeped from beneath her upper lip. But drawn across her shoulders was a black SpetzNaz uniform decorated with four captain's stars.

Silently, she beckoned Vlad onward and suddenly he found himself standing at the edge of a deep, dark cavern.

"Follow me, major," the ogre ordered. "Do not stray from the path. And keep one pace behind me — no more, no less."

Vlad obeyed, stepping out into the darkness as the Ogre moved forward. An invisible pathway met his feet, keeping him and the ogre from plunging into the abyss.

A few moments later the ogre suddenly stopped and Vlad had to pull himself up quickly to keep from bumping into her.

"The armory," the ogre said. "Choose, softskin."

Vlad saw nothing but dark shadows, pricked with gleaming eyes. But he could sense the ogre looming nearby.

"I need something to locate my enemy," Vlad said. "He's a cunning fellow and will be hard to find."

The darkness was lit by the ogre's grin as she exposed her gleaming white fangs. "Ah, ha! I know what is required, major. A spirit we call the 'Hound.'

"She was bred for nearly twenty years. An extraordinary thing, Major. Half spirit, half fairy and a thin layer of crystallized devilish luck. She can find any softskin or fiend."

The ogre laughed, as if she'd just made a joke.

"Crystallized luck?" Vlad asked. "What's that?"

"Thou doest not need to know, major," the ogre admonished him.

"Well, let's see it then," Vlad said.

He didn't have much time. Davyd had just upped his score by assassinating two combat wizards and a certain colonel who had been the head of a vital intelligence division. So now it was one hundred and three kills for Kells and one hundred and one for Vlad.

Moreover, Vlad had detected a subtle pattern in Davyd's choice of targets. Three kills on three different planets. The first was on a world just within the starry borders of the Russian empire. The second was deeper still. And the third was even more daring — less than three e-days journey from New Russia itself.

Vlad firmly believed that New Russia would be Davyd's next choice for a killing ground. But where exactly? New Russia was twice the size of Earth and had three times the population. How could Vlad find him among all those people?

"The Hound can also be a weapon herself," the ogre said, breaking into Vlad's thoughts.

The gloom was relieved by dim light and Vlad saw the ogre stretch out a scaly claw, pointing. "Look, softskin!" she commanded.

Vlad looked and saw the darkness unfold swiftly before him. And he caught a glimpse of something, or someone lurking behind a dark curtain.

Projogin couldn't tell exactly what it was. Subtle sensations floated through his mind: a faint pink flourish on the black velvet of an evening sky; the swift trembling of water in the small bowl of a bubbling spring; the whisper of white apple leaves in blossom ...

"Here to obey, major," whispered a voice.

Vlad shivered.

It was the voice of Tanya Lawson!

"She's pretty, isn't she?" the ogre said proudly.

"Oh yes," Vlad muttered "She's *very* pretty!"

*　*　*

The rest was not so interesting.

A half-alive weapon stuffed with various fiendish creatures. Swifter than bullets and more deadly than lasers. The device was one of very the latest models, as were the other weapons Vlad chose.

But these things were of no comfort to him. For his gut instinct told him that in the end he and Davyd would face each other with little more than their bare hands.

Surely, Vlad thought, Kells would be armed with the same sort of sophisticated weaponry. Then he suddenly imagined how he and his enemy would approach one other for the final battle.

Dropping their deadly devices one by one. Facing one another. And then …

"Be careful with this little baby, major," the ogre warned as she turned the Hound over to him.

"And good luck. This will be a good show. We'll all be watching thee."

The ogre laughed most evilly.

Vlad turned and exited without saying thank you, much less goodbye. His mind was churning with hundreds of half-formed thoughts.

He chased them away and went swiftly to the special little grav-van he'd ordered to be waiting for him upon his arrival in New Russia. Inside, he turned on the strong shielding system that blanked out all known snooping devices.

Then he chanted a spell and the Hound came to life. "Ready to search, master," said the invisible Tanya Lawson.

How could this be? How could this unseen creature possibly manage …

"You were thinking very intensely about this person, master," came the answer to Vlad's unspoken question. "I was searching your mind for clues, master."

"But …" Vlad blushed. There were too many hot dreams and visions for anyone to dig in …

"I'm staying out of what humans call 'moral areas,' master," the Hound said in Tanya's voice. "And you can eliminate all auxiliary material that would be dragged from your memory. But now … This Davyd Kells? Yes. The search has begun."

The world around Vlad became dim and gray and he felt as if he had been enveloped by a thick, dry mist. He shivered and clenched his teeth. Although he knew his refuge in the van was quite safe, he hated not being able to see what was going on.

It would be so easy for his enemy to find him and take aim!

Vlad stirred, but then the stern voice of the bodiless Investigator Lawson warned him:

"Remain motionless, master. I... must ... locate the astral trace ... according ... to the ... imprints in your memory ...

"Yes! Lock! Okay ... tracing ... locating ..."

At that moment Vlad broke into a cold sweat. Davyd was near! Dammit, he was near! Vlad could sense the Hound stretching out ... stretching out ...

Vlad's glands overflowed with combat hormones. Pumping them through his veins. And for a moment a red haze of hate obscured his view.

And then, through the Hound, he sensed Davyd shaking off the hook and escaping.

Vlad sucked in air, as if rising from cold, salty depths. He fought to return his system to normal.

"Search failure," Tanya's voice announced. Then: "New search, master?"

"No! Not yet." Vlad's mouth was as dry as desert sand in midday. "But can you check to see if a similar Hound system was used to detect us?"

"Of course." It seemed that the Hound was annoyed by his stupidity and lack of faith in her. Then: "Shall I establish a permanent guard circle, master?"

"No," Vlad said once more.

A nasty lump slipped down his throat. His stomach felt as if it was being squeezed in a vise.

To establish a permanent guard circle would be the ultimate stupid deed.

Surely Davyd would expect something like that. And surely he would possess tools of no less power than Vlad's. And surely Davyd had been alerted by Vlad's search.

And now Kells knew exactly what kind of weapon Vlad had used to find him. Davyd might not know exactly where Vlad was. But he'd discover his location soon enough.

Vlad had two choices: (1) Get the hell as fast as possible. Or, (2) Remain in the area — with all the fiendish systems shut down. And to use only his eyes and combat senses to guard him while he waited for Davyd.

Of course, Vlad had a few other aces up his sleeve. Such as several ancient spells the Church of The Sword had kept secret for hundreds of years. Perhaps these spells would be a good surprise even for the great Davyd Kells.

Vlad stuffed his gear into a self propelled hoverpack and exited the van. He looked up and down the street until he saw what he needed: It was a small hotel. A two-storied house with solid stone walls and narrow windows.

It was stylized after a medieval castle and the section facing the street had two small towers on each corner.

Casually, he strode down the street and went through the doors.

"How may I help you, sir?" asked the clerk behind the large counter.

"Do you have any rooms available in either of the towers?" Vlad asked. "They look charming, absolutely charming."

"Oh yes, sir, surely. On the second floor, the one to the right. The cost is quite reasonable …"

Playing his role, Vlad rented the room and paid in advance for three days. Although he was fairly certain he wouldn't need it for more than three hours. Well, nevertheless, he'd be ready.

The tower chamber was just as good as he expected — roomy, with an excellent sightline along the two main streets. It also boasted thick doors made of old oak.

Oak! That was excellent. The Church Of The Sword had the best of relations with the spirits of those ancient trees.

Vlad ordered the hoverpack to spill its contents on the bed.

And he swiftly got to work.

CHAPTER FORTY ONE

As the pirate ship prepared to land on GS-1, the *Hamilton* and *Rubin* lurked behind a screen of orbiting meteorites.

Aboard the *Hamilton*, Tanya monitored the renegade Engine Devil's instructions to the fiendish crew that operated the ship's systems.

Although obviously drunk, the demon displayed that breed's typical perfectionism as he barked orders to his spirit world charges.

Tanya heard him chant a snooping spell, then saw the lights of her monitor board blink madly as the spell swept through the meteorite swarm that hid the UWP ships.

She held her breath as the powerful magical particles penetrated the *Hamilton's* hull, making her skin crawl and her hair stand on end.

Then the spell passed harmlessly by, giving no alarm, and she heard the Engine Devil bark the all clear for landing.

Moon swiveled his control chair about, beaming a big grin and giving Tanya a thumb's up sign. Rhodes had just reported in from the *Rubin* that the ship's system had also dodged the spell and all was well to proceed.

Tanya breathed a sigh of relief. The two stealth ships had easily shrugged off the best magical snooping technology the sophisticated pirate vessel could bring to bear.

For the first time in what seemed like an eternity, her hopes were rising.

She motioned to Moon, giving him the "go" signal. They'd maintained complete silence since they'd spotted the pirate ship and would continue to do so until the crucial moment.

Their human prey wasn't so sensible. The minute the Engine Devil announced there was no danger, the pirates immediately started chattering like monkeys.

Through her old-fashioned electrical earphones, Tanya could hear them boasting about their most recent raid. And debating the merits of the different kinds of debauchery they'd be able to enjoy once they'd unloaded their ill-gotten gains.

The instant the pirate ship disappeared from sight — settling down through the thick mists that perpetually shrouded GS-1 — Moon signaled Rhodes via the deep-cover radio channel the stealth vessels favored. And the hunt began.

GS-1 was a smuggler's paradise. Eternally blanketed by heavy mists and fog, the small planet's several mountainous continents were covered by thick, fern-like forests. There were so many potential hiding places it would take years to investigate them all.

Tanya had heard stories about whole communities of criminals so well concealed that an unsuspecting person could amble halfway through one of the towns before realizing she was no longer in the middle of a wilderness.

As the *Hamilton* and *Rubin* swept down to the surface and the monitor screens revealed the great fern forests waving their fronds in the mist, Tanya saw for herself that those stories were not exaggerations.

Hot spots indicating thousands of living creatures red peppered her screen, yet when she looked through the *Hamilton's* wide viewing port all she could see was the gray humps of low mountain ranges and the shadowy, greenish black shapes of the forests that covered them.

For Tanya the experience was one more proof of her firm Luddite belief in the superiority of mechanical over magical technology. In her mind the only benefit magic had brought to human beings — and this was dubious, considering the ongoing crisis — was the ability to travel through space at post-light speed.

Since she was no use to Moon and Rubin during the stealth chase of the pirate ship, she let her mind roam over those sticky matters.

What would the present be like, she wondered if spirit world magic hadn't buried the technology of her ancestors?

There'd be no wizards — and what would be wrong with that? There'd also be no fiendish creatures occupying every household device. A blessing, as far as Tanya was concerned.

And she also wondered — taking her idle thoughts to the limit — if there'd even be a war between the Russians and Americans.

Was all the intense xenophobic hate that infected the human race the result of its total reliance on sorcery?

There was a time, she recalled from her history lessons, that Russia and America had nearly laid down their arms and embraced one another as brothers.

What had happened?

What had stopped the peace and propelled the Cold War forward for another thousand years?

Which brought her back to Davyd and Vlad and their mysterious exchange when they'd met in the neutral setting of her UWP chartered ship.

They'd evoked the names of George Bush and Vladimir Putin. Two national leaders assassinated during the first years of the Twenty First Century.

What the hell was that all about?

And, as impossible as it might seem, did it have something to do with what was going on now?

Tanya's pulse quickened as idle speculation suddenly began to solidify into something real. Something pertinent.

What if Davyd and Vlad were the assassins?

But that was impossible, you stupid woman. Neither of them looked more than thirty five. And Bush and Putin were killed a thousand years ago.

Except ... except ...

And then Moon abruptly signaled her, breaking her train of thought.

She felt suddenly emptied, bewildered and shattered as all her speculations turned to dust.

Moon signaled again, then pointed at her monitor. Dully, she looked down at the screen.

The pirate ship had landed.

Now the shooting was about to begin.

* * *

Many light years away — in land of red rolling plains and purple rivers — little Billy Ivanov danced about a campfire singing at the top of his lungs:

> *"O look and behold*
> *The Planets that love us*
> *All harnessed in gold!*
> *What chariots, what horses*
> *Against us shall bide*
> *While the Stars in their courses*
> *Do fight on our side?"*

Old Scratch scraped away a tear with his scaly claw, overcome with emotion.

The song, which he'd taught Billy, was from one of the Engine Devil's favorite Kipling poems: "The Astrologers Song." And the boy's high clear tenor gave it deeper meaning than it had ever held for Scratchy before.

Voice shimmering under the swirling stars, Billy sang on:

> *"All thought, all desires,*
> *That are under the sun,*
> *Are one with their fires,*
> *As we also are one:*
> *All matter, all spirit,*
> *All fashion, all frame,*

Receive and inherit
Their strength from the same."

Scratchy turned to look at his companions, who were gathered around the fire, gazing at Billy with misty eyes.

Most were escaped spirit world folk; fiends of every size and kind: tiny gremlins, misty goblins, electric DeathSpirits, great-mawed MotherDemons and on and on, too many to mention.

Twenty of them were humans who had fled repression on their home planets. They were dressed in the skins of exotic beasts hunted for their meat and hide on the rolling red plains.

It was a strange group — certainly stranger than any Scratch had seen in his long life. But they all had one thing in common: they were outcasts, hunted ones, with bounties on their heads.

Just like Scratch and Billy.

Scratch thought of the long, arduous flight that brought them to this rebel world, where fiends and humans lived side by side.

His friends had smuggled the Engine Devil and the boy aboard a rusty old freighter bound for GS-1 — the pirates' haven. Scratchy didn't trust those human criminals one bit and it was a good thing, because several thugs had attacked him and the boy in their sleeping places the first night.

Scratch had slain one of them — ripping the pirate from stem to stern with a mighty claw — and the others had fled, their ears burning from the hot swear words he'd hurled after them.

From GS-1, they'd hopped a rebel freighter his friends had provided and after many days they'd finally come to this outpost of the spirit world.

The renegade fiends and humans had given the boy and the Engine Devil a rousing welcome. Apparently the story of their deeds — defying both Rooskie and Amer wizards and warriors — had penetrated even to this wild place.

And so it was that they were given a home — only a hut, but quite comfortable, Scratchy thought — in a friendly village which sat upon the banks of a wide purple river teaming with things easy to hunt and good to eat.

Billy had charmed one and all with his kindness and boyish enthusiasm. Also, even the strongest fiends were impressed with his growing magical powers and they counted themselves lucky to have such a mighty human wizard — no matter how young — join their grand cause.

It was this cause, however, which gave Old Scratch pause about remaining among these beings. Wild idealists all, their oft-stated holy purpose was to rid the galaxy of the two great softskin empires who had kept all creatures under their thumbs.

Although Scratchy sympathized with them, he didn't see how it was possible and feared he and boy would be swept up in their doomed revolution against two such mighty giants.

What else could he do but remain among them? There was no place else he and Billy could go. At least not right away, that is. Scratch had half-formed ideas about getting Billy and himself to the star system of his birth, where wild Engine Devils still roamed.

But as yet he hadn't figured out how to get his hands on a ship that would take them there.

There was also a large dead goblin floating in that idea soup. Once they arrived, what would Billy do? The atmosphere of Scratchy's home planet was hostile to softskins. The boy couldn't live in a magical protective bubble all his life.

And even if a way could be found to overcome that problem, Billy would soon become lonely for his own kind.

Scratchy sighed, feeling very sorry for Billy — and himself. But then the boy's voice broke through his depression and he smiled as he listened to the last thrilling verses of the song:

> *"... Though terrors o'ertake us*
> *We'll not be afraid.*
> *No power can unmake us*
> *Save that which has made.*
> *Nor yet beyond reason*
> *Or hope shall we fall —*
> *All things have their season,*
> *And Mercy crowns all!*
>
> *Then, doubt not, ye fearful —*
> *The Eternal is King —*
> *Up, heart, and be cheerful,*
> *And lustily sing:—*
> *What chariots, what horses*
> *Against us shall bide*
> *While the Stars in their courses*
> *Do fight on our side?"*

The fiends and humans applauded Billy's performance with much enthusiasm. He blushed and grinned, bobbing his head in thanks.

Then he ran to Old Scratch's side, crying: "Isn't this grand, Scratchy? I'll bet there's not another boy in the whole galaxy who's had such a great adventure!"

Scratchy wanted to tell the boy everything was not as good as it appeared. That awful men were hunting them and he feared they'd come on them soon.

He opened his mouth to speak those words of caution, but then Billy threw himself into the Engine Devil's arms, saying, "Oh, thank you, Scratchy! Thank you! I've never had a *real* family before. And now you've given me one!"

Old Scratch bit back his warning. And he clumsily patted the boy with a huge claw.

"It's good to see thee happy, O Little Friend of the World," he said instead. "And I am pleased to be the cause of so much joy."

* * *

Tanya coldly surveyed the line of prisoners drawn up before her. Most ducked their heads in fear as her narrowed eyes fell upon them, then swept onward. A few glowered defiance and her eyes stopped, fixing each unruly felon with a soul-piercing glare.

Invariably she'd win this contest of wills and soon the pirate's eyes would become frightened and he'd quickly shift his gaze downward, as if he'd suddenly found something of absorbing interest about his feet.

Her UWO marines stood guard over the prisoners, their weapons at the ready, their eyes almost as fierce and intimidating as Tanya's.

Framing the prisoners was the bullet-chewed corpse of the freighter they'd tracked to this landing zone. To the left was a large hangar — once artfully camouflaged to blend in with the forest. Now shattered by the guns of the *Hamilton* and *Rubin*.

The two ships hung above the scene, gunports peeled back to show their teeth. Wood smoke columned upward, flowing around the narrow bellies of the vessels. The smoke was rising off the blackened remains of the trees the two fighting ships had blasted into fiery splinters during the initial attack.

Unfortunately for the pirates, their commanders had tried to resist when the *Hamilton* and *Rubin* had swooped down into the clearing — loudspeakers blaring demands for their immediate surrender to the United Worlds Police.

The felons had answered that lawfully delivered demand with a barrage of fire. They'd even gotten off one missile.

Moon and Rhodes had replied with overpowering return fire. The chainguns spitting out lead bullets like death-dealing hailstones and the missile — along with its battery of DeathSpirits — had been blown to pieces.

The same thing had happened to the men and rebel fiends who had fired upon the UWP vessels.

Tanya didn't know how many pirates had died during the brief engagement. No one had counted them yet, nor did she think anyone would have time. She certainly had no interest in such figures, since her sole concern was the whereabouts of the three fugitives she sought: Kriegworm, Billy Ivanov and Old Scratch.

So far, none of the pirates had confessed that they'd seen them. But Tanya knew they were lying. When she'd asked the question her cop's senses read the lies in the shifty gazes and body language the prisoners displayed.

She needed to get the truth out of them damned fast, but wasn't certain how to go about it. There wasn't any time for individual interrogation. Torture was a possibility, although it was forbidden under the UWP charter.

Still, some rogue cops had been known to torture their suspects. Tanya had never considered using those tactics. She thought torture not only inhumane, but believed the answers gained were unreliable.

Even so, time was so short and the stakes were so high that for the first time in her career, Tanya was contemplating what had once been unthinkable.

As she flipped through her mental book of black ops torture methods, she suddenly caught a metal flash winking at the wrist of one the prisoners.

Tanya stalked over to the man. She remembered that he was one of the pirates who'd glowered at her.

"You!" she growled. "What's that you've got?" She pointed at the antique gold Rolex on his wrist.

The felon gave her a gap-toothed grin. "What's it look like to youse, major? Just me watch, is all."

"Where'd you get it?" she demanded.

The felon shrugged. "Can't say as I remember," he said.

"Let's see if I can jog your sorry-assed excuse for a memory, then," Tanya said.

She stepped back. "Drop your pants!" Tanya ordered.

The pirate turned pale. "What does youse want me to do that for?" he gulped.

Tanya slipped her combat knife from its sheath. "Seemed as good a time as any," she said, "to add to my collection. You should see it — six pickle jars packed to the brim and a seventh two-thirds full."

The pirate took a step backward, but one of the marines prodded him forward with his bayonet.

"You heard the major," the marine said. "Drop your pants, bub!"

The pirate started crying. "Okay, okay," he blubbered. "I'll tell youse what youse wanna know."

Tanya sighed. "Damn!" she said. "Another chance gone."

Then she grinned, running her thumb along the knife blade. "Of course, I can always hope, can't I?" she said. "Maybe you'll lie to me. I'd like that. I really, really, would."

The pirate started talking just as fast as he could.

CHAPTER FORTY TWO

The problem is that I'm too hyped for this job, Davyd thought.

Man, did that sound familiar. But he'd felt like that from the very beginning of the game. The three kills test ... the infamous generalisimo ... the apprentice assassin ...

Not so long ago, but so damned far away. Far, far, goddamned away!

Shit, he should've killed the little S.O.B. for freezing and almost spoiling the mission. If only out of mercy so that someday he wouldn't have to face what Davyd was facing now.

Davyd swallowed. An old habit: he never spat. Saliva was a precious tool for those bastards who called themselves "wizards."

He hated those sons of bitches, but he'd never been dumb enough to ignore a clear and present danger. Can't leave spit hanging around for the wizards to gather up and hunt you down and barbecue your lily white with their spells.

Davyd's solo command post for this job was a sewer drain. And just now he was sitting absolutely motionless, filthy water swirling around him; thick, foul odors testing his rebreather to the max.

Good old Vlad had fallen for his little ploy. Davyd had strewn the trail with dead men like the fairy tale kids had scattered crumbs when they were on their way to the witch's big damned gingerbread house.

Okay, so he'd drawn Vlad out. Gotten him to look for the gingerbread house. But this house was full of the blood and blasted bones of Vlad's comrades.

And he'd known from the start that the Russian couldn't resist trying to make Davyd pay for his crimes.

Like Odysseus Corps, the Church Of The Sword was intent on revenging any perceived wrongs. And Davyd had spent ten centuries making them mad as hell.

Pity he had to pull that trick on Vlad. Not a bad guy, when you got to know him.

Then Davyd realized that Vlad was the only person he'd known throughout his entire Odysseus-prolonged life. They'd met as very young men. They'd been the best their respective countries had to offer in the military pentathlon. And they'd gone head-to-head in a pre-Olympics match.

Vlad had equaled Davyd in every event. Dead even in the pistol shoot, hitting target after target for hours. Finally, after a record length of time, Vlad had missed a shot and Davyd had been declared the victor.

But then Vlad had evened the score by winning the fencing contest. Again, it had been such a close contest that both knew mere chance had made Vlad the victor. And that it would very well turn out differently if they fought a second time.

Their scores remained equal in the three other events: swimming, plus cross-country running and horseback riding.

In the end, it had been a tie and they were both awarded a gold medal.

Afterwards, they'd both gotten very drunk toasting each other for displaying such skill and sportsmanship. And they had been looking forward to meeting again in the 2004 Olympics. But their respective leaders had other plans for Vlad and Davyd that were less than Olympian.

Much less.

Now — a thousand years later — they were about to meet in another competition. Except this time it was a death match. And the only toasting that would be done would be Davyd drinking Vlad's soul to hell after he'd killed him.

Too bad, but that's the way it had to be.

Watch yourself, Kells, Davyd suddenly warned himself. You're getting soft on the guy. The very thought triggered a flood of angry juices into the American's veins.

And just like that, Vlad was transformed from a nice guy into a cunning, hated enemy.

He took pleasure as reviewed how he'd won the first, most difficult round. This gave him a better than average chance of accomplishing his mission.

Jesus, he'd already pinned Vlad's ass to the ground so he could blow it away at his leisure.

Gridded the war-mongering Rooskie creep in super tight coordinates with his gremlin box and now all he had to do was move on in and … boom!

Goodbye Comrade Vlad — and hello to many blissful tomorrows as Davyd slept in his shimmering magic tube for a century or more. Hardening his soul to all the men he'd had to kill just to get to this fateful moment.

Despair crept in behind that thought, but Davyd quickly shooed it away. He had to be alert. Guilt free, like Father Zorza had said. Put the asshole down for God, Country and the Odysseus Corps.

But it wouldn't be easy.

Vlad had surprised the holy hell out of Davyd even as he was chalking up the first round as his own.

That clever President killing S.O.B. had nearly turned the effing tables on him with his little game. Using that Hound device to locate him. A device that had sounded exactly like Tanya!

And oh, shit, and oh dear, Davyd had thought he was in trouble then. The Tanya device had nearly thrown him for a loop.

As soon as Davyd had heard her voice through the gremlin box his mind had gone into freeze mode. Mooning over her mental image like a schoolboy as Vlad got ready to toast his ass big time.

The Russian was clever, he had to give him that. And one helluva cheat, playing the Tanya card like that.

Still, Davyd had managed to shake him off and now he was sitting in the cat bird's seat.

At that thought, Davyd grinned ruefully and looked down at the chilly water, thick with particles he didn't even want to think about. Cold water running between his legs and getting his ass wet.

Some seat!

Regardless, he'd managed to break Vlad's grip just in time and now Davyd was ahead in the important opening of the deadly game they were playing.

It was only a one-step lead, but it was a precious step.

He'd located Vlad — up in that tower room in the little hotel. But Vlad didn't have the faintest idea where Davyd was.

Oh sure, he knew Davyd was close. But what of it? All Vlad could do was sit and wait for Davyd to come to him and deal out the Death Card.

Actually, in most cases Vlad's decision would've been damned smart. Holing up was the best thing to do. Davyd had done it many times himself.

Letting an artful enemy come to him while he prepared the ground.

But that tactic wouldn't work on Davyd Kells, who was a deep believer in the Odysseus Corps' motto: "Kill with the first blow!"

True, The Church of the Sword was cunning when it came to defense. However, there was no denying that a skilled attacker always has the advantage. This had been so since the days of Alexander. And Davyd was an ardent student of Alexander.

However, the last thing he wanted to do was fool himself into thinking his victory over Vlad was already in his pocket. That Rooskie was too damned good.

Davyd must not underestimate him.

Also, that first damned mistake was not Vlad's fault, he grudgingly admitted. The Hound had failed him. Giving Vlad away even as it had tracked Davyd.

Davyd had his own Odysseus Corps version of the Hound. But he'd decided not to use it, fearing it would behave exactly as Vlad's had done. Putting out so much magical energy that the device revealed its presence to his prey. Which is what had happened to Vlad. In spades, pal, in spades.

Instead, Davyd had turned his own mocking and swearing hound spirit to a passive waiting mode. And now he was damned glad he'd done so. The poor thing had been knocked into a coma when it had come up against Vlad's Tanya-voiced snooper.

Didn't matter. Davyd had dodged one psychological bullet and was more than ready for the next one.

He had all the weapons he needed. With luck, his duel with Vlad would be over in less than an hour.

The actual fight itself shouldn't take longer than thirty seconds.

That's how these matters usually unfolded. Maneuvering for a long period of time. Then a blazingly quick exchange and someone would be dead.

Davyd remembered that he'd gone through that sort of thing before with Vlad aboard the *Borodino*. The memory of that incident worried him for a minute, then he put it aside.

It was different this time. On the *Borodino*, Vlad had the advantage because he was on his own turf, backed by hundreds of soldiers.

But this was neutral ground. And the fight would be between the two of them, with no help lurking in the background.

It didn't matter that Vlad believed he was choosing the battle field once again by holing up in that tower. Keep on thinking that, pal. Because I sure as hell have a big surprise for you.

The main thing was that Davyd had to keep his cool and not deviate from his plan.

One shot and then Vlad would be dead.

Maybe two.

But don't think about that.

Jesus, the guy was good!

Breathe deep. Breathe long.

He's good. But not as good as you are.

Okay fine? Okay goddamned sure?

All Davyd had to do was keep his focus. Chill out, Kells. Chill out.

Davyd closed his eyes, centering himself. Thinking how nice the wait was. Making himself enjoy the anticipation. Imagining the shot. Yeah, pressing the trigger nice and slow and sweet.

And …

Okay, so in reality the wait wasn't so nice.

It was cold in the sewer and the stench was awful even filtered through his rebreather. However, to Davyd such discomforts didn't matter. He'd suffered through worse conditions in his thousand-year career as a killer.

So he ran Father Zorza's orders through his mind over and over again until they turned into a sort of litany. Almost like a spellcasting chant.

Zorza's orders had been simple: Make Odysseus Corps proud and kill that Rooskie bastard. Hero of the RGF. Assassin supreme. Etcetera, etcetera.

Davyd liked that "etcetera" business.

A good word to repeat … "etcetera, etcetera."

As he relaxed, he sighed. Calmly considering the game that was about to begin.

Okay, it really wasn't going to be that easy.

Hell, until a few hours ago he hadn't even known how he was going to kill the guy.

But now …

But now …

Davyd smiled in the darkness. Killing Vlad was going to be a supreme delight.

This was no fat-assed Generalisimo, for crying out loud. A guy you could take out in your sleep.

Vlad was a goddamned tiger, man. A tiger with a human's cunning brain. And no matter how well-armed Davyd was, no matter how well prepared, in the end they'd face each other as equals.

One stone-age man against the other.

To hell with the magic.

To hell with the special weapons.

Flint knife to flint knife was how it was going play out.

Yeah, and maybe fists against fists …

But, Jesus, what about Tanya?!

Ah, shit, where the hell did that thought come from?

Tanya!

Staring at him.

Measuring him.

Who did she love: Davyd or Vlad?

Okay, okay, okay. That was all stupid stuff. Not to be considered. Get thee behind me, Tanya Lawson!

But still … But still …

Davyd gritted his teeth. Forcing himself to think: Who the hell cares about Tanya Lawson? I've had plenty of women in my time. And I'll have more. Lots more. Blondes, brunettes, redheads … you name it.

And to hell with Tanya Lawson.

Because, my friend, if keep worrying about that woman Vlad will eat your lunch.

Concentrating, Davyd got his killing edge back. His blood was hot, his nerves singing with hunter's joy. But deep within the ghost of Tanya still haunted him.

Then the little green lights on his gremlin box flashed into life. And the little spirit said, "It's time, boss!"

Davyd rose, ready to get on with it.

Now go-go-go, Kells, he thought.

For Odysseus Corps and — like the little motor spirit said:

For Godblessamerica!

*   *   *

He's near, Vlad suddenly realized. He's even closer than I expected. He's really good!

Well, now it's time for absolute calm. Calm as a stone. Imagine that stone: old … covered with green moss … embedded in the turf … motionless … without self awareness … a remnant of a forgotten age.

Yes, that's how calm he'd be.

The Hound caught the scent of the approaching enemy. And Davyd's soundless steps boomed loud in the astral void because his battle desire was too great. Davyd Kells wanted to kill Vlad Projogin too much. And that was a big mistake.

For despite all of Kells' cloaking spells and masking fiends, his desire rang through. Especially after Vlad's preparations.

The walls of his tower room were freshly painted with strange runes. And there were several pentagrams and hexagrams scattered among the runes.

Black candles stood at the vertices of a star with five points. A six-pointed star had bowls of incense placed at each ray. Thirteen small pieces of brown birch bark had been set in the center of a design filled with lines written in old Russian.

These were spell chants created when there was no Empire, no Federation. When America itself was nothing but a vast unexplored continent. When Europe was a dozen small kingdoms.

When Grand Duke Yaroslav's daughter, Anna, became the queen of France because of an old Kiev tradition: the daughter of a strong ruler marries a weak one. A time when Kiev's power stretched from the Baltic to the Black Seas.

The ancient spells had been collected by the Church Of The Sword long ago and kept a carefully guarded secret. It was Vlad's hope that Davyd would be fooled by those powerful old spells.

Kells had expected to face something like the Hound: a tremendously evil weapon; the offspring of some grim wizard's mind. But not these old and odd chants from half-forgotten times.

Vlad's trap was well prepared and now all he had to do was wait for Kells to trigger it.

Davyd's footsteps came closer.

And closer.

Come on, you Amer bastard, Vlad thought.

Come on!

CHAPTER FORTY THREE

From his hilltop vantage point, Infeligo watched the rebel villagers go about their daily business. Several fiends were fishing in the river. A group of softskin women fetched water along a path that led to the communal cooking pot set up in the center of the village.

The human boy and the Engine Devil were squatting near the pot, scooping up food from big wooden bowls. All around them were many other fiends and softskins; some were eating, while others were engaged in tool and clothing making.

Using a spell of magnification, he could see them all quite clearly. Down to the color of the thread the village tailors were using.

Infeligo had half a mind to just go down the hill and kill all the villagers and capture the boy and the Engine Devil.

His ship was hidden at the bottom of a lake about five miles away. Once he'd captured Old Scratch and Billy Ivanov all he had to do was mentos order the ship up, put the two fugitives aboard, then head home.

He'd leave the interrogation of the softskin boy and Engine Devil to Apollion, who was highly skilled in the arts of torture. They'd soon break and then the traitor's identity would be revealed.

Infeligo was especially looking forward to what would happen after that. He hated all of his colleagues equally, so it didn't matter who the villain was.

The main thing was that the punishment would be painful and prolonged. If they went about it the right way, death might take a year or more.

The demon smacked his lips in anticipation, the red stone glowing brighter on his forehead as if it too relished the promise of so much pain.

Then Infeligo remembered his duty and reluctantly put away all those delicious thoughts. The main thing he had to concentrate on was the young softskin and the Engine Devil.

Should he take them now?

Or wait until night when everyone would be asleep?

The only trouble with immediate action was that one of the villagers might escape. If the escaped one carried the news of Infeligo's attack to others, there was a possibility the existence of the Council Of Eight would be exposed.

This was definitely to be avoided. Instead of being congratulated by his colleagues for his deeds, they'd most likely kill him along with the traitor for revealing their ancient secret.

Unfortunately, the villagers had been on the run for so many years that they were an incredibly wary lot. Making the odds even better that one or more might escape.

Although the sorcerous shields they'd erected would be easy enough for Infeligo to penetrate, they'd also created several fairly clever roaming spells that sniffed a mile-wide area constantly for signs of danger.

Infeligo had guarded himself against those, but once he started moving down the hill it would be extremely difficult to maintain the power of his counter spells.

No matter that he was disguised as a human. Or that the costume he wore — the loose flowing robes and turban of a desert warrior — was made of magical cloth which made him nearly invisible to the naked eye.

It wasn't those eyes that worried him, however, but the tricky and powerful snooping spells that guarded the rebel villagers. All commanded by curious little Brownies who ran this way and that with no seeming pattern — like ants just before a storm. Examining every particle of earth and atmosphere for signs of danger.

Very well, then. The answer was obvious. He'd wait until night. Then slip in. Overpower the Engine Devil and the boy. Then slip out with no one the wiser.

Later, to be absolutely safe, he'd see that word got out about the rebel village. And they'd all be killed, or put into bondage within a month.

Yes, that was the best way to proceed. He'd have to exercise a bit more patience. Something Infeligo rarely did. For the most part he agreed with that old softskin cynic, Ambrose Bierce, who'd defined patience as "… a minor form of despair disguised as a virtue."

In this case, however, a delay of several hours would be safer than taking immediate action.

But if he had to wait until nightfall there was no reason to crouch here on this sunbaked hill the entire day. He'd retire to his ship, drink a little brandy and smoke a pipe or two.

It had been a long journey to this disgusting planet where softskins and fiends mingled so easily. Flaunting every convention that kept the races separate.

He'd traveled many light years tracking the two fugitives and now he was rather weary. A good rest and a little sustenance would make him more alert for the job he had to do that night.

Infeligo rose to his feet, stretching and yawning. Already feeling the warmth of the soft flame bed that awaited. Mouth watering at the thought of the good brandy he'd drink.

Then, pressing the curved scimitar against his thigh so it wouldn't clang against the rocks, he started off for his ship. But before he'd taken more than a step or two a sudden chill prickled his spine.

He sensed a threatening presence behind him and he whirled around to confront his enemy, hand transforming into a huge fiendish claw as he lifted it to blast the intruder with magic.

Nothing!

Only the empty hilltop stretching out before him.

He looked down the long slope and saw the villagers were undisturbed. The softskin boy and Engine Devil still squatting beside the pot, calmly eating.

If there were danger, the snooping Brownies ought to have alerted them.

Thou art only imagining things, Infeligo, he thought. The result of so much weary travel.

Just the same, he transformed the rest of the way; his robes splitting and falling off as he traded his human disguise for his normal state: An immense, green-scaled demon with fiery eyes and long, glistening fangs.

Infeligo was a very powerful demon, indeed. His size and physique were more than a match for any mortal beast in the galaxy. His magic superior to all but his colleagues on the Council Of Eight. And he was certainly equal to them.

Otherwise they would have cut his share of the spoils long ago. Or have killed him.

There was no such thing as friendship — much less loyalty — among his colleagues. A condition Infeligo hardly regretted. Another of his favorite sayings — once again from a clever softskin, the Marquis de Sade, put pity into clear perspective:

"Humane sentiments," the decadent old softskin once wrote, "are baseless, mad, and improper. They are incredibly feeble; never do they withstand the gainsaying passions, never do they resist bare necessity."

Words to live and have others die for, indeed!

Confidence restored by the twin influences of Bierce and de Sade, Infeligo set out for his ship once more.

But to make certain there'd be no surprises he could not handle, the demon stripped the scabbard from his scimitar so he could carry the blade naked.

He also had a spell ready that would turn the sword into the deadliest weapon imaginable.

As he lifted his clawed foot to take his first step a black abyss suddenly opened up under it.

A scarlet bolt of lightning blasted upwards, catching him in the chest and slamming him backward.

And he found himself sitting awkwardly and shamefully on his haunches. Stunned. Humiliated.

Infeligo struggled desperately to rise and face his mysterious enemy. But then a strange voice whispered foul things in his ear and he felt a numbing coldness sweep up along his body, from clawed toe to ghastly head.

The spell words were so chilling that his sword blade turned from blue steel to glacier white, shattering in his hand. The pieces falling across his lap and on the ground, tinkling like metal snow.

On his forehead, the glowing red stone of duty winked out. Turning cold and lifeless black.

He tried to fight. Tried to cast several spells at once to protect himself. But they all hammered up against a shield without pity. And fell cold and frozen to the ground.

And then he realized that he himself was frozen in place. Not one muscle would twitch, no matter how hard he commanded it. He was completely helpless.

His head was bent slightly downward, staring in a single direction: he could see the village and nothing more.

And although he was cold, so cold, he became colder still as a frightening *presence* made itself known to him.

Although he could see nothing of his enemy, he knew it to be a beast of enormous proportions. A beast not of this world, or even the next. But of another, separate, and most dangerous place.

A beast whose astral body stretched through many dimensions. Collapsing time and space and even the slender line that divided living things from the dead.

Yes, yes, he thought. It's alive and dead at the same time. What could it be?

Then a shadow fell over him. A shadow cast by the incredible absence of anything at all.

A shadow swirling with pinpricks of light like the starry map of an unknown universe. A place where the rules of time and space were commanded by a single, evil entity.

More evil, Infeligo, the demon thought madly, than thou hast ever dreamed.

And that thought — that sudden, aching realization — frightened him more than anything that had gone before.

"Infeligo," the fierce voice whispered. "Now thy soul, thy substance, belongs to me!"

The demon wanted to speak. He wanted to beg for his life. But no words would come.

Footsteps crunched in the pebbled surface of the ground. Something bent forward and then he saw a huge ogre bending down to observe him with glowing red eyes.

It wasn't the beast. Of that Infeligo was certain. But a slave of the beast. Strangely, the ogre wore a dirty, badly torn three-piece suit that once must have been very expensive.

On his lapel was a small silver pin, bearing the symbol of the United Worlds Police.

"Shall I kill him, master?" the ogre asked the shadowy presence.

"In time," came the deadly voice, filling Infeligo with more soul-shuddering fear than he'd ever known in his long, long life.

"First, he must be interrogated about his friends on the Council Of Eight," the voice continued. "Then thy will is thine own. How thou slayest this fool is not my concern. Only that he be slain."

"It shall be done as thou sayest, master," replied the ogre. "What are thy instructions?"

A damp wind sprang from nowhere, lifting up pebbles and particles of dirt. Swirling them around in several miniature tornadoes.

"Doest thou see the softskin child and the Engine Devil in yon village, Kriegworm?" asked the voice.

The ogre stood upright, removing himself from Infeligo's view. But he didn't have to guess where the beast was directing Kriegworm's eyes. For the demon's own eyes were permanently, helplessly, aimed at the two fugitives he'd hunted for so long.

"I see them, master," Kriegworm said.

"I want them turned into dust," the beast said. "And the villagers as well. And their homes. When thou art done, I want no sign remaining that they ever existed. Are my desires clear to thee, little one?"

"Most clear, master," Kriegworm said. "This time, no one is to be blamed. Not the Amers. Not the Rooskies. No one!"

It was then that Infeligo finally understood what was happening. The beast was a Planetar Demon — a breed the Council had made certain arrangements with a thousand years or more ago. And apparently those arrangements were no longer satisfactory.

"Thou hast guessed how it is, Infeligo," the Planetar Demon whispered in the demon's ear.

"Thou hast ruled too long. As have thy comrades of the Council Of Eight. Thou hast taken all the spoils for thyselves and left nothing for me.

"Thee and thy comrades have ruled the softskins and spirit world folk too long. Thou hast denied me much. We had a bargain, Infeligo. Me and thee. And thy friends. If thou wisheth to call them friends.

"I, myself, have no trust in friends. Friends are for the weak. Colleagues for the less than weak. So canst thee see now, Infeligo, how impotent thy rule over the galaxy has become?

"And if thou doest not, know this: I, the Planetar Demon — the force that is astral and sorcerous glue of all thy power — have come to collect what is due me. Thy time has lapsed. And mine has begun. It's only right. For I am the one who makes Time, itself, in this realm.

"I make not only Time, but gravity to hold thy feet upon the ground. I make light — and null-light. And all the magical forces that give thee power.

"I captured these powers from stars that collapsed and died when Time was new. And I have allowed thee to share these powers.

"And now, my dear Infeligo, thou shouldst know before thy death that I have decided to take them back!"

"We will speak together again, foolish one. After I have done my business. And thou wilt tell me all that I need to know to complete my purpose.

"Which is the total destruction of all that I now command.

"I'm hungry, Infeligo. Very, very, hungry!"

Complete and total realization dawned for Infeligo — the demon who had been commanded by his colleagues on the Council Of Eight to fly far and wide to seek answers.

And although it was too late to make any use of those answers that were now rushing in, awareness dawned like a dying star's final explosion of light.

It was apparent to him now that there never was a traitor on the Council Of Eight. The attack on *HolidayOne* and the Russian base had been the work of the Planetar Demon. And no one else.

It was Planetar Demon who was intent on creating a war of total destruction between the Americans and the Russians.

It was the Planetar Demon who had returned to collect what he clearly believed was owed him.

Infeligo instinctively cast about for blame. And immediately fixed it on Apollion, who had always claimed the Planetar Demon was satisfied with their leavings.

Now Apollion's assurances were proven a lie.

Not only that, but the Planetar Demon felt he'd been denied his proper meal so long that he was intent on nothing less than a feeding frenzy.

Like sharks attacking the victims of a sinking warship. With all that blood smell infusing the water.

Or, more to the point, the bloody exploding bodies bursting into space when the Planetar Demon — not the men of *Borodino* — attacked the Amer liner.

And the Russian base. Not the work of the Amers, intent on revenging *HolidayOne*. But of the Planetar Demon, feeding once again.

Pressing the two sides to war.

Not so difficult, Infeligo thought, considering the Council Of Eight had kept the Amers and Rooskies at the terrible edge of all out war for ten full centuries and more.

Infeligo and the others had purposely set up the equivalent of an old-fashioned armory filled with kegs of gun powder.

And all that was ever needed to set that armory off was a stray spark.

The Planetar Demon had provided that spark.

And when he was done he would gorge himself on all the victims. Eating until few living or spirit world beings were left.

Consuming the entire — and previously steady — supply of victims the Council Of Eight had worked so carefully to create.

And when it was over the Planetar Demon would move in to gobble up whatever meat was left.

Turning this thriving galaxy into a lifeless wasteland.

To tell the truth, Infeligo couldn't help but admire the Planetar Demon's plan.

As the realizations sank in, his mouth watered in envy for all the good things that would be spread on the Planetar Demon's newly bounteous table.

Why, if Infeligo possessed that much power he might do something similar himself.

To eat, really eat well and without end, was a pleasure he'd never known.

It didn't matter if there was nothing left when the greedy banquet had ended. The main thing was to eat — to gorge oneself on all those mortal and spirit world souls until the last bit of marrow had been sucked out.

Reading his thoughts, the Planetar Demon whispered, "How unfortunate we didn't come to some kind of agreement earlier, Infeligo. Thy mind is cousin to mine!"

Infeligo wanted to cry out, "Let's bargain together, my friend! Spare me and I can give thee more. So much more."

But the Planetar Demon's attention had moved on and he did not "hear" Infeligo's thoughts.

And even if he had, Infeligo realized, it wouldn't have made any difference.

In a cold business sense what die he really have to offer that the Planetar Demon hadn't already grabbed?

The beast was already taking over everything he and the other seven members of the Council had worked for these many centuries.

"I'm ready, master," Kriegworm said, breaking through Infeligo's thoughts.

"Go then," the Planetar Demon commanded. "Kill them all. And kill them certainly. And remove all traces of their abominable presences. Doest thou understand me?"

"I understand, master," Kriegworm replied.

Then the ogre stepped into Infeligo's view again and he saw him descending the hill. At the same time a loud buzzing sound erupted in the demon's ears.

And suddenly hundreds of deadly creatures popped into existence. Filthy things. Murderous things. All intent on the rebel village.

Kriegworm shouted a hoarse, unintelligible war cry — the ancient traditional shout from the time when all ogres were wild and free.

Then he bounded down the hill, waving a long, ugly DeathSpirit hand-weapon.

And hundreds upon hundreds of swirling lights and jagged-edged shadows raced after him. Filling the air with their shrieks.

CHAPTER FORTY FOUR

Billy felt the cold, deadly presence of the Planetar Demon rushing in on him and jumped to his feet, crying, "He's back, Scratchy! He's back!"

But Old Scratch had felt it too and didn't need the warning. His head jerked up and he saw a huge ogre charging down the hill toward the village.

At the ogre's back were hundreds of ghastly shapes, shrieking a murderous song as they swept down the hill like a rogue wind.

"Help me, Little Friend of the World!" Scratchy shouted.

At the same time he hurled the most powerful killing spell he had in his Engine Devil's arsenal. A spell whose inspiration was straight from the vortex of a fierce collapsar he'd encountered in his youth.

It was full of death, death, death. All the death-dealing thoughts poor Old Scratch could muster. All the death Scratchy could bear to inflict. And he cursed his worst curses, filling the air with his foulest blasphemes.

Yet even as he cast the spell and shouted his awful oaths he knew his efforts were too weak and too late.

Then he felt the boy's powers suddenly join with his, strengthening the spell. And he formed it into the magical equivalent of grape shot blasting from the mouth of an ancient cannon.

Hundreds of the attacking DeathSpirits died in that blast.

But to Scratch's dismay, hundreds more survived. Their angry shrieks only growing louder and more determined.

Even more disheartening — somehow the ogre managed to escape the magical blast. He rushed onward, deadly as ever, shouting commands to his ghostly minions as they swooped down the hill.

Scratchy grasped Billy to him. Enfolding him in his arms and turning his back on the onslaught. Taking the brunt of the searing arrows of sorcery the DeathSpirits were firing.

He felt scores of hot stings pepper his thick hide. He flinched and moaned in terrible pain.

But in his agony he was glad that not one sorcerous missile struck the boy. He could sense the child was gathering his strength and wits — trying to form another spell to hurl at the enemy.

The boy, however, was too inexperienced in the ways of violence and the spell he cast did little to stem the deadly tide.

There was nothing Scratch could do to help him. The pain was too great for him to focus on Billy's attempt to save them.

All around him he heard the panicked cries of the villagers as they fled the oncoming hordes. He heard the voices of human friends cursing and begging as they died. He heard fiends who had called him brother only the night before shriek defiance as the enemy slew them.

It was too awful to bear. And there were so many dead and dying that all Scratchy could think about were the last moments on *HolidayOne* when the beings under his care were slaughtered by this same terrible presence who was supporting the ogre and his demons.

Instinctively he knew that the presence — a shape he was beginning to recognize — could not act on his own. That he relied on the ogre and other creatures who called him master to do his evil work.

This realization was no help to Old Scratch. All he could do was protect the boy as those fierce spirits closed in on him.

But at the last possible moment — just as he thought he was about to die — Scratch heard an incredible roar, like something from the hot guts of an enormous dragon. The ravaging pain suddenly lessened.

He looked up and saw two strange ships whirling overhead. White hot blasts of lightning poured from the ship's guns, riddling the fiends who besieged him.

And then, like a guardian angel, he saw a winged creature circling above him. Straddling its back was a woman with two big antique pistols in each hand.

Even as he watched the pistols bucked: Boom! Boom! Boom! and several spirits who were closing in on Scratch burst apart like balloons filled with green water.

But other DeathSpirits quickly took the place of their dead brothers and sisters. Gnashing their teeth as they swept toward Scratch and the boy.

The woman quickly holstered her pistols and drew out a long black weapon from the sheath dangling from the flying creature's saddle.

Then Scratch realized it wasn't a living creature at all the woman was riding — but some sort of strange flying machine powered by mechanics, rather than magic.

And then the woman opened fire again and all the hungry fiends around him shrilled agonizing cries, then burst apart and died.

A long shadow fell over him. Scratch looked up and saw the Ogre pacing forward. A big pistol clutched in his right claw.

The Ogre aimed the weapon at him and Scratchy could see the Death-Spirit grinning at him from the bottom of the barrel.

But just before he fired, a round from the woman's weapon smashed into the ogre's chest.

And the Ogre was flung backward, pin-wheeling away even as he triggered his pistol. The DeathSpirit bullets flying harmlessly into the sky.

Sudden silence descended on the scene.

Scratch was safe and so was the boy, who was struggling in his arms.

"Let me go, Scratchy," he demanded. "It's that woman again!"

And Old Scratch's belly turned inside out at this revelation. One enemy had been defeated, only to be replaced by another.

He looked up as Tanya brought her fly-flapper to the ground. She climbed off and stalked over to him, her expression grim, her weapon raised.

"You're under arrest," she announced.

And all poor Scratchy could do was sigh and hold Billy tighter to him in case she fired.

* * *

Infeligo saw the whole thing.

Frozen on the hilltop, fearing he was going to die any minute, he watched the ogre named Kriegworm lead the Planetar Demon's minions down the hill.

The subsequent death toll he witnessed didn't concern him. He was only worried about the softskin boy and the Engine Devil. If they were killed, he thought, it would leave him with no witnesses to his discovery.

But soon as that thought rose in his mind he cursed himself as a fool. Although the Planetar Demon was gone — vanishing the moment the strange fighting ships had appeared and opened fire — Infeligo was still incapacitated by the spell.

He couldn't move, he couldn't form his mind around a fighting spell of his own. He could only sit there as the woman, backed by a dozen uniformed men, led the Engine Devil and the boy up the hill toward him.

Infeligo was not accustomed to helplessness of any kind and his condition frightened him mightily. He finally realized what it was like for the beings he had made slaves to his will for hundreds of years.

And now the woman was standing in front of him. Her eyes examining him from scale-armored head to clawed toe.

"Who in the hell are you?" she asked.

Infeligo burned with anger at her rude tones. If only he could regain his powers, he'd teach her a painful lesson about addressing a member of the Council Of Eight in such a demeaning fashion.

Then, to his intense humiliation, one of the uniformed men prodded him with a bayonet.

"Answer the major, buttwipe," the man snarled.

Oh, how he ached to kill these foolish softskins. He would've gladly traded all he possessed to revenge himself on them. A foul curse formed in his throat, but he couldn't get it out. It stuck there like a hard knot, choking him.

Then it came to him who this softskin female was: Major Lawson, the UWP investigator. Once again fear roused itself in Infeligo's breast. Lawson was dangerous. As a detective she was a veritable Javert who would not give up the chase until she either captured her suspect or was killed.

He had to be careful not allow her the slightest clue about the existence of the Council Of Eight or all would be revealed.

Suddenly he was glad he couldn't reply to her questions.

The marine jabbed him again. "Speak, dammit!" he demanded.

Lawson intervened. "Hold on, Moon," she said. "As much as I'd like to see you keep sticking this filthy thing, I think there's something wrong with him. He not only can't talk but he can't move, either. He didn't even flinch when you jabbed him."

"What'll we do, then?" Infeligo heard the softskin named Moon ask.

"Let me try it a different way," Lawson replied.

Then she stepped very close to Infeligo, head lowering to stare into his eyes. Her own eyes started to glow and to Infeligo's dismay he suddenly felt the cold tendrils of a magical probe slithering through his mind.

Lawson nodded as she found what she was looking for and withdrew the probe.

She turned to Moon. "Just as I guessed, he's been immobilized by some sort of spell. Damned strong one, too. I sure as hell couldn't have done it myself."

Lawson frowned, thinking. After a long silence, she said, "Lay him out on the ground. I think I know how to go about this."

Moon and four of the other marines lifted the immense demon up, then unceremoniously dumped him on the hard earth. Now Infeligo was staring straight into the red sun, the hot rays burning his eyes.

He heard Lawson talking to the Engine Devil and the softskin boy.

"Do either of you know anything about this creature?" she asked.

"Why should we help you?" came Billy's hostile response. "You're just gonna throw us in jail, or something."

Tanya sighed. "Listen, Billy," she said. "In case you didn't notice, I just saved your life. There's no reason to be mad at me, you know. I wasn't trying to kill you. But I *am* trying to find out who was."

Billy, ever stubborn, just snorted.

Then Infeligo heard the Engine Devil speak. "Major Lawson is right, Little Friend of the World. She did save our lives. Perhaps we should cooperate with her."

Silence. Then Billy spoke up. "Okay, Scratchy," he said. "If you say so, I'll do it. But we shouldn't talk in front of this demon. He was hunting us too and the less he knows, the better."

Then the three withdrew out of earshot and Infeligo couldn't do anything but stare up at that angry sun. After while, his vision became blurry and he wondered if they were going to leave him here until he went blind.

What cruel creatures these softskins were, he thought, without realizing how ironic that thought was considering what he and his colleagues had done over the past ten centuries.

After what seemed like an eternity he heard the returning footsteps of his enemies.

A shadow fell across his face and Tanya stood over him. She was holding a thick black candle in her left hand with red runes painted on its side. The sight of the candle and runes made Infeligo's heart quicken.

"Like it or not," she said, "you're going to spill the beans, buddy. Before we're done with you, we'll have turned you inside out."

And then she crouched down out of sight and Infeligo heard her start the brain-probing chant he expected.

A second later the Engine Devil's rough voice joined in and he felt a powerful jolt of magic strike his body. He did his best to resist. Fighting them tooth and claw to retain his will.

But then the softskin boy piped up. And his added magic was so strong that the dam of Infeligo's will burst and all he knew surged forth.

CHAPTER FORTY FIVE

The Planetar Demon was not a creature of common emotions. Oh, yes it knew envy, anger and hate. But these feelings — if they could be called that in such an entity — were a thousand times more intense than any mortal or spirit world folk could experience.

All matter, all energy that entered his immortal "body" was squeezed and shattered into the smallest possible particles. Which were trapped forever. The Planetar Demon could not rid himself of these things. Not that he had ever desired to do so, for his power came from this constant, most potent subatomic brew.

Emotions, however, were an entirely different matter. The only love the creature had ever experienced was love of self — a matter of base desire for survival. He had certainly never known compassion.

But the other things — hate, anger and envy — had expanded over thousands upon thousands of years until the Planetar Demon could barely contain them. He had to grow — to increase his size — or he would surely implode and die.

The only solution was to overthrow the Council Of Eight and seize its enormous supply of mortal and spirit-world souls.

This had been his purpose from the very beginning when he'd destroyed the *HolidayOne*. Followed by the destruction of the super secret Russian base.

The result, he'd been certain, would not only doom the fiendish Council, but the resulting Galactic war would provide an enormous pool of souls heavily-spiced with fear and hate to satiate his hunger. And allow him to grow.

A growth he could then sustain for many thousands of years as he fed on the survivors.

What happened after that didn't concern him. After all, he'd have more than enough time to come up with other plans to nurture his immortality.

Everything had been going well until that softskin bitch, Tanya Lawson, had launched her surprise attack on the Planetar Demon's minions — led by the ogre, Kriegworm.

How could a mere mortal have managed such a thing? It defied all logic. The Demon's plan to cover up his presence by killing the human child and the Engine Devil were exploded in that single assault.

And now, he was certain, Lawson was surely working at breakneck speed to uncover the remainder of his plot.

At any other time the Planetar Demon would have reacted instantly and overwhelmingly. Hurling all his remaining forces at Lawson and her allies. Crushing her as easily as he'd destroyed the Russian base.

But his recent efforts had badly drained him of magical resources. Given time, he could muster still greater powers and kill not only the woman, but blast entire planets from the heavens.

That time, however, was not available to him. He had to act quickly and decisively before it was too late and his conspiracy was discovered.

Fortunately that opportunity was readily at hand: the ongoing duel between Davyd and Vlad.

Quickly, he shot through uttermost space and came to the place where the Russian and American warriors were preparing to face one another.

If he could have experienced humor, he would have smiled in deep satisfaction at what was occurring.

The two men were moments away from the final confrontation. They were assembling deadly magical weapons of both offense and defense.

Immediately, the Planetar Demon realized he could not only force the duel to much higher levels, but the power the combat released would go a long way to answer his immediate need for sustenance.

As he studied the two men, searching for weaknesses, the first thing he noticed was Vlad's use of the Hound to track Davyd.

The Hound that employed the voice of the Planetar Demon's nemesis: Tanya Lawson.

Both men were clearly smitten by the softskin detective. Their intense feelings for her undermined their wills. Confused their purpose.

New plans took shape in the Planetar Demon's mind as the duel between the two softskin warriors commenced.

*   *   *

Davyd was coming! His hatred was so intense that it beat like Poe's storied tell-tale heart against walls of guilt and remorse.

Vlad cast his first weapon — a sorcerous caldron of boiling oil.

To his immense aggravation, the spell was countered and Davyd dodged the red hot onslaught of many hungry mouths seeking out his flesh.

Vlad strained to catch further signs of his enemy. How would he come? Where would he go?

But all his efforts hammered against emptiness. Davyd had disappeared. Gone to ground. Waiting and looking. Vlad could almost feel his enemy's eyes upon him, although he knew this couldn't be so. His defenses were too good, too strong to be penetrated so easily.

He's back in his lair again, Vlad thought. Readying a new assault.

To his dismay, Vlad realized the first blow had not yet been struck. Davyd's approach had only been a minor foray to test Vlad's fortress.

Quickly, he reviewed his situation. To his relief, he realized he really hadn't given anything away. Davyd already knew his position. And Vlad's reaction to the foray had revealed nothing about his true arsenal.

He relaxed, steadying his nerves. Going over what had to be done to win this fight. Getting himself ready for the true battle to come.

As he prepared, Vlad once again determined that this fight had to be carried to a much higher level than the one he and Davyd had engaged in aboard the *Borodino*.

Then they'd only maneuvered to get off a killing shot at the other. That was nothing. Hardly worthy of an engagement between Church Of The Sword and Odysseus Corps soldiers.

After all, the whole combat would've been resolved by sheer chance. A miracle, favoring one or the other. A faint fluctuation in magic powers. Or merely an errant nail in the sole of a shoe.

He could not allow the coming fight to be governed by luck. The Church of the Sword certainly never relied on such thin matters as Fortune and her fickle minions. Each victory was the result of careful preparation. Nothing was ever left to chance.

Vlad thought of this as he reviewed his own careful preparations. He studied his little tower fortress for weaknesses. Where could a rat find its hole?

He felt sweat trickling down his back and suddenly thought how wise he'd been to take a newly improved magic-based deodorant with him. Surely he could not come to Tanya like this ...

Jackass, he immediately cursed himself. Dead or alive, you will never see her again.

Motionless, in the very middle of the small room, he waited for Davyd's next action.

His breath slowed, his pupils widened until his irises were barely noticeable. The darkness of the room was dissolved by dim light filtering in from small cracks beneath the door and shuttered windows.

The objects in the room were plain to him now. And through his heightened senses he could even make out the faint ethereal glow given off by his magical weapons.

Davyd, he thought, would have the advantage of the first blow. Even after his initial foray, he still enjoyed the advantage of being able to choose both the moment and the direction of the true assault.

But to Vlad's trained eyes, his position was practically impregnable. Practically — because there were no strongholds which could proudly proclaim themselves unassailable when tested by the best fighter Odysseus had to offer.

And then what would happen?

A good acolyte of the Church of the Sword ought not to think about such things before a fight. But Vlad no longer considered himself as faithful as he'd been before.

He'd violated many rules and regulations when he'd let his enemy escape from the *Borodino*. And now he must pay for it. Pay for Tanya's charms, for her warm hand above his own, for the thin fragrance of her perfume, for the wild dreams inside his own soul.

Now it was his turn to throw the dice. His, despite Davyd's active position and all the advantages of the first blow. Let Davyd believe he had that advantage. In truth, Vlad had excellent plans of his own.

Realistically speaking, it seemed to him that it was unlikely either would survive the duel. They were too evenly matched.

But then Vlad wondered, what would exist after the two dogs of war ripped each other apart? Without question, two colossal machines of destruction, both Rooskie and Amer, would instantly lurch into motion.

A war to the finish for both cultures. Welcomed by many because the release of such long pent up hostilities would certainly devastate the Old Earth and all the nearest colonies. Turn all the Fiendish plans upside-down.

And who knew what forces would be liberated after those savage blows?

Would the very fabric of the Universe remain intact? Could it support all those scorched planets and cold stars? Flame sucked out by the tremendous destruction unleashed by so many magical weapons of war?

He'd gladly sacrifice his own life to prevent it. Let Davyd win, if it would help. But all that would accomplish would be to give the Amers a new triumph, making them emotionally stronger for what was to come.

And the great wheel of conflict would not be stopped.

Vlad's heart raced as a sudden thought came to him. The wheel *must* be stopped!

Even if the price he paid was betrayal and the loss of his good name. What if … What if …

…They did not fight at all?

This thought penetrated through many layers of hatred and brainwashed loyalty.

It was a weakness suddenly revealed. And all of Vlad's experience and background railed against it.

He'd gladly give his life for the glory of Mother Russia. Surely Davyd would do the same for America.

But neither sacrifice would be of any help at all. And the guillotine-edged shadow over Earth and all its galactic dominions would fall without hesitation.

Dying is not an option, Major Vlad Projogin. You must find another way. You must!

Vlad made his fateful decision.

His fists clenched. And he pressed them hard against both temples. He was calling to Davyd.

Piercing his own battlements and trenches, his mental call shouted out wildly in all directions. Desperately seeking to be heard.

He knew very well that in whatever sheltered lair his enemy waited the refuge would be cloaked by all the possible warspells the infamous Odysseus Corps could muster.

Vlad's mentos knock on the door would most likely be answered with an instant and most violent reaction.

But he had to take that chance. Once the Duel began they would simply tear each other into pieces, with no remorse and no regret.

"Kells, I know you can hear me!" Vlad insisted in his mentos shout. "Truce! A moment's truce!"

"Coward," came a cold mentos answer.

The reply came immediately, but Vlad was incapable of detecting where his alter ego was hidden.

What a cool head, Vlad thought. He could understand. Despite his peaceful attempt, Vlad's own blood was boiling with combat readiness.

All the years of cunningly manipulated hatred were against him: pride, desire, medals of fame spilling down his dress-uniformed chest like armor against reason.

All these things were against one Major Vlad Projogin, thousand-year hero of the Church Of The Sword.

These objects and the symbolism they bore were so numerous that he was alone.

He didn't blame his enemy for refusing his plea. Davyd was too busy preparing his own assault spells. To be more accurate, at this moment Davyd Kells was little more than a combat spell himself.

Kells smelled the bait; he considered himself too big and too fanged a fish for this fisherman — and he couldn't stop himself now.

Being kept waiting for the enemy's offense helped to keep one's head clearer. That was Vlad's present advantage — but rather a weak one.

So Davyd wouldn't stop. Wouldn't allow talk of a truce. That was Vlad's answer. Combat juices spurted into his veins, but he desperately fought them back. Trying to think clearly. What the hell had been his aim?

He scratched at the veil of confusion and peered once more into the well of reason.

Okay, he thought, Davyd now was too hyped — to use the Amer's words — to be reasoned with.

Most likely Davyd firmly believed that Vlad was close to defeat even before the true duel began.

But perhaps it was something else behind all this violent thinking from Kells.

A sudden image of Tanya Lawson again intruded upon Vlad's mind.

A terrible jealousy was aroused. So intense he could barely control his fists from striking uselessly at the furniture in the room.

It was Tanya Davyd wanted. Not glory for himself, or a victory for his beloved America — that cursed place of misbegotten fools.

Very well, then. If that's what the Amer wanted!

And Vlad readied himself for the worst.

CHAPTER FORTY SIX

Vlad was still sitting in a deep trance, slowly floating upon the invisible waves of a fiendish sea, when Davyd's voice came again — still as cold as steel.

He said, "Let's quit playing games, Vlad. Hide and seek is for kids. We've gone one-on-one twice before. And each time it's been a draw.

"Why don't we settle things once and for all. No magic. No weapons. Hand-to-hand. What do you say?"

Vlad was stunned; amazed. What was this? A trick?

But Kells wouldn't toy with the most precious possession of a warrior — his reputation. Or would he?

The Odysseus Corps assassins were masters of swift assaults and withdrawals. Could this be a cunning maneuver to draw Vlad out of his refuge?

He heard Davyd chuckle. "I know what you're thinking, you Rooskie bastard. You're wondering if it's a trap. Well hell, it isn't. I'm making an honest offer.

"Besides, if we do this my way — the quiet way — we'll spare the people of this town. Why turn it into ashes? They've got nothing to do with our fight."

Still wary, Vlad considered. Kells was right about one thing: with the deadly arsenal they both had at their disposal the inhabitants of the city would suffer greatly.

Besides, if Vlad agreed, he'd have a chance to talk with Davyd face-to-face.

"I agree," Vlad finally answered. "No spells, no sidearms. Nothing except our bare hands."

"Sounds good to me," Davyd replied. "Come on then!

A pause, then: "Oh, yeah, one thing," Davyd added. "If you win, which I strongly doubt, I wish you luck with Tanya.

"You may be a Rooskie bastard, but outside of me you're the best man she's likely to meet in this life, or the next."

Vlad couldn't help smiling. "I also wish you luck with her as well, Davyd. I know you'll take care of her.

"But ... before we start ... can we stop and talk a little bit more? We can ..."

"No goddamned way, Vlad!" Davyd growled.

But there was real grief in that growl. Much regret. Menace and hatred buried for a priceless moment.

Then his voice hardened as he repeated: "No goddamned way!"

"Well, then," Vlad said. "Let the fight commence!"

And he broke the bonds of his trance, coming to his feet.

He waved a hand, dissolving his magical battlements.

A sudden chill crept into his bones, as if he were standing there naked, exposed, while cold eyes examined him.

Had he just made a terrible mistake?

* * *

The Planetar Demon heard Vlad's fearful thought. If he'd possessed lips to smile with, they would have curled back in an evil grin.

Yes indeed, my little softskin, the Planetar Demon thought. You've *both* made a very grave error. And now you shall pay for it.

He'd listened with deep interest as Kells had issued his challenge and Vlad had accepted it. Hand-to-hand combat. No magical defenses, or physical weapons.

Which meant they'd never suspect his presence. Much less his interference.

If the Planetar Demon had planned this moment — instead of impatiently waiting for his chance — it couldn't have turned out more perfectly.

The Demon swiveled his baleful gaze onto Davyd Kells, waiting … waiting …

* * *

…Davyd had retreated to his sewer tunnel hiding place before making his offer to Vlad.

It was the perfect place for a war rat, he thought as the cold slimy drops fell on his back. Quickly he stashed his weapons. Stripping himself for the coming fight.

Then he paused, heart quickening with fear as it suddenly wondered at what he'd just done.

What the hell was he doing? Better question, what the hell should he do now?

The first law of Odysseus was startlingly clear: the best way — the sure way — to win a fight was to fire a single shot into the head of your enemy. Fired from as great a distance as possible.

Instead, Davyd was not only forgoing that shot, but was carelessly tossing away all his careful plans for victory by giving Projogin the same chance.

He couldn't imagine why he was acting this way. It was not only dangerous, but irresponsible.

Then he thought of Tanya and instantly found his answer. It wouldn't make any difference to her, but he still felt it was necessary to make some gesture — a gesture of sacrifice placed on the altar of his love for her.

Very well, then, he thought. I'll go. Just like I said I would. Out to the very middle of the street. Defenseless except for my physical skills. With little hope of retreat.

It occurred to him that he might have just set a trap for himself. What if Vlad had several platoons of his crack Brown Bear troops standing by.

They could make things very hot for him. Especially with Vlad leading them on.

You must have just lost your teeny mind, Davyd Kells. Gone as mad as the proverbial hatter. A giddy question came to him: what made the hatters go crazy? Something to do with the solution of mercury they used to stiffen the brims? How's that for trivia, buddy boy? Trivia questions and answers in the face of destruction.

His mind whirled and he almost lost control. Something was hammering at him. Making him think silly things. Sucking at his focus. Bear down, Kells! Bear goddamn down!

Heart racing, he pressed on, climbing the iron ladder to the manhole cover. But just as a precaution, he grabbed his knapsack of weapons and hung it by the strap from a workman's hook, poking out of the concrete.

Then he braced himself on the rung and easily pushed the heavy iron cover aside with his great strength.

Just then, his gremlin box gave a fearful squeak: "Beware, master! Beware!"

Before he had time to react he felt a tremendous force suddenly descend on him. It was as if the whole sky was falling, falling, falling, crushing down upon him.

He struggled upward, pushing back with all his might. Then an ice flame seared him to the bone.

Shocked by the fierce pain, he still had the presence of mind to grab his knapsack.

There was a roaring sound in his ears and a powerful force ripped away the very concrete and steel surrounding him.

Davyd knelt on the ground, stunned and gasping under the cruel sky, fully exposed to Vlad's next assault.

He cursed himself for a fool. The Rooskie scum had fired first after all. And with a magical weapon, to boot!

The man had no honor! How could Davyd have been so blind not to see that from the very beginning?

The thought flashed in his mind and vanished as Davyd quickly set his own spells free.

Vlad wanted to fight dirty, die he? Well, by God the son of a bitch would get what he asked for! The horde of battle spells rushed forward to do his bidding.

Everything became very hazy to Davyd as swift waves of destruction altered time and space, swallowing the real world. He didn't feel pain or regret as he let the battle rage take him, lifting him to whole new levels of deadly awareness.

The transformation had begun and now not even Satan himself could keep Davyd from his purpose.

The Rooskie bastard would get what he deserved.

Goddamn his eyes!

CHAPTER FORTY SEVEN

Drawing on the intense hatred each man had for the other, the Planetar Demon unleashed simultaneous blows at the two softskin warriors.

But they were so carefully cloaked by clever spells that the men were unaware of the true source of the attack. Each thought the other was responsible …

…The first thing Vlad saw was a furious magical explosion in the street.

It was as if a huge invisible beast was burrowing into the concrete, hurling debris in every direction.

In his initial shock, he at first thought it might be an exploding artillery shell.

But that was impossible, he decided. No ordinary shellburst would be accompanied by the enormous waves of sorcery that were assaulting his senses.

It was cold, so cold it burned him to the marrow. And then a tremendous force bore down on him.

Vlad groaned in intolerable pain as a magical missile blasted toward him, with hundreds of hungry DeathSpirits howling for his blood.

Even before the missile struck, fantastic force waves rippled outward, battering him.

He dodged the oncoming weapon, hurling up a spell shield that absorbed most of the shock. Vlad fell to his knees, mortally wounded DeathSpirits wriggling on the floor all around him as they gasped their last cries of hatred.

Immediately, he was certain Kells had fired just as Vlad was emerging from his tower fortress. But Davyd had been so anxious for the kill that he'd fired too quickly — a tragic mistake!

The destruction in the street, Vlad was sure, came from the backblast of that too hasty shot.

His mind raged with anger. That damned lying Amer had tricked Vlad into revealing himself!

Not only that, but somehow Davyd had brought a whole contingent of Odysseus Corps fighters with him. Never mind the "man-to-man" duel the Amers had boasted about in the newsfeeds.

Vlad roared in blind fury. If Kells wanted to fight that way, Vlad would pay him back in kind.

And to hell with his Odysseus brothers!

Vlad rushed back to his pentagrams and ancient runes to let loose all the deadly magic he had at his command.

Davyd was poised on the very border of unreality and its countless magical domains. Major Projogin had broken the rules and now all taboos were removed.

Vlad's cunning lie so disgusted Davyd that he cheered when he saw the first collision of his just released fiendish army blast against the Rooskie bastard's battle lines.

Davyd was not a combat mage. In fact, he disdained that breed and had overcome and killed many of them during his long career as an Odysseus Corps assassin.

The spell weapons he was using against Vlad were only to keep his enemy occupied while he moved in to take him down.

If Father Zorza had witnessed this initial attack he'd be pleased, oh yes, yes, he'd be.

Homes along both sides of the street dissolved as Davyd's weapon exploded. Deep clouds of swiftly multiplying colors danced madly around him, heightening his joy.

Among them he clearly saw a red glowing globe, an entire circle of death surrounding the Rooskie son of a bitch. It'd be a miracle above all miracles if Vlad survived.

Davyd's magically enhanced eyes pierced the structure of Vlad's tower hideout. Walls of brick and stone gave way before his view.

But he couldn't find Vlad. Immediately he realized he was being blocked by a spell shield Vlad had somehow managed to erect. The cunning bastard had somehow survived!

Damn, damn, damn!

Instinctively, Davyd unleashed another assault before Vlad could recover enough to return fire.

His entire body turned into a deadly spear. An enormous shaft spread far beyond … stretching into the Void … pushing through time and space … while he, Davyd Kells, transformed into the shovel head of that spear.

The head was formed on a sorcerous anvil, white hot from the fierce flames of a magical forge.

And then a giant's hand hurled the spear at the place where Davyd believed Vlad was hiding.

But in mid-flight the burning spear head that was Davyd slammed against a super cold barricade. Thousands of magic-eating spirits devoured the force of his blow.

Yet Davyd pressed on. Hurling himself blindly against his enemy's battlements.

A near suicide attempt to quickly and decisively take Vlad out.

Father Zorza would not have been happy with Davyd's foolishly desperate attempt. It violated all the codes of the Corps.

But the damned enemy was so near ... so intolerably close ... that he couldn't resist.

The blow was savage but futile. Like hammering on the gates of the mightiest castle. Still he kept trying.

He drew back and crashed forward once more — the blow even more powerful than before.

But at the scant moment before the impact, Davyd suddenly heard a startlingly familiar voice:

"He's upon us!" Tanya Lawson shouted in perfect Russian.

At first, Davyd thought it was another one of Vlad's craven tricks. Using the Hound to mimic Tanya as he'd done before.

But then he heard another shout: "Kill, him, Vlad, kill him!"

And he knew it wasn't the Hound, but truly Tanya. She'd turned against him. Somehow Vlad had seduced the only woman Davyd had ever loved to turn against him. To join Vlad in battle against Davyd.

He burned with anger at this double betrayal. How could she? How could he? His rage overflowed and was instantly transformed into killing action.

Vlad Projogin must die.

He'd spare Tanya if he could. She'd made her choice — and he couldn't blame her, no matter what the reason.

But his wrath was so fierce against Vlad that all thoughts of Tanya's protection were swept aside.

He'd kill Vlad Projogin even if he had to die himself!

This was the last clear thought of Major Davyd Kells, hero of the Odysseus Corps.

*   *   *

When Vlad realized what had happened it was already too late to avoid Davyd's desperate blow.

All he and the Hound could do was face the assault square on. No matter how powerful Davyd's attack, Vlad must not allow himself to be beaten to his knees.

A cowering man was always the first to die and Major Vlad Projogin, the most prized warrior the Church Of The Sword possessed, was not a man to die easily.

With a terrible shriek, the Hound rushed forward, covering Vlad with its body, meeting the coming wave of violence.

This action won Vlad a precious millisecond. Allowing him to sweep through slow-floating time and to activate his own barriers and defenses.

The desperate Hound managed to fire not just once, but twice: a full load of BattleSpirits rushing out to ravage Davyd.

But the Hound's powerful counter assault drained the last of its magical resources. And so it had no shield to protect itself as Davyd's soul-blasting bullets ripped the creature into shreds.

The Hound's final cry of anguish was so damnably human, sounded so much like Tanya's cry, that for a moment Vlad believed the woman he loved had been slain.

On the very edge of his protective pentagram he saw his WarSpirits battling and dying one by one.

Davyd's assault was so fierce, so full of overwhelming hate that Vlad's first line of defense was smashed and burned with no hope of resurrection.

The second line of Vlad's defenses rushed forward to join the battle.

This was his most powerful arsenal — the ancient Church Of The Sword spells, used so sparingly that few knew they existed.

The flame around Vlad flared hotter and higher. Twisting and curling in on him. An enormous weight pressed down on the Russian, blood streamed from his nose and his bones felt like they were being strained to the breaking point.

But no matter how hard Davyd tried, he was unable to blast through Vlad's shield.

Vlad felt the pressure weaken slightly. This was his chance!

It was time for the counterstrike. Let this Amer be roasted in the very heart of Hell!

Vlad spat blood and burst forward, leaping into the flame.

And mad magic rushed over him.

*　*　*

An enormous purple and yellow globe rose, swirling crazily over the ruins of the small hotel.

All over the city hysterical people were fleeing the destruction wrought by the battle. Streets were jammed and the traffic was a hopeless snarl backed up for miles — the police had been among the first to flee the scene.

People were shouting their terror, screaming for someone — anyone — to help them.

But there was no help to be had.

Only the Planetar Demon, feeding hungrily on their fears. In turn, he fed still more power into the fight between Davyd and Vlad.

Lifting it to sorcerous levels unknown in all history ...

*   *   *

... Blackness fell from his eyes and the Archangel Michael raised his gaze.

Behind him were the green-blossoming leaves of an Eternal Eden. A heavenly universe filled with countless stars and worlds and living things stretched before him.

A wondrous universe, cunningly and lovingly forged by the Father of all things of lesser strength.

It was his duty, the duty of the Archangel, to keep and to protect this beauty — so fragile, so subtle, so defenseless.

And aye, there *was* something to protect it from. A shadow lurking in deep places, hiding beyond the dying stars. A Creeper, driven by pure evil to destroy all beauty, all wonders — all that was saintly and sweet.

A flaming sword suddenly appeared in Michael's hands. He peered deeper into the shadows, searching ... searching ...

And ... lo! What was happening? What was this terrible shape approaching this paradise of eternal rest where leaves never fell?

How dare this cursed Fiend, this enemy above all enemies, this Fallen One — how dare he spoil the surroundings of Eden's Garden with his foul breath?

Lucifer was approaching. Face twisted in anger, he was in the shape of the Horned One, his long red tail lashing back and forth.

Behind the fiend Michael saw an enormous army marching forward. A huge legion straight out the forces of Pandemonium.

The Archangel burned with anger, the flames leaping higher off his glowing sword. No matter how many, he would kill them all!

"Come forth Forces of Light!" Michael commanded.

And he stalked forward to meet the enemy, his own legions soaring up to support his attack.

The Devil roared in mockery. His clawed fist shot upright and a great yellow starburst imploded. Transforming into a supernova that swallowed all the surrounding planets.

Even from afar, Michael could hear the death cries of millions of tortured innocents.

"Forward!" he shouted, lifting his sword.

The two armies crashed together, thunderclap upon thunderclap rolling and rumbling through the starry skies.

Dark Sea met White Sea. Light and Darkness grappled in everlasting strife.

Michael's glittering sword clashed against Lucifer's flaming scimitar.

The blades shattered, unleashing an awful power that swept onward and upward in a great burning tidal wave.

Michael moaned in agony as he saw a whole galaxy collapse into itself.

"Oh, no!" he cried.

"Oh, aye!" mocked Lucifer.

Both enemies were now weaponless. But they still had tremendous powers at their command — powers steadily fed by the Planetar Demon who lurked just out of sight.

The two combatants advanced on one other. Now they would fight hand-to-hand.

Stars exploded one after another as the two warriors locked in a deadly embrace.

The Void itself caught fire when dark blood flowed into light.

And then there was a great shout:

"Stop! Stop, you fools!"

Michael felt his enemy's grip suddenly relax. He was so startled that his grasp weakened as well.

That voice! That voice!

She floated toward them, white garments flowing over lush curves. Face glowing. To Michael and Lucifer she was the queen of love and beauty. The one … the only one …

So powerful was their attraction to her that both combatants instantly ended their fight. And stepped apart.

"Look at each other!" cried the goddess of love. "Look close and see what is true and what is false!"

Michael obeyed — as did his opponent.

And what … what had happened?

Light cast off by the woman's shimmering garments dissolved Lucifer's evil mask.

And Michael found himself staring into the eyes of his heavenly twin!

"You are equal, don't you understand?" the woman demanded. "One and the same."

Equal? The same?

How could this be?

"I'll tell you," Tanya said.

And there was no doubt in either man that the woman standing before them was the true Tanya, not a ghostly clone created and manipulated by magic.

Then she took both their hands and the spell that had chained them suddenly fell away.

And Davyd and Vlad found themselves looking into one another's eyes.

Then they both turned and saw Tanya's beautiful face.

* * *

Angry and cursing oaths so fierce that they peeled away space and time, the Planetar Demon fled to his sanctuary.

Where had that woman come from? How was it possible for her to possess the magical power to interfere with his plans?

Suddenly, he became afraid.

It was absolutely necessary that he prepare to defend himself.

And for the first time in his long, long life, the Planetar Demon knew the true terrifying meaning of mortal time.

CHAPTER FORTY EIGHT

Davyd and Vlad suddenly found themselves standing on the command deck of an enormous spaceship whose gloomy interior stretched out in every direction.

Twin beams of ruby light spotlighted each man, puddling on the metal floor and flowing outward to illuminate Tanya standing between them.

Her arms were outstretched as if she were physically holding them apart, although she was positioned several feet away.

In one hand — raised to confront Vlad — she held a silver cross — the symbol of the Church Of The Sword. In the other was an Odysseus Corps medallion with a single blue eye glaring out of its center. This she presented for Davyd to see.

"I know your secret," she said to both men. "I know all about Odysseus Corps *and* the Church Of The Sword. As a matter of fact, I know more about them than either of you."

Neither Davyd or Vlad replied. Both of them were still in the throes of battle *must*. Every cell of their bodies infused with fighting hormones.

Tanya saw them struggling to break free of the spell she held them in and she called out to Billy and Scratch, who came forward out of the gloom.

"We have to the strengthen the spell," she said. "We've got to get them calmed down enough to hear me out."

Billy stared at the men, eyes wide in fearful awe of these two hate-driven warriors. He could feel his own magical powers weakening against the onslaught of their fierce wills to slay one another at any cost.

"Be strong, Little Friend of the World," Old Scratch said, gently placing a massive claw on his shoulder. "Together, the three of us can succeed."

"All right, Scratchy," Billy said, nervously licking his lips. "I'll try as hard as I can."

And then, with Tanya in the center, the three concentrated on bolstering their common spell. Light sparkled from the silver cross and medallion that Tanya held.

At the same time the ruby red spotlights that pinned Davyd and Vlad to the deck grew brighter and brighter, casting back the deep shadows that filled the immense chamber of the ship.

Gradually Vlad and Davyd became more aware of their surroundings. They were still filled with hate for each other, but now they could see Tanya more clearly. And the tide of their combative emotions began to retreat.

It was only a slight retreat, but it had the effect of allowing their love for her to flow into the gap. And slowly, ever so slowly, that love gained sway over them.

Both men suddenly felt exhausted. Drained of all energy. First Davyd, then Vlad slumped to the floor, unconscious.

Immediately, Tanya broke the spell and the beams of light vanished.

"Let them rest for awhile," she said to Billy and Scratch. "Then we'll tell them what's going on."

Billy shook his head, feeling very sorry for the men. "Boy, are they gonna be surprised," he said. "But not a nice surprise, that's for sure. They've been cheated their whole lives. I sure wouldn't want to wake up and find that out!"

"At least they now have the chance to put things right," Tanya said. "But first we have to pray they shake off a thousand years of brainwashing."

The boy smiled up at her. She was so pretty, he thought. And so nice. And brave, too. In a way, maybe even braver than Davyd and Vlad. It seemed strange to him that not long ago he'd believed Tanya to be one of his worst enemies.

But now they were the best of friends. This thought made his hurt about the death of his grandparents and Lupe lessen somewhat. Also, now it seemed there was finally a chance to revenge what had been done to them.

As if reading his thoughts, Scratch said, "More things may be accomplished than just revenge, Little Friend of the World. More things, indeed!"

*   *   *

When the two men regained consciousness, Tanya led them through the ship, whose name was the *Centaur*. They were both dazed and very weak and made no protest, trailing behind her like two obedient children.

They were not so dazed, however, that they didn't notice the strangeness of the enormous ship. To begin with the command deck of the *Centaur* possessed none of the usual operating instruments. Instead, there were mysterious, many colored runes that crawled over and through a huge hologram of the ship.

When Old Scratch saw their puzzled expressions, he felt moved to explain "As you both can see," the Engine Devil said, "this ship was not designed by softskins. It was constructed long ago by spiritworld folk using principles unknown to human wizards."

Davyd shook his head. "I don't see how that's possible," he said.

"Nor do I," agreed Vlad.

"Nonetheless, it is true," Scratchy replied. "Thine own eyes cannot deny what is set before them."

Davyd nodded in grudging admission. The huge, oddly formed seats scattered about the bridge of the *Centaur* underscored Scratchy's statement. It didn't take much imagination to realize they were built to receive the weighty bulk of large demons. And the controls built into the long armrests were shaped to fit talons, not fingers.

"Who were these creatures?" Vlad demanded. "And what do they have to do with us?"

"You'll find out soon enough," Tanya said. "Just be patient and follow me."

They did what she said and soon they were moving along wide corridors with high vaulted ceilings. As they walked, light bloomed all around, illuminating the way.

The light revealed that the walls and ceilings of the corridors were covered with livid scenes — some quite horrifying — of ferocious creatures and strange, other worldly landscapes.

They passed many chambers with open doorways large enough to accommodate a race of giants. The lights bloomed into life in some of those rooms and Davyd and Vlad saw all sorts of bizarre objects:

Racks of ancient human weapons, ranging from primitive clubs to great battle axes and exotic swords and armor. Displays of human skeletons and bubbling jars filled with heads and other body parts.

Black magic apothecaries crammed with evil-smelling ingredients in odd containers with mysterious symbols carved on their surfaces.

"Gives you the shivers, doesn't it?" Billy commented.

Both Davyd and Vlad reflexively shuddered in reaction to his statement. But they said nothing in reply.

Finally, Tanya came to a closed door decorated with a series of freshly painted red runes. She stopped there and turned to the two men.

"I must warn you," she said, "that this isn't going to be easy for either of you to bear. So brace yourselves for the biggest damned shock of your lives."

She palmed a switch and the door hissed open. Davyd and Vlad jolted when they saw the ferocious figure lying on a long couch. A large dark stone fixed on his forehead.

Their hands instinctively went to their belts, itching to grab weapons that were no longer there and defend themselves.

Then they relaxed when they noticed the creature was stiff as a board. As if he were dead. Then they saw his red eyes swivel toward them.

Other than the movement of those eyes, the creature was completely helpless.

"Let me introduce you to one of the biggest sons of bitches the Universe has ever created," Tanya said.

"His name is Infeligo. And he's your real boss! Or, should I say, your ex-boss, if you either of you have a particle of reason in your brains."

CHAPTER FORTY NINE

The *Centaur* was an old ship, a weary ship, but as Scratch pushed it through Uttermost Space his thoughts were full of youthful joy.

He was doing good work — Engine Devil's work — once again. And with tremendous overlight speed he was pushing the ancient starship deeper into the Void.

Beside him, contained in a protective bubble, Billy Ivanov chortled in boyish glee as he helped Scratch cut through the very flesh of The Continuum.

Commanding hundreds of thousands of spirits, contained in huge armored tubes, to throw back thick spurs of overheated plasma.

Along with his demon friend the child gloried in the shimmering of the uncounted stars that flowed past. Stars with fiercely burning crowns that filled the eyes and soul with their beauty.

He was learning what it was like to love the storms of hard x-rays swirling around the enormous Black Holes that press through the very fabric of space. And all the planets, the many-colored planets: blue, purple, yellow, red or green.

Billy experienced the musical voices of remote Engine Devil friends floating in upon the wings of FastSpells. And the many, many other wondrous things that make up the very core of an Engine Devil's life.

"Oh, this is wonderful, Scratchy," he said. "This is supreme. This is … Well, I can't think of all things it is, but it sure beats being a stupid softskin ship's captain. Who doesn't do anything at all, except maybe eat dinner with the big shot passengers."

"But thou art a softskin thyself, Little Friend of the World," Scratch replied. He was troubled by the boy's remarks. "It is not good to so malign thine own people."

"I don't want to be a softskin, Scratchy," the child responded, his young brow wrinkling in displeasure. "I want to be a fiend, just like you. Fiendish people are true and honest and they never betray their friends. Softskin people are liars and only care about themselves."

For emphasis, he thumped the ship's co-pilot controls Scratch had built into his protective bubble.

"Human beings suck," he declared. "Suck, suck, suck! And I don't want to have anything to do with them. I want to be an Engine Devil, just like you!"

Although old Scratch was complimented by the child's remarks, he was also worried. And torn in his thinking. Other than this softskin boy, he loathed human beings. They'd never done anything but try to enslave him.

Only his Engine Devil's pride and will had resisted this enslavement. Like all his much-valued kind, he had managed to maintain his independence. Using his curses, his force of fierce Engine Devil personality, to stave off his softskin masters.

Still, it was not good that this softskin boy should hate his own kind as deeply as Scratchy despised them.

"All softskins are not the same, Little Friend of the World," he ventured. "Some have goodness in their souls. Some are to be admired.

"Consider, son of my old age, the softskins that we carry in this very ship. The woman, Tanya Lawson, whose name is quite familiar to thee.

"Thou calleth her friend, but I see the light in thy young eyes and I, Scratchy, know quite well that thy young mating organs are budding when I see that look.

"Then there are the men — the warriors for whom thou hast expressed much admiration for their skills. Although I despise softskins, other than thyself, Little Friend of the World, these men have also captured my loyalty and admiration. Their names are writ large in my personal scrolls: Davyd Kells and Vlad Projogin.

"Are these three not worthy softskins? Are they not creatures of grander purpose than the norm? Surely, thou must grant them the noble qualities I suggest.

"They fight for all of us. Softskin and fiend. They fight against Time, itself. Three mortals against time! What greater purpose could one ask of anyone?"

Billy considered, then nodded. "Okay, Scratchy," he said. "I guess you're sort of right. Except, it's more than three, isn't it? Aren't we in this fight too?"

Scratch exposed his fangs in an enormous grin of pleasure. Only a softskin like Billy, who loved the Engine Devil more than life itself, would not have been horrified by his ghastly grimace of affection.

But then his grimace vanished and his horned brow wrinkled in concern.

"I do not like this mission, Little Friend of the World," he said. "I do not fear for my own sake. I am old and of little importance in the scheme of things. I fear for thee, my young Friend of the Heart.

"Many years are ahead of thee, even in the miserably shortened span of softskins. We may not succeed in our mission. And even if we do, the chances of our survival are slim, indeed.

"This Planetar Demon is most powerful. We will attack him in his lair, which will make him more powerful still."

"I don't give a darn about the Planetar Demon," Billy said, quite coldly. "We'll find him and we'll kill him. Just you wait and see."

Then he hesitated, his smooth forehead suddenly running into scars of worry.

After a time, he said, "It's those other guys who bother me. They didn't kill my grandparents ... or Lupe. But they might as well have. They're the ones responsible for this whole Cold War thing.

"Making everybody hate everybody. Stopping peace every chance it had.

"I gotta say, I don't know who I'm madder at. The Planetar Demon, who killed everything I loved. Or those dirty rotten bastards on the Council Of Eight who set it up.

"Those are the guys I wanna get, Scratchy. Damn and double damn, they're the ones we ought to do in. Not just the stupid Planetar Demon."

Old Scratch was amazed at the child's adult reasoning. Billy had elicited feelings that Scratch shared deep in his own breast.

But there were other considerations that overweighed these feelings. How could Scratchy possibly explain Tanya's plan to the boy? How could he make him see the light of weary adult expedience over truth, truth and nothing but the truth?

The very ship they were flying had been seized from a member of the group Billy despised so much: Infeligo.

Scratch and Billy had overpowered Infeligo's spirit crew, reducing them to the mere spirit world slaves that Scratch so detested.

At this moment, Infeligo was frozen and chained by powerful spells created by Scratch, Billy and the three softskins who were making a daring gamble to solve the whole catastrophic problem.

He started to explain this to Billy, hunting for reasonable words that would press past the boy's most reasonable instinct for revenge.

But every word that came into his mind was weak. Words that held logic, but no real power.

At that very moment a transmission came streaming in from the Void. The message they had all been waiting for.

Old Scratch wasn't certain whether he'd just been blessed or cursed by the intervention of that transmission.

It was from the Council Of Eight.

Swiftly, Scratch keyed it through to the waiting softskins.

CHAPTER FIFTY

Although the two enemy camps were physically separated by millions of light years, magical transmission waves collapsed that distance into a scant few yards.

Apollion and his fiendish comrades glared at the holo images of Tanya and the two softskin traitors. While Davyd and Vlad, feeling totally betrayed — the underpinnings of ten centuries of faith ripped from under them — glowered back in return.

In the background, Infeligo, who had been propped upright on the couch, seethed in helpless fury at his predicament.

Tanya spoke first: "Greetings, gentlemen," she said to the fiendish Council Of Eight. "Before we begin, I want to say that I am addressing you as the independent representative of the United Worlds Police.

"As you know, I was charged by my superiors — at the mandate of the United Worlds Organization — to investigate the causes of the attack on the civilian cruise ship, the *HolidayOne*.

"The good news, gentlemen, is that I have not only solved that crime, but also the collateral crime of the attack on the Russian military base.

"The bad news is that I've uncovered another crime as well. Your conspiracy to enslave and exploit billions of human beings and spirit world creatures all across the galaxy."

Apollion, ever the diplomat, brushed this last charge aside.

"Thou art to be congratulated, Major Lawson," he said, "for getting to the bottom of those two evil deeds. We've studied the preliminary report thou hast already broadcast to the UWP. And it is clear that neither the Russians or the Americans were to blame for these incidents.

"As we speak, thy news is being relayed to the appropriate government authorities and I expect there will be a joint declaration of peace announced very shortly."

Tanya nodded with visible satisfaction. "Then the war is over?" she said.

"Indeed it is, Major Lawson," Apollion replied. "And it is my understanding that thou wilt be rewarded mightily for thy efforts. Thou wilt surely be promoted vastly in grade. A general with several stars at the very least."

He smiled. "There is even serious discussion," Apollion went on, "Of making thee supreme commander of the United Worlds Police."

For the briefest of moments Tanya saw all her dreams come true. She had a flash of Harry's look of terrible disappointment and fear as he realized his subordinate was being promoted over him. A subordinate he'd treated rather shoddily over the years.

She savored the victory, then she threw all those dreams away.

"It's more likely," she said, "that you gentlemen will do your best to kill me. After all, I not only know your dirty little secret, but have absolute proof of the conspiracy you've engaged in."

She jabbed a thumb at Infeligo. "I've brain scanned your colleague, here," she said. "And have recorded all his darkest thoughts."

There were angry mutterings from the other Council members. Frozen though he was, Infeligo rolled his eyes in shame and fear.

Pilyardock spoke up. "What if we were to inform thee, Major," he said, "that a powerful ship has been dispatched to deal with thee."

Auerkhan added. "And those two traitors as well. All of you shall pay for your crimes!"

Tanya laughed at them. "So much for your generous offers of vast rewards and promotions," she mocked.

Davyd broke in. "Send your soldiers," he taunted. "Send all you like. And I'll return them to you in caskets."

Vlad stepped forward. "Then I'll come for you myself," he declared. "To cut your throats one by one. I'm well-trained at such work, you know. After all, I have you to thank for that training."

More angry mutterings from the Council. Then Apollion waved them into silence.

"These threats are foolish on both sides, gentle lady," he said to Tanya. "As I'm sure thou must agree. And I doubt such remarks were ever thy intention.

"After all, thou hast not sent the report of our ... activities ... to your superiors. But have withheld it for some purpose of thy own.

"A bargaining chip, perhaps? To save thy life and the lives of thy noble friends?"

Tanya smiled back. "You're partly correct," she replied. "We have withheld the records for a bargaining chip. But not only to save our lives — but yours as well.

"Although I don't much care about any of you. However, we are all much concerned about our fellow citizens of the galaxy.

"It's true that you are a grave danger to them. Have been so for a thousand years when you foiled all those hopes to end the great Cold War between the Americans and Russians.

"However, my comrades and I are all convinced that a still greater — and more pressing threat — exists."

Apollion grinned understanding. "Thou must mean the Planetar Demon," he said.

"The very same," Tanya replied.

"Art thou proposing an alliance?" Apollion asked.

"A temporary one," Tanya said.

"Why should we agree to this, gentle lady?" Apollion asked. "What purpose would this alliance serve?"

"You can't kill the Planetar Demon on your own," Tanya said. "As a matter of fact, using the sorcerous computers on this ship — your own ship — I firmly believe if you engaged in direct conflict with him that the Planetar Demon would most likely prevail."

A dead silence descended on the Council Of Eight. Not one of the fiends moved, or even fidgeted in stressful reaction to Tanya's words.

Apollion himself became as pale as a corpse.

"Am I not correct in this assumption?" Tanya pressed.

Apollion nervously plucked at his lip. Then, instead of answering directly, he asked, "Doest thou think thee and thy friends can do better?"

"Absolutely," Tanya said quite firmly. "I've run those progs as well."

"Then tell me, gentle lady," Apollion said, "what doest thou proposeth?"

And Tanya spelled out her plan.

*　　*　　*

After Apollion and the others had agreed to Lawson's proposal and the Council was once again alone and unobserved, the members looked at one another uneasily.

Then Simionte said, "If this woman and her companions succeed in killing the Planetar Demon, it may very well be that she also possesses the power to defeat us as well."

Auerkhan nodded. "I was thinking those very thoughts myself, noble Simionte."

Mamri said, "I suggest, noble ones, that we prepare an alternate plan. I have no doubt this softskin woman will reveal our presence and purpose to one and all, once the Planetar Demon is defeated."

"Assuming she is successful," Syrr weighed in. "Her chances are quite slender."

"Unfortunately, noble ones," Simionte said, "we must pray for her success. I shudder to think what the Planetar Demon will do if he finally breaks his bonds and comes after us."

"Gentlemen, gentlemen," admonished Apollion, "there is no cause for panic. We've have been through greater crises before, have we not?

"After all, it was we who overthrew the softskin way of things and took control of their lives. And have we not fed well all these years?"

"Yes, but now we are faced with a threat of revolt from the wild ones," Mamri reminded him. "Our own kind will certainly be aroused by this woman's statements."

"Noble Mamri, noble colleagues," Apollion said. "I considered all these things whilst we were discussing — and agreeing upon — Major Lawson's plan.

"We must simplify the tasks before us: First, to defeat the Planetar Demon. This is of the utmost importance, do you all agree?"

"Aye," chorused the frightened others.

"Secondly, we must then act quickly to remove the threat of Tanya Lawson and our former vassals, Davyd Kells and Vlad Projogin.

"Do you agree with this as well?"

Another chorus of ayes echoed across the chamber.

And, to the immense satisfaction of the council members, Apollion once again proved his worth as their leader by laying out a most satisfactory plan.

After they'd considered and agreed, the council members faithfully complied with the first part of Tanya Lawson's bargain.

Actually, it was something Davyd and Vlad had insisted upon in no uncertain terms.

Apollion summoned Father Zorza and his Church Of The Sword counterpart, Father Onphim.

The two quaking softskins were led into the chamber by a squad of fierce demons, with yellow eyes, long fangs and sharp claws.

There were the usual protestations of innocence, loyalty and pleas for mercy based on long and faithful service.

The members of the Council Of Eight enjoyed the misery of the two priests immensely — feeding on their fear and pain as if they were a large tubs of fine caviar.

In the end, they had the fiendish squad hang them both.

Kicking and screaming, loops were placed over their necks, and they were hauled up on the chamber's ancient beams. But that was only a temporary measure. Next, they pierced their heels with meat hooks and let them dangle like squealing pigs from the ceiling.

They recorded the priest's deaths with much close attention to their agonies.

Then transmitted the scene to Davyd and Vlad: the softskins who had demanded this price for their participation.

Davyd forced himself to stare with an unwavering gaze at Father Zorza's final agonies.

But he felt no satisfaction.

Instead he was sickened by the hateful desires of his own dark soul. Scarred and notched so many times by so many sins, that Davyd wished that it was he who was being drawn up by the strangling rope.

Vlad had a similar reaction to the scene. He felt as if he were killing himself as Father Onphim gasped his last pleas for mercy, brothers, mercy.

Tanya, seeing their pale looks, intervened, leaning forward to palm the switch that cut off the last agonizing throes of the two priests.

Forcing a cold calmness on herself that belied her inner torment, she said, quite cruelly, "You're both bastards, I hope you know that. You have a shitty way of getting your revenge.

"And if that scene is what makes you happy, I don't want to have another thing to do with either of you when this is over!"

Both men were abject, saying they were sorry, sorry, sorry.

"Sorries don't cut it!" the UWP detective snapped.

"The two of you are serial killers, as far as I'm concerned. Hell, you've both got a longer string of murders to your names than any other psycho in history."

Davyd bowed his head. "I've always known that, Tanya," he said. "And right now my only consolation is that finally, I get to die.

"They've kept me alive for a thousand years as their personal assassin. And by damn, I was good at it. And by damn and double damn I was bound for Hell. I always knew that.

"At least, now I get to go to some kind of peace. Paybacks, big time, for yours truly, David Kells."

Vlad was looking at Davyd the whole time he spoke. Tears of empathy jutted in his eyes, but he fought them back. Then he looked at Tanya.

"As Davyd said … and you said," he added in a hoarse whisper, "we deserve whatever terrible things await us, once our souls are set free. And I hope to God that my own soul is bound in chains so hot they burn right through. For even then I could not repay my transgressions."

Tanya was stunned at their reaction to her accusations. She'd been angry. Disgusted at the price they'd demanded from the Council Of Eight.

But all along she'd known it wasn't their fault. They'd been pawns, just as the human and spirit-world race had been pawns, of the creatures who'd seized control of a whole galaxy's destiny — even before the galaxy could be accurately described.

Comforting words rose up. She wanted to tell them they'd been brainwashed and manipulated, just like several billion others — including herself.

Tools and ensorcelled fools, bent to the deadly purpose of the Council Of Eight.

It had been a coup above all coups.

The whole human and spirit world race enslaved in a sudden overturning of reason, just when reason and hope had coincided to change the course of all the events that were to follow.

She started to explain this ... to haltingly offer shattered sentences of comfort.

But as she looked into their faces, she knew there was no comfort she could ever offer that would salve the wounds that had been suffered by these much violated men.

At that moment — as she looked at them — a strange and indescribable thing bloomed in her heart. It was so deep and overwhelming that it nearly carried her away.

Shaking her all the way down to her upcurling toes.

And Tanya snorted and said, "Jesus Christ! Apparently I've fallen in love with *both* of you guys! Now what in the hell are we gonna do about that?"

Vlad and Davyd glazed at her, astounded by her announcement. Neither man knew what to say, although they both stuttered some remarkably silly words of reaction.

Tanya stared at the two foolish men she'd been cursed to fall in love with, and shook her head.

"I am the dumbest broad in all creation," she said. "To fall for two mass murderers. Well, read 'em and weep, those were the cards I was handed and I don't have any time at all left to figure out how to play the hand the fates dealt me."

Then she became very stern, standing over them.

"The only thing is," she said, "is that I have to ask you both to do it one more time."

Vlad shrugged. "If you love me, Tanya," he said, "I'll kill the whole fucking galaxy."

"Jesus, Mary and Joseph," Davyd broke in. "All she's asking is that we kill the Planetar Demon! Not the whole galaxy. What the hell is the problem with you?"

Vlad gave a Russian shrug, saying, "My only wonderment is who shall she love when this is done?"

Tanya laughed at his reply. "Don't worry about it," she said. "Assuming I survive — and get back into my right mind — I'll probably tell both of you to get the hell out of my life!"

"That's fair," Davyd said.

"An even chance," Vlad agreed, suddenly feeling much better.

Tanya snorted in displeasure at both of them.

"Okay, say we survive the Planetar Demon," she said. "A big damned assumption. But after that …"

"The Council of Eight is going to want to wipe us off the face of the Galaxy," Vlad provided.

"You've got that straight," added Davyd. "They're probably plotting our demise at this very minute."

Both men looked up at Tanya. Eyes full of many, many questions.

Davyd was the first to ask: "What do we do after that?" he asked. "Assuming we take out the Planetar Demon?"

Tanya shrugged. "I've got it all figured out," she said. "If for some reason, by some goof up on the part of the deadliest power in the galaxy we happen to survive …

"Here's what we do: we run like hell!"

"That's the plan?" Davyd asked, aghast.

Another shrug from Tanya. "Under the circumstances — and given the time I'd had to consider … Yep!

"Do either of you have an alternate suggestion?"

One by one, both men shook their heads — No.

CHAPTER FIFTY ONE

The *Hamilton* and *Rubin* were doing some first-class lurking as the strange ship approached the *Centaur*. It was a smaller version of the vessel Lawson had seized, but reeked of the same ancient sorcery.

The name painted on its side — The *Hesperos* — matched the ID engraved on all the main engine parts, plus it coincided with the mag-computer-driven messages the ship was beaming out to the *Centaur*, notifying Lawson of its approach.

Moon and Rhodes carefully scanned the *Hesperos* with the powerful null-magic devices their stealth ships carried and noted that so far the Council Of Eight was keeping its side of the bargain.

Rhodes and Moon conferred, then shot a chaos-frequency message to Tanya, who had a duplicate non magical com system which they'd installed on the *Centaur*:

The approaching ship was as advertised: it contained a powerful planet-busting mag bomb; plus — and this was the main thing — there were no lurking spirit-world soldiers on board — not even an Engine Devil.

The *Hesperos* was programmed to meet the *Centaur* at the mutually agreed upon coordinates without mortal assistance.

Tanya received the message and turned to Davyd and Vlad.

"We're on," she announced.

Then she signaled Scratch and Billy and the odd team lashed a magical tractor beam onto the *Hesperos* and took full control.

Down in the engine room Billy hooted in glee. "Now, we get to run two ships Scratchy!" he chortled. "Two, count 'em, two, to ram down that Planetar Demon's filthy throat!"

Old Scratch didn't answer. He was too busy sending a stream of mentos commands to his fiendish crews. But he did share the boy's delight. This was going to be something he could boast about at the "Hanged Monks" for many and many a day.

Assuming they lived to see that day. But he shut down that bit of pessimism and directed the boy in his copilot's work.

Meanwhile, Tanya gave Moon and Rhodes some commands of her own. Quickly, they ducked their two stealth vessels into the magical shadow of the two great ships.

And some minutes later the mini-fleet shot through a worm hole and bored toward its destination.

* * *

When he got the first warning of the approaching enemy, the Planetar Demon was nursing the wounds of his humiliation and drawing in as much as power as he could to recharge his badly depleted energies.

His first reaction was amazement — and just a bit of panic. How had he been tracked to his lair, deep, deep in Uttermost Space?

The answer quickly came back to him as he sucked in a small fiery swarm of free electrons — much like a great whale scooping up plankton in the frigid polar seas on Earth.

There were millions upon millions of little "pops!" — like dying bubbles in a gigantic champagne glass — as he devoured the electrons. And as the electrons ceased to be, what remained were the empty places they'd formerly occupied.

The Planetar Demon understood his problem when he saw the many pinpricks in the magical and physical fabric of space left by the consumed electrons.

Tiny holes that amounted to nothing when considered individually. But a great shining trail with other dimensions glaring through the pinpricks when considered in such numbers.

Now that he'd been found he didn't bother trying to correct the problem and cover his tracks.

Instead, he immediately sucked up an enormous quantity of light beams, gravitational waves, doppler shifts in color, old acts of sorcery gone wild in space — anything that would feed his most urgent hunger for power.

As he digested, he studied the coming enemy. Two warships from the Council Of Eight. Aboard them: Lawson and the two assassins.

Oh, yes, and the Engine Devil and boy he'd sought.

Not only that, there was also an enormous arsenal of deadly things aboard those two ships that was clearly meant to destroy him.

He thought of flight — playing for time as he replenished his powers, then turning on his hunters and attacking them.

But he quickly dismissed that plan. Chances were they'd be able to follow close to his heels, harrying him as he drained himself of still more energy in his attempts to escape.

Undoubtedly, they'd attack him each time he stopped to feed. And retreat every time he tried to strike back.

Eventually, he'd be so weak and helpless that they'd be able to kill him at their leisure.

The Planetar Demon considered other options. Swiftly running all the progs on each idea that came to mind.

Then, to his intense and angry delight, he saw the best solution. Not only to these creatures who were bedeviling him, but to all that kept him from his final purpose.

There was just enough magical power contained in the two ships to bring him up to minimum strength.

Not only that — and this was the deciding factor in his equation — if he added the agonies he could cause Lawson and her lovers while killing them, he'd get a tremendous boost when he devoured their souls.

He sent out sensory feelers to examine the individuals in question more closely. And came back with still one more potential bonus:

Davyd and Vlad's tormented confusion. Hate and love and betrayal. All mixed up into a delicious tonic.

More testing of the ethereal atmospheres brought in Scratch and Billy as well. Their hopes so high. Against the backdrop of injuries so deep. All their powers and emotional baggage directed against him.

If he destroyed them he could feed on all those things and fill himself with so much power that he could attack the Council Of Eight full force.

True, it would be one against many.

But the many would have no hope against the one.

How could the Council Of Eight and these softskins have been so foolish that they'd dare bring such a bounty to his table?

The Planetar Demon boomed forward.

Eager to fight.

His passions and hate so intense that unbeknownst to him they flared out like the trail of a null-worm suddenly appearing to bore a new hole in Uttermost Space.

When he made his decision to attack the Planetar Demon made two mistakes. Not necessarily fatal, but they were rather large mistakes.

The first thing he didn't count on was the heightened combat awareness of Davyd and Vlad.

The second involved the two stealth ships — the *Hamilton* and *Rubin* — which hovered just out of his magical view.

Waiting for him to take Tanya's bait.

*   *   *

The Planetar Demon's initial attack nearly ended the deadly game.

Long before he physically reached the sensors that tripped the ships' alarms, his awful presence was upon them.

A sudden feeling of cold, cold dread afflicted every being aboard the little fleet.

Navigation Spirits, Control Brownies and Fueling Goblins shrieked in terror, abandoning their duties to flee in every direction.

Scratch and Billy froze in their positions, every thought wiped away by the bitter, probing eye that examined them.

Read them through and through.

It was the *HolidayOne* all over again. Ever muscle, every sinew, every nerve cell shivering in helpless fear.

A tremendous feeling of fatalism drowning their will to fight and live.

Up on the command deck, Tanya, Davyd and Vlad were reduced to frail butterflies, quivering and flapping weakly on the points of a collector's pins.

Resigned to their coming deaths.

So powerful was the Planetar Demon's bow wave of hate that even the captains and crews of the *Hamilton* and *Rubin* were affected. Although their presence still hadn't been noted by the attacking fiend.

Rhodes and Moon moaned in agony as ice needles penetrated the hulls of the ships; then their flesh; then their bones; then their very souls.

All around them their crew shouted in terror as the unseen enemy powered onward, blasting everything in his path with an ice storm of will-freezing magic.

If it wasn't for Billy Ivanov, they all would have died in the Planetar Demon's first rush.

The battle lost before it had even begun.

CHAPTER FIFTY TWO

Billy was back on board the *HolidayOne*. He was asleep in his bunk, dreaming dreams of the beautiful Lupe. And, just as before, those dreams turned grim and he was uneasy.

Then a sudden sense of cruelty roughed his senses and he shot up in bed.

The beast was rushing down on him with slavering jaws. Instinct took over and as he threw up his hands he hurled a hard spell!

And then ... boom!

Billy closed his eyes. Fire scorching and hammering all around. But this time he didn't flee the ship. And he didn't shout Lupe's name.

Instead he shouted defiance, "Come on, you ... you ... bastard! This time I'm gonna get you! Just you wait and see!"

At the sound of his young's friend's frantic voice, Scratch shook off the Planetar Demon's spell and roused himself into action.

Unleashing a red hot lava of fierce oaths, he halted the Brownies and Gremlins in their tracks and forced them back to work.

Trembling — now more in fear of Scratchy than the Planetar Demon — the fiendish crew rushed into action, hurling up the ship's defensive shields.

Old Scratch's mentos commands were so fierce they rattled Tanya's teeth, like a spacequake thundering through the material world when a star goes nova.

Instantly, she threw up her own shields, crying out to Davyd and Vlad at the same time.

The two warriors leaped to their feet, combat systems exploding into life just as the Planetar Demon let loose with a barrage of thousands of fierce DeathSpirits.

Flaming swords appeared in their hands as the first wave of Death-Spirits — the shock troops — pierced the ship's hull and raged toward them.

Tanya slammed her fist against the com button, setting off shrieking alarms aboard the *Hamilton* and *Rubin*.

Attack signals shrilled in the ears of Moon and Rhodes, who fought off the Demon's spell, then harangued their crews into motion.

The two stealth ships shot out from under the protective shadows of the *Centaur* and *Hesperos*, separating to take on the Planetar Demon from two different sides.

Their chain guns roared, hammering the Planetar Demon with hundreds of collapsed anti-matter bullets.

The Demon howled in pain and fury. He tried to absorb the energy of the bullets and use it against his attackers. But they were dead things and could not be digested.

Blindly, he lashed out at the little ships, but Moon and Rhodes deftly maneuvered out of his reach — pouring on more fire. Tanya's voice urging them on through the com lines.

To Tanya's dismay, the shields dissolved like butter exposed to flame. Giving way to the Planetar Demon's minions.

Vlad and Davyd waded into them, laying waste right and left. Slashing at the creatures with their fiery swords. Ripping them apart with every blow they struck.

The command deck quickly became was a welter of green, luminescent gore. But the DeathSpirits kept coming, never letting up.

Slowly, Davyd and Vlad were backed against the raised platform of command central where Tanya rushed along the bank of controls. Slapping buttons, hissing commands. Shifting resources here and there.

Conducting the battle as if she were the leader of a ghastly orchestra that dealt out death instead of music.

The two men took their stand at that point, protecting her from the onslaught.

Tanya shot a quick glance over her shoulder and what she saw made her heart beat triple time. Both men were visibly tiring. And every blow they struck weakened them more.

To her it seemed as if they could hardly hold the magical sword blades at waist height. She even heard Vlad groan as he lifted his sword to fight off a DeathSpirit.

Although the two men had rested after the great duel they'd fought, they hadn't had enough time to recover fully. And now they were paying for it — maybe even fatally — as the Demon's hordes hammered at them.

Cracking against their shields and sniping from every side.

But there wasn't anything she could do to help them. What David and Vlad were facing was only the Planetar Demon's initial strike force. Meant to soften his enemies for the final, killing blow that was sure to follow.

And at this precise moment it was all Tanya could do to ward off that attack.

This isn't working, she thought. This isn't how I planned it!

She struggled to regain calm control. Leaching fearful thoughts from her system as quickly as they arose.

Tanya steadied her self. Returned to her role of the cool observer.

The Planetar Demon was on her center screen. A great beastly face the size of Jupiter. So angry that his color spectrums swiftly ran up and down an unimaginable scale that ranged from the blindingly white hot visible to a cold, black nothingness that sucked the mind from its rational bearings.

Tanya fought that defeatist thinking off. Returned to her most rational, observing mind. Weighing the complications. And how she should deal with them.

It was easy to note that at least one part of her plan was working.

The only things keeping the Planetar Demon from unleashing its murderous best — which would send a thousand times more DeathSpirits against the *Centaur* — were Moon and Rhodes' tiny stealth ships.

As the men who loved her fought to keep her from harm, Tanya pressed the attack.

Directed by Tanya, the two stealth ships ripped at the Planetar Demon like hungry sharks. Sending stream after blazing stream of collapsed anti-matter bullets into his thick hide.

But she quickly realized that Moon and Rhodes couldn't keep up the pressure much longer. Just like Davyd and Vlad, they were losing the advantage of surprise as their energies were diminished.

Already the Planetar Demon was starting to get the range of the stealth ships, pouring on all the magical weapons he had at his disposal.

And now, instead of flailing wildly about, he was firing off enormous magical spears that exploded with space warping strength. Blistering the skin of the two stealth ships. Flipping them over with the force of the blasts.

Then coming in to strike at their exposed bellies with the next blows.

Tanya knew this battle would eventually be a losing one. In a little while, the Planetar Demon would get Moon and Rhodes in his sights and blast them into perdition.

Then he'd turn on the *Centaur* and kill her and all she loved.

Tanya called on all her powers to regain her confidence. Reminding herself that she'd never intended this fight to be anything more than a diversion.

The crucial blow — her true attack — was yet to come. Patience, she urged herself. And courage. Damn it woman, you need more courage than you've ever had before.

At that moment Davyd's sword was ripped away by a shrieking DeathSpirit. Kells grabbed the creature by the throat, sorcerous fire shooting up his arms. Bubbling and boiling and eating away at his skin.

The pain was so intense he could barely keep his grip. But he persisted, squeezing with all his might.

Then the fiend's neck snapped under his curling fingers and he hurled its lifeless body into the face of another attacker.

Meanwhile, Vlad was having troubles of his own.

Three DeathSpirits were howling and gnashing at him. Dodging this way and that as he struck out at them with his blade.

Swooping in at every opportunity to ravage him with their fangs. Blood dripped from bite wounds in his chest and shoulders.

He reached deep inside for the last reserves of strength. Then, bellowing like an enraged bull, he charged forward.

At the last instant, he vaulted over the DeathSpirits, then reversed course and came at them from behind.

He slew them before they had time to whirl around and defend themselves.

Panting and dazed, he looked around to see where the next enemy might come from. Holding his sword up to fend off a surprise blow.

And then he saw Davyd slay the last fiend and kick its body aside.

Davyd looked up at Vlad, grinning at him through bloody teeth.

"In our next lives," he said, "maybe we ought to think about becoming accountants. Business consultants … whatever."

Vlad grinned back. "Mathematics," he said, "was never one of my best subjects."

Davyd laughed. "Me either," he said. "But at least they don't kill you if you fuck up!"

"An excellent point," Vlad agreed. "Business consultant it is, then. Let's get together on this. We'll call it Projogin & Kells Inc. Murder and taxes are our business."

Davyd laughed, feeling a little giddy. "You're on, buddy," he said. "You can even put your name first. For when the cops come to arrest us."

Tanya broke in. "It's not over, yet," she snapped. "Jesus Christ, this is definitely not the damned time for male bonding!

"Look at what this son of a bitch is doing now!"

They looked up and saw that the huge vid-screen image of the Planetar Demon had changed. He was opening his mouth … and it kept opening … and opening … until he became an enormous maw.

Nuclear explosions bloomed to make the teeth. White hot particles of burning plasma formed the lips.

And at that moment an enormous wave of sorcerous energy blasted outward, grabbing the *Centaur* by its roots and hurling it away.

Davyd and Vlad were thrown violently against the ship's walls. They slammed against plas-metal, then slid to the floor, stunned.

To their amazement, they heard Tanya calmly announce: "Moon and Rhodes got away just in time. At least they're goddamned safe!"

From their prone positions they saw the enormous mouth that was the Planetar Demon powering straight toward them. Millions upon millions of DeathSpirits pouring out to consume them.

"This is where it gets tricky," Tanya said.

And as they pondered those words, she slammed her palm down onto a switch, signaling Scratch and Billy …

…In the engine chamber, the boy and his fiendish friend heard the howl of Tanya's command.

"Now, Scratchy, now!" Billy shouted.

On his own vidscreen he could see the enormous maw that was the Planetar Demon speeding toward them. The fiery lights of shrieking DeathSpirits pouring out to overwhelm them.

But Old Scratch was unmoved by the emergency. "Do not get thy softskin bowels into an uproar, Little Friend of the World," he said, cool as could be. "Calm thyself, so thou canst do the proper work of an Engine Devil."

Then, to Billy's amazement, Scratch flicked a switch with a long talon. And at the same time, he issued a stream of mentos orders that came so fast Billy could barely decipher them.

Thousands of little fiends raced to do Scratch's bidding and in an instant the *Centaur* was hurled aside.

The action was so quick and violent that Billy was pinned to the invisible walls of his protective bubble. Before his eyes he witnessed the ship veering straight across the Planetar Demon's open mouth.

There was a violent rocking as the fiend tried to suck them into his black hole innards. Then a quick feeling of freedom as they broke the gravitational bond and swooped past the ferocious visage.

And then Scratchy said, "The killing is thy prerogative, Little Friend of the World. I give thee this gift of revenge."

Billy's mouth fell open. "What are you saying? What do you want me to do?"

Old Scratch shrugged. "Kill him, what else? Was that not the plan?"

Billy gulped and nodded. His hand hovered over the large button that would do the rest. This was it. This was his final revenge. He looked up at the screen and saw the huge jaws of the Planetar Demon beginning to snap shut in surprise as their ship evaded him.

At the slap of the button, revenge was his. Revenge for his grandparents. For the lovely Lupe. For all the wrongs that had been committed against him in his short life as a half-breed orphan.

All the hate for all the wrongs he'd suffered surged forward. His heart was so full of hate he thought it would burst.

Then he hesitated.

And in that hesitation, all hate fled. His hand dropped to the side of the button.

"I can't do it, Scratchy," he said. "I can't kill him." His head dropped low. "I guess I'm a coward."

And Old Scratch replied, "Thou art no coward, Little Friend of the World. Thou art a brave boy, indeed, to make this decision.

"I loathed to give thee this chance for revenge. He is too young, I thought, to carry such a burden. But it was my love for thee that could not deny thee the opportunity."

Billy was bewildered. "So what do we do, then, Scratchy? What next?"

And Scratch said, "We kill him, what else?"

Then he slammed his taloned fist down on the huge button.

Immediately, the *Centaur* swooped off in the opposite direction. Releasing the planet bomb carrying *Hesperos* from the traction beam.

The *Hesperos* shot forward. And at the same time Scratchy mentos shouted commands to its crew to flee, flee, flee for their lives.

Then, he swung the *Centaur* back around to watch what he had caused. Little Brownies and Gremlins from the *Hesperos* were already crowding into the engine room and Scratchy had to shout for silence, because they were so happily and noisily gossiping.

"Damned Brownies," he growled. "A decent Engine Devil can't think over their noise."

He only commented in a futile attempt to distract Billy, who was watching the *Hesperos* blast toward the Planetar Demon.

The fiend saw a quick victory, rather than a threat, and swallowed the ship whole.

At that moment Scratch toggled another switch with his fore-talon.

And that was the end of the Planetar Demon.

It was a terrible thing to witness. Not just for Billy, but also for Old Scratch, who was at heart a peaceful demon who meant no harm to anyone.

There was a series of incredible explosions, of course. But the gore that followed would haunt one and all for the rest of their lives.

Terrible shrieks wrapped around gobs of meat. Crying, crying, crying. Leaping flames that moaned and wailed so pitifully that they even made Scratchy weep.

He witnessed other things as well, too gruesome to relate.

He was so shaken that when the deed was done it was Billy, not Scratch, who signaled Tanya.

She turned to Davyd and Vlad, saying, "Well, it's finally over. We won, in case you're keeping score."

Davyd and Vlad were nearly overcome by what the horrible thing they had just witnessed.

Vlad recovered first. "What do we do now?" he asked.

Tanya sighed and palmed a switch. The giant vid screen swirled for a moment, then cleared.

Filling the screen from edge to edge was an enormous war ship of ancient design and hateful intent. It was swiftly moving in on the *Centaur*.

As they looked, they saw the deadly gunports open.

"You're looking at a little present from the Council of Eight," Tanya said. "Good job, boys, now we're gonna kill you."

"No problem," Davyd said. "My suggestion is that we get the hell out of Dodge."

And so that is what they did.

CHAPTER FIFTY THREE

It was in a world far and far away and at the very edges of the Galaxy …

…The gathered tribes sat about a roaring campfire, sparks shooting up to meet the starry night.

There were softskins of every age — from suckling babes to cackling crones — as well as spirit world folk of every shape and sex and variety.

And they all listened intently as the wise old Engine Devil told the tale of his great adventures.

His name was Scratch and as Old Scratch he was known to rebels throughout the Galaxy. Crouched beside him was his constant friend and companion, the softskin boy known to one and all as "Little Friend of the World."

Scratchy spun a remarkable yarn of marvelous feats and terrible sacrifices and fabulous deeds of derring do.

He told them about Tanya Lawson, the fearless police detective who ferreted out the dread conspiracy of the evil Council Of Eight.

And of the two bitter foes, David Kells and Vlad Projogin, the two mighty warriors who had fought the greatest duel in all history. Only to lay down their arms for the love of a woman and join together to defeat the dreaded Planetar Demon.

The softskin and spirit world clans hung on Scratchy's every word, murmuring in amazement as he recounted all that had occurred.

When he was done, many toasts were drunk to the health and well-being of Tanya and her companions.

Scratchy waited until the proper time, then he made his recruiting pitch. One which he'd perfected over many nights such as this on countless worlds.

He told the gathered clans that a still greater fight was being waged by Tanya, Vlad and Davyd.

It was battle not just for their own lives, but for the freedom of beings everywhere. Softskin as well as spirit world folk.

Scratchy pointed a gnarled talon at the blazing night sky. "They are somewhere out there even now," the Engine Devil said, "raising the tribes to bring down the Council Of Eight and end their tyranny.

"But everywhere they go, those devils who rule the council are hard at the heels of our three heroes. Intent on bringing them to ground and slaying them."

There were angry mutters at this news. Fierce curses hurled at the Council Of Eight that delighted Old Scratch and Billy.

He said, "I wish I could report to thee that all is well and that our friends are gaining the upper hand.

"Alas, that would be a lie. And all of you know, an Engine Devil never lies.

"Perhaps those evil ones will eventually capture the brave three who carry our banner high. Who can say? I must admit the odds do not favor them.

"The devils who rule the council command many fiends. And, as all of you know, they are ancient lords of terror who have fostered hate among the races wherever they go.

"But even if they do, my friends, many of us have pledged ourselves to carry on that brave fight.

"And with thy help we can march forward and take the battle to the very doors of the evil ones who have enslaved us all for lo these many centuries.

"So, what say you, O gracious hosts? Will you join me and my Little Friend of the World in this final fight to cast off the chains of our enslavement?"

Again he gestured at the sky, where the two stealth ships hovered, waiting to gather up recruits and fly them away to the many raging battle zones.

"You only have to say the word and make the sacred pledge to join our growing band of brave heroes. I cannot promise riches, or even sufficient food. Only hardship awaits you if thou chooseth to join us.

"However, when the scrolls of freedom are unfurled at the end time — and Judgment Day is upon us — your names will be written large for the eyes of the gods who love us to marvel upon.

"So what say you, brave folk? Will you come away with us. And fight the good fight?"

There was a loud and defiant clamoring of voices as young fiends and softskins leaped up to pledge their very lives to the cause.

This pleased Scratchy mightily, but also saddened him. For he knew that many of them would never again return to sit by the campfire with their friends and families.

But such things must be done if the galaxy were to be made a better place.

Then Billy rose up to sing his Kipling song and seal the moment. His clear boy's soprano floating through the sweet night air:

> *"O look and behold*
> *The Planets that love us*
> *All harnessed in gold!*
> *What chariots, what horses*

Against us shall bide
While the Stars in their courses
Do fight on our side?..."

And Scratchy knuckled away a stray tear, feeling just a little sorry for himself.

For he was an old devil.

A tired devil.

Whose vacation was long, long overdue.

And he wondered if Avalon had been lost to him forever.

THE END

www.ingramcontent.com/pod-product-compliance
Lightning Source LLC
Chambersburg PA
CBHW030930260626
47169CB00002B/434